THE BLACK SHIP

GERRY WILLIAM

First Printing

Library and Archives Canada Cataloguing in Publication

William, Gerry, 1952-, author
The black ship / Gerry William.

Expanded version of book published in 1994.
ISBN 978-1-926886-38-1 (paperback)

I. Title.

PS8595.I544B53 2015 C813'.54 C2015-907574-2

Printed in Canada

www.theytus.com

Book Design: Ann Doyon

Patrimoine canadien Canadian Heritage

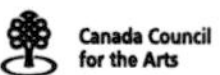
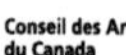
Canada Council for the Arts Conseil des Arts du Canada

We acknowledge the financial support of The Government of Canada through the Department of Canadian heritage for our publishing activities. We acknowledge the support of the Canada Council for the Arts, which last year invested $154 million to bring the arts to Canadians throughout the country. *Nous remercions le Conseil des arts du Canada de son soutien. L'an dernier, le Conseil a investi 154 millions de dollars pour mettre de l'art dans la vie des Canadiennes et des Canadiens de tout le pays.* We acknowledge the support of the Province of British Columbia through the British Columbia Arts Council

The Black Ship

Gerry William

I would like to thank my ever patient wife, Beth Cuthand,
for her support during the writing and editing of this.
I would also like to dedicate this novel to my brother,
Raymond, who went to meet the Creator on May 1, 2015.

But if any man is overmuch desirous to depart homewards,
let him lay his hand upon his decked black ship, that
before all men he may encounter death and fate.

Homer
The Iliad

Acknowledgements

I would like to thank my ever patient wife, Beth Cuthand, for her support during the writing and editing of this. I would also like to dedicate this novel to my brother, Raymond, who went to meet the Creator on May 1, 2015.

Introduction

The timely republication of The Black Ship opens ground for a whole new wave of Indigenous writing in Canada. There are great shifts in social consciousness which have been occurring: the recent Idle No More movement, the Truth and Reconciliation Commission and the general attention given to the well-being of Indigenous women and men. A vibrant rebirth of Indigenous consciousness is unfolding part of this rebirth is a rethinking of the past, and also a reimagining of the future. The power of science fiction is that it allows us to do both of these things. The Black Ship does both, and its republication could not occur at a better time.

The book was originally published in 1994, and was ahead of its time. This rewritten version of the Black Ship has been expanded to continue the story beyond the original 1994 publication. With the new additions and changes, this is a novel which is twice the length of the original publication. In 1994, the period of contemporary Indigenous literary renaissance was still largely focused on traditional narratives. In addition to this, there were also anthologies, which were compiling and publishing Indigenous fiction and poetry. In this context, the possibilities of science fiction within Indigenous literature was largely unrealized. Yet, the themes touched on in the book show the power of mystery (as in the old stories), and also, like a great deal of contemporary writing in the 1990s, embodied an Indigenous poetics. In the case of The Black Ship, it is a beautiful poetics of space as experienced and embodied by future Indigenous people: it is eluded to in the book that the Repletians are descendants of the Indigenous people of the earth.

The Black Ship provides an opportunity to rethink Indigenous past histories. Enid Blue Starbreaks is a Repletian who survives a mass killing of her people on the Pegasus. She is later adopted and raised by an Amphorian family. With the recent attention given to the 60s scoop of Indigenous people in Canada, the parallels in the novel are quite striking. Despite the attempt to erase Enid's memory, and despite being integrated into the Amphorian society, the older, lingering memories of who she was shadow her, but also at the same time light a path for her across the stars. Despite the racism she experiences, she rises up the ranks of the Amphorian navy, and eventually becomes an admiral of the fourth fleet. Eventually, her uncle Leon Three Starbreaks connects with her, and her circle back to her people is complete although somewhat fractured.

The central character of Enid demonstrates strength and resilience in the face of great changes and challenges. Despite the upheavals and difficulties faced by her, there is something of a thread of continuity in the backdrop of the foreverness of the stars. Part of this is the sense of mystery and the unknown which lay at the edges of the story. While in some ways this goes against the "scientific" aspect of science fiction, mystery is presented in the book, in regards to Korel's world and also the Black Ship itself. This is done in such a way that is it could not be seen as unexplainable, but rather explainable and understandable, through the characters and the mysteries effect. The Black Ship and Korel's ship function something like the wind: they move and shape characters as the wind moves and shapes the trees and branches, and causes grass to sway.

The book also maps out the future, far beyond the confines of today's realities. This has always been one of the powerful driving possibilities of science fiction- and indeed it is the great promise of Indigenous science fiction to reshape possibilities. A world of planet of mystery is encountered by Enid's uncle, the Black Ship holds a mystery of bending time and space, and the book creates a galaxy where Indigenous people become an Empire- and a strong empire at that.

It is by portraying Indigenous people in these futuristic possibilities, that a map is presented where the great potential of Indigenous people rests in the stars, and the stretches of the galaxy. With the republication of this book, other Indigenous writers can build upon the legacy left by Gerry William; as we look forward to the author's sequel, which is currently a work in progress.

-Neal McLeod
nîhtawîcikanisihk,
Saskatchewan, 2015

WRAP-AROUND

It starts with light.

Annie Clerk sits back. She watches the student write her notes. The recorder hums, copying only the words Annie wants it to copy. The student doesn't know this.

Light?

Annie ignores the student's question. She leans forward in her rocking chair. Stirs the fire, sparks flying, small billows of grey-blue smoke puffing up the chimney flue.

I knew a woman once. I can tell her story, if you like.

The student hesitates, her pen tip an inch from the paper.

Is it a traditional story?

Annie laughs low, the long scar on her left cheek exposed in the glowing reflection of the flames.

All stories are traditional. This one happens maybe a long time ago, maybe now, maybe not yet. I sometimes do get confused. Not often, but sometimes.

This woman. Do I know her? Have I heard of her?

The syilx know her. She once saved two children in the time before the sha-mas, the white people, rode into our lands. The story starts big, then gets bigger.

So it's history.

With a worn alder staff Annie stirs the fire. Sparks flare and the sizzling wood crackles; a puff of smoke fills the room with the smell of burning pine.

You want answers. Stories have answers. Not maybe the answers you're looking for. I know that my people have made their homes among the stars.

But that's the future.

A future. Yes. Do you want to hear the story?

I have to go home soon.

Annie stares at the student. When she sees what she sees, she giggles and reclines back in her chair, begins rocking.

You got time.

The student looks down at the words she's written, line after line, page after page. She's confused. Her hundred page notepad is almost full and yet she came here with a blank pad only a couple of hours ago. She looks up. Her eyes grow round with surprise and a touch of fear as the rocking chair sits empty. As her mind registers this, Annie carefully places the teapot onto a coaster on her coffee table. Somehow two cups have appeared on the table, along with a plate of biscuits, a bowl of sugar cubes and a creamer.

When did you...I mean, how could you...?

Annie pours tea into each cup and then eases herself back into her chair, begins rocking, sips from her teacup, nibbles on the biscuit.

Now, where was I? Oh, yes, the story. There are two women in this story. Follow me closely.

*

The stars kept Sam Nordell from losing his mind. He drank the light from those beacons each time he felt empty. Their colors washed through him in gentle filaments. Light from both the past, present and the future. Time was contemporaneous in the universe. His discovery was one Sam would take to the grave. Humanity wasn't ready for its next great humbling, not ready to know that its view of the universe was dependent upon, and relative to, the human condition. Sam knew this from the planet he had just visited.

Sam eased his lifter down into a clearing. Five-trunked crystal trees scattered across a landscape where the smallest things were the oldest. Objects moved, some so striking that Sam saw only a faint reflection of their real form. His mind rebelled. As iron-willed as he was, Sam felt on the verge of lunacy, of screaming, gibbering madly. Nothing moved or looked like anything in Sam's long human experience.

The planet circled a triple star, not unusual. But there was no carbon. DNA was not the foundation of the things that jerked, heaved, limped, waddled, swayed and thumped across a land carpeted in a rug of black, coal black. Things that could have been grass, clover, wheat, trees, bushes, but refused to be any of them.

The light from the two visible suns cast the world in a shade of steel blue and green marble with an edge that circled into Sam's eyes and felt like needles. In the first few moments outside of his lifter Sam heard women wailing in sorrow combined with notes that struck deep deep chords in his soul, notes that scattered music, tore metal iron striking wood in a cacophony of delirium. Sam desperately turned his suit to audio mute, only to find the sounds continuing on another level, a whale's death agonies booming through the Celtic notes of a deranged wolverine yelping shrill through the roof of a warehouse. And at one point the soft throated chuckle of a coyote could be heard.

Sam staggered back into his lifter, yanked off his helmet. After several minutes of gasping breaths his computer spoke.

Please do not yell and continue to sing the Ancient Mariner in G-Major.

Sam stared at the metal floor. It was wet. Only then did Sam realize that he was soaked, in his own sweat.

Sam spent an hour in a shower of alternate cold and scalding hot, twice stepping from the shower to don clothes that quickly became drenched with his continued perspiration. His lifter, while small by military standards, still topped out at a hundred yards, ten of them devoted to the zero-point tachyon drive unit. Sam eased into his command chair. Mercifully the translucent titanium windows were scaled against outside light.

Sam shivered, and it wasn't because he had to walk around nude. In shock he spoke to his computer.

Did you see that? Did you ... see that ... I can't go out there, I can't...the pain...Please take a deep breath. Take a deep breath.

Sam surged to his feet. For a wild second he swayed between singing Happy Birthday and repeating the valedictorian speech, which he'd forgotten seventy years ago.

Take a deep breath. Like that. Another. Yes, like that. Another. Now, please talk.

Two hours later the computer was making variations to Sam's survival suit. It studied the recording made by the suit, the audio and visual elements. It then delivered Sam a restructured suit.

The second time out, Sam's suit guided him across the terrain by using an improvised radar sensory sweep. His visual and auditory devices had been muted fifty fold and even at this level Sam heard and felt things he would remember the rest of his life. Great gusts of wind surged to the surface, yet no back draft occurred. The air simply seemed to pour into the ground.

In five minutes Sam reached the dome he had first scanned from space.

Silence.

The first step into the great half dome (Sam presumed the other half of the dome extended below the surface). Sam's viewer opened. His audio crackled into normalcy.

Sam cautiously turned to face the exterior. Outside. Something like a flying anaconda with dozens of feet and an appendage like an arm that ended in a waffle iron hovered at the entrance. Behind it his lifter was framed in its isolation by a brown carpet crystal flowing over it and dancing a dirge of happiness that sent Sam's mind yammering into the longhouse raven dance he'd witnessed if the dancer had a serrated eye and then *Turn away, Sam*, came the gentle strong voice of his computer.

Turn away now.

Sam hesitated and something seemed to turn behind the anaconda, something dead gold and it smiled.

He turned around and almost fell. And it took several seconds to realize the thunderous sound he heard was his own breath, a whistle just this side of endless screaming.

I've revamped your visual. The air is breathable.

So my helmet?

Off. Leave it. It will be a beacon to track your return.

All too soon, and forever, Sam began the recorded journey into the dome. The journey that became a conversation occupying a large portion of the Ten Confederacies of Humanity.

THE BLACK SHIP

CHAPTER 1

Standard Year 2478

"Fucking Repletians!" Vice Admiral Hubert Tyrel, Commander of the Fifth Fleet, swiveled in his commander's chair to get a better look at the small craft racing ahead of the Kirilovnich, his flagship. "Can you identify its origin?"

"We're fairly certain it's a Repletian ship. But it's light years from the nearest inhabited home planet in Sector Five. What's it doing out here?"

Tyrel shrugged and stared down his First Officer. "Who the fuck cares?" he repeated an old curse that had recently surfaced in the Navy, keeping its primal potency over the ages. His First Officer backed up two steps, repelled by the Vice Admiral's physical size and intensity. Tyrel snorted and turned back. "What is it?"

"As near as we can tell, it's a scout ship."

"A scout ship? This far from any base? What the hell's going on?"

Tyrel didn't wait. Instead he studied the readouts on the Repletian vessel. As he watched the small ship, it flared into a brilliant fireball, flinging debris that struck the flagship's shields and disintegrated. A slight shudder ran through the ship's massive hull.

"Is there any damage to us?"

"Negative, Admiral."

Tyrel returned to his commander's chair to contemplate this encounter. He hadn't planned to meet a Repletian so soon after departure from Leginial IV, an agricultural food planet. They were five Standard hours away from Artel's Star.

"Take over the bridge," Tyrel told his First Officer. Without waiting for a response he strode swiftly from the bridge into the corridors of the ten-mile-long vessel. His guards, an elite composite of the best soldiers in the Fifth Fleet, followed his swift confident strides as he made his way to his personal quarters less than twenty yards from the bridge.

Once in his quarters, Tyrel secured the inner doors and went to his personal holograph console. He linked with the Anphorian Home Base he had left some five years before. With any luck he could complete this last mission and head home on relief within the next Standard month. Now wasn't the time to get sloppy; he knew what failure meant to his career. He made a few terse comments that were sent through coded channels, where they would be read by the Admiralty. Tyrel eased back in his chair and took a customary survey of his quarters. Nothing looked awry but he never took chances; his military training told him to distrust the obvious. Everything appeared unmoved so he took out his journal to carefully write down the events of the day. On occasion he paused in his writing long enough to stare at the opposite wall. His brows furrowed in thought as he weighed how to word each sentence. He liked to be brief without losing anything important. During his pauses the writing tool he held in his left hand hovered a few inches above the page. Tyrel never stopped for more than ten seconds. When he returned to writing, the frown he wore during his pauses quickly disappeared, leaving a face as blank and unlined as the new pages confronting him every ten minutes.

The small clear bell tone signaled a message coming in over coded channels. Tyrel stopped writing. He showed no relief over the interruption. He lowered his pen into the journal's creased center to keep it from closing, smoothed his grey uniform and squared his broad shoulders. Closing his eyes, he slowly counted to three under his breath, then voice-activated the viewing holograph.

"Tyrel, hello."

"Greetings, sir."

"The Admiralty received your message. Give me your assessment."

"It was a scout ship. From its design it was Repletian."

"And yet there are no Repletian planets nor battle cruisers in the neighborhood," the figure mused, half to itself.

"We have no signs of other Repletians for light years around."

"Is there any indication your crew knows about the Black Ship?"

"No, sir. I haven't told them of the mission, our destination."

"Excellent. Tyrel, I count on you to maintain security. How soon before contact?"

"We should reach the Black Ship in less than five Standard hours."

"Tyrel, you know the ship is alien?"

"Aye, sir. The Repletians are good, but we'd know if they'd been working on anything like the Black Ship."

"I agree. Still, if we're going to pull this off, we have to agree it's Repletian."

"To justify our invasion of Repletian space?"

"Exactly!" Admiral Lexington smiled. "We need to capture that thing before the Repletians do."

"I"ll get it for you, Admiral."

"Excellent. Please inform your fleet of what they're dealing with. My transmission will end with a ten minute briefing tape you can use to explain the mission goals as well as the need for tight security. Have you secured communications?"

"The only transmissions I've allowed are local ship-to-ship. All other messages need my personal authorization."

"Excellent. You've done well."

Tyrel waited patiently for Lexington to go on. After an awkward pause, Lexington sighed and lowered his voice. "Are you convinced of this need for secrecy?"

"Sir, you make those calls."

Lexington laughed, thinking sadly Tyrel meant every word he said. Yes, Tyrel followed his orders, no questions asked. And nothing Lexington could do would help his friend at this distance.

"Tyrel, make the necessary preparations and report to me in two Standard hours."

"Aye, sir." Tyrel watched the image fade and then he left his quarters to return. When he got there Lexington's coded message was being received. Tyrel sat in his commander's chair, punched a few numbers to uncode the message then called his bridge officers from their posts for a briefing. They watched the holograph of Lexington and Tyrel watched them. He knew what the message was. He wanted to observe his officers when their attentions focused on other things. If they were aware of his attention they didn't show it. Their faces remained neutral or slightly tense as they listened to Admiral Lexington's message. Tyrel turned away from them half way through their briefing. He knew his officers were all right.

Tyrel spent the next few minutes looking at the analysts' reports, each report showing its separate style and bias. He heard the holograph tape come to an end and then the faint pattern of footsteps; he looked up from his reading to see the single row of officers standing two paces away.

"Well, you've heard the Admiral. We're proceeding into Repletian territory and should reach our destination at Artel's Star in less than four hours. We have much to do, so take your posts. Make certain we're ready for battle and our research teams are prepared for any outcome. Any questions?"

Second Lieutenant Daniel Peters spoke out: "What's this Black Ship the Admiral mentioned?"

"Ten weeks ago one of our scanners malfunctioned. Before anyone noticed it was missing it had veered into Artel's Star system. It sent back pictures of a most remarkable object. Observe this, all of you."

Tyrel brought up a holograph image of a black object that floated in space. Its shape was odd and changed as they watched.

"As you can see, its structure is artificial."

"Could it be Repletian?" Peters persisted.

"Our best scientists think so; some of them believe it's a new Repletian weapons system and had the scanner initiate a series of tests on the ship. The results surprised them. That ship, if it's a ship in our meaning of the word, changes as we observe it. Its shape, its weight, and its mass transforms in random patterns."

His officers looked at each other skeptically.

"By every standard we know, that ship doesn't exist in our universe. And yet there it floats. Nothing we have matches it."

"And so it's Repletian?" His aide asked the question the other bridge officers were silently asking themselves.

"Yes, it's Repletian."

"Perhaps it's alien."

Tyrel turned to the speaker, a lieutenant normally quiet. "If it's alien, gentlemen, we might as well sue for peace now before they take over our Home Worlds."

The normally quiet officer refused to be cowed. "I don't see what this ship has to do with our border wars against Repletia."

"Maybe nothing," Tyrel answered patiently. "Maybe everything. The Admiralty and the President have called it the Black Ship for obvious reasons. Anything making that structure could theoretically kick the tar out of us."

Tyrel ordered his ships to prepare for battle. As his bridge crew went about their duties, Tyrel left his post to stride through the ship. He passed scores of soldiers, recognizing only the most senior officers. The rest formed a huge conglomeration of faces and personalities Tyrel had nothing in common with. Once he took a wrong turn and a junior officer pointed out the correct way, Tyrel thanked him and turned down another in a long series of corridors.

Finally he reached one of the nine docks where the flagship kept its fleet of lethal fighters. He stood to one side and watched as maintenance crews went about overhauling each fighter, checking every component of each fighter. They replaced any suspect parts. Parts were cheap and the Navy prided itself on keeping intact its greatest asset, its weapons.

Tyrel had once manned a fighter during the Trask Incident. The Anphorians suffered a ninety percent casualty rate against the Repletians in that skirmish. This forced the Admiralty into retraining its corps of fighters. It was an expensive year-long overhaul and when it was over Tyrel had climbed two ranks.

Of course, no one knew what damage they inflicted upon the Repletians at Trask. By the time the Navy returned with reinforcements the Repletians had left.

Tyrel soon became too valuable to let him fly fighters. His promotions were as much self-interest on the Navy's part as it was for recognition of his courage and dedication.

A generation later Tyrel enjoyed watching his battle crews go through their drills. If he couldn't fly the latest generation of ship-to-ship fighters he could observe those who did. He enjoyed the mingled smell of oil, grease, sweat, and booster fluids. Drills and hammers and wrenches filled the bay with sound, while light coruscated from welding tools. He listened to the shouts and curses of men and women as they worked on their assigned duties. Flight crew members came in five minutes after Tyrel. They were oblivious to his presence and stood in a ragged line, facing the machines they would soon command. Tyrel heard their laughter and comments and found himself again missing the comradery he had known as a flyer.

For an endless time he stood beside a fighter closest to the bay's inner doors. Across from these inner doors was a giant sliding panel with room for two fighters at a time to leave wing tip to wing tip. This panel opened to a pair of sliding doors forming part of the outer hull. When these outer doors opened, the cargo bay would be empty except for the fighters warming their engines; the din would be enormous except in space nothing resembled sound.

As Tyrel watched his men focused on their tasks, a sergeant-at-arms walked up to him, briskly saluted, and told him a message awaited him from the Admiralty.

Back in his quarters Tyrel made himself a hot brew of noodle soup, which he sipped gingerly, reveling in the hot smooth taste of it. He poured the soup from its container into a large mug. Next, he made himself comfortable in his work desk chair, placed the mug without looking next to the holograph computer, then keyed in his command code. As the holograph image sprang to life he took a pen from its holder and occasionally jotted notes on a writing pad. Writing was one of the few archaic luxuries he permitted himself. He remembered Lexington's penchant for the same habit and felt connected in some fashion to a man he considered his friend despite the five-year absence from Home Base.

The sharp, clear, life-like focus on the woman who faced him did nothing to dispel the faint sense of fear he felt each time he saw her image. He knew this fear was unfounded; after all, what could she do to him this far from Home Base? The rationalization, of course, didn't work; her steady unwavering gaze unnerved him. It wasn't just the power she wielded, but the sheer force of her icy personality.

The President's face was smooth despite her age. Her black eyes calmly stared at Tyrel for several seconds. Short black hair framed her small face. Not for the first time did Tyrell wonder how she had climbed to the Presidency, especially given no one became president without defeating the incumbent president in a hand-to-hand combat to the death. Katina Patriloney looked no larger than Tyrell's eldest daughter. There seemed nothing lethal about Katina's appearance, yet in her reign she had already killed three challengers to the presidency. Each fight had been different, and yet none had lasted more than two or three minutes. Stories had grown about how Katina could kill warriors twice and three times her physical size. People who saw the recordings could not understand how she did it, even in slow frame.

"Greetings, Tyrel. I received your latest dispatch." Tyrel noted her refusal to formally acknowledge his rank. It was her way of reinforcing her position. As Tyrel mused over this she continued. "I suggest we keep to our primary goals. The Black Ship is top priority. Everything else is secondary and expendable as per the Navy's First Directive."

"Madame President, I . . ."

She held up a hand, stopping him in mid-sentence. "I repeat, everything else is secondary and expendable. Follow our Prime Directive to the letter. No one must interfere with your mission to retrieve as much information as you can about the Black Ship. Do I make myself clear?"

"Yes, Madame President."

"Fine. I knew we could come to an understanding. Lexington will have further details on how you are to proceed."

"If we meet Repletians? It's their territory we must enter."

The President paused in the act of turning away. "Tyrel, under no circumstances is the Black Ship to fall into Repletian hands. Under NO circumstances. You are to get access to the Black Ship at any cost. *At any cost.* If that's impossible, destroy it. See to it."

Her image winked out before Tyrel could say anything. He felt both chagrin and relief; chagrin from the curtness with which she dismissed him, relief from the tension he felt whenever in communication with her. Tyrel took a few minutes to jot briefing notes before he felt ready to talk with Lexington.

As soon as his image appeared, joy washed over him. Despite

Lexington's imposing size and his role as Chairman of the Joint Fleets of the Admiralty, Lexington's brisk self-confidence and gruff nature were worlds away from Katina's icy demeanor. Tyrel and Lexington had gone through the Officers Academy together and they relied on each other's judgements and skills.

"You've talked to Madame President," Lexington confirmed in his brusque manner. "We cannot have anything interfere with gaining access to the Black Ship and whatever secrets it holds."

Tyrel nodded. "Madame President was firm in stating this includes any Repletians we happen to find on the way."

Lexington paused for a slow second, then nodded. "Including Repletians. We cannot have them gain access to the Black Ship. They can do irreparable harm to it with their mystical absurdity. Savages, all of them."

"You've had a chance to observe the ship?"

"Yes. Our technicians are still assessing the data you sent us. It's no accident we stumbled onto the Black Ship inside Repletian territory. We must assume a connection between the two."

"We should assume the Repletians may have found the Black Ship already."

"Nonsense. For one, despite their primitive belief systems, if they had found the Black Ship they would've had ample time to capitalize on it. We wouldn't be having this conversation outside a cell. No, this isn't a scenario we have to worry about."

Tyrel took a sip from his mug. Lexington watched him, keeping a stoic expression as Tyrel placed his mug next to the console, and finally said, "There's one outcome you must prepare for."

Tyrel stared at the solid image of Lexington and waited.

"Have you heard of Colonel Enid Blue Starbreaks?"

Tyrel sucked in his breath and stifled a gasp. Lexington saw Tyrel's expression.

"She can answer the dilemmas we face. If it's the Repletians who are responsible for the Black Ship, her background may cause them to hesitate."

"And what of our Navy? A Repletian in charge of a fleet will cause a stir."

"Indeed, I expect so. I've based my plans on the impact she'll create."

"Can you trust her?"

Lexington kept his composure. "With my life. But that won't happen. She'll flush out those whom we don't know enough to worry about."

Tyrel nodded. "You're willing to waste such a person to flush out others?"

Lexington gave a slight smile. "We do what we must. No one expects us to come out of this without some sacrifices. But we'll be stronger than we are now if we play our cards right."

"You think that little of her?"

"No, under other circumstances she would make a hell of an Admiral and a hell of a replacement for me. But we don't live in such tolerant times. There's so much she doesn't know. We've taken extraordinary steps to keep her from anything we can't control. She's only what we've made her. No, Tyrel, my friend, you'll do best to be cautious yourself. We don't have the facts. You're in a precarious position. We can't save you if something unforeseen happens."

As Lexington's image faded Tyrel leaned back in his chair to take a few minutes to reflect. He needed to feel the control back in his hands. Let anything happen, he had a force that could cope with anything short of a supernova.

Tyrel was on the bridge when the fleet met the Black Ship. As everyone scrambled to battle stations, he remembered the young woman he met ten years ago in the Officers Academy, a tall, slim green-eyed figure of twenty-seven who still haunted him. Enid Blue Starbreaks had been a quiet young cadet but the Admiralty knew it had someone special. She inspired fear, hatred and awe among the other cadets, both for her abilities and for her ancestry. Definitely leadership material. Tyrel wondered how she would handle the situation he was heading into if he wasn't successful.

"Admiral, we cannot get a fix on that ship."

Tyrel stared at the impossible ship. Again his senses hurt to see it waver in and out of sight, its form changing from moment to moment like black water. Nothing they threw at it in terms of probes could decipher the least bit of useful information from it. Its mass shifted between zero and super-neutron density in temporal spans too small to record. It acted as if momentum didn't exist, flowing from one point to another without a pattern. And, in the vacuum of space, Tyrel swore he heard bizarre notes and rhythms emanate from whatever hull the Black Ship had, bizarre because the chords on which Humanity's musical understandings were built were absent from the Black Ship's sounds.

For precious minutes the dark ship led the fleet. The Admiral couldn't control its eagerness. Nor did he try to do so. There were hundreds of millions of people scattered among a thousand main battle cruisers, ten thousand lighter ships, hundreds of thousands of single-occupant fighters, and countless support ships. The sight of so many fighters breaking ranks to engage in battle, had cowed more than one enemy fleet.

What was surprising was the sudden appearance of a dozen Repletian ships. Housing no more than a few dozen thousand crew members apiece, they were certainly no threat to the power of a single Anphorian battle cruiser. The Repletian ships hovered a hundred light seconds from the Fifth Fleet, making no threatening motions. They were observers, for which Tyrel cursed them. They were an uncomfortable distraction when Tyrel could least afford to be occupied by anything except the task at hand.

"Sir, our ships request the authority to fire on the enemy."

Tyrel nodded his assent. "Permission is granted but only from the leading fighters. I want sustained bursts for about ten seconds and then they're to cease firing. Have them acknowledge my orders."

Acknowledgements came in quickly. Tyrel watched with the rest of the fleet as the ten lead ships fired their weapons. The Black Ship stopped in the path of the firestorm, which dissipated into the Black Ship's hull without a ripple.

The Black Ship engulfed a Class III fighter, which had a crew of thirty thousand people. Amazingly the Black Ship, which dwarfed the small fighter, covered only half of its hull. The pictures, which now came from the fighter's internal holographs, shocked Tyrel into stillness.

Muffled explosions and screams came from beyond the bridge's reinforced doors. The Captain of the ship was yelling orders while an elite group of guards circled him. As they completed this maneuver, the main bridge doors sagged inwards and then melted from immense heat. A tide of red swept inwards, engulfing everything. The sight confused Tyrel. Was it some toxic fluid, some poisonous liquid or gas?

This scarlet incandescence streamed to the spot where the soldiers formed a circle about their Captain. The soldiers fired repeatedly, each energy wave creating a massive ring of blackness and smoke against the walls and surfaces of the bridge, only to be covered again by it almost as fast as the eye could register the blackness. As the red tide circulated, cascading up the legs of every person on the bridge, Tyrel realized no liquid or gas could do this. And then the guards on the bridge fell as millions of Anphorians watched and understood from the sudden dark redness the guards were being buried in their own blood. Blood flowed from their bodies as creatures smaller than ants consumed them. In moments the guards were red mounds that shrank in size, while the rest of the fleet watched in horrified silence.

Within half a minute the red tide swiftly ebbed from the bridge to reveal the white skeletal frames of bodies, each stripped of flesh as though they had been bleached ten years in the desert.

In the shocked stillness of the flagship's bridge Tyrel drew himself up in his seat. "Where's the goddamn ship?" he bellowed. Tyrel's voice stirred his bridge officers into action.

"It's gone!" came back the swift answer.

Suddenly aware of their acute danger, officers throughout the fleet scrambled back to their duties. Communication links became a hubbub of sound as messages quickly engulfed each other. In this storm of confusion Tyrel ordered his flagship to cut off all channels except their internal ones. His officers tried to locate the Black Ship. For precious moments they came up with no answers.

When the Black Ship appeared next to the *Kirilovnich's* hull, panic followed. Officers screamed at one another and Tyrel, unused to this loss of discipline, fought to regain command of the bridge. And then turned to the screen as the Black Ship radiated shafts of multi-hued light that speared through the fleet in ever-increasing numbers. The Black Ship became a sphere and the tonal music Tyrel heard earlier resounded through his flagship, through every ship, a tonal pattern so mesmerizing Tyrel never moved even as he watched the familiar galactic core waver in form. The great yellow Centre of All Worlds quickly faded until his screen was blackness itself, blackness made darker in contrast to those shafts of light in a pattern Tyrel recognized from the tonal music.

And then the shafts of light disappeared, the music stilled and stars swam back into view. They clustered around a galactic core which Tyrel, because he had grown to love the sight, knew wasn't the galactic core of the Milky Way galaxy.

"Where the fuck are we?" Tyrel demanded of his bridge officers. "Where the fuck's the Milky Way galaxy?"

"I don't know. Admiral. Our computers don't register any familiar systems."

"They must! They have to!" But Admiral Tyrel knew they weren't in their own home galaxy; the stars were different and so too was the shape of the galactic center he saw on his screen. "We're lost! Where the fuck are we?"

Tyrel sank into his seat as a feeling of hopelessness rose in him. "We're lost," he said to no one in particular.

CHAPTER 2

Standard Year 2478

Katina Patriloney stared out at the rain. Behind her the steady click of the grandfather clock's hand went unheard. It was something she had listened to for almost all her eighty years, paying no attention to it now unless she needed to check the time. Tonight she felt a sense of peace and calm.

The rain slanted from the angled window before her, running down the thick panes of template glass to the distant ground fifty floors below. Most lights of the city were out at this time of night. She stared into the night, waiting for something, anything to break the hold of the darkness that held her. Discomforting whispers of motion and sound were out there.

When the soft bell-like chime of the holograph panel rang true and clear in the room behind her, she straightened her posture, squared her shoulders, briefly and lovingly touched the glass barrier with a left hand, and then turned swiftly to take the incoming message.

"Sorry to disturb you, Madame President."

"Lexington, you knew I was awake. What is it?"

"We've received transmissions which are the last we'll receive from Tyrel in some time, if ever."

"Lexington, you know I don't enjoy riddles. Come to the point."

"It seems the Fifth Fleet's no longer where it should be."

"I take it you mean Tyrel didn't reach the Black Ship. Was it the Repletians?"

"We're not sure. Messages before the fleet stopped sending showed a group of Repletian ships appearing. But they were too small; they shouldn't have been able to hurt us in any significant way."

"Yes, it was the Black Ship."

Admiral Lexington paused, caught off guard by her certainty.

How did she know? He had just received the message himself.

"It's too early to say with any conclusion but, yes, I'd guess it was the Black Ship or something like it. But a single ship! The fleet had enough fire power to level a dozen systems."

"As I said earlier, Lexington, I don't like riddles. You followed my earlier instructions?"

"Yes, Madame President. The orders have gone out. The Fourth Fleet's rendezvousing at Baradine's Planet in four days, enough time for its Admiral to be appointed and sent."

"Good news, Admiral. And of Enid Blue Starbreaks?"

"She"ll be told about her interview when she shows up for duty tomorrow afternoon."

Katina stared at Lexington's holograph image and waited, knowing there was more. And there was.

"Madame President, are you certain we're making the right move? We won't be able to retract ourselves once word is out."

"Lexington, please leave the thinking to me. Enid Blue Starbreaks is where she is because of what I saw in her a long time before you were Admiral. She's a known quantity and perhaps the Repletians aren't as canny as they seem."

"As you wish, Madame President."

Just before Lexington terminated his link she held up her left hand, making him stop.

"Admiral, after we interview the Colonel I'll send my seal of authorization to you."

She turned off her link and moved from her chair to look out again at the never-ending streams of rain flowing down her slanted window. Her mind slowly sank into the past. Her smile faded as she recalled another rain fifty years ago in another place.

Standard Year 2425

Lawrence (everyone called him Lawrence) stared at her in that cruel mocking way she had grown to love. His devil-may-care attitude drew her to him. At twenty-seven she had the slim figure of an athlete; he stared at her and nodded with approval. The others in his small group of followers waited until they saw how he treated her. They were always uncertain of how to treat the daughter of the President, taking their cues from Lawrence.

"Repletians probably deserve as good a fate as we gave the Thetans five hundred years ago," a student continued his argument. A storm of protests rose as Katina sat next to Lawrence. He put one arm around her and then pulled it away to lean forward in his seat. The uproar slowly died and Lawrence looked at the student who started the argument.

"Paul, we gave the Thetans the breaks and look what happened. Like our leaders said, they were assimilated into Anphoria. Nowadays you can't find anyone claiming ancestry to Theta or its satellites. Our policies were right. Take away their citizenship, teach them our ways and language, and they make better citizens."

"I don't know. Last week I found old records from a planet said to be the Home Planet for our species. Some of their records sounded like what we did to the Thetans."

Lawrence guffawed and slapped the table, hard. "Wake up, Paul. The problem here isn't the Thetans or useless history books. The problem is these Repletians. Sooner or later they'll interfere with us and we'll have to deal with them. If you ask me, it's about time we eliminate that crew and their mystic lunacy."

Paul was stubborn. "What about your insistence on logic over emotions? If we don't need the Repletians, we can let things stay the way they are now."

Lawrence shook his head. "Come on, Paul, you aren't scared

of a bunch of barbarians and their mumbo-jumbo, are you? They need what we've got. I say it's about time they stopped trying to get in our way."

Katina heard no more as she made her way to the bar for more drinks. Lawrence could get wrapped up and excited about things but she knew he never meant half of what he said. She thought his cruelty was a show, masking his need to belong. Of that Katina was certain. She looked around the room as her drinks were made. Nothing exceptional. A half dozen other people were in their own quiet worlds. It was too early for the party crowd and for this Katina was thankful. Later the bar would fill with smoke and noise, which often gave her splitting migraines the next day.

In one corner, by himself, a Repletian nursed a drink. Katina sensed his gloom from where she stood. The Repletian was tall, taller than her Lawrence, and more slender than Lawrence's bulky frame. He paid attention to no one.

He looked up and Katina turned her head quickly to avoid meeting his glance. A shiver of distaste went down her spine. Once the sight of any Repletian in a bar would have caused a sensation. But as the border wars dragged on Repletian survivors began to show up deeper in Anphorian space. Since they were loners and caused no trouble, the Navy and the Council left them alone, too busy gaining territory to worry about the casualties of their efforts. This didn't stop ordinary people from feeling resentful about the influx of Repletians, especially on those worlds where the immigrants tended to collect. Katina found them odd creatures, each lost and yet fiercely independent.

Back at the table, Lawrence, as usual, grabbed his frothy mug without looking at her or giving his thanks. He took a long sip of the copper-colored ale before he turned his attention to her. He studied her raven hair and ivory skin; sometimes she caught him rapturously entranced, lost in her long, thick locks of gleaming hair.

"How's your father?"

"He's all right. Off to another Council meeting tonight."

"For what it's worth, your father is the best President we've had in two hundred years. He doesn't take guff from Repletia."

"I wish he'd stay home more often."

Lawrence shrugged as if to say there was nothing he could do about that. He studied Katina's pale face for another second then returned to his diatribe against giving Repletians special status or services.

"After all, none of us receive special services so why should they? It's their problem if they're losing the border wars. If they can't find work, that's their tough luck. We have to sacrifice in tough times. They're bums; you can't trust them because they're animals. None of them know what a good day's work is."

Katina felt eyes on her and she turned to the far table where the lone Repletian sat quietly gazing at her. At first Lawrence didn't see her look away, so intent was he in convincing Paul of his beliefs. Only when he turned to ask her for support did he find her staring across the room. He followed her gaze and saw the single man staring back.

"Fucking Repletian!"

These words startled Katina for, despite his arrogance, Lawrence rarely swore. She turned to him but he was incensed. At the top of his voice he yelled at the Repletian, "What the fuck are you looking at, Plete?"

"Baby, I'm sure he means no harm." Katina tried to soften Lawrence from his discomfort but Lawrence would have none of it. He shook her hand off and stood up, his chest expanding as he yelled again at the Repletian, "You want her? Come over here and I'll show you something, Plete!"

Amazingly, the Repletian, who looked so glum moments before, was now amused. He continued to stare at the table, but his expression now of frank curiosity. This further angered Lawrence. He grabbed his mug and stormed over to the table where the Repletian waited. The others at the table followed Lawrence, their eyes bright with anticipation. Lawrence had a reputation for street-fighting Katina had never seen. The students knew the Repletian faced danger.

"I said, were you looking at my girlfriend, Plete?" Lawrence now towered over the Repletian, who looked up at the angry student and said nothing.

"What, are you deaf?" Lawrence bellowed. A few others in the bar looked to the corner where the commotion was, but no one moved from their table. Let the management of the bar take care of matters if they wanted to.

The Repletian stayed calm, waiting in his seat. Lawrence became more incensed by this indifference. He reached over to grab the Repletian's tattered lapel. Without losing his faint smile, the Repletian knocked Lawrence's hand away and for the first time he spoke.

"I was merely curious about you Anphorians. I intend no harm or insult towards you. Will you accept my apologies?"

"Come on, Lawrence, let's go. It's nothing." Katina attempted to pull Lawrence by his arm but Lawrence refused to budge. He stared down at the Repletian. "What gives you Pletes the right to come into our bars and feed off our good natures? Why aren't you in the Plete section of town where you belong?"

"I'm grieved I cause you such discomfort." The Repletian made a move to leave but Lawrence, seeing the anticipation in the other students' eyes, felt the chance to prove himself slipping away. He shoved the Repletian down into his seat again and said, "Oh, no, you don't. You owe an apology to my girlfriend and to me. You were making eyes at her"

"I was merely curious about your group."

"What are we to you, freaks? You a spy? Yeah, I'll bet you're a spy."

The Repletian looked puzzled. "A spy? No, I… don't blend in too well. I'm from the border worlds."

"A deserter then? My dad told me about your kind. Nothing but scum who wouldn't hesitate to rape an Anphorian."

The Repletian looked from one student to the other but they made no moves; their bright eyes had a rapacious look the Repletian understood too well. It was never going to be easy. But he tried, knowing he had to try.

"I apologize for any insult you may have felt."

"We can't trust any of you," Lawrence spat. Then, as the Repletian made another move to get up Lawrence broke his mug against the hard tabletop and brandished it in front of him, waving it inches from the Repletian's eyes.

"You want some of this, huh?" Lawrence imitated the weave and bob of a boxer, his feet stumbling a quick unsteady pattern on the wooden floor. When the Repletian merely stared at him another student sneered. "Fucking Repletian!" Lawrence shrieked at the top of his voice and made a lunging jab, his hand arcing up in a wicked curve towards the Repletian's face. The Repletian grabbed Lawrence's arm to deflect his blow. Lawrence, off balance, fought against the hold and his momentum carried him into the edges of the mug. He gave a stifled gasp and clutched at his neck, where blood spurted, gushing onto the floor. The Repletian gently lowered Lawrence's shuddering frame to the floor. Katina witnessed Lawrence's final spasms as blood continued to pump from his neck, so much blood. For several shocked moments, she cradled Lawrence's head in her bloodied lap, but Lawrence spoke not a word, his eyes slowly losing their luster, and then she felt him leave as a last gurgled choking rattle emanated from his mouth, along with a seeming endless outflow of blood. Before the first responders arrived, Katina found herself out in the night.

The rain poured from the skies, streaming along the gutters and falling along worn paths, gathering in great puddles everywhere she looked. In moments she was soaked, but it was not the rain. Blood sluiced down her clothes. Her eyes scanned the streets in search of the beast. Not knowing which way to go, she blindly set out in pursuit, her legs aching as she pushed herself in a way she never thought possible. She quickly left the few other students behind. When she rounded the corner and stared down the street she saw nothing. But she ran and ran against the pain rising from somewhere deep inside herself.

Finally, she collapsed against a wall and let the rain and wind beat against her. Her mind focused only on Lawrence's words, " . . . they're animals . . ." Lawrence and her father were right after all. What good was their mysticism if it let them kill someone like Lawrence?

And gradually Katina felt her anger shrink into a cold dark rage that tightened and threatened to choke her. She was on her feet again, moving swiftly back to the bar she had left. As she neared the pub, now bathed in the red lights of emergency lifters and security forces, Katina felt the anger sink deep into a place in her soul to which she promised to return to for as long as it took to take her revenge. Repletians would pay for this outrage against Lawrence. If she couldn't find the one who did it, she would make sure other Repletians paid dearly for her dear Lawrence.

Her father was standing in a group of other people, most of them bodyguards. When he saw her, he held up a hand to stop the others from talking and hurried to meet her.

"Honey, I came as soon as I heard. Are you all right?"

Katina collapsed into her father's arms. "Oh, dad, I hate them. I hate them. They killed Lawrence."

"My men tell me it was a Repletian who did this. Don't worry, honey. We'll find him."

Katina shook her head. "No, father, he's gone. He's gone back into the slums. You'll never find him now."

Her father stroked her wet face and looked into her eyes. “Honey, we’ll get him. We’ll get him if it takes ten years.”

“And if you don’t find him? If you don’t get the animal that killed my Lawrence?”

“I’ll stake my career on finding the killer.”

“They’ll pay. With their blood they’ll pay dearly.”

Her father, shocked at the intensity of her voice, gently reassured her, “We’ll find him.”

Katina’s eyes narrowed and her face drained of color. “They’ll pay, father,” she whispered. “They’ll pay in blood if it takes all my life.”

CHAPTER 3

Standard Year 2478

Katina stared out the window and felt the wonder of her position, the surprise that while it had taken generations to plan and carry out such revenge she now felt nothing but a weariness where joy should have filled her soul. A few short years after Lawrence's death, when her father died, the Council was thrown into confusion, a confusion into which she'd stepped to become first Council Member and then, with the sudden death of Jonas Palmer (her father's successor), She had set up everything so carefully, spinning webs over the years to form a maze she couldn't get out of. In nine days, the Repletians would indeed pay for the death of Lawrence but she had a hard time picturing his face. She had an even harder time recalling his voice and mannerisms. Perhaps, she keenly felt this loss because she could say nothing to his soul as her moment of revenge neared.

The old woman swam into focus from the darkness of Katina's living room. Katina felt the woman's presence. She turned.

"It's been awhile."

The old woman shrugged, her face shrouded in the dimness.

"I haven't decided whether you exist or not." Katina sat on the sectional couch.

The old woman smiled, saying nothing.

"One day you'll tell me about that scar."

Katina leaned forward to pour a cup of tea. When she looked up, the old woman was seated across from her.

"It's from berry picking."

"Must be some berries to do that to you."

The old woman nodded. "Some berries."

Katina sipped her tea, her dark eyes studying the woman. She tested. "I don't know your name."

"It's Annie."

"Annie, what do you do? Are you Anphorian?"

"Aside from you, do you know any Anphorian as small as me?"

"We do tend to be tall."

Annie smiled. "Not me. And certainly not you."

"You haven't answered my question."

"If you asked the right question, I would answer."

Katina closed her eyes. The ticking of her longcase clock allowed her to relax. Otherwise nothing. Her quarters were soundproofed. After a while she opened her eyes. Annie was gone. Katina finished her tea before preparing for sleep. The next morning Katina was up before sunrise and waited in her study. The three men entered under the escort of her slave, a Repletian male whom she had the pleasure of neutering thirty years ago when they had escorted him from the Pegasus Revolt. She enjoyed the task of beating down the will to resist from a strong body over the ten years it took to train him. She was aided by the pain simulators, they surgically installed.

Once she had enjoyed watching his reactions. But over the years, she grew weary of torturing him and eventually grew used to him. He no longer played anything but a minor role in her daily routines. As her personal slave he was everywhere she was in the house but he might have been a piece of furniture for the attention she gave him.

As the three men seated themselves, Katina spoke and a life-size holograph appeared ten feet in front of them. Katina watched the men study the image as it rotated to show the woman's figure. Katina had taken care to show the woman in the grey uniform she would soon wear. Katina knew the figure from memory, having watched the girl grow into a woman. Each passing day solidifying Katina's confidence she had made the right choice in selecting and carefully shaping the events around Enid and securing her position as successor.

The tallest of the men wore the black overcoat he always wore, a coat long and bulky enough to hide gutting knives, strangling cords, and other portable tools of his trade. Katina had used him a few times over the years but this was his last job for her, although he didn't know it. She had taken steps to ensure she never saw him again. For this, she was willing to put up with a great deal from him. The recording ended. Enid's image flickered and then disappeared. The wall lights brightened.

"So, gentlemen, you have your target."

The leader turned his eyes from the holograph to stare at Katina with an insolence that brought a deep flush to her face. How dare he have the gall to look at her with such boldness! She took a deep breath for control.

"Lexington has contacted you?" she asked, knowing the answer but wanting time to consider their reactions.

The one who stared at her nodded. "Yes, the Admiral thinks he found us on his own. Of course we planted our names into the system through a few discreet channels. It proved to be an interesting exercise. I've always wondered if we could manipulate the Navy."

Katina nodded but she knew they wouldn't live to use their information. Nevertheless, Lexington must be distracted into thinking he controlled events. And once these three were dead no one would be the wiser. No one would know she was using Enid Blue Starbreaks as a smoke screen.

"So she's the one we kill?" The leader spoke with a contemptuous tone of voice. "She doesn't look like much. Should we worry about her?"

Katina sprang the half-truth on them. "I understand she'll be an Admiral by the time you kill her."

The leader frowned. "Say, you aren't pulling a fast one on us, are you?"

"The Navy runs its own shop."

"But you contacted us two months ago."

"I have my sources of information. Stopping her is important. "

The leader was stubborn. "It don't make sense."

"The Navy figures it will have an advantage if it can use a Repletian in the border wars."

The leader thought for a few seconds. "I see your problem."

Later, after she detailed the plans she made for them, they left and Katina took a deep breath as she closed the door behind them. She was infuriated by the leader's casual arrogance. Her father had never put up with such insolence when he was President. She thought about this as she turned from the door and almost bumped into the slave. She hadn't heard him approach and she hissed at him. He backed away to the side to allow her to pass. She looked hard at him but his face and eyes expressed no emotion, not even fear. She coolly grunted and continued on her way, quickly putting him from her mind as she hurried to her communications center. She had duties to perform and more calls to make to set everything into motion.

Hours passed in her study, where the silence was complete. She typed her commands into the quaint keyboard. She could have verbally entered them but she liked to keep her fingers nimble. It kept her young.

When she finished her duties and logged her commands for the day, sending them to her office for processing, she took time to walk back to her window, the same window out of which she had stared the previous night. This time her mind was focused on the disappearance of the Fifth Fleet and Vice Admiral Tyrel. The tapes showing the final visual moments of the fleet were received but her scientists and technicians hadn't worked through to any useful analysis of the incident. Many were shocked by the images Tyrel had seen the day before.

Katina didn't for a second believe the Black Ship was human. But by sending Starbreaks after the Black Ship, Katina hoped to create confusion, affording her the necessary time to complete the operation. In another nine days, while the war raged along the borders between

Anphoria and Repletia, her star bomb drones would reach the centers of every star that housed the ten Home Worlds of Repletia. If Enid could distract the Repletians for that length of time then Katina would win the war. Whatever happened to Enid then didn't matter. Katina supposed Enid would lose her officer's rank, a small sacrifice for a greater cause.

"Madame President?"

Katina recognized Lexington's voice. "Yes, Admiral?"

"I have set up the interview for the Vice Admiral's position. It begins in less than forty minutes at thirteen hundred hours. Can you be here?"

"I'm on my way."

And for the next few minutes she hummed to herself as she went about preparing a simple meal. She was famished and ate it with great gusto, relishing in the exhilaration of the day

CHAPTER 4

Standard Year 2478

Enid Blue Starbreaks felt sick when she woke up at noon. Disturbing dreams (whose details eluded her the more she tried to remember them) plagued her. Most of the major muscles in her body had the familiar ache, which she was quick to shrug off. A tree near her bedroom balcony swayed under the overcast sky. In the distance a ray of dull red sunlight managed to break through the clouds to light part of the storm-tossed ocean. Enid hastily wrapped herself in a large thick night robe, scrambled out of bed and made her way to the washroom.

As Enid turned on the shower she glanced at her lean military build through one of the mirrors that covered the walls. The three-month survival course she completed four days ago made her naturally brown skin darker. Her blue-green eyes became brighter in the light. A few scratches from yesterday's cross-country march marked the lower part of her arms and several of her long slender fingers but they were nothing serious. At sixty kilograms she was light set as an Anphorian, but her five-foot eleven-inch height turned her weight into an advantage. She was small for a Repletian, but tall for an Anphorian. With this thought she stepped into the shower and turned it to the coolest setting. She gasped as the icy water chilled her body, raising goose bumps on her tanned leathery skin.

Enid shivered from the shock and suddenly, without stopping to reason why, she reached down and shifted the temperature until steam was billowing from her lithe body. Feeling a moment of delicious defiance, she reveled in the heat. Damn the military with its need for Spartan frugality. She deserved to treat herself once in a while.

After the shower, Enid quickly dried herself; her no-nonsense military buzzcut was easy to take care of, and methodically went through the rest of her morning rituals. Before long she was ready for work. Her grey two-piece uniform, except for its single Colonel's double-slash red insignia on one shoulder, could have been that of any senior officer below Admiral rank.

The trip to her ninetieth story office was uneventful. Enid spent most of her time reviewing the documents Daegan Markowitz had given her to study over the weekend. She looked up once to see the driver studying her through the reflective mirror; he quickly hid his look of distaste as he looked away.

Enid was used to this look. She ignored it as she ignored similar looks from others. Soon she was making her way through a maze of corridors and flights of stairs to reach her small office on the ninety-fourth floor of Naval Headquarters.

Daegan was waiting for her. She closed the door, took her chair, and accepted the cup of warm liquid from him. She asked him to seat himself at the table dominating the room and pushed the files she had brought with her toward him.

"Well, Daegan, I've read them but I'm not certain why the Admiral wants me to review them. They have nothing to do with my present posting."

Daegan looked at her and chose his words carefully. "I'm not certain myself why the Admiral gave you those files. There have been rumors . . ."

Enid winced and Daegan stopped in mid-sentence. "Daegan, you know how I don't like rumors. They've ruined fine officers in the past and I don't want to become one."

Daegan shrugged. "How's the coffee?" he asked.

"Is that what it is? I wondered. It's been so long since I had any I've almost forgotten what it smelled and tasted like."

They smiled at each other. "Come on, Daegan, what's up? It's unlike you to spoil me like this. You're hiding something."

Daegan grinned and pushed Enid's schedule towards her. She glanced at it and saw the blank page.

"I don't understand this." Enid frowned. "What happened to my meeting with Colonel Marks? Weren't we supposed to review the logs for *Stars End*?

Daegan stood up before he spoke. "I'm to take you upstairs to see Admiral Lexington."

Daegan reached for the files Enid had passed to him and tucked them under one arm. "The Admiral said you could come as you are. That means your coffee as well."

Enid was flustered as she followed Daegan up the single flight of stairs. The thin doors innocuously slid open but Enid knew the two-inch barrier of metal was an alloy that could withstand a nuclear blast at close range. The entire building was made of the same alloy found among the ruins of a civilization long since extinct.

Lexington's Aide was a tall man Enid recognized from her survival course. He saluted her and led her into the Admiral's quarters.

Enid wasn't sure what to expect but the single large desk and the man behind it were dwarfed by the size of the room. A series of priceless first edition prints by a Canopian artist lined the walls. Other than that the only furniture in the room was a large conference table and a dozen chairs placed in one corner of the room.

What caused the sense of infinite space was the thirty-feet-high walls of glass overlooking the city. Since this building was by far the tallest structure in the city, she could see the whole city and the lands beyond it all the way to the white peaks of the Magnusson Range shimmering in the distance.

As she entered Admiral Lexington stood and moved from behind his desk. "Please," he said, indicating the conference table. "Let's have some room to talk. Daegan, you're excused."

Daegan saluted and left.

Enid sat nervously at one end of the table and waited. The Admiral sat beside her. The entrance door opened and a small woman in her early eighties walked in unannounced, but she needed no introduction. Enid stifled a gasp and quickly stood up to salute, as did Admiral Lexington.

"At ease, both of you," Katina smiled as she seated herself at the head of the table. Enid tried not to appear nervous so close to the President.

"I can see I should have told you I was part of your interview process," Katina gave Enid a warm smile. "I don't stand on formalities, so shall I begin by saying I hope you know why you're here?"

Enid shook her head and Katina turned to Admiral Lexington. "Why Admiral, I thought you'd have told Colonel Blue Starbreaks by now."

The Admiral looked confused by her smile and in turn he also shook his head.

"No matter," Katina said. She turned to Enid. "I've read your file."

"Madame President, if there's anything out of the ordinary I can explain."

"Can you? Well, I didn't bring you here for any impropriety. Far from it. You have a record of accomplishment for your age. You have a way of getting things done with the minimum of fuss and attention. I like that in an officer. I'm looking for that in the next Vice Admiral of the Navy."

"Thank you, Madame President."

Katina opened a file, spreading its contents in front of herself. Her blue-black hair looked striking in the room's light. It starkly contrasted with Katina's skin, which was so white it looked like marble, and yet her veins were uncannily invisible under her translucent skin. Her mouth was rimmed by a slash of light blue lipstick. She studied the file for a few seconds and then looked up at Enid.

"It says here both of your adopted parents are dead."

"Yes, Madame President."

Katina leaned back in her chair before continuing. "Tell me about them."

"Madame President, I don't know where to start."

Katina shrugged. "Please...proceed. And, call me Katina."

Enid glanced at Admiral Lexington, who looked baffled. She'd get no support from him. She wanted to try to keep this meeting as formal as she could, relying on the confidence this would give her.

"Well, Madame President, I mean, Katina. I was young when they were killed. I don't remember much about them because I don't want to remember. It's too painful."

"Even now?"

"Yes, even now. I loved them."

"It states in your file they died in an accident involving their lifter. You mentioned the word *killed*. Can you elaborate? Do you see their deaths differently from the autopsy?"

"I do, sir."

Katina stared at Enid, her black eyes unreadable but her face showing curiosity. "Enid, I need to know everything you know of yourself, especially anything that bothers you. Do you understand me?"

"Aye, sir."

"What you tell me is between us."

Enid took a deep breath and averted her eyes from Katina's intense gaze. "Well, sir, they died in the lifter but no one ever found the flight recorder. Dad was the best flyer I ever knew and the weather was perfect. There was no reason for them to die like that. It was horrible."

"Something unexpected happened?"

"Sir, if you're as thorough as they say you are, you know my father had a medical scan and you know the results of that."

Katina smiled and waited.

"My mother was found in the driver's seat. She was good but

she wouldn't operate the cruiser if Dad was there."

"Let's move on. You received outstanding grades in your class but you weren't sociable."

"Sir, after my parents died, I wasn't the same person I was before."

Katina studied Enid for a few seconds. Whatever she saw, she looked grave as she came to a decision. "Have you read the files you were given on Sector Five?"

"Aye, sir, I have."

"Give me your assessment of the situation."

"Well, sir, Sector Five's one of the disputed border systems between us and the Repletians. There are less than ninety major Repletian settlements and barely twice that number of Repletian battle ships."

"Ah, yes, the Repletians. We didn't think they would expand their settlements into that sector so quickly. Until recently we thought they were expanding their settlements into Sector Nineteen, on the other side of their Home Worlds."

"Sir, we were probably correct twenty years ago. I understand the situation has changed since then."

"Many things can change in twenty years," Katina agreed. "A lot can also stay the same, especially if things are planned ahead of time. Putting all that aside, let's get to the real point that this sector became strategically important with the discovery of the Black Ship. We want access to that ship but the Repletians won't cooperate."

Enid watched Katina; it surprised her when Katina placed a file bearing her name on its label onto the table and opened it. A photo of her as a small child slid across the smooth table to a point midway between them. Enid looked at the picture and noted her frightened eyes and disheveled appearance. She was clutching a doll in her arms; behind her was the silhouette of a tree shattered by weapons.

For a moment the room swayed and Enid grasped the arms of her chair to keep her balance. Memories of those days threatened to overwhelm her. With great effort Enid kept her seat. Katina, seeing her look of dismay, reached over to take the picture and replace it into her file.

"I have to know, Colonel, how you feel about Repletians."

Enid took a deep breath and averted her eyes from Katina's.

"Sir, I barely remember those final days. I remember sadness; something to do with my natural parents but I can't remember."

"Yes, my files shows they were unfortunate victims during the Pegasus Revolt. Of course the revolt was stopped and we found the ringleaders. But losses were unavoidable. After the Navy sorted everything out your foster parents were happy to adopt you. These things happen."

"Sir, it'd be best if you came to the point of this meeting."

"All right. Knowing what you know about Sector Five, tell me in your words how you would see yourself in charge. What would you do and in what order?"

Enid suspected something like this would happen and went into hard core interview mode. But, mid-sentence, she was immediately curtailed as Katina's eyes shifted to a holograph image which popped up from the table.

"Yesterday Vice Admiral Hubert Tyrel was on assignment to Artel's Star in Sector Five. As you know, he was in command of the Fifth Fleet. We normally receive transmissions every hour from his flagship, the *Kirilovnich.* Again, as you know, standard operating procedure. But whenever the ship goes into a status alert higher than green, it sends us continuous transmissions until the ship or events themselves end the transmission. Watch this."

At first the images showed the command deck of the *Kirilovnich.* Officers were scrambling to reach their stations. The three-dimensional holographs enabled Enid and Katina to see every officer on the bridge. Tyrel was rushing to his commander's chair when the picture shook and the deck's lights dimmed. Enid gasped because she knew what it took to shake the deck of a ten mile long ship that way.

The Vice Admiral shouted at his crew as brilliant hues of light flooded the bridge. Enid heard a strange series of sounds running up and down the scales and reminded her oddly of music, although it was music she never heard. The deck again shook and a great blackness showed in one wall, a blackness opening into spaces Enid didn't recognize. Mercifully the image went blank then, although Enid shook as she thought of the stars, which lay beyond that blackness.

Enid found herself on the edge of her chair. As the image faded, Katina passed Enid a small drink. Enid was fascinated by Katina's slender fingers. They ended in the longest fingernails Enid had ever seen. Katina had painted her fingernails a pale blue to match her lipstick. Enid looked up sharply at Katina's face and Katina smiled. "The water's for you," she said. "You look like you could use it."

Enid gave a nervous laugh and suddenly, for no reason she understood, she felt comforted by Katina's concern. She drank the much appreciated offering in one great gulp. Katina took the empty cup from Enid's hands and without looking tossed it into a disposal unit twenty feet away. Enid returned Katina's smile and Katina resumed the rigorous questioning.

"Colonel, there have been no reports from that Sector since then."

Enid looked at Katina to see if she was joking, hoping that she was joking.

"But sir, did you say this was taken yesterday?"

"I did. And to anticipate your questions, we've started to assemble the Fourth Fleet off Baradine's Planet. Isn't that correct, Admiral?"

"That's correct," Admiral Lexington agreed, his expression unreadable.

Enid looked at Katina's bright black eyes in the low light, waiting for the words she had worked for since she first entered the fleet.

"Colonel, I don't know what caused the disappearance of the Fifth Fleet but we must find out, and soon. When word of this gets out we'll be hard put to contain the damage."

"The damage, sir?"

"Please, as I said, call me Katina. As for the damage, you've taken enough training in human psychology, Colonel, to know that once people see something's possible, it's only a matter of time. The Fifth Fleet's disappearance has compromised our fleet's reputation. The sooner we can discover how the Repletians and that Black Ship did what it did, the more we can control the effects. I'm not fool enough to believe we can return to the past. Whatever the outcome, our fleet's role has been changed forever. Once I know what we're dealing with I can make whatever plans we need."

Katina noted her close attention and smiled. "You're wondering how I can keep calm, aren't you?"

Enid felt herself blush and Katina laughed. "That's okay," she said. "I've seen that look once before. In fact, I believe I was sitting where you were when Jonas Palmer did what I'm doing."

"You knew President Palmer?"

"Knew him? He was my father's successor for a brief time. I'm surprised you don't know this."

"I don't follow politics much. There's enough to being an officer."

Katina smiled. "I guess I knew him better than any person ever knew him. He wasn't open to speculation; he never let anyone except his wife know who he was. I doubt if even she understood what he was while she was alive."

"Aye, sir, I mean, Katina. That was a regrettable accident."

"She was a fine woman. Tough as nails, something like you. Which brings me to my main point. Colonel, I've seen enough of you to offer you command of the Fourth Fleet. Most importantly, I'd like you to find out what happened in Sector Five."

"Sir, I would love to but . . ."

"Yes, I know. As of this moment I'm promoting you to the rank of Vice Admiral. Admiral Lexington, if you will?"

The Admiral stood and Enid followed suit. He moved around the table to face her. The outer door slid open and the Admiral's Aide came in. He marched to the Admiral's side and handed him a small case which Lexington opened. The Aide turned to Enid and removed the stripes from her shoulder. Admiral Lexington reached into the case he was holding, took from it a thin red stripe shaped like a lightning bolt, and pinned it onto Enid's uniform over her heart. The insignia molded into the fabric. The Aide held some documents for the Admiral to sign.

Simple, straightforward. Enid had expected a lavish ceremony. Again, the Admiral smiled. He gestured for his Aide to leave and then he handed Enid another file.

"Admiral Blue Starbreaks, here's the information we have on the event you witnessed. No one below our rank is to see this file. Therefore, once you've read it you're to destroy its contents. Do you understand me?"

"Aye, sir."

Katina stood up to leave. She came around the table to shake Enid's hand. Enid, a head taller, looked down at the President, and felt the shorter woman's presence as a physical force. "Congratulations, Admiral. I'm certain you'll do fine. I have other matters to take care of. I wish you God's speed on your assignment. Admiral Lexington will fill you in."

The two Admirals saluted as Katina left the room. In the following silence Admiral Lexington turned to Enid. "Admiral, you're to leave for Sector Five tomorrow. Take *Stars End.* You've read her files and know her thoroughly. The only task I want you to complete before your departure is your selection of an Aide. And before you choose, let me warn you. People are seldom what they seem. When you read the file you'll understand. Send me the name of your selection for final approval. That person will need the rank of Colonel if they aren't already. Dismissed."

The next few moments were confusing ones for Enid. As she left the room she thought she heard the Admiral say "Good luck" in a low voice. His Aide stood at attention outside the door. He saluted her and led her to one of three offices opposite the Admiral's. Already her name was on the door. The Admiral's Aide led her to her desk and smiled tightly.

"Sir, congratulations are in order. The Admiral has instructed me to assist you until you've confirmed the appointment of your Aide. Can I get you anything?"

"No, thank you, Major. I'll be fine. I'll summon you if I need you. That will be all."

"Aye, sir."

As he left, Enid began to realize the enormity of what was taking place. She collapsed into her chair and simply stared at the wall opposite her. So much to think about. Her thoughts were a welter of confusion, part joy, part puzzlement, part disbelief, part fear.

Finally, needing something to take her mind off everything, Enid toured her office. It was large; smaller than the Admiral's, but large by any standards she knew. In one corner, a sectional couch arced around a circular template glass table. In the middle of this table, a squat blue flower vase contained a dozen roses.

Eight swivel chairs in another corner of the room formed

a semicircle around a low oval black platform whose purpose eluded Enid. She noticed the central chair was slightly larger than the rest and she sat in it. As soon as she did, a holograph sprang to life from the depths of the oval platform. A young officer saluted her.

"Greetings, Admiral. Your entire office is now encoding to your identity pattern. I entered your retinal patterns, fingerprints, blood type, DNA, voice pattern and handwriting samples into your personalized office system. You will be automatically classified as soon as you enter the building. Authorized entry into your office and access to your office system by any person other than you will not be permitted without the official approval of yourself or at least two other persons of the rank of Admiral or higher. A copy of approval has been forwarded to the President's office and to the Central High Council. Only the President and the Council are permitted access to your files. For confirmation of your identity and to initiate code protections please answer the following questions."

Enid patiently answered the questions, only once pausing when the machine asked her for a clearance code, which only she knew, to activate her office system. Enid thought about this and finally decided on using a word only those who knew her would understand the significance of *Pegasus*.

As she completed the security process Enid felt tired. She looked at a screen she hadn't noticed before. It held a list of her priorities for the day. The first item was something she had put out of her mind until now. It was a sentence asking her to select her second-in-command. Enid punched the number and the screen showed a one page summary of the skills required of the person, and a short list of candidates.

Enid scanned the list and felt pleased to see Daegan's name was among the selected candidates. She knew better than to assume Daegan was the best for the position; at least, not until she saw the other candidates.

She glanced at the timepiece on the opposite wall, gave herself an hour and began to scan each file in the program, verbally making notes recorded for her use only.

The first candidate was Captain James Hollinger, a man with fifteen years of field experience. His holograph showed him in combat action. Enid read the dossier detailing his decision-making processes. Enid knew what to expect; fighting men tended to be cautious in their normal lives, choosing to be safe. Taking risks would draw attention to them. They preferred silence, ready when needed. But the Captain also had a sadistic side to his nature he thought only he knew about. Others could use this sadism against him. Enid moved on.

The second person was Jenara Carstairs, an Anphorian Combat Major said to be without peer in strategy. The holograph image revealed a six-foot six-inch tall warrior. She was savage in battle, never leaving her assailants alive. In strategy, she always went for the jugular. But this was disconcerting for her; a warrior who always attacked an enemy's weaknesses was easy to manipulate into prepared traps. Her savagery might result in casualties, but a determined foe would take casualties if it meant victory.

And then there was Daegan. Again, although she knew Daegan, she reviewed his file as carefully as she had done with the others. Daegan preferred to follow leadership he believed in. He never took chances and was unshakeable in his loyalty to his superiors. His combat and fighting skills were conventional and predictable. Because of this, he wasn't Admiral material.

But Daegan had an uncanny ability to second-guess his commanding officer. Knowing what his superior wanted, he worked without directions to finish tasks, often freeing his Commanding Officer for more important issues.

After she read the last file, Enid asked Lexington's aide to set up appointments for each candidate. She sat back in her chair to relax for the first time in hours. A movement in the far corner of the room startled her. She found a tray of food on a food lift, and the full import of her promotion hit her for the first time. No more waiting in the Officer's Mess for lunch. They knew her food preferences, of course, and she took the tray to her desk and enjoyed a leisurely lunch while she called up a review of the latest news, taking in what she saw at a superficial level.

After her lunch, Enid lay on the couch and looked out through the great bay windows. The sun shone through the glass, its brightness muted by the glass's tint. A slight draft from the air conditioning kept the heat in the room at a comfortable sixty-eight degrees. Enid felt the tension ease from her body and her last conscious thought was how soothing the clock sounded above her head.

*

She was on the bridge of her ship. The hull was breached. Daegan yelled something at her. In the great hurricane of air rushing into empty space, taking with it screaming men and women, she couldn't hear Daegan. He held onto a rail on the other side of the bridge and even as she watched the rail he held onto tore loose. Her heart stopped as she watched Daegan helplessly swept into space. She reached out for him but the computer held her in its force field grip.

"Goddamn you!" she yelled at the Computer. "Goddamn you, let me go! I have to help Daegan! I have to help Daegan!"

And then a quiet voice came from behind her, a voice so powerful that despite the wind she heard every word clearly.

"You cannot help him. You were lost from the start."

She turned in her mourning and he stood before her, an old man she had seen in her recurring dreams of the mountain. He smiled as his image faded and his last words echoed in her mind.

"You must return to the beginning. You aren't in your element."

"My element? What are you talking about?"

And then she was staring at an old woman. A scar ran the length of the woman's face.

"It's about the light."

"The light? I don't understand." Enid found herself shouting, and didn't know why.

"You have to give her the light. It's the only way."

"Who? Who do I have to give the light to?"

"She's the light bringer. Her gift is the darkness. Use it. Let her use it. Push her into the light."

"I don't understand," Enid repeated.

"She's the darkness. She's the hope of humanity. There isn't much time."

"Who are you?"

The woman turned away, and as the darkness of space encompassed her, enfolded her, it grew so dark that Enid's eyes hurt. She tried to scream and at that moment she woke up to the soft muted chimes of her wall clock. Someone was calling for her. She groaned as she sat up, the stiffness in her bones draining her of strength. An hour had passed. There was so much to do and for once she didn't know where to begin.

"Admiral, are you all right?"

She recognized the Aide's voice. "Yes, I was having a rest. Please come in."

He walked in without Enid hearing him and was standing on the other side of her desk when she turned around. She smiled at this; he reminded her of Daegan and his patience. "Have you managed to contact the three candidates?"

"Aye, sir, I have. They are scheduled to see you starting at sixteen hundred hours this evening, if that's to your satisfaction?"

"Thank you for your efforts. Yes, that'll be fine. I'll be in the recreational area for the next hour if anyone wishes to talk with me.

Then I'm going home until fifteen thirty hours. Dismissed."

The lake was eight miles around; as Enid walked towards it she felt excitement stir within her at the thought of running the entire course. There were a few people who walked or jogged by her as she did her warm-up routine. She ignored them as she reviewed the course in her mind.

She knew every man who passed her was distracted by her dark skin and slim figure. She had grown used to the stares as she grew used to the looks of disgust when they saw her brown skin was due to more than suntan. That was okay for it gave her an edge they didn't have.

As she ran along the cinder path she felt good and picked up her pace. She had settled into the rhythm when she became distantly aware of someone quickly coming up behind her. She leaned into her run as she climbed a steep hill, putting her energy into conquering it, when the figure drew up beside her. To her surprise, it was another woman running the same course. Few men Enid knew could keep up with her, so the woman proved to be unsettling. Enid worked harder, trying to ignore the other woman, but the other woman easily kept pace. Enid reached the peak and briefly marveled at the beauty of the lake, which lay some three hundred feet below her. Then the woman effortlessly passed by her, moving at an inhuman speed.

During the rest of her run, Enid found herself wondering who the woman was. When she reached the end in a time better than anything she had done before the other woman was nowhere to be seen.

At home, Enid had a quick light meal composed of a salad and water and sat back in her balcony chair by the side of her painting easel to eat her meal at leisure. She enjoyed the sensation of the sun on her body and the sounds of the wind stirring the trees below her. Occasionally she sketched something that drew her attention and when she did her hands were quick and confident, showing the results of years of practice.

The red jewel she had been given by her first mother, whom she could hardly remember, glinted in the sunlight. She felt comfortable with it, although she only wore it during her leisure hours.

CHAPTER 5

Standard Year 2478

At sixteen hundred hours Captain James Hollinger came in the room without a sound. Enid marveled such a heavy man was so light on his feet. He strode to her desk and saluted.

"At your command, sir!"

Enid gestured at the chair. "At ease, Captain. Have a seat."

Hollinger sat and quickly looked about the room, taking in every detail. His eyes paused once when he saw a small holograph depicting the six planets of System 1397. He returned his attention to Enid as she spoke.

"Captain, you know why you're here. I'm going to ask you a series of questions. I want you to be as candid as you can. If I feel you aren't honest or forthright in any of your responses I'll end this interview. Do you understand?"

"Aye, sir."

Enid opened a file, which lay before her. She scanned the contents, which she knew by memory. She picked up a gold pen and drew a pad of paper to herself before she asked the Captain, "What interests you in being my Aide?"

"Sir, your record speaks for itself. I applied because I know you're going into Repletian territory. Three years ago I fought the Repletians; somehow they won without beating us in battle. This time around I know how they think. I can be of invaluable service to you."

"Captain, you're aware of my ancestry, aren't you?"

"Aye, sir."

"How do you feel working for me? Do you doubt my allegiances? My integrity?"

"Sir, I won't second guess the Admiralty."

Enid leaned forward, searching his eyes for reactions. "What do you think about Repletians?"

Her green eyes took Hollinger backwards in time.

He sat at the viewing screen that covered the entire front of the Meridien's bridge. His officers were busy preparing for battle conditions. Orders flew from the main computers. For the past three weeks human crews had gone over every option the computer forecast, feeding their new plans back into the computer. Now, as details came in, the ship's computer systems chose from the options given it.

Everything went according to plan. Hollinger swiveled in his commander's chair, rolling with the shock wave of the blast coming from the port side.

Ships usually were out of visual range of one another, relying on their equipment. They sometimes passed one another but at the relatively slow pace of ten percent of the local speed of light, even a flagship could travel the five thousand mile field of sight in less than one sixth of a second, so quickly the human eye would barely register the movement.

It was therefore discomforting to watch a battle ship, its weapons in full use, quickly expand on the viewing screen. Hollinger hesitated, transfixed by the sight of the strange vessel. Almost too late he snapped out of his hypnotized state and yelled at a nearby lieutenant, "Evasive action, Lieutenant."

The lieutenant, only the second Repletian after Enid Blue Starbreaks to become lieutenant, looked down at his screen and punched a red button. As he did so Hollinger bolted over the railing. It was too late. The first jolt shook the entire ship as its defensive screens went down.

Hollinger barely recalled the next few minutes. A mad scramble to abandon ship followed, but not before he killed the lieutenant.

As he studied the Admiral's eyes watching him he remembered the feel of life ebbing from the lieutenant. Enid was a formidable opponent so for now he played the game.

"There isn't much to say. Repletians are like any other culture; there are good and bad Repletians."

"I see. Tell me, is it standard practice to snap someone's neck in the line of duty?"

The Captain kept his face neutral, even as he wondered how she knew. Until now, it had been a secret known only to his friends. He would re-evaluate his friendships. Someone near him had let out information he or she should not have. Their time would come.

Enid saw the small tick betray some inner shock and knew she had hit close to home. His file showed a penchant for killing people with his bare hands in situations where a weapon was cleaner and quieter. So the rumors were true. She knew better than to pursue this line of questioning. He wouldn't make another such mistake again.

"I do what I have to do in the line of duty, sir."

"I'm sure you do, Captain. I'm sure you do."

Enid brought the interview to a quick end and he left after again scanning her office. She sat back in her chair and gathered her thoughts. She would keep an eye on the Captain. He was dangerous around her but he was even more dangerous out of her sight. The ancient saying crossed her mind: "Keep your friends close but your enemies closer." She spoke to her computer, making notes and recommendations. Then she asked for the second candidate to be sent in.

Aside from Jenara Carstairs' six-foot six-inch tall frame she looked unremarkable. She walked briskly to the table and, instead of saluting, leaned over the desktop and extended her left hand.

Enid, startled by this gesture, automatically reached out her left hand to shake the Major's. It was then Enid recognized her as the woman who ran by her on the course earlier that day. Jenara's hand engulfed Enid's, and Enid caught the bemused look that flashed in Jenara's brown eyes.

"Good day, sir."

"At ease, Major."

"Thank you, sir."

Enid's initial impressions of the Major changed when the Major smiled. Enid had imagined a tight-lipped stern person who brooked no nonsense. But the Major's warm smile belied any rumored toughness.

The Major saw Enid's expression and said in a low voice, "You were expecting perhaps a female version of the Captain. Do I disappoint you?"

Enid laughed at this. The Major seated herself and looked around the room to show Enid she was interested in where Enid worked. Enid saw the almost invisible scar tracing down the Major's left cheek. Jenara's cheekbones were high and she had a military haircut that looked natural on her. There were women in the Services who hated military haircuts but the Major was clearly not one of them.

"Shall we begin?" The Major's voice kept its low level yet Enid felt the certainty behind it. Jenara Carstairs would be good in a command position.

Enid shrugged. "Why not? You know the procedures. If you fail to be honest in your answers to my questions I'll end the interview."

The Major nodded her head. "I understand," she said as she leaned back into her chair.

"You were an aide for General Anthony Stewart. It's unusual for someone in Ground Forces to want to transfer to the fleet."

"Yes, I suppose it is. Shall we say I'm looking for new challenges?" The Major smiled again and Enid found herself drawn by Jenara's confidence.

"I doubt if you'll find any challenges to equal the Seavian Incident. That was some campaign, from the reports I've read."

"Yes, I imagine you're curious to have my version of the events?"

"Especially your personal thoughts. I've read the military reports but so much is left out of them. What did you feel during those two months?"

Jenara straightened in her chair, took a deep breath, and answered Enid's question in a quick rush of words. "I don't know what to think of it. To think the creatures living in the Seavian system could so blithely ignore us as if we were nothing to them."

Enid leaned towards the Major. "Perhaps we are in their eyes. They may ignore us as we ignored the ants back on our First Home World. Tell me, have you thought about why they ignored us even after they knew of our presence?"

The Major nodded. "The theory is once they neutralized our military threat they could go on with their own fighting. We had nothing they needed."

"And so what did you learn from that experience?"

"I'm not sure of its meanings. The creatures who fought those battles operate from beliefs alien to ours. We don't even know what was at stake. Certainly not the planet, for they had already ruined it for a thousand years to come, maybe more. Their probe of us must have told them we weren't threats to them. Now they know of us." The Major shrugged. "What we do about it is something outside my realm of expertise."

Enid jotted a few notes, aware the Major followed her every move. "Do you have questions, Major?"

"I do but they should be asked later when you're more comfortable in your role as Admiral."

Enid laughed. "Don't you think I'm comfortable now?"

The Major looked at Enid: "You misunderstand my motives. I meant you'll know more about them as time passes."

Enid returned the Major's candid gaze. "I'm not sure we want to know either Seavian species any more than we do now. Their goals seem to be different from ours."

The Major nodded her agreement and added, "Yes, and in any event they won't want anything we have. They'll probably ignore us."

"Tell me, Major, why should I hire you as my aide?"

The Major leaned towards Enid and responded in a low voice that forced Enid to lean forward to hear the words. "Sir, I know what you're thinking. You believe I'm too bloodthirsty, too eager to kill. This interview is to go through the motions. You have your mind made up but cannot afford to let Admiral Lexington know that. Am I hitting the mark?"

Enid waited for the Major to continue. When the Major saw this, she smiled. "I enjoy games with the best of them. You don't know what I can do, despite the files you've read on me. I'm what they used to call a 'loose phaser' back home."

"In the next few weeks and months we'll find more than we expected. I want to be there when it happens and right now you're it. Everything seems to focus on what you'll do out there. Whether I get this promotion I have signed on as an officer in the Fourth Fleet. My transfer came in two days ago."

Enid was surprised. The Admiral must have known of this and yet he chose not to tell her. What else didn't she know?

"Sir, you should hire me because I am the best there is below Admiral's rank. Battle for its own sake no longer interests me. The real fighting happens at another level I want to see and learn from."

I am the best. That phrase played back in Enid's mind long after the Major had returned to her quarters. Jenara Carstairs' frankness attracted Enid. The certainty within that tough body was a contrast to Enid's personal doubts. What did other people see in her to move her ahead of people like the Major?

*

"Let me tell you how this'll play out, sir." Daegan gestured towards the window. "They need someone out there now and they've found themselves at a loss. There are things out there involving more than the Repletians, tough as your people may be. Whatever it is, it scares the shit out of them. They need someone who's both good and expendable to take the heat for the next while until they can regroup and figure out what to do. But whatever they plan, it'll probably fail."

"Daegan, why will their plans fail, assuming there are such plans?"

"I've read and analyzed the latest Black Ship reports. Whatever that thing is, it's too big to hold in check. We may be too late to do anything about it already."

"Too late?"

"Yes, it's like a runaway flagship; we need to sidetrack it or we can kiss everything goodbye."

"We're a bit melodramatic, aren't we, Daegan?"

"No, I'm not. If anything, I've understated the situation. If the Black Ship and what it represents wants what we have it'll get it despite our best efforts."

"Let's get back to more mundane matters, Daegan. Tell me, why should I hire you as my aide?"

Daegan gestured towards the window and the outside world: "Sir, as I've said, there are things happening out there that require your full and undivided attention. I'm not much of a fan of our High Council but it beats anarchy. Science is the only thing holding us together. You'll have things to say about whether this continues to hold true or not. In the meantime, I can watch your back for you and let you spend the time you need to figure out what's happening."

After Daegan left Enid moved to her desk. She thumbed through the file and scanned a few pages but found herself unable to recall what she read. There were other things on her mind. She returned to the interview table and reviewed both the files and the holograph recordings she had made of each interview.

Her decision was now clouded. The files she reviewed before the interviews and the interviews themselves didn't match each other.

After fifteen minutes of indecision, Enid made up her mind to get some sleep before making her decision. Too much had happened today. She didn't want to be hasty in her actions.

Later, at home, she stood on her outdoor patio and watched the great red disk of the sun slide below the horizon. Night was nearing and daylight quickly faded. A cool breeze blew in from the sea and carried with it a sharpness Enid welcomed. A few lights began appearing from houses that dotted the coastline. None of them were close to her and for this Enid was thankful. She treasured her privacy and made a ritual of watching the day's end from her balcony.

She wondered what stories lay behind those lights, what people moved behind those unseen walls. Below her patio she heard the hoot of an owl. She looked at the stars and marveled at how many of them supported oxygen worlds suitable for the settlement of humanity and the other creatures from humanity's First Home World.

A sudden movement in a clump of trees a hundred yards from her house interrupted Enid's thoughts. The growing darkness made it difficult to make out the figure that skirted in and out of sight within the line of trees. Whomever it was moved slowly and often doubled back on his or her path, a path that took the person to within fifty feet of where Enid stood without moving a muscle in her body.

Enid waited until the figure was within speaking distance and then she spoke: "Stop and identify yourself."

The figure turned towards her in surprise, not seeing her still form until Enid spoke.

"Sir, Corporal Reynolds."

"Corporal, what are you doing on my property?"

"Sir, we've been posted to be your guards until you're off-planet. Admiral Lexington's orders."

"I see. Just how many of you are there?"

"There are twenty men on every four-hour shift."

"Why wasn't I told of this?"

"Sir, your schedule today made it impossible to notify you. We secured the building an hour before you got here. Now we're patrolling."

Enid was about to carry on the conversation when she saw the Corporal looking ill at ease. She thought better of keeping him from his duties: "Carry on, Corporal."

"Aye, sir."

As Enid watched the Corporal quickly blend back into the trees and the darkness the full impact of her day began to sink in. Guards meant protection and protection meant someone wanted to ensure her safety. In turn, that implied there were now other people who thought nothing of killing her if the opportunity presented itself.

Enid found herself longing for that time so recently when she was a Colonel; the safety there was no longer hers. In a few short hours she had become an Admiral, and that thought alone tired her.

As Enid got ready for bed she found herself looking through her windows into the night. She felt so tired she skipped her usual ritual of tea before bed. Instead, she climbed under the light covers and fell asleep within moments. She never heard the whispers of motion as her unseen guards went about their rounds. Nor did she know about the machine hovering two hundred feet above her house. It watched the house through its infrared sensors.

It was the first night in a long while Enid slept soundly. The next morning she was unable to recall the dreams that had bothered her so often lately.

The Black Ship

CHAPTER 6

Standard Year 2478

Admiral Lexington slowed as he came to the wood-framed door. When he reached it the door silently slid open to reveal a small conference room. The Admiral walked in and sank into the closest chair. He was tired and chose to wait. He looked at the room, surprised Katina had redone it in a Spartan taste not to his tastes. A single picture hung on the wall and its sweep of primal colors clashed with the rest of the room. The Admiral knew enough about art to recognize this painting as one of Picasso's great works. The Admiral also knew enough about the person who owned this room to know the painting was genuine, one of the few originals preserved over the ages through a special processing suspending the canvas in a complete vacuum seal.

The conference table was small because its owner never met with more than two or three people at a time. In the middle of the table a crystal vase of pale black flowers sat, the crystal forming a dark reflection of light dancing about the room at the smallest motion of the table. The chairs were the same size, black leather with padded arms for comfort. This elegance was false. Something wasn't right in the way the room looked since his last meeting here.

The Admiral heard footsteps and recognized their beat as the door opposite to the one he had entered opened in the same silent way. He stood at attention until the woman who entered told him to sit.

Katina Patriloney was eighty years old but the intensity of her gaze showed she retained full use of her faculties. She kept her thick hair cropped short. She moved deceptively slow. Her clothes were simple. A black loose-fitting tunic covered her to her ankles, making it impossible to know her weight. She returned the Admiral's gaze with the same candor as her father, whom the Admiral had known well. When she spoke, her low voice was clear.

"Things are proceeding as scheduled?"

The Admiral chose to answer this rhetorical question with a small nod of his head. She watched him for several seconds and then reached for her panel. A holograph sprang to life before the Admiral. He recognized Enid as she spoke to a Combat Major in her chambers. The Admiral knew the Major was a candidate for the Aide's position. He couldn't help gazing at Enid's slim figure, although he knew Katina was studying him.

"What is your assessment of Enid Blue Starbreaks?"

The Admiral expected this; he turned his gaze away from the holograph.

"She did as she was supposed to do. She had some hesitation when you asked about her ancestry."

Katina nodded and said in a musing voice, "No, she would have no memories of that time. We gave her some strong drugs to impair her memories. She has feelings but no memories of that time."

The Admiral hadn't heard about this. He waited for her to speak but she watched him with a slight smile on her face. He decided to probe further.

"You were there?"

"Directly there? No. Others carried out the necessary actions."

"I didn't know you were in the Forces then."

The old woman looked shocked. Then she broke into a laugh.

"Admiral, you sometimes surprise me. The military does not control everything. No, I need more satisfaction and power than the armed forces can provide me. Did you know there are only two people who know who I am? You, of course, are one of them. The other one doesn't count."

The Admiral knew better than to try to pursue this line of talk. He decided to talk about Enid's situation.

"The Vice Admiral seemed surprised by her interview. She didn't expect her promotion. Nor am I sure I agree with it. There are so many variables to weigh."

"Yes, exciting, isn't it, not to know everything in advance?"

The Admiral eased back into his chair. "Interesting and dangerous. The Vice Admiral walks a tightrope she doesn't know. We may live to regret our choice."

"Yes, we may. But there are changes coming, changes that require answers. No choice we make guarantees a satisfying ending for ourselves. And yet the risks must be taken. While we can make choices we have a chance of winning."

"That sounds idealistic."

"Why, Admiral, are you calling me on my plans? You are becoming a pleasant surprise. Tell me, does she know of our plans for her?"

"Which plans?"

"Cat and mouse time, Admiral? Be careful of the cat. As you well know, I have claws."

"During the interview, she was remarkably composed. I don't think she knows. If she does then she should be in my seat."

Katina smiled for the first time and the Admiral felt a chill run down his spine as she spoke. "That's good. We can't have her knowing everything, can we? Too much knowledge is a dangerous thing, a poet once said."

The Admiral shrugged. He always felt inadequate when he was in her company and no more so than today. Katina gestured at the Vice Admiral's image. "She will, of course, choose Daegan as her aide."

"Of that I have no doubt," the Admiral agreed.

Katina smiled again, the blue lipstick giving the smile a predatory gesture. The Admiral quelled an urge to scream. "Have you arranged matters?"

"I have. It involves three people; they will . . ."

Katina shook her head and said, "Admiral, I trust in your abilities. I don't need to know the details. Results are all that matter to me."

The Admiral decided this was the last chance he had so he continued: "Are you sure this is the best way to go? It seems so drastic. Good people will be hurt by this."

The old woman turned her black eyes away from the holograph images and stared at the Admiral for a few seconds. "Admiral, there's no simple or painless way to do this. Because of our hurry, we haven't been able to test her through our normal processes. While I don't doubt she's physically up to her new posting, we cannot leave it up to chance. We've seen her administrative skills during her interview, but we must know what she's like under a crisis and before she runs into whatever awaits her out there. The Pegasus Revolt taught us much in the way of planning. You recall your role in the Revolt, don't you?"

The Admiral sucked in his breath at the rush of returning memories.

He was a Second Lieutenant at the time of the Revolt in 2446. The *Pegasus's* great bays held over a billion Repletians, survivors of the destruction of what Anphoria at the time thought was one of the Repletian Home Worlds. Anphoria hailed it as a great victory; no one knew then the planet they destroyed was simply a frontier world on the edge of the Repletian borders.

Engineers had built the *Pegasus* over five years; their designs called for the *Pegasus* to house five billion people. It was the first ship of its kind, a giant prototype that, if successful, would lead to the building of more such ships to resettle captured Repletians to less strategically important areas deeper within Anphorian space.

Engineers carved the *Pegasus* from a giant asteroid, leaving its outer shell intact as they gutted its insides. What remained was a shell inside which they carved twenty spheres, the smallest sixteen miles in radius. Great reinforced braces extended from the center of the asteroid through each sphere to the outer shell. These pillars held the whole ship together. Each sphere was three miles greater in radius than the sphere below it. Each sphere was at once the ground on which people lived and the ceiling within which a smaller sphere was built. Each sphere was eight hundred yards thick, which allowed for lakes of up to one hundred feet deep to be built. Thousand-foot hills dotted the landscapes of each sphere. Every odd-numbered sphere contained housing units. Every even-numbered sphere contained food production centers. The result was the most humane prison facilities Anphorians could build. They were proud of it. It was a move away from the type of prisons they had depended upon for a thousand years, prisons the more liberal of them recently were complaining about.

No one knew how the trouble started. There were the inevitable rumors afterwards, rumors that the revolt may have received inside help to get as far as it did. Some said groups in the military, unhappy the project used resources for keeping the enemy alive, supported the revolt.

On Level Five Commander Grady was impatient. On this level five million Repletians formed long lines. Soldiers separated men, women, and children. Guards kept wary eyes on the prisoners who quietly shuffled past the myriad stations. Their silence added to the tension. Grady stood above the processing units to keep order. Word was already filtering down that this wasn't the major victory originally thought. The planet they had reduced to rubble was a minor agricultural planet that had put up little struggle against the military might thrown at them. Victory was sudden and shocking in its quickness. Many Anphorian soldiers felt cheated. They had hoped for a glorious war but the quick defeat of the planet's people sickened them. They were contemptuous of the captured Repletians; didn't they have any backbone, any spirit?

Their nervousness also stemmed from the feeling that the victory was too easy; there had to be more than this involved. Surely the Repletians weren't this easy to defeat? Legends of their ferocity and take-no-prisoner attitudes formed the grist for many a table talk among the Anphorian troops. Tales of atrocities to curdle the blood were common; everyone knew the Repletians were bloodthirsty savages who raped and pillaged entire planets. Even now, there were those who waited for the other shoe to drop, who expected to have to fend off the hordes of savage Repletian warriors who would show up to rescue their people.

Grady turned to his Aide, a young lieutenant who stood unusually quiet as he watched the people below the stage on which they stood. Grady wondered again about this man. There was a certain distance in the man, a certain point beyond which he didn't allow anyone close to him. He was good (Grady had read his record), but the man called no one a confidant, let alone a friend. This concerned Grady but nothing he could do would change the way his aide was. And Lexington often guessed Grady's own actions before Grady himself knew, making Grady's job easier.

"Lieutenant, how are things proceeding down there in the lines?"

Lexington turned from watching the people below him, "Sir, things are going as well as they can under the circumstances."

Grady sighed, "You're talking of our deadline?"

"Respectfully, sir, we could handle this situation and ease tensions if we had ten more hours to process the prisoners. We're making a mistake by hurrying so quickly."

"Yes, yes, I understand. But, Lieutenant, I have my orders and they include leaving for the nearest home base by 0-nine hundred hours tomorrow. That gives me no time for dilly-dallying."

A commotion on the floor directly below them drew the two men's attention. A young girl was trying to pull away from a processing officer.

"Mommy, mommy, don't let him take Dolly away." Her voice pierced the low hum of voices around her. Clutching the doll in her hands, the small girl turned to run. The processing officer swore.

"Give me that thing, you fucking Plete."

He lunged for her but too slowly. The girl evaded his reach and he tumbled to the floor.

The next few seconds exploded with action. As the officer came to his feet he drew his weapon. The girl, followed by a pair of frantic parents, darted past the tables. The blast of the weapon in such close quarters ignited the people in the same line as the young girl.

Before the Commander or Lexington could get to the main floor the processing officer who fired the weapon was buried under a mass of Repletians who went for his weapon. Lexington ran as fast as he could to reach the pile of people. With the aid of other troops he managed to pull the officer from the struggle. A Repletian had recovered the officer's weapon and Lexington said, "Give the gun to me. You won't be hurt, I promise you."

His officers tensed but the man slowly relaxed his posture and smiled. Under the watchful eyes of everyone, he passed the weapon, handle first, towards Lexington's outstretching hand. He never finished his motion, his chest exploding under the impact of a laser from behind Lexington.

"Fucking Repletians! No one does that to me!"

In slow time Lexington watched as first shock and then pain filled the Repletian's face. The man fell to the floor as the officer behind Lexington fired again, this time hitting a teenage girl who stood in the next lineup. Lexington heard the screams and then began to fight for his life as the entire platform exploded into a frenzy of rage. Scores, then hundreds, of Repletians fell before the soldiers. But they also wrestled dozens of soldiers to the ground, taking their weapons. Fighting quickly became more equal as the troops found themselves facing their own weapons.

Grady, surrounded by a group of soldiers, got to Lexington within moments after the fighting began. Troops quickly herded the two senior officers back to the platform. The fighting spread as Repletians broke past the processing units into the general living quarter areas. Grady ordered the soldiers to pull back to regroup but this took time.

Twenty minutes later Lexington watched the soldiers form combat lines. The Repletians had spread into the housing complexes. Many of them carried weapons taken in the fights. Grady brought forces from four other levels to help him regain control of Level Five.

Reports later told of sporadic fighting put up by the prisoners during this phase. Lexington knew better. The prisoners who had weapons formed a ragged line of resistance behind which the unarmed prisoners hid. They were no match for the Anphorian soldiers who moved on them. The soldiers hid behind shields that repelled the firepower turned on them. The Repletians, many of them farmers, knew their fight was useless as hundreds of them fell to the Anphorian's first attack.

Surrender was total. Repletians slowly came out from their hiding places to walk between the lines of soldiers to a holding area. Lexington and the Commander stood on the platform watching this process; Grady was silent, pacing back and forth. Lexington could get no answers from Grady. This was fine for he kept going over the original incident, kept seeing himself between the Repletian farmer and the Anphorian soldier. He could still smell the acrid odour of burning flesh from the Repletian who gasped at the hole in his chest, still saw the teenage girl falling in a cloud of blood and charred flesh.

A soldier said something in Grady's ear. Grady nodded and as he walked away from the platform he told everyone to stay where they were. Ten minutes passed. Lexington watched the lines of Repletians still walking between the troops. He saw the monitors spread throughout the area come to life. The lines of Repletians stopped as Grady's image swam into focus.

"May I have your attention please? This is Commander Grady. I'm in the quarters of Living Unit Seventeen. We've captured the family responsible for the initial cause of the riots."

Grady gestured and the camera showed a line of soldiers and three people whom Lexington recognized as the young child and the parents who had gone after her. The young girl still held the doll in one arm but she also looked at the line of soldiers with fear and uncertainty. Her other arm was wrapped around her mother's knees for support. Behind the people the housing complex enclosed a park.

The camera returned to Grady, who continued: "As Commander of Level Five, I won't allow further conduct such as that we saw. You're prisoners of war and as such we'll treat you with respect if you respect our rules. If you don't obey, we'll take any measures we see fit to correct your behavior."

And with that, Grady signaled and the line of soldiers fired upon the buildings. Even without the monitors, the citizens shuddered from the recoil of the blasts as the deep booming reverberated through the intervening space between the Unit and the platform. The housing units were reduced to flaming rubble in a matter of minutes. Clouds of black smoke curled upwards towards the ceiling three miles above them.

Grady's impassive face looked into the camera. "I want you to watch this."

The Commander turned from the camera and barked an order. Five soldiers stepped from their ranks and quickly forced the small girl from her parents. One of them held the girl in a tight embrace while the others led the weeping mother and the struggling father to a tree where the soldiers bound both tightly to the tree trunk. Grady gave another order and ten soldiers lined up fifty feet from the tree.

"Ready." The soldiers stood at attention. Lexington couldn't take his eyes from the camera. The Repletians on the platform began to realize what was happening and a hum of voices increased. Everyone heard the small girl's cries, "Mommy, Daddy! Come back. Don't leave me. I need you!"

"Aim." The soldiers brought their weapons to bear, regardless of the protests from the platform.

"Fire!" The tree and its captives exploded in a sea of blood and wood as Lexington turned from the cameras. When the guns stopped thousands of Repletians stood in silence as the screams of the small girl burned into their minds. Her screams died and she stood alone, clutching her doll against the background of the still smoldering fragments where the tree had once stood.

A great wail erupted from the Repletians, a keening song whose volume pierced the ears. What Grady said next was drowned by the singing on the platform. And not for the last time Lexington wondered whether what they had done was the right thing to do.

*

Katina's words broke through the Admiral's reflections. "We all have ghosts to deal with, Admiral. But we can't allow them to cloud our minds, can we?"

She moved on to more mundane topics. When she finished she stood up and leaned across the table. Lexington sucked in his breath as she touched him with her right hand. He heard her long fingernails click. She smiled and her fingers lingered a moment longer than usual, the cold glow from her nail polish reflecting the room's light.

Back in his quarters the Admiral spent a few minutes making a coded record of his meeting. He tried to interpret what was said, the way it was said, and what wasn't said. He also made some preliminary conclusions for later review.

The computer drew his attention with its low modulated voice: "Admiral, your appointment is here."

The Admiral saved his file and then told the computer to let the Major in.

She came through the door with an easy familiarity, her posture informal. Her height was always pleasantly astonishing to the Admiral but today the Admiral needed information.

"Did your interview with the Vice Admiral go well?"

The Major nodded and waited.

The Admiral noted this with a secret pride; he had trained her well. He tossed a small disk to her: "This allows you to temporarily disable the personal security systems in the Vice Admiral's quarters. The disk self-destructs and fits into any terminal outlet on board the flagship. Once inserted, this disk gives ancillary orders to those others involved. You don't need to know their names."

The Major showed no outward reaction. "Sir, may I be frank?"

"You may be as frank as you wish. I've secured this office."

"Sir, she makes quite an Admiral. Will she be hurt?"

"No. There are backups to this plan. I trust you will carry out your duties as well as you can. You know what you need to know."

"Sir, if there are consequences?"

"You know enough to improvise. You know the end goals of your mission and they are what count. Is there anything more?"

"No, sir!"

"Then you are dismissed, Major."

The Admiral worked long into the night and when he finished his paperwork he left the building to walk through the quiet streets. No one seemed to be around but the Admiral knew his guards were invisible to everyone, including himself, unless danger threatened.

The streets were still slick with a sheen of water from an earlier rainfall. A cool breeze rippled the few puddles that hadn't yet drained. The Admiral's feet sounded a steady muted beat as he made his way home. Early in his walk he reached the canal and followed its long pedestrian pathway. His mind was elsewhere but at some point the small sounds from the canal relaxed his military pace. He slowed and soon stopped to sit on an almost dry bench.

He relived the events of the day, plagued by the notion that something wasn't right, something disturbing that left him ill-at-ease.

What was it? What had he missed? It had to do with the Vice Admiral, of that he was sure.

The Admiral didn't fool himself; he knew Katina had plans he knew nothing of. He could do nothing about it. And yet, why the plans involving the Vice Admiral? Something didn't add up. No logical reason existed for such complex planning. Surely Katina knew the more steps there were the more unpredictable the outcome. Why not simply use him? Why use Enid, who had issues that needed resolving? It would take all the Navy's resources to clean up after this one.

The Admiral wrestled with these problems until a raindrop drew him from his internal reverie. Bemused, he watched as a man walked by, his pace slow and hesitant. The man was obviously a poor Repletian, one of thousands who littered the streets of the cities and worlds within the Anphorian Empire. Anphorians thought them lazy and unreliable workers who kept to themselves.

The Admiral didn't think of himself as biased. But so many issues involved the Repletians. He wondered whether they could ever be overcome. The best the Admiral could hope for was a quick end to the war so Anphoria could turn its attention to pressing social issues such as the plight of the Repletian poor.

The Admiral waited until the Repletian, who appeared to be an old man, had gone some distance the other way. Satisfied, he resumed his walk. The rain returned with a silken whisper, washing over the streets and the canal. The Admiral found it oddly comforting as he reflected on why he was consumed with such uncertainty and upset. What was he missing? And for the first time in a long time, why did he feel fear move through his body like the rain?

His wife was asleep in the large antique bed. Her small body was lost among the blankets covering her body. The Admiral, seeing her asleep, moved away from the bed, the carpeted floor muffling his footsteps. He closed the bedroom door, advancing down the curved stairwell into the study where a small door lead to the outside balcony overlooking the city. He stood on the balcony for some time listening to the sounds that drifted up the slopes.

The rain fell in sporadic bursts, making the small trees and bushes below the balcony come alive with a soft hiss and rustle. A shadow moved at the corner of his sight but the Admiral knew it was a guard floating from tree to tree along the perimeter of the property. He thought of the troops he had dispatched to Enid's house earlier in the day. Hopefully they were dressed for the weather and weren't too cold. He fondly recalled the times he had stood guard over superior officers.

The Admiral sometimes felt, as he did now, he was at a natural disadvantage against someone like Katina who had the freedom to move without military restrictions. Her inner strength was born and forged by a process outside the military. This didn't make her better or worse, simply someone who worked with different assumptions than the Admiral.

Lexington mulled over Katina's words, trying to decipher her intentions from what she had said and not said; wrestled with the coded implications of her actions. It was a process fraught with danger, for the Admiral knew her powers reached into areas well beyond the military. If he read her wrong, he would pay. He knew this. The skies to the west began to lighten with the pending day. He saw the clouds break and knew the day would be warm and cloudless. His last thoughts as he moved from the balcony were of Enid Blue Starbreaks. What lay in *her* future?

CHAPTER 7

"If there are gods, they have their paths far from the understanding or knowing of men."
-Theresa Kuang Hsia, Thetan Philosopher.

Standard Year 2455
Among the Repletian miners and traders who lived along the outer borders of Repletia, Leon Three Starbreaks was one of the richest, strongest and ablest. At seven-foot one-inch and three hundred and ten pounds, Leon's hard, travel-worn body was a testament to his travels into uncharted systems. He wasn't ready to retire to become an academic archaeologist like scores of his elders. In the past fifty years of his young life he had opened up a dozen systems for Repletian settlement, and he looked forward to at least another sixty years of exploration.

Leon spent his free time mostly alone but sometimes, new outposts drew him their way. Other miners lived at these outposts, loners who enjoyed doing things their way. Leon loved talk of new star systems, of perils met by Repletians as they worked to gain the wealth needed to hold their Rapac Naming ceremonies. Those who knew Leon wondered why he hadn't held his ceremony. But Leon always shrugged and turned the talk to other topics.

The truth of the matter was Leon wanted to gather enough wealth to give the best Rapac Naming ceremony he could. When he had accumulated enough, he'd gather the remnants of his small family and do the Ceremony in his tribe's traditional ways.

During one of Leon's trips to an outpost, he heard of Korel's World again. Corlin Blackbones, an ex-miner turned storyteller, was telling one of his stories about the Frontier when a voice asked him about Korel's World. Leon, who silently nursed a Sour Nat, lifted his head. Corlin stopped and searched for the right words, unusual for someone with such a flair for telling stories.

"It's said in the early days of our coming into this part of the galaxy, explorers found a planet in the Ursa Landine system. They spent months on this planet and whatever they found changed them."

"Aw, come on there, Corlin. That's a bit much even for you."

Corlin glared in the direction of the man who had spoken. The man, undaunted by Corlin's glare, snorted and shook his head. "A planet that changes people. Now I've heard everything!"

"Perhaps you can tell this story better?"

The other man shrugged. "Everyone's heard of Korel's World but how many have seen it with their own eyes? They say it's haunted."

Leon exclaimed, "Haunted? How so?"

The other man turned, ready to argue. Leon's large frame and blue-green eyes stopped the man from saying what he was about to say. Instead, he licked his upper lip and chose his next words carefully.

"Things there aren't what they seem. Those who've ventured there have told different stories of what they found. That is, any who didn't go mad. It's a mean planet. Only the savvy survive."

Corlin nodded, "Lad, the likes of you and me, we'll never see such a sight."

Leon, who felt the conversation taking a turn, pushed further. "So why do they call it Korel's World?"

Corlin shrugged: "It's said the planet has its own mind. The few who've spent any time on it come back with the oddest stories, unbelievable stories. But whatever happens seems to scare the piss out of them."

"How come no one seems to have met any of these brave explorers?" The man with the questioning voice nudged his friend and grinned at Corlin, awaiting his response.

"For one, it isn't a planet full of riches. For another, it's in a remote part of the Arm, away from the shipping lanes."

The other man refused to let up. "Guess that means you'll

never go to Korel's World. I've seen you scared shitless going down a dark flight of stairs. No explorer's stuff there, if you know what I mean?"

Argument over Corlin's courage raged on for a good hour, after which, with no final verdict, the Repletians separated, going their own ways. But just as he was about to step out, Leon held him back with the promise of a free ale.

"I know what you want, Leon, but you're talking to the wrong man. No one knows much about the planet."

"Corlin, all I'm looking for are facts. Any facts you have are better than nothing. I need an edge."

Corlin took a pull of his ale and squinted at Leon, looking at him long enough to make Leon nervous.

"You know," Corlin said as he made a gesture enveloping the entire pub. "Most of these people are going nowhere. They'll be here a hundred years from now moaning about lost chances or how cruel fate was to them. And I'll be here showing them as much sympathy as I showed today, all for the price of a good ale. There's a price to be paid for anything."

Leon waited. Corlin smiled, reading Leon's thoughts. "I have to change my habits. You know me too well."

Leon laughed. "There are those who say you're as welcome to a lost soul as the Formias Rash that brings people to adulthood."

Corlin agreed. "There is that rumor. Did you know some say before we came out from the first Home Worlds, puberty came on without any deaths at all? They say the Formias Rash was once a plague that wiped out most of the Mother World, if you believe the Mother World ever existed outside myths. All nonsense, of course. How can a rash extending human life come from a plague? It makes no sense."

Leon shook his head. "Is this going anywhere?"

"The point is there are things we know nothing of. If we

include those damn Anphorians who think they've a God-given right to rule the galaxy, we still haven't explored more than five percent of the galaxy. If there's a Korel's World it's not the strangest thing out there. There are things happening along the border that have the Elders worried. Nobody's talking but it means a change is coming for our people."

"Stories to scare the witless. I need facts, Corlin, something I can use to track down this Korel's World."

Corlin stared long at Leon before he spoke. "How come you haven't held your Rapac Ceremony yet?"

Leon shrugged. "No reason except I'm not ready yet to hold one. In my travels I haven't found the time to look up my family."

Corlin shook his head. "You know, the thought of not knowing where I come from is scary. I don't know how you can stand not knowing who your family is."

Leon said angrily, "I didn't say I don't know who my family is. My brother's dead and so are my parents. I never bothered looking for the rest of my family, if there are any left."

Corlin decided to return to his subject. "It's said the last person visited Korel's World some three hundred years ago. She went crazy and died about fifty years ago. She never got over what she found on the planet. She did the same thing you're trying to do, find a planet not meant for you to find."

"Corlin, that's a ghost story for young ones. I don't scare easily. Nor do I need anyone to help me. I've gotten on fine by myself."

"Yes, that's a shame, isn't it?" Corlin drained his mug and stood up to leave. "Leon, you've always been a loner. But a man can't always live by relying only on himself. If you still want to find Korel's World there are two things you should know about it. First, you need to go in with an open mind. No one knows what you'll find there, but rest assured, it'll be a shock to your beliefs."

"Second, look to your past to find what you need. If answers are there you'll find them only by knowing who you are. That's all I know. A word of warning, you may not be ready for what you'll find out there. Good luck."

Leon was about to pursue Corlin and then thought better of it. Corlin wouldn't tell him more than what he did. And no one could stir Corlin from a path once he chose to do something.

Leon carefully prepared for his journey. First, he picked up enough supplies to last two years. He then had his ship overhauled to meet his needs for the trip. This included the buying of a Radtic computer, the latest of its kind and illegal on most Repletian Home Worlds. Leon had no plans of staying near such worlds; his search would be along the frontier where people didn't ask questions.

When he ordered a survival course to be put into his ship, the construction crew gave him some puzzled looks. It took more credits to persuade them to install the various modifications he gave them. This included forty miles of jogging paths, which wound in staggered loops through the length and breadth of Leon's ship. Since he needed one giant cargo bay to keep his personal belongings, he adapted the other five cargo bays to hold the turf that formed the paths themselves.

Leon then bought holograph recordings on both Korel's World and his family tree. He scooped information, which even remotely dealt with either. Later, of course, he'd have the time to read what he had and decide what was relevant.

Finally, Leon had over a ton of hardcover books delivered to his ship. The price was steep, for few people read books any more. Most people preferred holograph recordings of ancient classics like *Moby Dick* and the latest works of the great modern Thetan philosopher, Theresa Kuang Hsia, whose works on divinity were stirring a revolution among the ten Groups of Humanity.

Buying books also gave him a chance to see Red Dawn, a retired doctor who loved good books and kept a stock on hand rivalling those in the main libraries of the Repletian Home Worlds. When Leon gave her the list of books he wanted to take with him, Red Dawn smiled. “You have enough material here to keep you for a while.”

Leon laughed and pointed at a title on the first page. “If you have this one, you should have no problem getting me the rest.”

Red Dawn looked at the title and grinned. “No problem. Although I must say few people I know have ever read her works.”

“Yes,” Leon agreed, “They’re missing so much.”

“This’ll take until tomorrow to fill out.”

“That’s fine by me.”

Red Dawn handed his order to an assistant, giving instructions on what to do. The assistant hurried off and Red Dawn relaxed.

“Leon, you hardly come around here. I don’t see enough of you.”

Leon laughed. “How much of me do you want to see?”

Red Dawn gave him a mischievous look. “Well, let’s hope it’s more than you showed me the last time.”

Later that night, after they’d made love for the second time, Leon lay on his back, falling in and out of sleep.

“Dear?”

“What is it?”

“Why so many books? Where are you going?”

The tone of her voice brought Leon to full consciousness. “I’m going to check out a lead.”

“What lead?”

“There’s a planet I need to find.”

“Oh, Leon, there’s a million planets out there, a billion, a trilllion. Why do you have to be the one to find them all? Why can’t you and I settle down somewhere? Get out of this mad house and settle into something more comfortable. Maybe you could get a teaching job somewhere. Not many people know half as much as you do.”

Leon stared up into Red Dawn's green eyes. "I can't. You know that. I'm too young. I'm only fifty."

"You'll get yourself killed and then where'll I be? We should have children, a place to call home."

Leon poked Red Dawn in the ribs. "Now you're sounding like my mother. Come on, dear. There's plenty of time to settle down. God, I wonder how many other people have said what I've said?"

Red Dawn brushed a damp strand of black hair from Leon's face and hugged him: "It's just I don't want to lose you. You're always risking yourself. You must have a small fortune by now. And I have money saved up from my medical practice, too, so we'll never starve."

"I don't want to depend on your money. If we're going to be together, the only way it'll work is if we both don't depend on each other that way."

Red Dawn sighed and lowered her head onto his bare chest, using him as a pillow. "I wish one day we could be together forever."

"We will, my dear. We will."

As Red Dawn fell asleep on his chest Leon thought about what they'd said. As a specialist, Red Dawn had made a great deal of money from her thirty years of medical practice. She wouldn't have to worry about money for the rest of her natural life, no matter how long she lived or how poorly her shop did. Maybe after this next trip he'd take her up on her offer. She was right. He had money enough to retire for the rest of his life, what with the finder's fees and mineral rights he'd gleaned from the systems he'd opened up.

The next day Red Dawn, who was gone by the time he woke up, was waiting for him when he came into her shop. Without a word she led him into the back where he found himself shivering in the cold air of a vast warehouse whose size always staggered his imagination. Books upon books lined shelves towering forty feet over his head. The humidity was carefully controlled to ensure the preservation of these books for many lifetimes.

When Leon had first seen the storefront years ago, he had thought it a joke; it was too small to hold what his sources told him was the biggest supply of books in this part of the galaxy. The store was a small building whose back ended against the great wall of a mountainside.

The woman who had met him on that first visit smiled at his initial reactions. He stuttered about looking for some books and she silently took his list from his hand and led him into the back, where the next few hours were a fog in Leon's memory. He remembered only spending a seemingly infinite amount of time thumbing through books he thought extinct, reading thoughts from men and women from cultures lost in the haze of civilization's long and chequered past.

Now, as he looked at the boxes on boxes of packed books, Leon grinned; this was one trip for which he had plenty to read. Out of respect for Red Dawn, he watched as the machines loaded the books into his waiting carrier before paying her in credits. He was about to leave when, he hesitantly confessed, "You know this journey...may take months, years."

Red Dawn knew this. And looked deep into his eyes and kissed him hard, whispering the standard Repletian greeting, "When I give to you, I give myself." Then forcing a smile, professed, "I'll be waiting."

He cupped her face gently and licked the tear that gently slid down her check; the trace of which, he knew he would carry with him, eternally.

And with that he got into his lifter. In seconds he was up and away, he went about the last of his preparations, which took him the better part of another day to complete. At the end he felt he was ready for anything.

*

After setting his course for Korel's World through his new computer, Leon sank into his chair and was staring blankly at the view screen when the computer startled him: "There's a minor problem in my navigation program."

A jolt shook the ship and Leon yelled "What problem?"

"A power surge momentarily disrupted the navigation program. We are now off course."

Tachyon drive units, commonly called star drives, were simple in their operations. The only thing affecting them was the mass of the ship or ships. A single ship such as Leon's was easy to control. Fleets the size put out by the Anphorian Confederacy took much longer because of the immense relative mass of their combined armada. So Leon was confident when he ordered the computer to shut down the star drive.

Stars swam into focus to confirm the computer's statements. Leon took a close look at the stars and smiled to himself. At last, a problem to occupy him! He studied the local star maps and then said to the computer, "No problem. Set your course coordinates as follows." Leon read his calculations aloud and sank back into his chair. A slight lurch told him his ship had restarted its star drive unit. The stars again became streaks of light centered on the middle of the view screen. Satisfied, Leon sat back to think about his past.

For days the ship plowed towards the last known whereabouts of Korel's World. Each day Leon woke up and went through a ritual set of exercises. His ship, moderate for its class, was still a good mile in length, giving him considerable space for his morning jog. Normally the six large bays were full of cargo which Leon moved from system to system. Their relative emptiness left echoes of his strides as Leon went on his exercise routes.

His younger brother had once teased Leon about not putting this space to the best of uses, a charge which Leon ignored as he ignored other things about his brother. The two had gone their ways; Leon learned of his brother's death in the Pegasus Revolt four years after the Revolt.

To trace his family's roots, each morning after a cold shower and a quick meal Leon linked into the central files he had bought. He downloaded the files bearing his family name, settled into a comfortable chair, and listened to the computer read from those files.

Sometimes he stopped the voice when he felt its progress was in the wrong direction. He learned of his great grandmother's penchant for chocolates. Her sister was a medicine woman who made some major steps in analyzing the Formias Rash. Still, no one knew how or why the Rash struck at puberty. Nor did anyone know why or how genetic changes during this stage extended human life by some hundred years. And no one could stop the Rash's twenty percent death rate.

For hours every day Leon pored over more knowledge about his family than he had thought existed. It was during the fifth day when a casual note from the computer puzzled him. He backtracked and within moments the picture of a small frail girl came onto the screen. The holograph screen read, "Enid Blue Starbreaks." Leon could barely contain his excitement. There was no doubt about it. She was his niece, a niece he hadn't known about. His brother had no children when the two brothers last saw one another.

Leon stared long and hard at the picture, the only known picture on file before the girl's disappearance into adoption. She had a small doll under one arm and in the background was the terrible devastation left from the crushing of the Pegasus Revolt. Anphorians whose names were hidden in military files later adopted the girl.

Leon was so intent on the image of his niece that the screen blinked before he noticed the computer was trying to draw his attention. Annoyed, he asked what the urgency was. In its flat voice the computer said, "There's a Class M planet off the starboard side of our ship. It's Korel's World."

As the planet's image appeared on the computer's screens Leon was awed by its beauty, the great blue patches of ocean, the long river systems, which wound their way through green lands.

Leon knew better than to venture unprepared onto the planet's surface. He called up the files the computer had been collating for three days. Corlin was right in his comments on a woman being the last person on the planet's surface three hundred years ago. Ten weeks after she had landed and placed her marker, a distress signal from her mother ship forced a freighter from its routine path. By the time they arrived the woman was insane. When they found her, she was wandering in the middle of a vast plain some thirty miles from her lifter.

After some discussions, the freighter's crew decided to leave the marker on the planet's surface. When the Repletian scout ship later showed up at the coordinates left by the freighter, the marker was nowhere to be found.

Leon knew he had to land on the planet and decided the first thing he would search for was that marker. Given its structure it would be easy to find. After that, he would explore the planet; there had to be some reason for the planet's mystery and he wanted to find out.

Most of the records the computer read out were rumors and speculations. There were no records available from Major Korel, who had led the first explorers onto the planet named after him. They were thorough in their removal of anything that linked them to the planet. But, Leon found one piece of evidence that puzzled him. No one from the present Council had been to the planet. It was five hundred Standard years since an Elder had last visited Korel's World.

Leon filled his lifter with the necessary supplies and placed his ship into orbit around the planet. There it would circle until Leon called for it. Should anything happen to the lifter or to him, his ship would send out a distress beacon. Leon didn't know how long it would take him to find the remains of the marker or the reasons why people shunned this planet but he was determined to find the answers to both before he left.

CHAPTER 8

Standard Year 2457

The plains were deceptive. Their flatness hid hundreds of gullies and the rolling hills in the distance were flattened by perspective. Over the months Leon had grown to love this land but there were times when he missed the salt air and the sound of breakers on rocky shores. The fatigue he felt now was different from how he felt when travelling along the shores of the great ocean five days west of where he was.

Somehow when he walked along the seashore, he never begrudged the long days. He loved the feel of the hard sand underfoot, the call of the waves in their eternal rhythms, the spray which sometimes swept inland to cover him in a fine sheen of moisture that quickly evaporated in the heat of the red sun.

For what seemed a lifetime, he scrambled through this desolate country, seeking the site he knew was here, the site for which he bore endless jokes, ridicule in nameless bars throughout this arm of the galaxy. And because of his desperation he hadn't had a drink in so long, too long for his liking. He was on a mission.

Leon chose to ignore the warnings, experts who dedicated lifetimes siphoning through ancient records that over the ages, had acquired the status of myth.

He had to find the site. But God, was it hot! He squinted into the distance, watched for any movement, any telltale sign he was right. The grass and the trees in the near vicinity swayed to the unseen rhythm of the warm breeze as they must've done for untold years.

It didn't make sense. He moved down the gentle slope. Once he had done so with every nerve, every muscle tense with fear. But one operated only so long on nervous energy, only so long on adrenalin.

Leon shifted his rifle into a more comfortable position. He had come prepared for violence, remembering the crazed eyes of the last visitor, the woman who kept screaming about endless fields of grain, grain that (if the scientists were to be trusted) never existed.

By his reckoning that was twenty months ago. The lifter had settled its twenty tons onto soil that buckled as it gave way to the tons of metal and plastic. Several minutes later Leon walked into the bright sunlight, stopping for a few seconds to take in the great fields of what looked like wild grass. The hot breeze swept past the ship on its way to its own destination. It was that breeze which puzzled the few scientists who ventured near the planet; it was a breeze that should've dried everything into a desert-like aridity.

There was no reason to the breeze; it uniformly swept the planet's whole surface. From all accounts, it may've been doing so for the past ten days or the past ten million years; there was no way of knowing. It blew west at fifteen miles per hour over land and water, over flat plains and mountain ranges. It defied all known laws of meteorology. With such winds there should be storms, clouds, signs of erosion, wear and tear on the land, movement of animals bred to the planet's idiosyncrasies.

The first Repletians, as they moved into this arm of the galaxy, spent years mapping the planet, digging for clues, looking for animal life. Sonar probes, seismic readings, infrared and ultraviolet scans, radio wave and x-ray searches, everything led to nothing.

There was no logic, no explanation for the geological and atmospheric features, and most expeditions moved on. No one wanted to place their roots here. The last one, the woman, left her marker, a small capsule parked in the exact geometric center of the largest plain on the planet.

It was made from imperishable plastic and emitted radio waves at one megahertz every ten seconds. Those signals recorded the air temperature and the wind velocity. Even if the marker was buried under a mile of rock its signals were strong enough to be read by any orbiting space vessel.

Leon had landed his probe within a mile of where the marker should be. Once he became used to the heat he set out at a slow jog.

His heart was racing. Intoxicated with the potency of all he might find there, he finally reached the site.

There was nothing there.

Perhaps the radio was broken? Leon searched the area for two hours, a search which seemed increasingly futile. For, when he raised his eyes, he could see the horizon. Losing his temper, Leon used his blaster to dig down some forty feet. Nothing. No radiation, not a whisper of radio waves. The wind moved through the trees and grass with a gentle rustling sound. It moved through his hair, ruffling it in the same way it moved the trees and grass.

On that first day Leon ran back to his lifter, certain something watched him. Only when he was inside the lifter did he feel safe. Safe and foolish. What was there to be afraid of? There were no large animals on the planet's surface. Hell, there were no animals at all, not even birds or worms. Just the trees, the grass, and the wind. Ecologically impossible.

*

The next morning, after a large breakfast, Leon ventured onto the plains again. He reached the site he had left and felt sheepish at the large gaping hole dug with his blaster. It was an unsightly mess. For the first time Leon giggled, then broke into laughter. What the hell was he afraid of? A herd of ancient bull elephants from the Mother World?

For two minutes Leon laughed as he stood at the edge of the hole he had dug. Laughed into the wind. Laughed and bared his teeth. And felt himself watched.

Cursing, Leon spun around, lifting his rifle to his shoulder. In the distance his lifter occupied its stolid space. The green-brown stalks of grass and the clumps of trees swayed in the breeze. Leon held his pose for a few seconds then lowered his rifle. The hairs at the back of his neck stood on end.

Leon aimed at a nearby tree and fired three rounds at the

small base. All three were hits and he saw the chips fly from the target. The sound of the bullets faded quickly into the endless plains of grass. The feeling of being watched receded. Leon laughed again, this time nonstop until he became too tired to continue.

He walked over to the tree and admired the three perfect vertical bullet holes that went through the tree's base. Say what you will, Leon thought, but he hadn't lost his touch with a weapon.

Leon touched the holes and decided to take a picture of them. It would be his distinctive mark to be left on the planet.

Following a final survey of the site where the capsule was supposed to be, Leon walked back to the lifter. Perhaps the woman had made a mistake in marking the location. Leon shrugged. What could he do about it anyway?

Inside the vessel Leon had a quick lunch and then recorded his notes on the computer. His remarks were short and concise, the result of years of training. Any detail, however small, could decide a life-or-death situation. Leon noted everything, the bullet holes, the pit he had dug the previous day and, after some hesitation, the odd feeling of being watched. He beamed his comments to his ship in orbit as per safety procedures, which Leon would follow until he was sure of his safety.

Leon took his lifter seven hundred miles north of the original site to the edge of the plains. His lifter nestled among the small foothills below the five-thousand-meter mountain range.

Leon, despite his daily workouts on the trip here, was out of shape and knew it. Working out in the ship's holds was different from scaling hills. So he began with four and five hour hikes. As his strength improved he took longer hikes.

Within a month Leon scaled his first mountain. It was a grey slab of what looked like granite. He loved the challenge of the mountain; there was nothing like contact with a planet's terrain. And Leon's first mountain almost proved fatal. Halfway up a thousand-foot slope Leon's mind was on other matters when he should've been paying attention to his footing. In a moment he found himself tumbling down the slope. He thought this was it until he slammed into a large rock that broke his fall. His hiking gear saved him from more bruises and cracked bones but he limped for two days afterwards and gained more respect for the planet.

From that point on Leon spent his time searching; climbing hills, mountains, making aerial scans of canyons, scanning shorelines and once taking his lifter to the bottom of the deepest ocean trench on the planet. It didn't help his search knowing former visitors to this planet had kept silent about whatever they discovered; the few scraps of information collected over the years came mostly from inference and occasional hints from explorers. Leon only knew he would know what he was looking for when he came upon it.

Each night Leon recorded his thoughts and observations before going to sleep. As the months passed these entries decreased. At the same time Leon's obsession with the plains grew. Their unchanging nature was daunting. The winds that blew through his hair became a memory waking him from restless dreams in the night. The trees scattered over the landscape looked small one moment and in the next, were armies spilling across the plains like the fabled herds of buffalo from the First Home World. The tall grass was an ocean of green in a land where things should've been parched by the ceaseless winds.

Leon often woke up at night on some barren stretch of rock and gazed down into the deep blackness, which lay below him. He heard the wind as it moved across the unseen lands and he wondered how long this planet had gone through such nights. Where were the animals? Where was the change that was a hallmark on every planet humanity had found? What forces kept the wind in its constant course? Where had the trees and the grass come from? Why was there no other mobile life form around?

The wind brushed through his hair in these moments of thought. Overhead, the great disk of the Milky Way speckled the entire sky in a single band of light. From wherever he stood, Leon could spot the central galactic bulge only now being explored by a few daring explorers. Among those stars a trillion people slept and dreamed in never ending cycles.

Leon was a loner and proud of it. He felt contempt for most people, whose only desires in life were to be like one another, to belong to each other. They needed each other to share their fragile emotions, needed each other because they knew nightfall was only a breath away. Leon knew real people were like him, the ones who dared to think for themselves despite race or ancestry. Such people, the scientists, poets, thinkers, explorers, were the ones who kept nightfall away. They were the only ones who mattered. Leon cared not for normalcy. He cared even less for being a herd animal. He lived for such moments as now, lived for seeing a beauty beyond civilization's own making. And it was in one such moment Leon had his second accident.

A year had passed since he first landed on Korel's World. Leon still searched the plains for clues among the trees, the grass, and the wind. He ate some grass a few times when he ran out of food too far away to make it safely back to his lifter. The first time he became ill and had thrown up much of what he had eaten. For a day he lay there feeling nauseous and too weak to move. But even that passed. These days, Leon found himself not caring to take food from his ship, knowing the grass, while tasting slightly bitter, was edible. Leon also found the trees bore leaves with a slightly less bitter taste than the grass. Once he was used to their taste they proved more consumable.

He walked for five days, exploring each gully, each ravine, each waterhole. On the fifth day he was backtracking out of a dead end ravine and rounded a familiar bend in the path. Behind him, a clump of small trees stirred in the wind. It was a pleasant sound and he was drifting with its music when he fell over a limb he didn't remember seeing half-an-hour ago. The fall was nothing, but as he climbed back to his feet, the communicator linking him to his lifter fell from his knapsack.

Leon spent the next hours piecing the parts back but the lifter refused to answer his communicator. He finally lost his patience and threw the communicator against a tree trunk, shattering the communicator into small shards of metal and plastic. The only thing he could do was start the treacherous hike back to the lifter.

He moved his backpack into a more comfortable position, filled his canteen with water from a nearby stream, and set out at a brisk pace, one he could keep up for two days without undue strain, something he couldn't have done six months before.

To occupy the time, Leon took to singing every song he remembered. His wasn't the best voice in the galaxy but no one was around to care. Perhaps the trees cared but they were only trees, no more to him than the endless stretches of grass through which he hiked. Leon felt good and his anger and frustration about the communicator drained from him well before the end of the first day.

Once at the ship, Leon managed to wire the doors open. Behind him he heard the swaying of the grass. Leon stood up to wipe the sweat from his brow. The next moment he faced the plains, his gun levelled and the hair at the back of his neck standing on end. He had felt something. But the grass continued its waved motions for as far as the eyes could see.

Leon fired a few rounds. He felt a grim satisfaction in levelling some nearby trees. The sound of the bullets were reassuring and felt wonderful after listening for so long to the wind among the trees and grass. He went back and that night, within the womb of his lifter, Leon had his first deep sleep in a long time. And, the next day Leon recorded his comments about the set of events.

*

A year and some again passed without note. During this time he went to the coast a dozen times. Each time he enjoyed the cold salt water against his skin. Uncannily, he enjoyed even more that he was the only human occupant in this water, the only human challenging the waves as they crashed along the shoreline attempting to beat them. And with each meeting of the ocean, he lost more of his human inhibitions.

As time passed Leon began to lose interest in wearing clothes. Eventually, the time came when he chose to forego the rituals of dressing. While the lifter could make any clothes he might want, Leon saw no need for them, especially in that the temperature stood at a balmy twenty-eight degrees centigrade.

On one of these travels to the coast, Leon was swimming back to shore when something grabbed his legs and pulled him under. He fought to the surface for breath and saw the rocks rushing towards him. The current pulled him under again and again; each time he managed to surface and each time he felt more tired from his struggles. In less than a minute he was close enough to the rocks he felt he could touch them. He felt another tug and the current pulled him from the jagged outcrop. Leon made a desperate grab for a low-lying tree limb but it slipped from his grasp, badly cutting his hands. The current swept him in a great arc to a point four hundred yards further than the rock outcrop. Again he made a grab for some tree limbs and again they slipped from his grasp. Three more times he was swept shoreward and then away. He kept swallowing bitter salt water, choking as he flailed about, losing any self-control. Each time he thought it was the last time and each time, as he felt his energy slip away, the current slowed enough for him to struggle to the surface again.

Finally, the current came close enough to the beach so that he was lifted to shore by a large wave. He crawled up the beach as far as he could before passing out.

When Leon regained his senses the sun hovered on the horizon and the tide lapped at his cold feet. He ached in every bone and muscle. For a time he stared up at the sky, waiting to gain enough energy to start the trip back to his base camp. In his mind he went over everything he knew of the terrain, planning his route. At least there were no animals.

Leon steeled himself; climbed to his feet, but the pain made him wince and grit his teeth. But an age-old instinct kept him quiet, an instinct born in times when a sound, any sound, would have brought grief upon him. Leon hobbled to a nearby tree and took several deep breaths to gather the strength to break off a nine-foot branch. The branch was tougher than it seemed but after several tries it finally snapped off, scraping Leon's hands in the process. He trimmed the leaves from it and the gnarled and crooked limb became his crutch; one he found he needed more than he at first thought. Taking another focused and deep breath, he began the walk back.

The rock outcrop was the major barrier. In Leon's weakened condition he couldn't take the extra time to find a way around it; he had no choice but to scale the hundred-foot obstacle.

Each boulder presented its own pain, its own test. Every time he managed to climb over or around one rock another rock reared over his head. At times he had to place his cane on top of a boulder and forcibly hoist himself up the rock with his bare hands. Soon his hands were bloody again. The growing darkness made his efforts harder and often he found himself pausing to wonder if he could go on. The sound of the waves crashing against the rocks a few feet from where he climbed upwards filled Leon's mind and made it difficult for him to focus. Once he thought he heard something in the wind but after stopping for a minute with bated breath Leon continued his slow climb upwards.

The next hours were a blur in time, a growing litany of pain with no relief. Leon was deliriously singing when he emerged from the last of the rocks to totter on the edge of the great plains. A beacon of light, flashing every ten seconds from his base camp, guided Leon through the night but he grit his teeth against the pain and guarded his footing over the treacherous terrain. There was no way he could afford another injury and so he was as careful as he could be in the circumstances. He sang off-key to the songs he heard in his head or in the air; he was never sure what they were although there were moments in that climb over the rocks when Leon heard the music come from around him and he knew he was hallucinating.

The cuts and bruises took a week to heal. But the incident at the beach haunted him. If he had been seriously hurt away from the base camp no one and nothing would have helped him. His thoughts strayed to the promise he had made to Louise Red Dawn so long ago. But, he had made a promise to himself too, and needed to make a difference here.

When he had the idea, its scope staggered him. The ship had the equipment he needed, simple equipment, which only took time to set up. He went about his tasks with a single-minded fury. And when it was done, Leon stood one morning at the eastern edge of the largest plain, the plain where he had started from nearly three years ago. If the planet would give him no answers he would make it pay. The wind blew in his hair and he laughed. For once the wind served his purpose. This planet would notice him or he would move on with a clear conscience.

He planted the last of the explosives and synchronized the timers through the lifter's computers. With a gleeful twist he inserted the final wire into its terminal and waited.

It took time, but he had time. Soon he saw the first plumes of smoke north and south of him. Each device ignited thirty kilograms of explosive chemicals over a square mile of grass. With the help of the planet's eternal winds and the three hundred bombs strung over a four-hundred-mile arch, the fires grew and overlapped each other. Leon landed his lifter on a mountain plateau four thousand feet above the plains, where he scrambled out to watch the explosions reach the spot he had vacated.

Hours passed as the winds swept the fires westward to form a single hundred-foot wall of hunger. The sun dimmed and then became invisible as columns of smoke and ash rose in thick plumes. And then for the first time in Leon's memory the winds changed speed as they quickened into gale force winds that howled and swirled into the vacuums created by the fire.

Leon watched the flames reach express train speeds. He screamed: prancing about in his excitement, reveling in the dying of the plains, reveling in the scale of destruction. The lurid orange and red light from the flames cast his thin frame into a grotesque dancing creature whose manic laughter rang against the hills and flew into the wall of sound that was the fire and wind.

Leon boarded his lifter and moved as the flames moved. He had seen many things in his lifetime but nothing on this scale. In five hours, flames consumed an area half-the-size of his home country. Over the millions of tons of ash, heat, smoke and winds, thunderclouds blossomed upwards, their shadows racing ahead of the smoke and winds to break against the western mountain slopes.

Into the night the fires raged, fighting against the black storm cloud shadows. Sheet lightning jumped from cloud to cloud, followed by deafening claps of thunder. Pushed ahead and up by the heat the storm clouds boiled into the mountains to the west of the plains. Leon ran from screen to screen; sweat beading his forehead as he watched his creation run its course.

The first tornadoes funneled their way towards the ground, each struggling against the blasts of heated air roaring through the night sky like demons. These tornadoes were large, but nothing like the one that twisted from the clouds over Leon's lifter. Its nightmarish winds and awful changes in atmospheric pressure threw Leon's lifter about like a cork in a storm. Leon fought the controls, cursing himself for letting his lifter get too near the storm. The twister jumped like a berserk puppet on a string, carrying Leon's lifter with it.

The flames licked at the mountain slopes that ringed the plains. With nothing left to devour, the flames wavered and then flickered out so quickly Leon, still struggling with the controls, saw spots in front of him.

The storm raged on, unleashing torrents of rain over a land now robbed of every blade of grass and tree, every trace of life except that within the lifter. Fuses blew as the lifter's engines strained under the constant shifts in the ship's balance.

The twister hit the ground and blew up a plume of ashes and dust. Torrential rains were sucked into the funnel. Leon howled as the lifter's frame fought forces it wasn't built to deal with; rivets popped from the outer frame, as the great shifts in air pressure sucked the life from the lifter and blew it apart.

Leon activated the distress signal aboard his ship circling far above him. As winds pulled his lifter apart around him, he began to sing a song he heard come out of nowhere, a song from the beaches reached into his heart and made him weep. When he saw the God in its awful blackness, a blackness that shifted impossibly and shaped the winds as it filled his mind with its presence, he slipped into unconsciousness and remembered nothing else.

*

The starship landed in the area where Leon's lifter had broadcast its final signals. Troops poured from the great bay doors and spread out in a semicircle, their weapons pointed outwards over the plains. The Elder surveyed the troops and the plains and then he spotted the naked form of a man lying one hundred yards away. The man rolled onto his back and made a feeble cry for help.

Next out of the ship were the scientists. As the Elder signaled for the still man to be carried into the ship, the scientists quickly covered the plains with their instruments. Several of them ventured further from the ship but returned with puzzled looks.

The Elder waited until the ranking scientist was ready.

"Well, Arthur, anything?"

"I don't understand this. There should be something, some trace of what we witnessed from Leon's recordings."

"Could he have imagined this?"

"No way. You saw the fires, the storm, the final moments of the lifter. There should be something."

The Elder sighed. He had been afraid of this ever since the Council assigned him to follow up on Leon's distress signals. On the way to answer this call, he had read Leon's files. Leon was among the best and strangest of the Repletian traders, traders who owed nothing to anyone but themselves. The Elder wondered what led Leon to make the journey here. It wasn't like him. Maybe the loneliness had finally won out, finally took him over that edge he had always skirted between privacy and madness. Of course, the Elder knew better. He had watched the final cataclysm with everyone else aboard his ship. Nothing on that scale could be faked.

"Arthur, what did your colleagues find?"

"Nothing. There's no trace of Leon's lifter nor of the fire. How Leon survived I don't know."

The Elder felt the steady wind brush through his hair. Neither he nor any other living Elder had visited Korel's World. The planet had chosen to reveal itself to a trader and that meant something important the Council and Leon would discuss over the next months and years. But that was in the future. For now, the Elder felt strange. He turned to Arthur. "Is that possible? The tapes were made only three days ago."

"No, it shouldn't be possible. There'd be traces of nuclear matter, traces of the hull made of the same material our ship's made of. Damn it, there'd be traces of that hellish fire Leon started. We can't even find the ashes. All we have is that grass you can see as well as we can."

"What would you like to do next, you and your team?"

"I think we should take the hint and leave this place. There doesn't seem to be anything of value here. My best instruments came up with the same readings the first Science Expedition came up with. Nothing."

The Elder disliked loose ends but he had no choice. He gave orders and watched as his people packed their instruments.

"You know, there's something here that feels uncomfortable. It's as though this whole planet has its own mind. Arthur, did your men find anything on Leon?"

Arthur showed the Elder a photograph. "We found this lying beside Leon's body."

It showed Leon beside the tree with the three perfect bullet holes in the tree's trunk, the photo seemed to be taken in his first days on the planet. In the background were the other trees.

Arthur felt the wind tug at his hair and watched the endless seas of grass sway in great ripples to the distant horizons.

"Other than that photo, there's nothing. My men have surveyed the entire planet. Leon's fire covered only eight percent of the planet's surface. We have pictures of Leon in other areas away from this plain." Arthur pointed to the picture in the Elder's hand. "But what is rather troubling is, nowhere is there any sign of those trees. To the best of our measurements they never existed. And yet we have the pictures; we have Leon's personal logs and tapes."

The Elder turned from Arthur and gazed over the plains. He felt the winds and saw the grass; listened to its gentle rustling as it bent and swayed to the perpetual winds. He would always remember the grass and the winds. And wonder about the trees.

He shivered in the warm breeze. “Let’s get out of here.” He turned and had a difficult time walking instead of running back into the ship. The winds continued blowing over the plains, moving around the hull of the ship as it lifted from the ground. The ship caused a brief disturbance but it didn’t last long and that was good. The winds had their memories as did the grass. And long after the ship had left the star system the winds continued their journeys. And remembered the trees. As did the grass.

CHAPTER 9

Standard Year 2478

"Of course we can always replace him."

Enid turned from her pilot to stare at Daegan, not understanding him.

"I beg your pardon. You said what? You said to replace . . ."

Daegan smiled. Enid hesitated, then returned his smile and turned to the waiting pilot. "You're dismissed. Report your recalibrations in ten minutes."

"Aye, sir." The pilot retreated, his tone of defiance replaced with confusion. That's not what he wanted to happen. Her anger should've triggered other bridge officers, who watched the confrontation with great interest. He had only ten minutes to get this done, no time to talk with anyone. He fled to his computer terminal and punched in codes and commands at a rate that brooked no disturbance.

Enid returned to her seat overlooking the pit where her crew was busy going through last minute checks and safety maneuvers. They were a day out of port, halfway to Baradine's Planet, and she let them know she was unhappy at how much planning they still had to do, to assume command of the fleet.

Daegan left his console and stood to her immediate left. Enid took a few breaths and then, while keeping her eyes on her busy crew, said in a low voice, "Thank you, Daegan."

"Sir, you're welcome. The situation called for some quick thinking."

"Well, keep improvising, Daegan."

"Sir, if I might speak, the crew's a bit edgy. They need to feel the Admiral is in control. We're entering unknown territory and more than three-quarters of the fleet have never been in this position before."

"I take your point."

Enid waited for a few minutes and then the pilot approached her with a single sheet of paper.

"Excuse me, sir."

"Make your report, pilot."

"Sir, your calibrations have been entered. All fleet vessels have encoded them into their systems."

"Well done, pilot. Send my compliments to their captains. And pilot?"

The pilot looked up at her expectantly, his body tensing as hers had done moments before. "Sir?"

"Pilot, we're in this together. We go where this ship goes. And the bridge is no place for private matters. Do you understand me?"

"Aye, sir!" The pilot noted the Admiral's inclusion of herself in her statements and saluted before he turned to his console.

"Sir, you've gained an ally."

"Have I, Daegan? I wonder. Prejudice isn't as simple as I thought it was."

"Nevertheless, sir, you're here."

Enid shrugged and lowered her voice. "I wonder why. I wonder why."

The next hour was hectic as reports streamed in from other ships in the fleet; Enid quickly lost track of time. She was signing a log entry when she felt a light tap on her left shoulder. She looked up to see Daegan standing over her.

"Sir, it's ten hundred hours. Time for your rest."

Enid knew better than to argue; at this moment she felt whatever energy she had leave. She transferred the commander's chair to Daegan and swiftly left the bridge.

As she slid through the connecting corridor towards her quarters, Enid felt a cold draught of air. Of course, no one was there. Yet she couldn't shake the feeling of being watched. The corridor was short by ship standards, a narrow umbilical cord connecting the flagship's bridge directly to her living quarters. Above her head and to her left the transparent walls let her see the center of the Milky Way.

Enid paused to stare at this sight. Red giants streamed through the outer arms of the galaxy; stars ranging in color from blue to ultramarine speckled the great dome forming the galaxy's center. She saw great patches of darkness like spider webs dimming the stars that lay beyond. Ribbons of light emanated from the center in cartwheel patterns, forming arms like those of a starfish. Enid continually wondered how patterns as simple as a starfish were repeated in objects as unimaginably large as a galaxy.

The great ridge of light brought back memories of her distant home. There had been mornings when Enid sat on her balcony and read a book as she enjoyed the heat from the yellow sun. Below her, she could hear the breakers crash onto a shoreline that existed long before man had ventured beyond his First Home World. Sometimes a breeze stirred the pages she held in her hand. She changed her grip on the book to keep the pages still. More than once, others commented on this odd habit; book reading was considered archaic, a poor version of the holograph readings people used everywhere. Enid took pleasure in its visceral materiality; cherished having the hardcover books of authors.

Reading Philosopher Reynold's theories on the widespread existence of Terran-type planets, Yuzuki's childhood memories, or the Seventeen Cantos of Antonia Myers provided one of the few pleasures Enid allowed herself. She recalled the aghast looks the crew gave each other when the fifteen boxfuls of books were delivered to *Stars End.* And surprise greeted her request for bookshelves to be built in her living quarters. After much searching, a handyman was found who had done such work before. He was rapidly escorted to the flagship, where Enid found him deeply engrossed in measuring walls when she came on board. And when she returned two hours later she found one wall of her living quarters lined floor to ceiling by the shelves, and her books immaculately alphabetized. The handyman, whose name she forgot to ask, placed a copy of *War and Peace* onto a shelf. As he gathered his equipment he said to Enid, "Not many people have read your stuff. It's good." By the time Enid thought to thank him he was gone, becoming one of the hundreds of thousands of people on her flagship.

Now, as she watched the stars, Enid found herself wondering briefly who that man was, what his story was. Probably she would never know and yet it was people like him who carried out the commands set by people like Enid. Without them, nothing she did meant much.

Alone in this corridor, Enid shed the role that demanded so much energy each hour she was on duty. Compared to the stars out there her life span was meaningless. She sighed, feeling the strain of the past week soak into her bones. She needed rest, and needed it badly, but how was she going to manage the fleet of ships? She had been on her feet for some twenty hours.

Meetings with the various departments for the most part went well, even the one with the Science Department, whom Daegan jokingly called the Egghead Department. After that, the unofficial nickname for the Science Department was 'ED.' Enid, while officially frowning on such euphemisms, smiled inwardly whenever she heard the acronym.

"What are you laughing about?"

The words, seemingly out of nowhere, tore Enid from her thoughts. She turned as Daegan saluted.

"How are the boys in the Science Department doing?"

Daegan smiled, "So that's what you were laughing about."

"Your nickname seems to have leaked out and now everyone's calling them ED. A quadrillion credits of hardware and we continue to reduce the sublime to the ludicrous."

"Is that going into your memoirs?"

"Daegan, if I were going to add such trivia to "A Lonely Repletion among the Native of Anphoria", she jested, "they would have to go after the thirteen volumes dedicated to my memories of a certain officer I've known for ten years."

Daegan grimaced: "Touché."

"So are they treating you any better now that you're a Colonel and my direct aide?"

Daegan smiled but from his expression Enid knew Daegan was choosing his words carefully.

"Sir, are you certain I was the right choice? I've never seen combat before and from the sounds of it you'll need someone experienced in that area."

Enid told him to follow her to her personal quarters.

"Daegan, the best troops we had were among those who perished with the Fifth Fleet. We don't know what we're up against. It might be the death of us to go into this situation armed to the teeth. Consider us more as an exploratory team. We need to know what destroyed the Fifth Fleet. Until we know more, we assume we know nothing. No preconceived notions, no enemies." Enid momentarily paused before continuing. "Too many people think it's the Repletians. If it isn't, we could get ourselves killed without knowing the true enemy."

"In any case, Daegan, you're on White and Blue Watch. I'm on Red and White Watch, so I'll relieve you at eighteen hundred hours, okay? Dismissed."

Later, after a light meal and some concentrated Ra-Clestics exercises, Enid felt ready for her next task.

"Ship, do you have anything to report?"

Another voice, seemingly addressed to no one in particular, originated from a spot two feet in front of her in a soft, modulated voice impossible to hear more than five feet away.

"Reports indicate unusual amounts of gossip about you. There are rumors about your ancestry affecting your decisions."

"Yes, I'm aware of them. There's nothing I can do. Any protest will add fuel to the fire. Best to remain silent for now..."

Enid left orders for the computer to wake her at seventeen

hundred hours. She took a long, hot shower and still dripping, moved towards her bed. She didn't bother to put on her undergarments. Clothes slowed her movements by split seconds, enough time in some cases to make it hard to live through the next moments. This time, though, her decision to not wear anything was more from fatigue than from caution. She felt she couldn't stay awake another moment.

One moment she was staring at the ceiling and in the next she was at the foot of a great mountain. The trees near her leaned before the blasts of searing gusts of wind. Enid had difficulty standing, so she anchored herself by holding onto a low branch. In the distance, further up the slope, a hooded figure stood at the edge of a precipice. Enid couldn't make out his features but from his bent posture, he looked old.

She struggled up the slope towards the still figure and then he was facing her. He said something but the wind drowned his voice. Enid yelled out "What?" and the man spoke again in his low voice. This time she heard every word, although the wind had increased.

"We won't reach the summit," he said, and pointed towards a peak hidden by great banks of clouds. Enid saw his green eyes and she was about to speak when the man nodded at her, turned, and disappeared as he limped forward into space. Enid screamed and found herself at the edge of the cliff. She gazed over the edge but the man was gone.

The ground shook; Enid backed away from the edge as it crumbled underfoot. The faster she backed away the more rapidly the ground gave way. Enid turned and ran up the slope. As she scrambled to the summit she found herself gazing at a sight that took her breath away.

A vast planet filled a full quarter of the sky. Enid saw countless asteroids forming a ring around the planet. She realized she stood on one of these great rocks for the ring stretched away from her in both directions. In the silence of this spectacle she stood speechless. And then she heard a faint sound, a warning sound that rang throughout the rings, a sound she had heard twice before in her life, a sound whose origins she didn't know.

She woke up at that point. The room was dark except for the dim glow of the wall clock reading fourteen hundred hours. White team was still on duty. Acrid smoke filled the room. In the same instant she became aware of this smoke she leaped from the bed, twisting into a defensive posture in the air. She almost made it to the floor when she felt the cold metal blade cut into her ribcage.

She knew better than to stop. She continued her forward roll, letting her momentum tear the blade from her assailant's grasp. In the silence she heard the blade snap from its handle. She landed on her side and swung her entire momentum into a continued arc driving her left foot up and out. It wasn't pretty but it was accurate and lethal. She heard the gasp as her blow landed; felt the assailant's rib cage break with the force of her blow; saw him lifted from the floor as she completed her kick, throwing him a dozen feet.

Enid twisted again in a reflex action, her mind refusing to register the pain of the imbedded blade.

The bright beam of light stabbed at the spot where she had lain. She heard the low curse as she twisted again; "Fucking Repletian! Just like a snake." The second voice, low and to her left, hissed, "Watch out for the alarm . . ."

Enid rolled to her feet in one blurred motion, throwing her weight into a counterpunch aimed two feet beyond the second man's nose, delivering a punch that drove broken cartilage into the attacker's brain.

"Ship!" she yelled as she turned in the dark to face her last attacker. Her voice triggered the computer's defense systems; two beams of light, brighter than any hand-held weapon, stabbed out from the wall. A choked gasp was all the third assailant managed before a puff of evil-smelling black smoke marked the spots where the ship's laser beams hit him in his chest.

As Major Carstairs and a swarm of other officers poured into the room Enid leaned against the library opposite to the broken doors to the hallway. She clutched her side to stop the bleeding. In a glance Jenara took in the scene and grabbed at the towel a medic carried. She knocked away an officer's hand as he reached to touch a body. "That's evidence, you fool!" she hissed at him. "Everyone except the medic, out. Now! That's an order. Computer, seal this room and give me an analysis of the situation."

Jenara's security officers followed her commands without question or hesitation. In emergencies people who thought about orders slowed things down, usually with fatal results. She moved towards Enid and the medic. The computer performed a series of electromagnetic scans of the corpses and everything else in the room in less than one Standard second. It did a molecular breakdown of scents within the room and examined every fingerprint.

When the medic completed his initial assessment of Enid's injury Jenara lifted Enid and carried her to her chair, a chair copying the functions of the commander's chair on the main bridge. In seconds a local anesthetic allowed the medic to remove the broken blade from her ribs and spray the ruptured area with a gel. The gel rapidly configured to her DNA structure and began replacing damaged cells.

Jenara waited until the medic finished his treatment. She watched him leave before she dared to move away from Enid to gaze out of the view screen at the center of the galaxy. They had come close to killing the Vice Admiral under Jenara's watch. She couldn't let Enid see her until she had regained her composure.

"It was planned, of course." Enid said in a low tired voice.

Ready now, Jenara turned from her view. "Yes, I'm afraid you're right. There were three of them."

Enid looked at Jenara. "Tell me, Jenara. Who wanted to warn me?"

"Warn you? I don't understand."

Enid pointed to where one of them, the first one killed, lay. "They weren't military. Their methods were crude; it was inevitable they would be caught. Blasting a door like that was bound to wake me and alert you." She touched a console button and Jenara watched as the cameras replayed the scene. She heard the second one swear at Enid before he died. "Fucking Repletians!"

Those words stuck in Jenara's mind, replaying themselves and clearing her mind. She became aware of Enid's stare and knew the Vice Admiral was waiting for some response from her. Jenara stared back and the look in the Vice Admiral's eyes as she studied Jenara told Jenara she should say something, anything.

"We weren't ready. They, or someone, deactivated the security systems in this section."

Enid turned from her and Jenara knew then her words weren't the words the Vice Admiral wanted or expected from her. She watched the Vice Admiral, held back by forces she didn't fully understand.

"Major," Enid said. Jenara heard the formality and felt weak. She wanted to say something, anything, but again she couldn't. "Major, I want you to schedule a meeting of my senior officers for eighteen thirty hours. Red Team should be on duty by then."

"Aye, sir."

"Good." Enid reached for a small red necklace that sat on the glass table next to her. She turned it and in the soft light of the room the jewel threw beautiful red arcs of light onto the walls. She sighed.

Military code was clear and so she ordered Jenara to relieve Daegan of command. As per regulations, he would be under house arrest until a complete investigation had either cleared him of any complicity or condemned him to a life of slavery.

"Major, you're in command until I relieve you at eighteen hundred hours."

After Jenara left Enid sat in the darkness of her bedroom for thirty minutes, replaying in her mind the previous twenty hours and thinking of the struggle she had with the pilot.

"Ship, pipe me through to Admiral Lexington. Priority One."

Enid waited while the tachyon signals leaped across space. As she waited Enid thought of Daegan. She couldn't believe Daegan was part of this conspiracy but she recalled Lexington's words before her departure for the flagship: "Trust no one except yourself."

At the time Enid had rejected his advice out of hand. Its implicit cynicism reflected a view of life alien to Enid. But, given the past hour, Enid's faith was shaken. Against her best plans, things were happening around her over which she had no control. There was a traitor, more likely several traitors, within her ship. To disable her alarm system was beyond the reach of everyone but her senior staff.

"Admiral Starbreaks."

Lexington's voice broke through Enid's thoughts. Enid didn't know how to start.

"You want some advice on what to do now?"

Enid watched him but his face was hard to read.

"Then you know of the attempt on my life?"

The Admiral nodded. "Yes. And, like you, I wonder who has the balls to send you this type of warning. I take it you weren't seriously hurt?"

"I sustained a knife wound but the blade broke on my ribs. They were clumsy and I killed two of them. The computer took care of the third."

"Yes, a setup. The assassins themselves probably never knew they weren't expected to live. The setup ensured they wouldn't."

"Well, Admiral, what now?"

Admiral Lexington gestured at his console. "Your computer has received my program. Listen to it carefully and then use your best judgement. I'll back you up in whatever course you take."

Before Enid could answer the connection was cut off. The voice of the ship's computer replaced the Admiral's voice.

"Admiral, do you wish to hear the Admiral's message?"

"Proceed."

What followed was an analysis of the situation with the Fourth Fleet under Enid's command. Enid listened carefully, at points asking the computer to halt while she jotted notes.

In the end, Enid had several choices, each of which had its risks. She needed more information from her senior staff. Their input would form the basis for Enid's next decisions.

For the second time that day, Enid made her way to her bed. But sleep evaded her. A pain deeper than her knife wound sank into her soul. The thought of Daegan imprisoned tore at her, forcing her into a fetal position. She closed her eyes to the darkness of her room. And as she lay on the hard mattress, Enid's last thoughts were of that mountain with its mysterious figure she had dreamed three times in the past week.

At eighteen hundred hours, Enid walked onto the bridge as fast as her healing body allowed her. As ordered, Jenara had assembled the bridge crew. Daegan was led in under guard.

"As you know," Enid said, "there was an aborted attempt on my life earlier today. The assailants were neutralized. As per military procedures, I've relieved Colonel Daegan Markowitz of his command." Enid ignored the gasps from several directions and continued. "Combat Major Jenara Carstairs, as First Officer, is promoted to Colonel. An investigation into the assassination attempt is now underway. You'll be notified of the results."

Daegan approached her. She wanted to reach out and hug him

but she waited while he took off his officer's insignia and handed it to her. Only a slight shaking in his hands betrayed what he felt. He stepped back, saluted, and the guards led him from the bridge. Enid refused to watch; instead, she turned her attention to the woman who stood before her.

"Major, I promote you to the rank of Colonel. You are hereby appointed as my Second-In-Command."

Enid saw the look of uncertainty on Jenara's face as Enid pinned the double red slash onto her uniform.

"See me in five minutes in my quarters, Colonel. Carry on."

The crew waited until Enid left the bridge before they broke into applause, surrounding the Colonel to congratulate her. It took Jenara the full five minutes to pull herself away from the crew to make her way to the Admiral's quarters, where she waited until Enid answered the door.

"Reporting as requested, sir."

Enid turned from the display view and gestured towards a seat. The Colonel sat and waited as Enid brushed an invisible speck from her own grey uniform.

"Colonel, you're now my Aide. Our fleet will follow your orders as though they were mine but I need more than that."

"Aye, sir."

"When you and I are alone, drop your formality. I won't tolerate any aide who is formal when alone with me."

Enid sat in a chair opposite to the Colonel's and gazed into the Colonel's eyes. Jenara returned her gaze and Enid smiled. "Always the fighter, eh, Jenara? My question to you over the next few days and weeks is whether you can be as tough as you are in combat."

"I don't understand, sir."

"'Enid' in my quarters, Colonel. Tell me, do you play chess?"

"Well, I've watched but I've never played."

"Chess is a variation of an older game called Go. Go combines strategy and sacrifice; a good player knows when to bluff---when to hide their true motives. You must be at least three moves ahead of your competitor to survive. Do you see my point, Jenara?"

The continued use of her name made the Colonel blink. Enid smiled and waited for Jenara's answer. Jenara Carstairs thought for a few moments and then she caught her breath. "Daegan!"

"Yes, you see my point, do you not?"

"But he's your friend!"

Enid shook her head: "That's why I've removed him from my side. If things work, I'll have the same talk with him as I'm having with you."

"Does he know?"

"Don't be foolish, Jenara. Knowledge is dangerous if it's used improperly."

Jenara thought for a few more seconds. "Enid, you asked me in here for a reason and I'm sure it wasn't to tell me about Daegan."

"Jenara, if you were the enemy and wanted me neutralized, how would you go about doing it in the most effective way?"

"Well, I wouldn't kill you if I thought I knew you. I'd try to discredit you or use your heritage as a weapon. Prejudice is still an awfully easy weapon to use. You can't argue with it and you can't get rid of it by killing your enemies."

"You've been on this ship for the past four days now, before even I boarded her, Jenara. What have you found out?"

"Nothing. Daegan's part of the game now, isn't he?"

"As a fleet officer, Daegan is always part of the game; he knows that as much as you know it. It's going to be rough on him for the next while; they probably hadn't thought I would move so quickly. "

"So they're playing a delaying game. But why? Why do they need to delay things? For what?"

Enid shook her head in puzzlement. "I don't know and neither does the Admiralty. Clearly I'm not the end goal here but if I'm not, who or what is?"

"My part in this is what?"

Enid saw Jenara's worried face and laughed. "Don't worry. Whatever happens, your promotion to Colonel will stick. You deserve it. No, your role in this is to follow my lead. Don't go overboard in your treatment of Daegan but don't let down your guard either. You understand me?"

"Aye, sir."

"One more question. For the record, Colonel, where do your loyalties lie? And be careful how you answer."

Jenara looked into the Admiral's eyes again. She thought back to her meeting with Admiral Lexington. "Sir, my loyalties are first to the fleet and, second, to you and your orders, so long as they don't compromise my first loyalty."

Enid stood up and the Colonel did the same. Enid hugged her and then stood back, "Welcome aboard, Colonel. Your schedule for the day is waiting for you on the bridge. I'm glad you're here."

"Thank you, sir."

After Colonel Carstairs left, Enid returned to her view of the Galaxy. She felt uneasy, as though she had forgotten something vital. As she looked out at the stars, Enid wondered what the next period in her life would bring. Whatever it was, she had a feeling it wasn't what she expected. There were too many unknowns here and for the first time she asked herself if the Repletians were her worst enemy. And why did she keep seeing Katina Patriloney smiling at her?

CHAPTER 10

Standard Year 2478

In the dream, Leon sensed the deadness around the shrouded woman. She made her home in the belly of a vast metal mausoleum, commanding the dead souls therein. She turned towards him; he waited for her to speak but she moved forward and passed through his senses to stand before the window looking out at the Mother of All Worlds, its great center taking up half the view.

He felt her confusion and still he couldn't make out her face. As she faded from sight he knew she was from his tribe, and he felt her loneliness. His bones ached as he struggled to a seated position. The sun hadn't risen and he felt pleased, knowing he could still wake up early. Each day was so precious, a communion with forces he would never fully understand but which he trusted with his soul.

Still, not all things unfolded in time without small nudges here and there. The dream demanded something of him and he needed guidance. He thought of himself as a tool, a small wedge to accomplish ends he wouldn't live to see, which no one lives to see.

He made his way from his tent to the small stream flowing from the mountain slopes. At the stream he cupped water in his hands and threw a handful in each of the four major directions before gently easing himself into the icy water. He thanked the spirits, for water had shown him both life and death in another time. As he finished the rim of the sun slowly pulled over the horizon's edge, bathing the flatlands in a light so gentle he shivered with warmth despite the cold water. He closed his eyes. His senses made contact with the world. A flock of Plicoths settled into a nearby tree and spoke back and forth to one another in a language as old as birds. Their chatter made him smile; such busy creatures with so little time in the day to do all they needed to do.

A muffled roar in the distance told him of the Riocets he had watched the previous day on their migratory travels over the plains. If he opened his eyes he could watch them as they travelled on their three hind limbs, their sight organs thirty feet above the land. He also knew his alien scent troubled the animals. They shied away from his camp and only the plant-eaters, gentle enough in themselves, came close enough to cast curious glances his way.

When he finally stood up to leave the stream his wife, Red Dawn, was waiting as he knew she would be. She returned his bow before handing him a towel.

"Thanks, Red Dawn."

"Leon, I gathered a bowl of berries for you."

He smiled for he knew Red Dawn had tasted the berries for him. Although she was a doctor before she met Leon, she now distrusted things made of science. For the same reason she was at home on a planet's surface and always suffered when they were en route to another System.

After a brief meal Leon pointed towards the mountain. "Red Dawn, I'll be gone for half a day. If you need me I'll be on Quarter Bluff."

Red Dawn nodded. Quarter Bluff was their name for a great slab of rock a quarter way towards the peak. They had found the rock on their fifth day of exploring the area around the Nordell dome. Neither had known what they sought until they saw the rock and knew they had reached their goal.

"Dear?" Red Dawn whispered. Leon turned his face half towards her, his blue-green eyes still gazing at the mountain. She reached out in a familiar gesture to touch his exposed face with her small fingers, brushing his skin with clean fingernails that traced a path of warmth and comfort.

"Yes?"

"Be careful."

Leon smiled and nodded. "When I give to you, I give myself."

He left Red Dawn to her work and slowly made his way up the slope, walking carefully, for he respected the mountain and its ways. He passed a small tree leaning to one side, its roots clinging to the barren soil with a tenacity that gave lessons in life to those who saw such things.

Red Dawn watched her husband painfully climb along the invisible trail. Leon was withdrawn and his distractions affected the life around him in ways she saw as just more proof of his connection with spiritual forces stronger than any weapon. Red Dawn had studied for years to become a doctor and to collect the library she had once owned, but the years with Leon taught her of the things forever beyond science. Leon had turned to archaeology over the past thirty years. Still, Red Dawn knew little of what Leon had done before she met him. There were rumors, some fantastic, but clearly Leon's standing as an Elder commanded respect in the highest councils of Repletia.

When her husband was as small as one of Red Dawn's fingernails held at arm's length, Red Dawn returned to her chores; she had much to do on their last day on the planet. But as she busied herself, a part of her mind was always aware of Leon. So much rested on such weary shoulders.

As he struggled up the steep slopes, Leon paused once to look back. Far below he saw the campfire not because of its flames and smoke, but because it created a small stir of difference in the land. Beyond the campsite, almost at the horizon, some eighty miles away, the ocean formed a crescent revealing the planet's edges.

Two hours later, as Leon passed a tree he used as a trail marker, the path narrowed. He let his feet follow the unseen trail. There were things you couldn't hurry. At these heights the air was cooler. A bird flew by, making a strange sound he hadn't heard before. When he looked up, it wheeled away, descending gently towards the valley floor until it grew too small to be seen.

Through the haze of the north, a dome rose seventy-five hundred yards into the air, a dark monolith of Nordellian origin. He and Red Dawn had spent months at the base of this dome, plumbing its depths many times in efforts to reveal the secret of the species which built it. They found a great deal but none of it meant much to either of them; the species was too dissimilar in size, shape and function to lend itself to easy perception.

Five hundred Standard years before, the Nordellians had occupied this sector of the galaxy. Their trademark domes were everywhere. But something had happened and the Nordellians were gone. Leon's most interesting discovery on this planet had come as he shifted through a pile of strange cloth-like material. Buried in the heart of the pile he came across a small sphere, a black object so opaque it hurt his eyes if he stared at it for too long. Protocol for such findings were strict, and a passing ship stopped to pick up the black sphere for transportation to the nearest Repletian Home World, where the artifact would be carefully studied.

A sudden gust of wind stirred the leaves of a sparse tree a short distance from where he had stopped for breath, bringing Leon back from his reflections. He felt in his blood, a thrill he hadn't felt for what was a lifetime ago. There were things unfolding that had their own life. He would be a part of this, but only a small part.

He sighed and struggled upwards again, his legs aching with the effort. Along the way he found a stout branch he used as a crutch to steady himself. Yet he found himself periodically distracted by the pain coming from his feet. He felt the dampness of a broken blister. But he could not, must not, stop from reaching Quarter Bluff.

After an eternity he rounded a corner of the trail that led onto a great flat rock. Quarter Bluff. At its edge he saw the valley from which he had climbed. He wiped the sweat from his face and stood still, feeling the wind envelop him in its warm embrace. A Plicoth, far from its natural habitat, floated in the winds, its long white wings shifting now and then to balance its flight as it stared at him, waiting with the vast patience of a bird.

And then he heard it, at first a faint sound scarcely audible in the wind. It faded in and out of hearing and transfixed him; he dared not move a muscle. He could've listened to it forever for it was the sound he had heard on Korel's World. This time it came from the distant black dome. As it continued, its melody changed from a hesitant rhythm to a persistent and undeniable beat insinuating itself into his blood, making his muscles and body feel a part of everything around him. His senses floated like the Plicoth; he felt inadequate next to the purity of this feeling.

He drifted and the music that flooded into him was accepted without the struggle he had exerted in his youth. He found himself singing a song he didn't know, a stronger and a crueler song for it told him of things that reached into his heart to draw tears. He knew he couldn't stop the pain he foresaw.

It was nightfall when he returned to the base site. Red Dawn helped him to the fire, where she fed him some soup. She used her experienced hands to check Leon's bad leg; it was inflamed at the knee joint so she massaged it until Leon told her it felt better. She then left Leon to his thoughts, satisfied he would speak to her when he needed to. But this Red Dawn knew; change was happening and the frail old miner-become-archaeologist sitting across the fire from her was at the center.

*

Three days later, on Sentus, a Repletian Home World, it was quiet. Leon heard the sound of the wind through the trees and for a moment he felt at peace, forgetting where he was. His mind went back to when wind had been a threat to conquer. Against the night sky his vision was blocked to the east by a shadow darker than the sky. The gusts of wind moving through his hair flowed towards that black shape.

"What are your thoughts, Elder?" The light musical voice lifted through the wind and became more a part of his mind than his hearing.

Leon looked at the speaker of these words. She stood ten feet away, a vague white shape pressed into the darkness of the trees behind her. It pained him to see it wasn't his wife.

"I've waited for you."

"Yes, and you'll say how you withheld food and drink from yourself to bring me here." The shape of her figure was the image of a small girl grown, an image he couldn't call by name for fear of offending her.

"Am I dreaming?"

"If you are, Elder, it matters not. The importance is in our words."

Leon turned again to stare at the night sky. He felt the presence of her spirit behind him and he drew comfort from it. The black shape lifted as he watched it, rising until it filled his sight.

The woman moved against the blackness of the trees, drawing Leon's attention. "There's much there to be used if understood. But much in there won't allow itself to be used except by those who are ready for what it is."

"You're saying the Amphibians aren't ready for the secrets within that ship?"

"Those who rely on their sciences won't unravel the secrets of what you call the Black Ship. And it's dangerous to try."

"You speak in riddles. Isn't there a better way?"

"I speak as simply as you can understand. For the same reason, I visit your dreams and visions. Nothing I say can be understood by your other self, which lies beyond your sleep."

"Are you part of the Black Ship?"

"I am both the Black Ship and what lies beyond."

"Am I to be the guardian of the Black Ship?"

"You're to do what you need to do. The Black Ship needs no guardians. You must find your brother's child. You've wasted time and there's so little time left to her."

"I don't know you and yet your shape's familiar."

"You will never know me but you'll find the woman whom I remind you of."

The sound of the wind moving through the lightly curtained windows woke Leon. He struggled from his bed, careful not to wake his wife, and limped into the next room to the great sunken tub, which he filled with steaming water before he lowered himself into it. The aches from yesterday's rigorous mental and physical exercises slowly soaked from his muscles and bones. But he reveled in the fatigue caused from yesterday because it made today seem valuable. As he lay in the water, his body half-afloat, he pondered the words of his dream. He wondered how to involve the real woman behind his dreams, she who moved from another world towards him.

Later, in the Elders Council Chambers, he listened as the younger warriors spoke of the great fleet bearing down towards the Black Ship that had sat off Artel's Star for forty years. They were angered the Anphorians had broken their treaty with Repletia to gain what they thought to be an advantage over the other human groups. So far the conflicts between Anphoria and Repletia had been limited to border fights with the more hot-headed warriors and soldiers on either side. But to break taboo and try to enter Artel's Star system was unforgivable. Artel's Star system, named after the first Repletian to explore its binary star system, was five parsecs inside what Repletians considered their territory.

"And what would you have us do?" Leon spoke for the first time. "Could we stop their advance if we had to?"

Black Snow, the leader of the young warriors, turned at Leon's voice. "No, we can't stop them but we can slow them down until we can gather our people to crush them and any foolish enough to follow."

A chorus of agreement followed Black Snow's words. Leon looked at the other Elders but they waited for him to take the lead.

"Yes, I say we throw what we have at them and hurt them. Let them think twice about breaking an oath." Black Snow looked around at his followers and Leon recognized how he and Black Snow were uncannily alike. He lifted the Speaking Sphere and Black Snow became silent; those who held the Speaking Sphere held the floor.

Leon spoke of his vision, omitting only his certainty that he knew the woman. To speak of his suspicions would throw the Council into confusion. He finished and waited. He underestimated Black Snow, who looked at him with a gleam in his eyes. "Next you'd have us believe your brother's daughter brings us peace and salvation. I can't be so trusting."

The Council broke into an uproar, every Elder and warrior were speaking at once, and it took some moments for people to become aware the Senior Elder held the Speaking Sphere in her hands. She waited patiently until the cacophony died down. When she was satisfied she had everyone's attention, she spoke to Black Snow: "Explain yourself, warrior."

Black Snow looked up to where Three Starbreaks sat. "Senior Elder, I thought it common knowledge she who leads this Fourth Fleet is Three Starbreaks' niece."

Into the shocked silence the Senior Elder looked first at Three Starbreaks and then to Black Snow. "How can such a thing be so?" she asked.

Three Starbreaks listened as Black Snow spoke of truths Three Starbreaks thought had been his alone.

"Senior Elder, Three Starbreaks knows well the truth of my words. His blood niece survived the Pegasus Massacre and was brought up in their ways. She's now the Admiral of the fleet that comes to take its vengeance upon us."

"Your words sound ludicrous, Black Snow. What can they gain by putting one of us in charge of their Navy?"

Black Snow persisted. He reached into his robes and withdrew a slender crystal reed everyone recognized was an information bearer. He waved the slender crystal reed high in the air for everyone to see before continuing. "In this, Senior Elder, lies the truth of Three Starbreaks' family. And yet I can't say Three Starbreaks meant harm by the holding back of information. Until recently, everyone aboard the *Pegasus* was thought to be dead or worse, imprisoned forever within those hellholes the Anphorians call prison. But it seems one Enid Blue Starbreaks was an exception; the Anphorians identified her early, as a possible weapon to be used in the war against us."

"A weapon? How can one of our own be used as a weapon against us?"

"She's been brought up in their way. They tested her when she first arrived upon the Pegasus. They found what we'd have found if she entered our schools."

"You talk nonsense, Black Snow."

"Do I, Senior Elder? Here's the tape to prove what I say is true."

The Senior Elder sank deeper into her chair. "If true, Black Snow, why do you bring this to the Council now?"

"Isn't it obvious, Senior Elder? Elder Three Starbreaks has a vested interest in this matter and can't be counted on to make wise decisions for our people."

"This Council will adjourn for a private hearing. Black Snow, I want that reed. Do you have any objections?"

"No, Madame Senior Elder, I don't." Black Snow extended the reed, which the Senior Elder took gingerly into her hands. Black Snow was surprised by the strength with which she did this but he said nothing as she bowed to him and then asked for the Council Room to be cleared. When the last citizen had left, she turned to face Leon:

"Three Starbreaks, what have you to say for yourself?"

"There's nothing which will harm this Council or our people."

"Who made you the arbitrator of our well-being?"

Three Starbreaks winced at this bluntness. "If I did wrong, Senior Elder, I apologize to the Council."

"Before I play this on the holograph, is there anything you wish to say about this matter?"

"Only this, Senior Elder. I've known of Blue Starbreaks' existence since my brush with Korel's World years ago. I've tried to find her since then but only recently have I broken through the Anphorian's security systems. And, as you can see now, she's the Admiral of the Fourth Fleet, recently promoted to that position following the destruction of the Fifth. Someone with powerful connections has taken great pains to hide her existence from us until it was deemed all right to reveal her. There've been rumors for years of a Repletian being trained by the Anphorians but no one gave credence to them."

"I see. That will be all, Three Starbreaks. The Council of Elders will see the recording and come to decisions about what to do next."

CHAPTER 11

Standard Year 2478

For a year, Baradine's Planet had prepared for the fleet's arrival. Baradine's Planet was one of those planets, which specialized in growing food for the twenty three fleets which patrolled Anphorian borders. Providing enough food to last a fleet several years was a major undertaking. Each fleet with its support ships, supply ships, weapons ships, production ships, was responsible for hundreds of millions of mouths to feed. Given the choice of having food ships or of obtaining food supplies from Home World planets, the Navy chose the latter option, making their fleets more mobile and less vulnerable.

Typically, a fleet's needs strained the resources of the planet chosen to supply it. But the rewards were also immense. A chosen planet was honored above all others in its sector for years to come. The planet's coffers groaned with the credits which came from having its food crops taken in one great gulp. In addition, this was often the last time for several years the troops and crews could have shore leave on a planet's surface. Shore leave was freely granted and a fleet's on-board complement of personnel during these stopovers was often less than ten percent.

Baradine's Planet was particularly excited this year. Rumors Repletia was winning the war filtered through all levels of Anphorian society. News of the Fifth Fleet's fate sent shock waves through Anphoria. Nothing had ever wiped out an entire fleet before. There were those on Baradine's Planet who said they saw it coming; the Navy had become complacent and sloppy over the last hundred Standard years, but these sages were in the minority. However, most Anphorians were outraged and wanted a full measure of revenge. Anger towards Repletians, already bad, was at an all-time high. Anphorians, fuelled by the news media, wanted Repletia crushed once and for all times, no matter the cost.

For a generation Repletians had filtered into the border worlds of Anphoria as servants and laborers. For the most part they lived in housing units, which were overcrowded and run down. As news of the Fifth Fleet's end reached the border worlds, Anphorians rioted on several worlds, taking thousands of Repletian lives.

When people found the fleet coming in was commanded by a Repletian Admiral, at first it was met with stunned disbelief. One of their enemies in charge? A Repletian whose allegiances were suspect? What in hell was the Admiralty and the President thinking? The media dug up details of the Admiral's life. There wasn't much to be found. Her parents and her early life were shrouded by military secrecy; a secrecy which began when the military took custody of the child. Her life started at fifteen when her marks set new standards. She was touted to be the perfect warrior, cool and detached in the most hectic of situations, precise and accurate in her prognostications, fierce and deadly in combat situations.

*

Talbot O'Halliran turned on his holograph and stared at the latest image of the stern calm figure, which stood alone before an endless sea of soldiers. The soldiers wore the dark blue uniforms of the Navy and saluted the woman who stood with her arms at her sides. Enid Blue Starbreaks wore the grey uniform of the Admiralty. Talbot had seen other images of her but this was his favorite. He had followed her career since he was a ten-year-old child, dreaming one day he would stand by her side as her Aide. She was his role model. Talbot read everything he could find on her, keeping an album with his favorite stories and pictures. Now, as he stared at her, Talbot wondered what she thought as she stood before that assembled multitude. The Fourth Fleet had sworn allegiance to her command and to the mission, which would end in Artel's Star system.

"Talbot, get down here now."

Talbot sighed and turned the image off. "Coming, Dad," he yelled. He tied his work boots and threw on a tee-shirt. A quick run of his hands through his hair to smooth it down and he was ready, taking the stairs two at a time on his way down to the dining room. His mother looked up from the table as he entered the room.

"Talbot, you'll fall down those stairs one of these days, I swear."

The tall Repletian carried a full heavy tray into the room and set it onto the large circular table. Fascinated, Talbot watched the new servant. They had hired her two months ago and they still knew so little about her. Because she was dedicated and punctual, Talbot's parents weren't interested in her private life. But her quiet strength drew Talbot like a magnet. Every gesture she made showed a lack of self-consciousness Talbot had seen in one other person.

Those were the times when he caught his father leaning on a fence. Ed would watch the diggers, planters, and weeders crisscross his farmlands in their endless automated cycles. Sometimes a machine idled while others hurried to its side to spend whatever time it took to complete minor repairs. And always Ed transfixed, gazed over his land, his face filled with musing, anticipating a machine that needed repair.

While Ed waited, his eyes would be distant, blank. Once when Talbot was a child his father hadn't moved for ten minutes: Talbot had waited in vain for his father to show a sign of life and at last he'd given up and returned to playing with his toy flagship.

Talbot's father came into the house, interrupting Talbot's memories. Ed took a quick look at Talbot, and nodded approvingly. "I see you're ready to go to town."

Talbot nodded and gave his mother a kiss on the cheek as the servant returned to the kitchen, which was a room where only she, by an unspoken rule, roamed freely. It was not that she ever said anything outright, about coveting her own space, but it became increasingly evident in her refusal to talk whenever someone came into the kitchen.

Canyon Reach (who came to be known as CR) quietly went about her duties diverting anyone who happened to be in the way. Even Sakana, Talbot's mother, became uncomfortable anywhere near the kitchen and avoided it if she could. Sakana attributed it to respecting privacy but Talbot knew otherwise. His mother was not someone who backed down easily; but his mother was clearly baffled by her.

Just a few days before harvest Talbot had been putting up a poster of the Admiral, when he sensed someone in his room. He turned to find CR staring impassively at the picture. Curious, Talbot decided to ask her about the Admiral but the servant said nothing; she gathered Talbot's clothes for laundry and stopped only long enough to say the Admiral wasn't yet one of them.

The aroma, which rose from the food spread on the table, was irresistible and Talbot's thoughts of CR receded. Ed said a quick prayer of thanks and then dug in, scooping great chunks of food onto his plate. Both Sakana and her husband gleefully watched this spectacle.

After breakfast Talbot made his way to the backyard where his father was loading the last of the grain into their lifter's storage unit. The lifter towered over the tall lean figures of both men and not for the first time Talbot marveled such a huge machine could lift effortlessly. As Talbot helped his father tie down and bolt the storage unit, Sakana emerged from the house and seated herself in one of the four passenger seats. There she waited, humming a popular tune to herself until the two men joined her. Before Ed entered the lifter he took a final glance around the yard and then, seeing nothing they might've forgotten, made himself comfortable at the controls and gripped the steering wheel with an easy control. The lifter rose ten feet, spun a quarter-turn, and then shot forward with a low hum.

The transmitter/receiver was full of news of the fleet now in orbit around Baradine's Planet. That morning Enid Blue Starbreaks had met with the planet's leading citizens to complete loading and leave schedules. The Fourth Fleet was using Baradine's Planet as the rendezvous point and warships were hourly joining the fleet, swelling its ranks and creating their own needs. Last night Talbot thad looked into the dark clear skies and saw moving lights everywhere, each a ship in orbit around the planet. He hadn't slept much, wondering throughout the night which of those lights marked the flagship and what the Admiral aboard ship was doing. One day, he knew, he would be up there; he had received the letter of acceptance into the Naval Training Academy.

Ed watched his son, sensing Talbot's excitement. Ed had wanted his son to take over the farm when he came of age but that was gone with the letter they received yesterday. He and his wife knew it was coming because of Talbot's growing fascination with the Navy and with the Admiral he followed. Last night, after Talbot went to bed, Sakana and he talked into the small hours of the morning, but the taste of disappointment was still there, coloring what should've been a happy day.

The farm had produced its best crop ever, a bumper crop for which the fleet had agreed to pay top dollar. The sale would set the family up for life because they had been frugal over the years, saving most of their money from three previous fleet visits. But the future he had worked for no longer included his son, who would spend the next few years or decades among people and on planets Ed would never see. For the first time since his mother's death Ed cried while Sakana held him in her arms, comforting him until he fell into an uneasy sleep.

A sudden lurch brought Ed's mind back to his flight controls. A warning light flashed from the console. The lifter lurched again and Ed began to steer it to the nearest large clearing while Sakana bit her lip to keep from crying out. Talbot said not to worry, holding her tightly, but inside he fretted that the engines would give out before they reached the clearing. If they did, the massive cargo holds would break apart upon impact, crushing the three humans under hundreds of tons of grain and metal, snuffing out their lives as easily as gnats. Both he and his mother breathed easier as Ed fought the controls to steer the lifter onto the flat barren plateau.

They scrambled from the lifter as soon as it touched down. Ed looked at the motor and shook his head: "Damned if I know what's wrong." Talbot pointed to a small disk component. Ed saw the slight crack in its gleaming silver surface. "Dad, it's like the mower back home. I can fix it in no time."

Ed said nothing and moved aside as Talbot placed his heavy toolbox to one side of the engine frame. Talbot dabbed a small streak of liquid onto the crack and then covered the liquid with a chalky-grey paste, which he squeezed from a tube.

"Be careful, son. That's strong stuff."

"Don't worry, Dad. This is easy." Talbot applied a last smear of paste, then ran his right thumb over the crack until the paste covered the thin line. Talbot took a live wire and touched the paste with the wire. A light sprang up which made the day seem dark; Ed and his son had already turned their backs to the engine. When the light faded they turned to see the fused metal disk. Ed started the engine and after a brief shudder, the motor purred to life. Ed glanced at his watch as they scrambled back into their seats. As they lifted off, he said, "We're late. I'll have to meet with the buyers as soon as we get there."

Nearing the port town of Myopia the O'Hallirans gazed silently at the hundreds and thousands of ships which flickered from the town, from beyond the upper atmosphere. There were so many that at this distance Talbot thought of a host of spiders building webs from a tree to the grass below. Through the open windows they heard the growing hubbub of sound. The acrid odor of burnt fuel increased with each mile.

Ed steered their lifter to a loading site outside Myopia. As the lifter circled to land, Talbot recognized Myopia's Deputy Mayor standing at the edge of the loading site. Just beyond the Deputy Mayor a small needle-nosed cruiser idled its engines. Ed saw the ship and he nudged his wife. Sakana stared intently at the cruiser for some moments, studying its black form as though she were trying to see into its interior.

The Deputy Mayor was a familiar sight. He made a habit of visiting the major farms around Myopia and had dinner with Ed's family every year after the first harvest.

"Ed, how are you?"

"Great, Mike. What brings you here today? I'm running late. Ran into a bit of engine problems on the way in."

"That's why I came to see you. You've had a fine crop this year, outstanding. The buyers were most impressed. They've asked you to dine with them."

"Hmmph. I see. Which ship bought the grain this year?"

The Deputy Mayor paused and Ed looked up. The Deputy Mayor was behaving strangely today. Ed wondered what troubled his friend.

"I've come to get you and prepare you for dinner."

"Mike, I don't have time for this nonsense. My family and I want to spend some time together before Talbot goes into the Navy. This'll be one of the last times we'll have together for a long time."

"I know that. Talbot, congratulations. I oversaw your application. With your outstanding school marks it was easy to do."

Talbot knew the Deputy Mayor was nervous so he was cautious. "Thank you, sir. I intend to work hard to get good marks."

"Yes, I'm certain of that, my boy. Certain of that."

Ed turned to his wife and raised an eyebrow; he stamped his feet as he circled his lifter for a final visual check, making sure the Deputy Mayor heard his impatience. The Deputy Mayor paused and waited patiently for Ed to finish his scan.

"I'm sorry, Ed, if I seem evasive. I've never had to handle a request like this before. I mean, it's the Admiral herself."

Ed stopped his check to look at the Deputy Mayor. "Are you telling me the flagship bought my crop?"

"More than that," the Deputy Mayor hurried on, as though afraid Ed would interrupt before he could finish. "The Admiral thought it would be a good public relations move to have a meal with the planet's best farmer; after all, it will be our food which feeds the fleet for the next few months. Your crop yields impressed the last fleet and someone passed the word to the Admiral."

Sakana nudged her husband. "Ed, you know we didn't bring anything for that kind of dinner. I'm not dressed for it."

Before Ed could answer the Deputy Mayor hurried on. "Of course the city would be proud to supply whatever clothes and other things you need to get ready for the dinner. More than proud, extremely pleased to have our best farmer there. The Admiral wants to keep this as informal as possible."

Ed was about to make a retort to this when he caught the gleam in Talbot's eyes. Talbot was in a daze; all he had heard was the word Admiral and that somehow, by some miracle, he would get to meet the Admiral herself. Sakana noticed her husband pause. Without stopping to think further she knew she had to agree to this dinner.

"Well, if you can get us suitable clothes I don't see why we couldn't spend a couple of hours away from our own business. As long as it's informal, where's the harm done?"

Ed blustered but he knew defeat when he saw it. "Mike, I'm holding you to your promise. Make the arrangements."

The Deputy Mayor beamed and hurried towards his craft. "You won't be sorry for this, I promise you," he said as he reached the black shape of his ship. "The Mayor will be so pleased to hear this. Pleased and grateful for your attendance. Go anywhere you please.

Arrangements have been made with Myopia's best shops; all you have to do is show up."

*

Enid was tired. She felt the strain of meeting with trade delegates and parties whose main intentions, it seemed, were to get close to her so they could later tell stories of meeting her with anyone who cared to listen. Any bickering and negotiation had been settled long ago but the Mayor assured her formalities had to be observed, and one of these was to go through negotiations in the time-honored traditions of Baradine's Planet.

It was getting late and she glanced at her timepiece as the last of the delegates disappeared through the doors. Her own guards stood against the walls, ten feet apart from each other. Given the size of the hall, several hundred soldiers stood guard; everyone had heard of the recent riots on other planets and no one was taking chances with the Admiral's safety. Baradine's Planet, of course, was unaware of the personal attack on Enid two days before; that matter was being investigated but Enid knew they would come up with nothing now.

The Mayor and his deputy bowed to Enid. "Yes, what is it?" she asked, impatient with the formality the planet's citizens cherished. She felt the dull pain in her side, a reminder of the near-fatal stab wound, which wasn't healed.

"Sir, we're pleased to announce the dinner has been arranged as per your personal request."

"Thank you. How many guests have been confirmed?"

The Deputy Mayor handed the Mayor a sheet of paper which the Mayor glanced at, a gesture which Enid knew was yet another formality. The Mayor would've known of the list before bringing it to her attention.

"At your request, sir, there are three guests. It appears two others contacted couldn't make it due to other, ahem, extenuating circumstances."

"That's fine, Mayor. Tell me, who agreed to meet me?"

"The O'Halliran family from the Eastern Sections will be here."

"Ah, yes, the farmers. When is the dinner?"

"In three hours, sir."

When Enid entered the dining hall she admired the tapestries strung against each wall. They depicted the early days of this planet's colonization, when there were still herds of four-legged creatures which Baradine Thompson, the original settler, had nicknamed Blandsheeps. Enid recalled one story. After the shipwreck Baradine needed to hunt for food. He noticed these peculiar creatures and their lurching walk; before long he also noticed their herd instincts and killed one of them for food. One day as he herded a group of them, he watched, astonished, as they panicked and bolted off a cliff to their deaths. Hence the name he gave them.

A swift glance about the hall revealed more tapestries than Enid could count. They were made from some material which reflected the shifting patterns of color. The huge wood table in the center of the room was covered with cloth. A host of candles, which provided the illumination of the room, lined the center of the table.

Enid waited, ignoring the awed looks of her guests, while her guards checked the room. Finding nothing, the guards posted themselves along the walls as the main doors swung shut. When she heard the bolts slide into place Enid strode towards the table. Her guests rose to their feet, their quiet conversation having stopped as she entered the room. The Mayor bowed and Enid returned this bow. She was amused to see that the farmers simply stood beside their places. Their son was dressed in a cadet uniform. Jenara had told Enid that Talbot had been accepted into the Naval Training Academy. He saluted as she looked at him.

"You haven't started your training yet, have you, young man?"

"No, sir, I haven't."

"Then drop the formalities." Enid's voice was low and intense. Talbot stared at her dark still form; she contrasted sharply with the larger figure, which stood a pace behind the Admiral. It was hard to believe he was in the presence of someone he had seen only in holographs, a person who commanded a fleet fifty times larger than the entire population of Baradine's Planet. He stared at the single red jewel that hung on a gold chain around the Admiral's neck.

Enid reached out her right hand to shake Ed's hand. She noted the firm grip he returned as well as his uncompromising and shrewd look. She kept her left elbow close to her ribs, trying to ignore the pain. Caught flat-footed by Enid's lack of formality, the Mayor made his introductions after the fact: "Edward O'Halliran, I'd like you to meet the Admiral. Admiral, Edward O'Halliran. This is his wife, Sakana, and their son, Talbot."

Enid shook their hands and then seated herself. The move was so sudden that again the Mayor was caught off-guard. The only thing he could do was to gesture for the others to follow suit. Enid noted the small smile, which appeared on Edward O'Halliran's face and decided this was a man she liked. His moves were self-assured, lacking the self-conscious gestures she had met in others through the long busy day.

"I understand you didn't receive my invitation until you arrived in Myopia. For this I apologize. I should've given your Mayor more warning."

Ed looked up from the soup they had served. Sakana looked up as well, watching her husband. Sakana's faith in this man was apparent by her gaze.

"Well, we had planned other things tonight."

Enid heard the barely restrained gasp from the Mayor but Ed continued as if he hadn't heard the sharp intake of breath. "But my son would have killed me if I hadn't agreed to this dinner."

"Your son?" Enid turned towards the young man, who squirmed in his seat.

"Yes, he's been in love with the Navy ever since he turned ten. There wasn't much Sakana or I could do about that."

The red tapestry behind Talbot's nervous figure drew Enid's attention and she closed her eyes against it. She stared at Talbot, surprised that his angular face reminded her of Daegan. The boy had the same wary look as Daegan's. From the way he stared back at her he also had the same candor. Enid felt a terrible emptiness at the thought of Daegan.

Sakana spoke up, again surprising Enid. "My son thinks the world of you."

Talbot blurted out, ""Mom, you didn't have to tell her that." He stopped, aware of how loud his voice was in this room with its soldiers and its tapestries of the past.

"Nonsense, son. It wouldn't hurt a bit. I'm sure the Admiral has heard much worse."

Ed took a sip from his bowl and then pointed with his spoon at the hall around them. "Truth to tell, Admiral, this isn't my first choice for a good dinner setting."

Enid smiled for the first time, admiring Ed's directness; he was a refreshing change and Enid was glad she had decided to have this dinner.

"No," Enid agreed. "Nor mine. But we make do with what we have, do we not?"

"Aye, that we do. I expect you wanted to see us for more than our social company."

"Yes, in fact, I did want to meet you. I checked back over your services to the Navy and I must say I was impressed, and wanted to meet the man who could make such quality grain without drawing attention."

"We do what we can to get by. I suspect I wouldn't be much good as a soldier and you wouldn't be much good as a farmer."

The Mayor tried to interrupt but Enid waved him still. "No, I expect you're right about that. I wouldn't make much of a farmer. That's why I'm happy to have people like you helping the Navy."

They became quieter as more food was served. Several times during the rest of the meal Enid found Talbot staring at her, studying her every move. He began to copy her. Amused, she returned Talbot's gaze as the meal ended. She pushed her plate away, and her left rib cage ached with the sudden movement. Her sight dimmed and she struggled to hide the pain.

Sakana's voice broke through to Talbot as he stared at Enid.

"Talbot, don't stare so. It's rude."

Talbot looked down and Enid turned to Sakana, again pleased by Sakana's quiet strength. "Talbot was wondering about me being Repletian, weren't you, Talbot?"

"Aye, sir. I was wondering that."

"What were you wondering in particular?"

"Well, sir, it must be hard for you as an Admiral. I mean, what with you being Repletian and all."

Enid laughed. "Talbot, it's hard at times but we all have burdens to bear, don't we?"

"No, ma'am, not like yours. I mean, there must be lots of people who hate you for what you are."

Enid nodded. "Yes, but there are also those who see me and not my DNA." As she said this Enid stole a glance at Jenara's impassive face. Talbot hesitated.

"What is it, Talbot? Whatever it is, feel free to ask."

As Enid waited the servants came in, clearing the dishes and utensils.

"Does it make it hard for you to be going against your own people?"

"Well, Talbot, I've thought about this before. Of course we don't know yet if it's the Repletians we need to be worried about. There are questions which need to be answered before the Navy decides on what course of action to take."

"But say you do find out it's the Repletians who did that thing to the last fleet. Or say the Council orders you to attack the Repletians anyway, what'll you do?"

"Talbot, where did you hear that?" Sakana looked shocked.

"I heard it through the news. They say that big of a force could only mean war. Wouldn't they have a diplomat on board if all they wanted were answers?"

Enid, about to continue the discussion, stopped and grabbed the table with one hand. The pain of her wound returned, and Talbot's words, which she knew were important, were forgotten as she drew in a great breath of air as quietly as she could.

"Are you all right, Admiral?" Ed's voice was ahead of the same question asked by another voice from behind Enid.

"Yes, yes. I'm all right. Let's proceed. I have an award to present to you and your family for your outstanding services to the Navy."

The Mayor handed Enid a small gold plaque framed in silver. She moved around the table and gave it to Ed, who had risen from his seat.

"Since we aren't standing on formality, I will only say 'Thank you' to you and your family on behalf of the Navy. Along with this award is a bonus payment of a thousand credits."

Both Ed and Sakana gasped, for the bonus was double the price of their crop and would give them more comfort in their retirement than they had ever thought possible.

"Admiral, there's no need for such a large bonus. My wife and I can live on much less than this."

Enid shook her head. "Ed, we know your son's going into the Academy. You probably had plans for your son. The bonus is small reward for the great things we expect from your son. Talbot, can you come here?"

As Talbot stood nervously before her Enid was handed another item, this one a small document which she gravely extended to Talbot.

"Talbot O'Halliran. On behalf of the Academy I congratulate you. With your marks and your references you've been formally accepted into the Officers Training Corps of the Third Fleet as of oh nine hundred hours five days hence, at which time you'll report for duty aboard the *Lexington III*, which is rendezvousing with the Third Fleet. Congratulations."

Talbot's mind was still on the red jewel as the O'Hallirans left the dining hall to return to their hotel.

"Talbot O'Halliran, I never thought you would have the audacity to challenge the Admiral like that."

Talbot winced at his mother's voice but stood his ground as they lifted off from the grey monolith of City Hall and headed to their hotel. "Mom, she asked me to continue."

"There was still no need for it. You'll have to watch yourself more closely in the Academy. Not everyone shares our views on matters. Not everyone should be trusted the way you trust us."

CHAPTER 12

Standard Year 2478

Three days out from Baradine's Planet Enid woke up and did some light exercise before she went to her kitchen to make a sandwich. After a few bites, she lost her appetite and decided to dress. The steel grey uniform she put on carried the three-inch red lightning slash over her heart.

On her way to the bridge, Enid gazed at the stars that swelled into the great central Galactic dome. Watching the light from those distant stars gave Enid a sense of peace difficult to find for the past several years. As she stared at the stars she wondered again why she was promoted; it had caused great controversy and several transfer requests from senior officers. Why her? What was she missing?

Just then, a star from the other side of the galaxy flared and grew brighter. The shields of her viewing port softened the light but the star's radiance increased until the shields were forced to dim out everything else. Enid knew the star had exploded several dozens of thousands of years ago. Still, the majesty and sheer scale of the explosion made her take a deep breath. The light grew until the entire screen was pitch black except for the star's single burning light. A small brilliant point washed the corridor in white. After a few seconds its intensity faded and the screen slowly returned to normal. Where the star had been a red glow reminded Enid of nothing so much as an open wound.

She had to turn away. Only then did she see the warning light flashing. Enid hurried to the bridge, where the port side viewer showed the close-up of a system's sun, a red star whose solar flares twisted millions of miles into space. Between the fleet and that star was a ship, or what could only be called a ship, for no naturally occurring object could do what that object was doing. It stopped and turned at speeds that would turn a human into sludge.

The ship was impossibly shaped, angles, corners, and curves defying human logic. Enid looked at it and laughed, startling her officers. Answering their puzzled looks, she pointed at the ship that flowed across the screen.

"Gentlemen, that may be the enemy but it certainly isn't a Repletian ship. They couldn't build that ship if they tried. We couldn't."

She turned from the screen to look at her officers, who waited for her to say something, anything.

"Lieutenant Commander?"

"Aye, sir?"

"Note for the record we encountered a Repletian ship at 1345 hours this date."

"Sir?"

"You heard me, Mister. We've encountered our first Repletians. Don't engage them. I want to see what they do."

Having given her orders, Enid watched with some satisfaction as her officers scrambled to obey. One thing could be said for military discipline; her officers were trained to follow orders to the death if necessary. Perhaps they would have to give their lives but that moment hadn't yet arrived. She watched as the dark shape twisted into a new shape, glowing a dull red that shifted to pale blue and then to a blackness that defied words. Whatever that thing was out there Enid didn't want its attention until she had more data on it.

And as they watched and gathered information on the ship it vanished before their eyes.

"Lieutenant Commander, report!"

"Sir, the Repletian ship is gone."

"I can see that, Mister. Where did it go to?"

"Unknown, sir. Our instruments report it simply isn't there."

"Is that possible?"

"Not with our technology, sir."

"You're saying it vanished without a trace?"

"Aye, sir, I guess that's what I'm saying."

Enid felt a chill run down her spine and she abruptly got up from her seat.

"Keep an eye out for it and let me know if it returns."

On those orders Enid transferred her command to Jenara and left the bridge. Once she reached the safety of her quarters Enid leaned against the door and took deep breaths. It was one thing to know about the Black Ship; it was another to see its impossibility. She moved from the door to the couch, where she lay down and closed her eyes. She wondered if the supernova was an omen of the Black Ship. Whatever race it came from, its appearance wasn't accidental; there was a reason, a purpose for showing itself. What was that purpose? Was the ship Nordellian? Was an invasion pending? Was this the reason for the Admiralty's secrecy? Enid felt herself panicking.

"Turn the lights off, please."

The computer dimmed the lights. Enid felt relief. But the memory of Baradine's Planet, that boy soldier, and then Daegan sent a shock through her system. His angular face drove her to her feet. Moments later she was making her way through the endless corridors of the flagship towards Daegan's cell. She never noticed the lack of guards around her but other officers in the corridors did. Several of them, after their first shock of recognition, fell in behind her to keep guard. With this retinue trailing her at a discreet distance, Enid reached her destination in fifteen minutes, doors and barriers swiftly opening before her.

Daegan was seated on the edge of his cot. He showed no surprise at her appearance, indeed seemed to be waiting for her. He stared at her with that look which sometimes infuriated her, as it did now. They had known each other for years and yet he sometimes acted as though they had met. Enid waved her escort back and leaned against the bars. She thought of the irony that after thousands of years of human development they still relied on mechanisms as archaic and yet as effective as steel poles sunken into floors to prevent escape. Their dull glint was similar in color and texture to so many other things on the flagship, a nondescript grey, which she resented.

"They're only bars."

Enid looked up from the floor, "I beg your pardon?"

"They're only bars."

"But they keep you in here, in this small room".

Daegan continued to sit at the edge of the cot, which squeaked now as he leaned slightly forward, "I'm happy to have the time to think."

"Daegan, if there was any other way, you know I'd have taken it."

"Admiral, don't blame yourself. I should have foreseen the attempt on your life."

"The attack was only a warning."

"Admiral, do you think they would have hesitated to kill you if you couldn't defend yourself? No, they were good enough to get through our defenses into your quarters; if that were a warning, it was certainly a costly one."

Daegan stood up and Enid sensed the alertness in the officers behind her. Daegan threw a swift glance at them before he moved carefully towards her. She waited, unsure of his intentions and hating herself for the small moment of doubt she felt at his approaching figure. Daegan saw the wavering in her eyes and smiled, saying clearly as much for the ones behind her as for her, "Don't worry, Admiral. I won't touch you."

Why…why can't I say anything to him, tell him everything's all right? She waited, feeling her muscles tense against her will, hating herself for what she was doing. Daegan stopped two paces from the bars and for the first time in a long time Enid looked at his familiar figure, marveling at the stillness and security she felt within him. Whatever else Daegan might be, he still had an authority which Enid, in her moments of reflection, sometimes felt was greater than hers.

"Admiral," Daegan spoke in a voice low enough to be heard by the two of them. "Admiral, watch your back."

"Oh, Daegan. I wish I could do something, anything, to get you back onto the bridge."

"No, you did the right thing. There'd have been a mutiny on your hands if you ignored protocol. Your biggest worry isn't me. Don't you see? They wanted me removed. They chose a way to do this with no risk to themselves."

"If I find the bastards, I'll castrate them all."

"Perhaps that's what they hope."

"What's going on here, Daegan? What am I missing?"

"If I knew that, Admiral, perhaps I wouldn't be here now."

Enid heard the growing restlessness in the officers behind her and said farewell more hastily than she wanted. She spent the next hour prowling through the forepart of the ship. She ignored the people she met as she made her way through endless passages, up and down countless stairwells, and from one deck to another, and found herself endlessly amazed at the sheer size of the flagship. Yet, despite its labyrinthian chaos, never once did she lose her bearings. It was said with some pride by her officers that the only Admiral, perhaps the only person, who ever walked the length and breadth of the immense ship was Enid herself. And although her routes and times changed, she did it regularly, and her presence was a comfort. With her, they knew the ship was secure. Five days ago, after her attack, she missed a full day's duties and none were more missed by her crew than that daily walk.

Enid watched an engineer work on a small transport cart. Despite her presence, he worked at a steady confident pace, his hands moving swiftly over familiar parts of the machine as he removed and examined various parts of the cart. He found the damaged part, swiftly placed it aside and replaced it with a new part. Only then, as he stood up from his crouch, did he greet her.

"Admiral, sir."

"At ease, Corporal. You've done a fine job."

"Thank you, sir."

Enid returned to her walk, moving more quickly than she had before, making it difficult for her officers to keep up. She went through places most of them were only vaguely familiar with. Often they threw glances at one another, baffled. Only in the last five minutes, as she neared her quarters, did they see familiar faces and halls. Outside her quarters, Enid dismissed them.

In her room, Enid felt the strain from her walk take hold. She ran a bath and soaked blissfully in the suds and soothing warmth. The steam from the water filled the large room and mingled with the slow steady drip of the tap to give Enid a sense of peace. Slowly, slowly, her anxieties slipped into oblivion. She sighed, curled her toes, lifted one slim leg from the water and stared at its brown glistening skin. She ran a face cloth along her fine musculature, reveling in the heat that stretched and relaxed as she let her leg slip back beneath the surface of the water.

She thought of Daegan alone in his barren cell, and felt a twinge of grief she tried to quell; why did he have to be her Aide? So many things she could have said to him, so many things she wanted to say to him, all forbidden by protocol.

Enid placed the soft cloth over her eyes and sank into the water. Water, the one eternal comfort she had to look forward to after each day. Her mind went back to earlier days, past the beatings from her schoolmates at the military schools, past the ridicules of her teachers who said no Repletian was worth the ground they walked on, past the dumb stares of boys who talked in whispers to one another in dares to ask her for a date, not because they liked her but because they thought her exotic and everyone knew what Repletian girls were like, past the terrible moments of silence in that isolation ward where they put her when she fought against those groping hands and sneering voices, past everything to the memory she kept of her early days, a memory buried deeply so the psychologists would never taint it with their foul probing.

Enid's adult arms formed a circle around the small precious doll she remembered cuddling until the time they tore it away from her. She felt the tears course down her face but here in the silence of her room she didn't care, letting them flow into the bathwater; soaking in the grief she shared with no one. She remembered the long black hair and soft cradle of her birth mother's hugs and the great booming voice of her father when she squealed and ran into his waiting arms.

There was the awesome moment when she went aboard her first starship, misunderstanding her parents' grief and the unusual silence among her tribe as they were shuffled on board the ship called *Pegasus*. It was a magical name. And she felt a part of the magic of the stars that shone overhead on the planet where they had lived on for as long as Enid could remember. She remembered the long lines---the endless corridors that her mother said would be their new home. And then running through those corridors with a small girl's overwhelming excitement, clutching her doll in her arms and hearing the growing hubbub behind her as her parents broke lines to chase her.

Enid began to cry as these memories rose from where they had taken refuge. And then the great black hole of acrid black and red flesh, a gaunt creature that loomed from the water and threatened to overwhelm her. Enid staggered from her bath, dripping water as she fled to the safety of her bed. There she curled into a fetal position and shivered uncontrollably. She stifled the screams she knew would never end if she let them out.

After what seemed like days, she heard Jenara's low voice.

"Admiral?"

Enid uncurled herself, as her name rang in her ears. The

computer told her she had been asleep for two hours. A soft darkness faded as the lights within her personal quarters lit up. Scattered on a small table in one corner of the room were charcoal drawings and sketches, jagged lines etched into the surface features of familiar faces and scenes. Most of these sketches were stained from much handling.

"Admiral?"

"This is the Admiral. What is it?"

"Admiral, we've been contacted by a Repletian ship."

"I'll be there in five minutes."

"Aye, sir."

Enid sat up in her bed and felt weak. She needed more time but she didn't have it. She swore at the impassive wall before her. Although her knife wound was healed, she felt a dull pain in her lower ribs. Sometimes this became a sharp stab that threw her off-balance.

*

Jenara looked up from her console as she heard the Admiral enter. She immediately saw the Admiral's unsteady stride. Enid's eyes looked uncertainly about the bridge for a moment, then cautiously made her way towards Jenara. Extending a helping hand to steady the Admiral as she sat in her commander's chair, alarmedly she blurted out,

"Sir, are you all right?"

"I'm fine. I need some time to gather myself. Give me a status report."

"Well, sir, we made contact with the Repletian ship an hour ago. Or rather, it made contact with us. The ship's commander wants to meet with you at your earliest convenience."

"Is it alone?"

"As far as we can tell, yes, Admiral, it's alone. Moreover, from its size it's no threat."

Enid took a deep breath and noticed the look of concern on Jenara's face. "Colonel, I'll be all right."

Enid knew Jenara wasn't convinced. Enid could do nothing but move on, bluff her way through the next few hours. She needed to get her fleet into some semblance of order, to draft contingency plans for any event the fleet met. Moreover, she needed time to mull over things. If not the Repletians, then who should she be looking out for? That strange Black Ship was seen by almost every ship in the fleet. While most knew Repletia couldn't have built such a craft, others saw in the ship, a devastating new Repletian weapon.

Enid found herself moving in a way that showed her stress, the fear of that dream returning to claim her. This time she wouldn't have the strength to fight off those images. She knew she would lose her sanity if she were stretched too far.

The small ship continued its leisurely course towards *Stars End*, past the great battleships around the flagship. Enid ordered her Commanders to be with her when she met with the Repletians. She also ordered the Great Central Hall (buried deep within the bosom of her flagship) to be prepared to host the meeting in thirty minutes. Jenara hurried off to secure the Hall with the team charged with the safety of the Admiral and her Commanders. No one was certain what to expect from the Repletians but Jenara wasn't taking chances; Daegan's arrest was one the crew would not soon forget.

Thirty minutes quickly flowed by. Long before Enid would have liked it she entered the Hall at the head of her military aides, all in their formal uniforms. Enid, as always, wore her plain Admiral's uniform, in stark contrast to the more colorful uniforms of her subordinates. She also wore her scarlet ruby on a thin gold necklace. As she walked to the raised dais where she would be seated a quick glance told Enid that, despite the short notice, Jenara had done a first rate job in securing the Hall.

With grim satisfaction, Enid noticed Jenara wore the gaudiest uniform. A string of medals covered the Colonel's left breast. The bright red two-piece uniform bore a deep blue stripe down its sides. The bottom half of it was synched at the waist by a belt with a large buckle flashing silver in the bright lights, emphasizing her tiny waist and the flare of her hips. The tight uniform drew the awed stares of most of the men in the Hall. Enid stifled a smile, pleased that Jenara's uniform successfully distinguished them.

People quickly took their positions in the Hall. Jenara strode to the raised dais and sat in the great throne that dominated the Hall. The Commanders of the various ships formed lines along each side of the wide aisle leading from the throne to the great doors that would open for the Repletians. Behind each line of Commanders security guards formed five rows, each row separated from one another by seven feet. The result was a show of force that was deliberately intimidating. Enid took her place ten feet behind where the Colonel sat, mingling with other Commanders, striving to be as invisible as she could manage.

Enid was uncomfortable with this ritual. She had seen delays after guests found the person sitting on the throne was merely a decoy for the ranking officer. The last attempt on an Admiral's life had been over five hundred Standard years ago. But the Navy persisted in the habit and it was one Enid had to respect. It was a habit deeply engrained in the military ethos.

So Enid stood behind the Colonel as they waited for the entry of the Repletian delegation. The Anphorians were nervous. What would the Repletians do or say? Were they as fierce as rumor had it?

When the guard at the door announced the pending entry of the delegation, the officers closed rank around Enid, while allowing her full view of the massive throne on which Jenara sat. The Hall's low hubbub subsided so abruptly Enid's ears rang with the sudden drop in volume.

Jenara straightened her posture. Her bright uniform, a distraction carefully crafted to add to the way she dominated the Hall, was worn proudly and Enid envied the Colonel her poise and imposing size. Certainly anyone unfamiliar with her would automatically assume Jenara was the Admiral.

Enid looked down the rows of soldiers to where the great entrance doors swung open and she waited, humming an old song under her breath no one else heard. The song relaxed her and she smiled, feeling a great calm enter her soul from the direction of the door.

CHAPTER 13

Standard Year 2478

The great entrance doors opened to usher in the delegation. The Repletians wore brown hooded robes, which rustled on the smooth metal floor. In the lead, the huge man's limp was noticeable and Enid found herself wondering where he had developed it. Anphorians rarely suffered ailments or disabilities. Medical practices and procedures cured all but the most severely injured or aged.

The music Enid heard came from three Repletian musicians who trailed their leader by several steps. Enid knew she had heard the song played before but she couldn't place where. Colonel Carstairs sat still and dominant in the hall. When the delegation reached the dais every Anphorian soldier snapped to attention and the sound of their feet stamping the metal floor in unison was like thunder, echoing far overhead among the rafters.

The Repletians gave no signs they noticed this impressive show of military precision. They stood motionless until the echoes faded. Then in unison, they chanted, "When I give to you, I give myself."

Carstairs waited as the lead Repletian advanced towards her, his progress slowed by his limp. Three steps from her he threw back his hood, exposing a face lined with wrinkles. The Colonel gave a small bow and greeted the Repletian Elder: "Welcome to our ship. You're our guests and you'll be so honored during your stay."

The Elder gazed at her for several seconds and then returned her bow. He straightened and said, "When I give to you, I give myself." And waited.

Jenara also waited and when it was clear he would stay mute, she said, "We're happy to discuss matters with you. Do you have anything in mind before we begin?"

The Elder nodded. "We'd like to meet with your Admiral, if she's available. There's much she should know and there's not much time."

The Colonel was unfazed. "Come, let's not play games. You may speak your mind before us all."

"What I have to say is to be said only to the one in command. I'll wait for her."

Jenara felt flustered by his stubborn refusal to speak further. How did he know she wasn't the Admiral? No one in the Great Hall gave a sign she wasn't in command yet here he stood, quiet and patient. Before Carstairs could think of a response Enid stepped from the ranks where she was hidden. She moved forward and Carstairs made way for her. The guards around the dais tensed, not enough to alarm the Repletian delegation but enough to draw their attention.

Enid bowed as formally as the Elder. The Elder repeated his bow and then looked her in the eyes, a bold gaze, frank and curious. Enid let him study her; if he were attracted to her so much the better. He would put himself at a disadvantage that might later prove useful.

Something flickered in the Elder's eyes and then receded.

"I'm Leon Three Starbreaks. When I give to you, I give myself."

"Welcome, Leon Three Starbreaks. We would have more courtesy towards you and your delegation but time means too much. But while you're on board my flagship, you won't be harmed."

"It's a good way. I come on behalf of the Repletian Peoples in good faith; bearing news which I hope is of use."

Enid swept the vast collection of soldiers with her eyes and looked at Leon Three Starbreaks. "Leon Three Starbreaks, the people you represent have much to answer for. There's the matter of our last fleet in this area. It's known your people were involved in the fleet's disappearance. We demand answers."

The Elder standing before Enid closed his eyes for a few moments and chanted something under his breath that was so familiar Enid blinked, trying to remember the tune. The Elder opened his eyes to gaze at Enid with a frankness that again disturbed her.

"You've come a long way, you and your fleet, to find answers my people haven't answers for."

Enid nodded. "This is so. And yet you do know something, of that I'm certain."

"I know enough to ask your fleet to stop here. Great harm awaits you if you continue to seek that which you won't find."

Enid shrugged ever so slightly. "That may be so, and yet your people have many deaths for which you must pay."

"Our people wish to know if you're determined to chase down what you call the Black Ship. To reach it you violate our common borders and we won't control the consequences of this violation."

"Anphorians don't give way to threats," Enid interrupted. "You still haven't accounted for the disappearance of the Fifth Fleet. We hold you responsible for their deaths and for that there's a cost."

"Ah, threats. Would you believe me if I said we have no idea of where or what happened to your previous fleet? I can't control what is already determined."

"More mysticism, Three Starbreaks? Mysticism is a poor substitute for the lives of three hundred million human beings. Surely you feel something for the loss of so many people, despite their origins?"

"I would have you tell me, Admiral, what you believe happened to your predecessor?"

Enid sensed the increasing rage among her officers for what they saw as the Elder's insolence. After sweeping the hall with a cold glance of caution, she stared at Leon, her green eyes narrowing and focusing. She chose her next words carefully.

"Three Starbreaks, you tread in dangerous waters. We have records of some of your ships appearing after you launched whatever that weapon is which wiped out our Fifth Fleet. We won't tolerate such an affront to our people."

Enid paused, noticing the Elder flinch for the first time as a pained look crossed his face. He reached into his robes with one hand and a dozen weapons from the dais pointed at him. He smiled and slowly, cautiously, withdrew a small disc he handed to Enid.

"Your techs can verify that tape. It contains our records of the events when we first emerged near the Fifth Fleet. The story goes thus."

There had been no time to react. For months the Council of Elders was aware of the buildup of forces along the borders of the Fifth Sector. It had watched the Fifth Fleet, impressive in its power, assemble to make a foray into territory held to be Repletian space.

There were those on the Council who wanted a military confrontation, an assembly of all the forces Repletia could muster to turn away this wolf from their borders. Such a showdown would deter further Anphorian expeditions for a long time, so the argument ran. It would also give Repletian warriors a chance to prove themselves in combat.

The older members of the Council answered by saying the warriors might prove themselves but how many warriors would return? If Repletia sent its vessels against the Fifth Fleet and managed to defeat it, there would be no strength left to repel the next fleet.

In addition, the Fifth Fleet was headed into a sector of Repletian space that held no major Repletian Home World. Rather, it headed for Artel's Star system. Three Starbreaks assured the Council that if the Fifth Fleet reached its destination, it lacked the technology to unravel the secrets hidden within the great Black Ship.

An Elder from across the table spoke. "Yes, yes. We've read your analysis of the Black Ship. Tell us why the creatures that made such a ship chose to leave it behind for all else to see? What were they trying to achieve?"

"A warning, perhaps. You know, the Ozymandias Principle? Perhaps the Black Ship inhabits a place where physical and mental forces are unified. Operating within the limits shown by the Black Ship may render the physical plane meaningless."

A murmur ran through the room. Everyone on the Council had experienced their own visions by going through the Dianic Ceremonies or, in Three Starbreaks' case, through survival on Korel's World. But the Elder across the table was persistent.

"We must act. If we don't, we risk everything, including the loss of our Home Worlds. If they get into the Black Ship, if they discover the technology involved in its make, the sciences used to build that thing will be used to destroy us."

Three Starbreaks waited for the outbreak to die down before he replied to the other Elder's concerns.

"I have no words to say that can still the fears of those who can't hear. But this I say. There are forces in motion, which will demand our attention sooner than later. Our peoples are scattered over a million cubic parsecs; they don't know where to turn for guidance. We as Elders must do something to help our people. Anything less and we won't deserve to be called Elders."

Three Starbreaks was about to continue when a warrior strode into the room. He whispered something into an aide's ear and left after handing the aide a small reed. The Elders watched as the aide placed the reed into its holograph slot. The image that emerged showed the destruction of a small Repletian fighter. Some Elders in the room murmured in protest and anger until the rippling black object came onto the screen. It flowed first one way, then the other, its course both impossible and without evident logic. Behind it came the battle cruisers of the Anphorian Fifth Fleet, cruisers that stretched out of sight in a solid ribbon of light.

As the Elders watched, a horde of smaller fighters emerged from between the cruisers, each of them intent on being the first to reach the Black Ship. Brief flares of incandescence marked the spots where the lead fighters fired at the Black Ship.

Three Starbreaks shouted, "We must get there before it's too late!"

The group of ships that surrounded the Elders' ship turned in orbit 180 degrees, wavered, then winked out of vision as they raced for the edge of the Anphorian fleet. Within moments, their ships emerged beyond the edge of where the Fifth Fleet floated.

The Black Ship quickly inundated a single Anphorian hull. The Black Ship paused before it passed on, leaving a broken and shattered ship gaping into open space. The Black Ship vanished.

Three Starbreaks wasn't in the room, but on the bridge. It took him a few minutes before he could locate the Black Ship. It was no longer black now, but rapidly emitted electromagnetic energies ranging from radio wave to cosmic frequencies inundating the Anphorian fleet.

"What's happening?" Three Starbreaks asked a technical support staff member, who yelled back, "We don't know."

It was then Three Starbreaks realized that no one on the bridge could hear anything else. The great wave of music pounded into Leon's mind, taking him back to his youth the black rocks he had scaled for his life into the memories of great red flames engulfing a world and folding him into their embrace.

The place where the Black Ship floated among the battle cruisers of the Fifth Fleet sparkled with colors that paced the music they all heard. Stronger and stronger the light grew until it penetrated their massive hulls. Ships became fainter as the light and sound from the center of the maelstrom of chaos increased into a great whirlpool.

And then complete darkness and silence so complete their ears rang and their eyes struggled to focus. Then came the first incredulous murmurs from all parts of the small group of Repletian ships. "They're gone! They're all gone!"

*

"So you see, Admiral, we were unable to help the Fifth Fleet. But we didn't make that Black Ship."

"So you say, Elder. We say you're hiding something. Perhaps you made a break through and tested it out on the Fifth Fleet. Your arrival at the time of the fleet's destruction coincided with that Black Ship's unleashing of whatever weapons it had. Surely in the scheme of things you have much to answer for."

The Elder held Enid in his gaze. "One can't force a truth onto those who won't listen. We didn't call it into existence but there it is. It's not entirely of this universe; nothing of science can render it inoperable."

Enid stared back at the Elder. "Are you saying the Black Ship's indestructible?"

Three Starbreaks nodded and his next words confused Enid. "Is it true you're Repletian?"

Enid felt the tension among her soldiers increase, felt every eye on her as she thought about his question. The Elder had to know the truth. Perhaps, as Lexington had said, she had something that would make the Repletians pause before carrying out any assault on her fleet.

"Yes, I'm Repletian by birth. That doesn't affect my role as Admiral. My allegiances are to my fleet and to the Anphorian Confederacy."

And again the Elder gave her a piercing look. She waited, her green eyes staring at this older man, wondering what his real mission was. He stood three steps from her, waiting as she waited. The silence was finally broken by Three Starbreaks.

"This is not the time or place for the truth. But one day it will be there. I ask your leave to depart."

"Elder, we're committed to taking the Black Ship, whatever it takes."

"So you say," he said, echoing her earlier words. Who was he? "I'm here merely to warn you there are things we can't control. You have the right to choose your own path. What you find may not be to your liking. When I give to you, I give myself."

As the Elder turned to leave Enid spoke: "I warn you any resistance from the Black Ship will be considered an act of war and must be dealt with accordingly. And lest you think this a warning, I give you this gift to show you there are other ways for us."

Enid solemnly extended a hand bearing her small red jewel and gold chain. The Elder took it into his hands and stared at the bright red center of the jewel. It felt small in his large hands and he held it to the light, marveling at its cold radiance. He deeply bowed to Enid and as he walked out she wondered if it was her imagination or if he walked slower than when he entered. She couldn't tell; his figure was shrouded by his gown and his hood again covered his head.

Later, in the privacy of their Conference room, her Commanders went over the meeting. No one saw anything in what the Elder said that would prevent their continuing forward. The ships bearing the Repletians left and quickly vanished.

The scientists had come no closer to what the Black Ship was, although they had spent countless hours studying it. The one thing everyone agreed upon was to go ahead.

Given the Black Ship's Fifth Fleet encounter, Enid's fleet formed a cone-shaped wedge. At the front of this formation Enid placed *Stars End*. If the Black Ship attacked, her ship would bear the brunt of its first attack. She placed Carstairs in charge of the battle cruiser *Okada* - next to the flagship it was the most fearsome ship in the fleet. The *Okada* dropped to the rear to form the center of the crescent that connected the sides of the wedge of cruisers.

If *Stars End* went down, she would leave a gap large enough for the ships in that crescent to fire their weapons at the Black Ship.
Between each battle cruiser were the innumerable smaller fighting ships, each manned by several dozens of thousands of combat-ready men and women.

As Enid escorted Jenara Carstairs to the departure bays from which Jenara would leave for the *Okada*, her mind was in turmoil. The great sense of expectation among the crew of *Stars End* was an almost visible presence; the air of expectation grew with each passing hour. Enid fought to keep these feelings from overwhelming her.

"Admiral, everything will be all right."

Enid smiled at Jenara's attempts at reassurance. Jenara hesitated at the entrance to the pod that would take her from the flagship. Enid saluted and gave her second-in-command a hug.

"I know it'll be all right. You take care of yourself and I'll see you back on the bridge when this is over."

Carstairs shook her head. "No, that isn't what I meant, Admiral. I mean you should see Daegan before you do anything else."

"Daegan?" Enid hadn't thought of Daegan for several hours and Jenara's suggestion startled her.

"Yes, Daegan. And don't worry about morale. You had to do what you did but your visit will perk up your crew. Daegan's respected among the rank and file. It's what I would do. When this is over, we can share a Condrian drink, okay?"

"Okay. And thanks for your suggestion. I'll think about it." As Enid watched the pod door close, her mind was already made up. She told the bridge of her whereabouts and then made her way through the halls of her ship towards Daegan's quarters.

He was sitting up as she approached his cell door. They had stripped a wall down and converted it into these solid bars in the old style of prison cells. Most of Daegan's belongings were removed, leaving the small cot and a few personal effects that lined the sink.

He had lost weight and his looks were sharper, his eyes brighter than she remembered him having. His grey prison clothes were well ironed; whatever Daegan felt about his plight, he kept himself sharp. Her hands formed into fists she kept closely to her sides.

"Admiral?" his voice was ragged from fatigue.

And Enid found her reserves crumbling. "Oh, Daegan. What have I done to you?" She leaned against the bars, clutching them with her two slender hands.

"Admiral, it isn't your fault. Don't blame yourself. We all swore on oath to protect our superior officers and I failed in my duties. You had no choice."

"Daegan, I know that and yet it doesn't help. I hate this military code. I feel lost. There are things happening and I feel lost."

Daegan forced a smile. "Admiral, there are things you and I can't control. But you have to do your best. So many lives depend upon it."

His words brought back memories. "There was a man who said that to me," she blurted out. "A Repletian Elder. What is it I'm missing? Nothing makes sense any more…" Enid brushed a tear from her face and looked at Daegan, who moved towards her as she heard the guards hiss. She barked a command for them to withdraw. She had almost forgotten them but they were always there, hovering in the background of her ever-growing misery.

"Admiral, you're the wrong person for this mission. Someone has set you up."

"Set me up?" Enid was shocked. "Set me up? But who? Why? I don't understand."

"Admiral, I've given this much thought. You're good, very good. But you weren't due for promotion for another ten years. Someone has put you into your rank as a distraction. There are things happening around you which don't add up unless they've been planned."

Enid's mind swam. "But the only ones who could be, would be . . . but that's nonsense! I mean, what would they get out of it? Would he dare? Would she dare?"

Daegan stopped several feet from her and said in a low voice, “Tell me, have you decided the Black Ship we saw attacking the Fifth Fleet has nothing to do with the Repletians?”

Enid nodded. “Yes, our techs say there’s a ninety-five percent chance the Repletian Elder spoke the truth. We had our sensors on him during our meeting. We played back the tape he gave us and its authenticity is unquestionable. It was made when he said it was made.”

“Watch your back, Admiral. I’m not the only one in danger. Someone’s playing for large stakes.”

Enid breathed, “Do you mean the President is behind this?”

Daegan nodded once, almost imperceptibly, before he turned his back on her and made his way back to his cot. And his shoulders sagged; the pain struck her mute and she watched him with a horrified fascination. With the greatest effort of her life she pushed herself away from the bars and let them go. She couldn’t bear to watch him collapse and she fled the area, her strides swift and long.

Her mind was a fog as she wandered the halls in an effort to beat the anger and rage from herself. Her travels eventually took her to the bridge, which she entered after absent-mindedly smoothing her uniform.

She was in her command seat barely five minutes when a technician yelled, “There’s the Black Ship ahead of us!”

CHAPTER 14

Standard Year 2478

At her console Katina relished the soft glow from the dark touch screen. Normally the controls were hidden, but they always came to life when Katina approached, keyed as they were to her DNA signature. From this desk Katina could reach anyone in the galaxy. She had a habit of staring at the flat console for a few seconds before her long agile fingers rapidly played over its smooth surface, activating a number of commands and procedures.

Today she made a point of inputting data for ten minutes before she sat back in her chair and looked across her desk at the uniformed man. "I beg your pardon?" she asked.

The middle-aged officer stared at her. Today Katina wore fierce red lipstick, a long blue dress, and her hair, always dark, twisted in the subdued light. The officer repeated his question. "I asked, does Admiral Blue Starbreaks know of this?"

Katina snorted in disgust. "She thinks she's on an exploratory mission. The Repletians are incidental to that mission; she has the authority to use any means necessary to reach the Black Ship."

"Is the Black Ship so important to you?"

"I wouldn't care if it held the secrets to immortality. I need to divert the Navy's attentions long enough for us to carry out our own plans. After that, let the chips fall where they may. I'll be gone before anyone finds the truth."

"Yes, I don't doubt that. You don't leave anything to chance, do you?"

"Taking chances is for the young or the foolish. The galaxy is better without either."

"And so I'm to take this letter to a certain place tomorrow and leave it there for someone to retrieve?" The officer held up a small sealed letter as he spoke.

Katina nodded. "Yes. You won't know the contact person. Even if you're caught and confess, as I'm sure you will, given enough time, your confession will be useless because you don't know anything I haven't already told you."

The officer got up to leave. Katina said, "Leave the letter under the ashtray on Table Four at the Donato Nebula Restaurant at precisely nineteen hundred hours. After you've had a cup and a half of your favorite drink, leave and don't look back. No matter what you hear tomorrow about me, I want you to follow my orders. Am I clear?"

"Perfectly. Good afternoon, Madame President."

" Thank you for everything. When you retire you'll receive a handsome surprise to help you out. Should you die before then, your estate will be the beneficiary."

"I would have done this for free."

"Yes, I know you would have. But you haven't that option. And, of course, you don't even know what you're conspiring to do... Thank you for everything."

Katina had the table cleared. She walked the man through her kitchen and down some steps to her basement. He towered over her small frame, but she was clearly in control. And with a whispered command, a wall moved aside, revealing a long tunnel curving out of sight.

"Follow this tunnel to its end. It's about a fifteen minute walk. You have seventeen minutes to reach the other side. Once you shut the door at the other end or the seventeen minutes expire, whichever comes first, the tunnel will collapse."

Katina watched him until his lean military figure passed out of sight. She then closed the door. The great bolts slid into place and then fused, sealing the door to the building forever. She climbed the stairs to her third floor bedroom, where her slave had brought a pot of local tea and a small cup complete with saucer and spoon. She gave the tray a quick glance, threw back the covers of her bed, and slid beneath the covers, relaxing into a book. Once she looked up as she felt a small shudder. She thought, "There goes the tunnel" and she smiled. Everything was going as planned. She began reading her book again, putting these thoughts to rest.

Sometimes she stopped reading to take a sip of tea. This ritual lasted for an hour until the pot was empty. Finally, Katina closed her book and turned off her lights.

She didn't climb under her blankets to sleep, though. Instead, she crept out of bed and peered out of her darkened balcony window towards the kitchen area. The slave was still working late, as he had done for as long as she could remember.

Katina took grim satisfaction in knowing her slave would be the first of many Repletians to die. The same timer that had sealed the tunnel continued to count down to final self-destruction. Katina would leave nothing behind her; at 0300 hours a small quarter kiloton explosion would destroy her huge house and most of the nearby woods. It would take them days or weeks to gather any useful evidence. In the meantime, the letter the man carried with him would set in motion a chain of untraceable financial transactions that would allow her to comfortably take her time deciding her next moves.

Without turning from the window, Katina spoke. "Will you tell me why you're here?"

"So you think I'm real?"

"I could be dreaming, but the night is so perfect, so dark and cold."

"Not like the light, the heat."

"No, not like the light or the heat. Different, and yet I think they're the same to me. When I'm in complete darkness, I feel and see something brighter than a nova."

A breeze lifted and stirred the curtains. Near the horizon a streak of light marked a meteor's passage.

"It's time to go," Katina whispered, knowing that Annie had already gone.

She quickly got into her black-hooded outfit. Wearing it made her invisible except for her face, which she covered with a black shawl. She set the computer to turn on her bedroom lights at oh two thirty hours and arranged the holograph of herself to cross in front of the open window every five minutes. The holograph would convince anyone at a distance she was pacing back and forth in her bedroom. Katrina left nothing to chance; she knew what the military was capable of once alerted.

She took the survival pack from her closet and crept from her bedroom. She moved swiftly to the exit door farthest from where her slave still worked in the kitchen. He wouldn't know she was gone until it was far too late to do anything. If he followed his usual ritual, he would finish his work and be in bed by midnight. At 0300 hours the mechanism would create a molten slagheap of anything within five hundred feet. Everyone would assume the house blew up with her in it.

Eight hundred yards downhill from her house, on a path seldom used, Katina found the lifter covered with underbrush. She stripped this cover from the frame and climbed into the lifter. The black cockpit cover slid into place over her head. With barely a whisper, the lifter rose and then streaked into the night, leaving nothing but a faint heat trail that dissipated into the east winds.

In another part of the great house, a lone light shone from the kitchen area. The slave finished placing the last of the dishes gathered over the day into the cleaning machine. He closed the door and turned the machine on; a soft hum filled the room as the machine washed the dishes. The slave looked out of the window towards the part of the building where the President's bedroom could be seen. The lights were out, the President having turned them off as she settled in for the night. The slave hung up the cleaning towel he used and dried his hands. He then moved to the far side of the kitchen, out of sight of where the

President slept, and donned a light jacket. He turned out the lights and moved swiftly and surely through the darkness to the study where the President and her guest had met earlier. He removed the holograph recording from its invisible niche against one wall and tucked the small disk into his jacket pocket. Within moments he stood outside the great front doors, where he paused for a few seconds to get his orientation. Then, without a glance backwards, he faded into the darkness, leaving the building wrapped in its own seclusion. A small wind swept over the building, creaking and groaning as it settled under the new pressure.

*

Mykal Bridgeman felt tired towards the end of a twelve-hour shift. He looked forward to a meal and then a welcome bout of sleep. While Tryon's Cove was a small community there were times like today when activity jumped the scale and he had to be everywhere at once. The most serious had been a drunk who had kicked up a fuss at the local pub when management refused to serve him more liquor. Since this was the most exciting thing to happen in Tryon's Cove that week, two police lifters had shown up on the scene. The result was something of a comical overkill, three large police officers against a farmer who came no higher than their shoulders.

Mykal had served the Cove for a dozen years, four cycles which saw him rise from Sergeant to Captain. Other police officers could hardly wait to finish the minimum three-year cycle and then move on with their families to larger communities. Mykal wished them the best but he enjoyed living in Tryon's Cove. He loved the outdoors and the extra freedom in a community where the most exciting thing to happen in over five cycles had been the addition of the Cove's first Repletian police officer, Daniel Slow Dreams, a year ago.

Mykal had been ready for storms of protest but after the initial excitement the Cove returned to its own quiet lifestyle. Most of the citizens grew used to seeing the tall and slender whiplash of a figure stride along the streets. The only time Slow Dreams had been challenged he wisely waited for backup; Mykal had made the arrest before a small crowd of citizens while the Repletian, whose presence had kept the man at bay, discretely left.

Once Mykal and Slow Dreams were at the local store when Katina Patriloney, the Cove's most distinguished and reclusive citizen, walked in. Everyone knew of her hatred of Repletians but Mykal was surprised when she ignored Slow Dreams' presence and went about her business without acknowledging the police officers.

"Captain?" The Desk Sergeant interrupted Mykal's thoughts.

"Yes?"

"Captain, you should come to the front desk."

Mykal felt annoyed. "Is this another of your games, Sergeant?"

"I swear, Captain, it ain't. You should come out here."

Damn it! Mykal thought. Only fifteen more minutes and it would have been his relief's problem. Probably Lionel Chester again; the local drunk had a habit of showing up at the station to turn himself in for any crimes in the Cove. Mykal glanced at the clock. Fifteen minutes to eleven. He jotted this down in his logbook and headed for the front desk.

A tall Repletian stood there and at first Mykal mistook him for Slow Dreams, who wasn't due for two more shifts. But the Repletian wore no uniform nor did he have the scar that ran half the length of Slow Dream's face. As Mykal entered the front desk area, both the Desk Sergeant and the Repletian turned to watch him.

"Sergeant, who's this Repletian?"

"Captain, he says he's from the President's house."

Mykal squinted at the tall figure and then put on his glasses. "Who are you? Speak up."

The Repletian hesitated, then reached into his black jacket. The Sergeant tensed and Mykal yelled at the Repletian, "Slowly. Do it slowly." The Repletian, seeing the weapon in the Sergeant's hands, nodded and slowly withdrew a glittering silver object that flashed in the low light. Without pausing, he extended the disk towards Mykal. Only then did he speak.

"You must take this. It's important. Very important."

Mykal reached out to take the light object, recognizing it as a holograph disk. The Repletian let the disk drop into Mykal's hand and stood back to wait. Mykal made a quick decision. "Call Slow Dreams down to the station now, Sergeant. I won't accept excuses. Then bring the holograph recorder into my office."

Mykal sensed something huge was happening. While he waited for Slow Dreams to arrive, he tried to contact the President's house but got no answer. Odd, damned odd, Mykal thought. Normally the President's house was surrounded by security. How had this Repletian servant made it down that hill in the dark? How had he known where to find the station? To Mykal's knowledge, neither Katina nor any of her aides or servants ever visited; they had their own security forces. He made a call to the closest Naval Base and briefly explained his situation to a sleepy-eyed Corporal whose eyes quickly became alert. The Corporal, at the end of the conversation, promised to get back to Mykal after the Navy made its own quick follow up.

The Sergeant brought the small holograph recorder into the room and set it on the Captain's desk. "Is that all, sir?"

Mykal was about to let the Sergeant return to his desk and thought better of it. He shook his head. "Sergeant, if you aren't busy out there, I'd like you to stay here. I have a feeling I'm going to need all the help I can get. Who's on duty?"

"Well, Captain, four officers are due to come on shift in the next five minutes. Shall I get them?"

Mykal nodded and as the Sergeant hurried out of the office Slow Dreams walked in, dressed in a nondescript light blue outfit that made his tall figure taller. He glanced at the other Repletian and, without saying a word, took a seat in one corner of Mykal's office. As he seated himself, the Naval Corporal came back on holograph.

"Attempts to contact the President's house have failed. Under the Captain's authorization, traces have shown her residence is unguarded; shift schedules were changed under the President's direct orders, leaving the premises unguarded for five Standard hours. Reasons unknown. All enquiries have failed. The President has secured her personal channels. Reasons unknown."

The four officers who walked into Mykal's office heard the Corporal and turned puzzled looks towards the Captain and the unknown Repletian.

"Have a seat. It seems our guest here," Mykal gestured towards the Repletian, "is only the tip of the puzzle. Maybe what he has brought us will clarify matters." Mykal inserted the tape.

*

Admiral Lexington finished his mind exercises, a series of puzzles that sharpened his knowledge of Thetan diplomacy. Lexington admired the convoluted processes the Thetans had built over the past two thousand years. Challenging them on their own turf proved exciting. Lexington beat the holograph game three of the four times, each game lasting longer as the computer adjusted to Lexington's game and stepped up a challenge level.

"Admiral?"

"Yes, what is it?"

"We've received a puzzling message from Tryon's Cove."

Lexington thought for a moment. "Isn't that where Madame President lives?"

"It is."

"What does she want at this late hour?"

"Admiral, it's not from her. It's from their local Police Captain. A Mykal Bridgeman."

"Isn't it normal for you to deal with local officials?"

"Aye, sir. But the Captain insists on speaking to you directly."

Lexington frowned. "Does the Captain seem on the level?"

His aide hesitated as he groped for a clear response. "The Captain's excited but rational."

"Okay, put him through. And record him. Oh, yes. Try to get the President out of bed. This probably involves her."

Lexington leaned back in his chair as the holograph sprang into focus to show a middle-aged man with greying hair. The Captain had a smooth face but Lexington wasn't fooled by this; with genetic surgery anything could be covered, even worry lines. Lexington glanced at the clock. Just past 0100 hours; the Captain must have had a difficult time reaching through channels to get him. Lexington hoped he wouldn't prove to be a waste of time.

"Good morning, Admiral."

"What can I do for you, Captain?"

"Do you have a secured channel?"

Lexington sighed; everyone these days enjoyed the subterfuge of coded messages. "Yes, Captain, we have a secured line."

"Admiral, one of the President's servants walked into our station two hours ago and handed us this recording."

Lexington's holograph cleared and then he was in a small study of some sort; Lexington knew the President but the other figure was a stranger. Lexington listened to the conversation with growing astonishment and then anger. The tape's timer showed it had been filmed three months ago. As it ended another recording began playing, dating from the same period. A different figure was involved. And so the quick conversations, one after the other, each lasting two to three minutes, each with different individuals and the President, reinforced the first conversation and sent chills through Lexington. The President was planning genocide against the Repletians.

Despite the ongoing border wars with Repletia, genocidal warfare was forbidden. While Anphoria could hold its own against any two of the other major human groups, winning against the other nine combined groups was impossible. Through a signed Covenant of Agreement the ten groups of humanity had agreed several thousand years ago, after the so-called Genetic Wars, that genocide was the one crime forbidden of any group.

And yet here was the President herself, not only thinking of, but apparently about to commit such a horrific act against Repletia. And she was clever, oh, so clever. Lexington saw no one who met with the President knew of the others or of Katina's plans, which became self-evident after hearing the various snippets of conversation. As the last meeting, recorded hours ago, faded from view, Lexington sat back in stunned disbelief. Who would think of exterminating so many people?

"Admiral?" The Captain's voice shook Lexington from his thoughts. "Admiral, should we send some men up to the President's house to get her?"

"No, let me summon my troops. This is bigger than your police force can handle. Secure the property but don't go into the house. If she tries to leave, stop her with any force you deem necessary short of assassinating her. Do you understand, Captain?"

"Yes, Admiral."

"Good. My men will be there in thirty minutes."

The wind howled through the foliage surrounding Katina Patriloney's house. The five-hundred-year-old trees had been transplanted over eighty years ago by her parents. Looming far into the night sky, their sheer magnitude dwarfed the house, rendering it invisible from all but the closest inspection. During the hottest summers, their shade kept the house cool. And approach from the sky was impossible within five hundred yards, providing a natural barrier.

Through this barrier several hundred men and women moved quickly and quietly. They wore infrared contact lenses that allowed them to see each other. The soldiers were drilled on the plans and they didn't want to alert anyone near the house. Haunting winds far overhead colored the night as the trees swayed, rustling protectively.

The police officers stayed on the edge of this mini-forest, having arrived twenty minutes earlier to secure the premises. They watched with some chagrin as the soldiers disappeared into the estate; they felt they could have handled the raid much earlier and faster. But the Lieutenant Colonel who commanded the naval forces made it clear he was in charge. Upon the arrival of the first troop lifters he relieved the police officers of their guard duties and asked them to back up another four hundred yards downhill.

As the commander of the ground forces approached the house, through hand signals he had his forces lay down a pattern, a web through which no person could penetrate. Everything went as planned; as the clock ticked towards 0300 hours the commander was sure they would soon have the President safely in hand. He looked at his watch as the last man settled into position for the quick rush to the house. Another seven hundred men and women arrived to strengthen the forces already there. His forces moved to within a hundred yards of the mansion. Thirty seconds to go. He glanced at the property and noted a light on in what seemed to be the President's bedroom. He saw the shadow cross the light and whispered into his communicator that the President was awake. On his signal the thousand troops began their march through the trees and thick grassy terrain.

Just as Mykal Bridgeman turned to his police officers to let them know they would stay another half hour and then leave it to the military to continue their work alone, a brilliant flash of light from behind blinded him. He staggered and then felt himself lifted from his feet by a searing wall of heat and thrown. He landed thirty feet beyond the lifter and his last memory was of a sound that blew his eardrums and then everything else into silence.

*

"Admiral?" the urgent voice broke in as Lexington was in the middle of talking to his final Council Member, seeking her support. Most of the Council Members had first watched the tape with incredulity and then growing anger as they realized the depth of the President's betrayal.

"Admiral, there's been an explosion at the President's house."

"An explosion?"

"It appears," his aide said, "that Katina detonated a small atomic device that wiped out herself and most of the surrounding area. That includes the soldiers we sent to the scene. We're sending another force but the radiation count and the satellite pictures leave no doubt she decided to end things. We can't get within half-a-mile of the place without putting our men at great risk."

When Lexington returned to his conversation with the last Council Member, she looked at him anxiously.

"Admiral, bad news?"

"It's worse than I thought. The President has apparently killed herself along with several hundred soldiers and a number of local police officers. We must assume the worst."

The last Council Member gave an order to her holograph and the nine other remaining members of the Council appeared. Between them, they quickly chose an interim President, pending the formal selection process that involved hand-to-hand combat to the death. Selection of a President through a formal ritual ensured that succession to the Presidency happened within a structured process, rather than an endless free-for-all. A President never came from outside the ranks of the armed forces.

Katina was the single exception. Her emergence had shaken the Confederacy. Even though she was the daughter of the former President, Katina was small, ridiculously so when put against the seasoned combat veterans who challenged for the position. She had no military training people knew of, yet in fight after fight she killed each of her opponents, never in the same way but always so quickly often the fight was over before most people had settled in to watch.

Katina never chose the bulkier heavier weaponry of her opponents. In the ring, naked except for weapons that could be hand-held, Katina chose weapons that looked like toys compared to those of her opponents. In the first few fights, sometimes objected to by other challengers who hesitated to fight against such a small person, Katina in motion seemed slow. Yet when people turned to her challengers, and saw how quickly they moved, they were baffled by the disparity in speed. Somehow, no matter how quickly her opponents moved, they could never move fast enough. The few times they managed to strike flesh, draw blood, it was like striking a granite boulder. Katina wouldn't speak, wouldn't acknowledge the fearsome power of the blows that landed on her body. Power that should have crushed her. Rage that should have dispatched her. The red slashes of blood from her own body streaked flesh so pale the sight of blood against it was mesmerizing.

Katina flowed, moving through the flurry of blades, fists, hammers and shields, her dark hair flashing eerily in the light, her skin so pale it was whiter than marble, the odd lipstick framing her small face, the body with its small breasts, its muscles and tendons not nearly enough to survive. And always, abruptly, Katina killed her challengers with a speed and savagery that awed the spectators, showers of blood bathing the arena from falling warriors dying before they even felt the blows from Katina's knives, swords and spears. To the endless taunts thrown at her, to the increasingly desperate and angered moves of seasoned warriors, Katina's only answer was a violence that shook the most experienced of them.

Where had Katina learned to kill so savagely, learned to fight so oddly, learned to cut so deeply through skin, muscle, tendon and bone?

What sealed Katina's legend was in the final fight against an Admiral who had seen a dozen battles, had fought fifty hand-to-hand battles. The Admiral had studied Katina's moves. He wasn't a fool, so he watched her shifts, her changes in balance, in speed, in direction. He focused on how she handled knives with her right hand, how she used her left hands to wield spears and swords. He would not underestimate her. In that first battle which Katina won and which the Admiral watched, the Admiral instinctively knew she would be the obstacle to his goals. During the following week-long process of elimination, between his own fights, the Admiral spent every waking moment practicing his moves, every motion geared to combat those of the woman who moved through her challengers so memorably her image became emblazoned on millions and then billions of observers throughout the Anphorian Confederacy.

Which was how Katina's fearsome reputation became permanent.

The Admiral stripped as required, his six foot eight inch frame a lean pillar of muscle and speed. Across the arena Katina also stripped. A single red streak of dried blood ran the length of one arm, while another ran four inches along Katina's flat stomach, the result of the only two blades that managed to slice flesh in the seven fights to date. She wore bright green lipstick, a garish color. From where he stood the Admiral knew the woman he faced was the fiercest and deadliest warrior he had ever met. No mercy would be shown. The prize was the Presidency of the entire Confederacy. The Admiral had worked long and hard for this, and he would use his height and weight and speed to win.

At the signal he moved cautiously towards Katina, the five-foot long slim sword in his hand tempered sharper than a samurai sword. He wielded the fifteen pound weapon easily and lightly. Striking the woman with the speed and power of his arm would surely overwhelm her. Her body mass and weight were a third of his. A single slash would cut her in two. The Admiral knew she relied on slaying her opponents quickly, so he would be quicker. By the third or fourth sword stroke he would be in a position for the death cut, the slash or stab or thrust that would kill her.

As the Admiral chose only his sword as his weapon, so too did Katina choose a sword, one two feet short, surely no match for the longer blade. The Admiral sliced towards Katina's torso and then stepped left to strike his second blow and then left again, keeping counter to the moves he had studied and memorized. Each time he sliced, his blade met Katina's with a hard steel-on-steel sound that rang through the arena like a bell. As prepared as he was, the Admiral was surprised Katina could counter his moves. She was far too small to match the power of his sword and yet somehow, each time he sliced, her shorter sword was there. The Admiral then switched sword hand and stepped right, usually a move that took his opponents by surprise, the next moment feeling the blade cut their life away.

The Admiral knew if he could last the next thirty or so seconds he would be able to wear the woman out, so his next sword strokes were powerful, designed to sap the strength of any fighter. The blur of blade on blade silenced the huge audience, both in the arena and throughout the countless homes and offices where the fight was broadcast live. Parry, thrust, stab, slice, stroke, step. The Admiral felt his blood flow, his sword sing, and he kept up his furious pace. It was an awful display of swordsmanship, one no soldier in the Confederacy could match. And at the end of a minute he was still attacking, still testing, still trying to find the opening for his life ending thrust. He sometimes stepped into the strokes as Katina backed away. Her sword should have been broken by now by his heavier blade, but each time he attacked his blade encountered hers. He was sweating now, as was she, yet although he swore and grunted and called out at each stroke, Katina silently countered, her small pale body glistening with sweat, which in any other circumstance, would have been arousing.

Three minutes into the fight the Admiral turned and twisted his blade forward and sideways. A red streak appeared on Katina's left breast, above the nipple. The Admiral howled in triumph and pressed forward with all his power and speed. It took him several seconds and perhaps fifteen sword strokes to realize the sound of blade on blade had gone. Each time he parried and struck, his blade met empty air where either she or her sword should have been. The Admiral felt his skin stinging. Katina smiled, and in that smile the Admiral knew she had let him cut her, a proof rather than a denial of her skills. Then Katina was moving forward. In the next two minutes somehow she closed the distance between them even as he fought back, his sword still singing, but now gripped by hands slick with sweat. Everything about this was wrong. Katina killed her opponents in the first minute, which everyone took for her need to finish stronger warriors and avoid a prolonged fight she could not last.

Yet here she was, this ridiculously small woman, matching the Admiral's brute strength, slice by slice, stroke by stroke, when she should have long ago collapsed into exhaustion and death. As fast as the Admiral had pressed his attack a few moments before, Katina began to speed up her own sword strokes. The Admiral felt a thrill of fear as he felt the power of those strokes, power he could barely match. A dozen times the Admiral knew of, she could have broken through his defenses, and a dozen times she withheld, Each time he felt his skin sting more and then, crazily, Katina stepped back three paces. The Admiral staggered, puzzled and shocked, before he noticed her blade was bloody.

The Admiral ran his left hand along his stomach to wipe the sweat away, and looking down saw his hand streaked with blood. Stupefied, he saw his stomach and chest streaked with long shallow cuts. Dozens of cuts. A crisscross of bloody trails. In his efforts to break

Katina the Admiral never felt those cuts but now, as he looked down, he felt the stinging turning into real pain. Looking up he gazed into the pale sweating face of the woman standing with her sword raised vertically. And then he felt a horrible wrenching pain burst from his stomach and abdomen. She hadn't moved that he could see, but suddenly she had gutted him vertically from his sternum to mid abdomen, his life force pouring from the wicked eighteen-inch cut that severed his insides. He heard the singing blade of her sword for an eternity after she had sliced him open. In truth, the sound of her blade came at the same time as it cut through the intervening space at an inhuman speed and power. And even as the Admiral fell to his knees, Katina's sword flashed twice faster than the eye or camera could follow, once slicing his throat, once cutting horizontally across his stomach, forming a cross with her first cut. In less than a tenth of a second Katina had killed the Admiral, so quickly he was still conscious as he fell backwards, blood everywhere. He was dead, but he didn't know it yet. The brutality shocked everyone into stillness, and then a collective gasp as Katina stepped into the arterial flow of blood spurting from the Admiral's death cuts, her small body quickly turning red as she leaned forward over the body in its death spasms. A baptism of blood but, although this was traditional, it had never been done so ruthlessly outside of a Roman coliseum.

*

The new President turned to Lexington. Both felt the momentous occasion. The thought of Katina challenging either of them at some future date to reclaim her Presidency was the stuff of nightmares. Neither wanted the Presidency that badly.

"Admiral, you have a fleet already in Sector Five. Can you contact Admiral Blue Starbreaks and see what her forces can do? We must somehow warn the Repletians or we'll pay dearly."

And with that, Lexington gave the Council the news. "We lost contact with the Fourth Fleet four hours ago. Their Admiral met with one of Repletia's Elders and warned them the fleet would proceed to the Black Ship. After the meeting, the fleet went into communication's blackout as per the First Directive. They should be reaching the Black Ship at any time now."

CHAPTER 15

Standard Year 2478

The great string of ships lined the heavens in a single ribbon of light reaching as far as Enid's eyes could track. From this view it was larger than the Centre of All Worlds. Leading this armada was her flagship, *Stars End.*

And in front of *Stars End,* some twenty light seconds away, a black object reflecting the lights from the fleet, for one second, and the next absorbing it, created a spinning pyrotechnic display. It never altered its position, although its size changed with the same speed as its reflections, creating a sense of vertigo that wrenched fearfully at Enid's stomach.

Enid tore herself from the view screen and pulled the fleet into battle formation. The weapons on every ship had enough firepower to break the entire system apart but no one knew what the Black Ship was capable of. A study of its bizarre motions showed no patterns that made sense.

Enid waited until Jenara had arrived at the rear of the battle formation to take command of the *Okada.* The technicians confirmed Enid's thoughts; everything they sent out to record the Black Ship was sucked into oblivion hundreds of miles from its surface. It hovered in one place, shifting its shape in a process evident only because it blocked out the stars behind its hull. Perhaps it had no hull, Enid thought. Perhaps it was a force beyond Anphoria's current capacities.

Enid briefly regretted their self-imposed silence but she had no choice. As she geared up for this encounter with the Black Ship, she knew she must emerge the winner; loss of a second Anphorian fleet would prove crippling to Anphoria. Enid knew no one would make a better scapegoat than her if she lost this battle.

"Send in a probe. Make sure it's unarmed. Have it stop a light second from the Black Ship."

Enid waited as her command was carried out. The probe took thirty seconds to reach its destination, from where it sent back breathtaking visuals of the Black Ship's shifting shape. The hubbub of communications quickly died as ships turned their attentions to the holograph images of the Black Ship.

"Have the probe send a greeting in the ten languages of Humanity. Repeat the message until I tell you to stop."

Enid glanced at the readouts from the probe as it broadcast its welcome. The probe's readings were meaningless in any human frame of reference. One moment the ship was made of diffuse helium gas, the next of impenetrable neutrons. Its mass ranged from nullity to the mass of ten yellow stars. It was no single color; its colors were caused by absorbed or reflected electromagnetic energies at every frequency. The changes alone required energies that should have torn the Black Ship apart, yet its surface sometimes registered absolute zero. All this happened at speeds faster than anything the fleet's sensory devices could measure. It required energy to drive the center of a galaxy, and yet the fleet hovered safely light seconds from its presence. Nothing about the Black Ship made logical sense and yet, there it floated.

After fifteen minutes, during which the Black Ship acknowledged no messages sent, Enid told the fleet *Stars End* would move in closer.

"If we're harmed, you have my orders to open fire on the Black Ship until it's rendered inoperative."

Enid sensed the collective intake of breath as she ordered her ship to move forward. The deck beneath her shuddered as it pulsed with the power of the tachyon drive units. The Black Ship grew in the holograph screen. Enid found herself gripping the arms of her commander's chair and forced her arm muscles to relax. It wouldn't help her crew to see her so tense.

"Admiral, we have Repletian ships thirty light minutes away. They're hovering near our flank."

Enid recalled the last messages from Tyrel's Fifth Fleet. Tyrel had ignored the Repletians once he knew they posed no threat.

"Hail their commander," Enid ordered. "Let's see what they're doing there."

Three Starbreaks' face came into view. Enid pointed at the holograph image of the Black Ship, which now filled her central view screen. "Elder Starbreaks, do you have any advice or information you wish to share with us?"

Three Starbreaks shook his head. "There's nothing I can tell you except to turn around while you can. You can't overcome what you don't understand."

Enid lashed out in frustration. "You've said that already. I need more to go on. You know my orders. I have to seize the Black Ship at any cost. My personal safety's secondary as is that of my crew. Do you understand? Do you know how much we depend upon the First Directive?"

Enid was surprised when Three Starbreaks' face faded from the holograph, leaving the image of the background of his room, a wall, facing Enid. She was about to turn back to her other duties when he came back into view.

"Admiral, are you keeping the standard communication's blackout?"

"Of course, Elder. You know our procedures as well as we do, I dare say."

"Admiral, we're not under such restrictions. One of your leaders is trying to reach you."

"A ruse, Elder. Surely you can do better. I'll contact you when I have the chance."

"You can stop this now, before you get in over your head. Don't and you lose everything, including your fleet."

"If you have anything that can help us, tell me. Otherwise, stay out of my way, Elder."

Enid turned her attention back to the Black Ship. She ordered her ship to stop on the far side of the probe. She turned to Jenara on the *Okada*," Colonel, any suggestions?"

"None, Admiral. You're setting the ground rules as you go. I wish you luck."

"Send a message to that ship," Enid spoke to her Aide. "Tell it we're on a mission. Tell it we only want to talk and share information. We mean no harm but we can't let anything interfere with our mission. We'll move forward in two Standard minutes but we won't fire upon it unless it engages in hostile activities."

"Colonel, did you hear me?"

"Aye, sir. On your orders we'll follow your lead."

Two minutes quickly passed as Enid set about getting her ship in order; punctuated with tension releasing, steady and confident chatter, until she was again at her commander's chair. Her ship retrieved the probe and as soon as it was safely lodged in one of the landing bays, Enid took a deep breath and said to her pilot, "Move us forward at a hundred miles per second. Straight ahead on the coordinates of the Black Ship."

Behind her ship, an immense band of light, moved in unison, a huge wedge, half a star system in length and an eighth as wide.

The Black Ship remained in its location and then a great bell resounded simultaneously throughout the fleet. Each hull served as the surface on which the tone sounded, deafening nearly three hundred million people. Enid covered her ears but it was too late; her hearing was gone as she grabbed her chair for support. And then the stars behind the Black Ship blacked out, Enid felt a heart-stopping shift of motion, and she faced the Repletian Home World star of Leonith V, its stellar radiation patterns instantly recognized by the flagship's computers. Her pilot yelled out, "Our fleet's caught in the same spatial shift. They're in the same relative position to us as they were before the shift."

Enid yelled, "What in Creation's name are we doing here?" even as she realized her hearing had returned and she didn't have to speak with such force.

Her pilot bellowed back, "I don't know, sir."

And then a small object hurtled from the sun's chromosphere. In moments it was three hundred light minutes beyond the orbit of the outermost planet of Leonith V's system, where it exploded with a fury that matched the energy output of Leonith V's red sun.

Enid had barely registered this fact when she felt another gut-wrenching shift and found herself and her fleet on the edge of the Perin Home world system with its double-star. Again a small object emerged from the chromosphere of the largest star to explode harmlessly and magnificently beyond the Home World's system.

The fleet was flung into each of the ten Repletian Home World systems scattered over a million cubic parsecs of space. At the last Home Planet, Nulliel's Star, as the small object exploded at a safe distance, the tone of the bell changed from a deep bass to a thin high-pitch that rang eardrums like a wind chime. Enid felt like an hour had passed but her ship clock registered barely eighty seconds from the time the fleet was first moved to the moment those chimes sounded. The fastest stellar communications couldn't match the speed of their movement from one Repletian Home World to the next.

And now they hovered above Korel's World, a planet on the borders between Anphorian and Repletian space.

Enid refused to accept defeat. As Lexington insisted, nothing was possible, which lay beyond the realms of science. All forces, if examined long enough, were subject to natural laws.

"Report while you can," Enid ordered her fleet. The reports spilled into the computer, which collated the information and told her the fleet was in good condition.

Three Starbreaks said, "You can still stop this. Don't fire. Don't move."

Enid fumed. "You know I can't do that, Elder. Our mission is to get the Black Ship at any cost."

"Don't you understand what's happened?"

"Three Starbreaks, I haven't time for your mysticism. There's a ship out there which has attacked us without provocation."

"Admiral, that Black Ship rotated us past our Home Worlds and destroyed bombs meant to wipe out our area of the galaxy."

"Now you're talking nonsense. Nothing could have done what we saw. Somehow that thing can delude our senses into seeing what it wants us to see."

Before Three Starbreaks could answer Enid cut him off and turned to her view screen. The Black Ship emitted a beam of light like that from a lighthouse, washing the entire fleet in its sweep. The beam of light rotated in a great circle back to the fleet, even as it widened and changed hue from a deep purplish-blue to a bright red. Enid watched the technicolor display for a moment and then ordered her ships forward.

"Lay down a barrage this side of that ship. I want coverage for our ships going in. I want enough firepower to blind the Black Ship."

An awesome and silent pyrotechnic display of firepower splashed the stars, increasing in intensity until no one could see anything of the Black Ship. Thousands of ships fired their weapons but when the black shape began to dampen the explosions, a shudder of primeval fear ran through the fleet.

"Admiral, we have trouble!"

The Black Ship flowed in uneven style towards the fleet, blackening the stars behind it. "Fire everything we have," Enid ordered (she didn't have to say at what), and felt the shudder as her ship replied. Weapon upon weapon, missile upon missile, the entire fury of the fleet was unleashed. For minutes the spot where the Black Ship was flared into an incandescence greater than the light from the nearby star. Great shock waves rippled through the fleet, making it hard to keep smaller vessels steady in their positions.

Enid finally gave the order to cease firing and the fleet waited for the enormous patch of energy to dissipate. Enid checked *Stars End*'s status and noted with pride the flagship had expended only a tenth of its firepower. She felt her uncertainty slip away and in its place a growing pride in the job her fleet had done. They would yet get to plumb the secrets of the Black Ship. Three Starbreaks was wrong in his belief the Anphorian fleet could be stymied in their goals by any single ship, no matter the technology that guided it.

The fleet's Commanders checked in with their status reports. The *Okada* was the last to report in. Colonel Carstairs kept a watchful eye on the small group of Repletians but they kept a respectful distance. Enid ordered Carstairs to continue her vigil on the Repletians while Enid's techs tried to get readouts from the area where the Black Ship had disappeared.

These readouts became increasingly bizarre, a clear signal which Enid didn't miss. She ordered her fleet to fire again on her orders. As she completed her orders the final remnants of radiation lifted from where they had fired and the fleet again faced the Black Ship. Enid felt as much as heard the great collective intake of breath and the sense of disbelief that washed through her flagship as stellar signals indicated the planet ahead of them was Korel's World. Enid made a quick decision and turned to her Aide.

"Mister, take our flagship in towards that planet. Prepare for landfall."

Enid felt *Stars End* shudder as its engines began to move the ship towards the planet. On her orders hundreds of thousands of troops within the flagship raced to don their combat gear in preparation for landfall. She knew they were ready. They had gone through countless drills on their way here. Her attentions returned to the Black Ship. As *Stars End* accelerated, she watched as the distance between the two ships rapidly closed.

"Hold on and fire with everything we have if that fucker makes any hostile moves."

As the acid words left her lips, Enid saw the tightening of postures from her bridge officers. Her use of the words Tyrel had used had the desired effect of shocking her officers into greater attention. And in seeing this, a fierce certainty washed through Enid. She couldn't turn back now.

When her monitors showed a scant ten thousand miles separated the two ships, Enid yelled to her pilot, "Now! Full speed through that bastard!" And was pushed deeper into her seat as the flagship underwent a brutal acceleration that knocked several bridge officers from their feet.

And felt the great beam of light stab through the flagship's hull. And heard the screams as something seized the ship and twisted it from its path, throwing it directly towards the planet's surface. And felt the computers kick in to break the ship's free fall towards the planet, whose surface rushed at a dizzying pace towards them, promising to crush them against its surface.

For a moment the flagship stabilized and slowed its fall. Enid saw the Black Ship spear its light through the Fourth Fleet's far-flung formation. She blinked in disbelief, distrusting her sight as that great host flickered in and out of sight. She managed to scream an order to escape even as she realized the reason for her shouting; the bass bell-tone rang through the hull of her ship as another beam of all-encompassing red light went impossibly through the hull and everything in it. Instinctively she reached for the self-destruct button as her ship faded around her and the last thought she had, was a grim satisfaction the technology aboard her ship wouldn't fall to the enemy. If that were the last thing she could do then she would do it with a flourish of defiance.

*

Moments later Leon Three Starbreaks received the news he

already knew in his heart. The Fourth Fleet had disappeared without a trace. As far as their Repletian sensors could reach, the Black Ship was gone. Everything had apparently gone up in an explosion of light and sound that both awed and terrified the small group of Repletian ships. And yet no debris, no shattered hulks or swaths of radiation marked the end of the Fourth Fleet or the ship it had tried to seize.

The rest of the Elder's Council saw everything from the Home Planet ten parsecs away and they were quiet, waiting for Leon to speak. When he did it was to request approval to return home because he could do nothing more. Things were out of their control. Approval was quickly given and Leon shut down the communication link to his Home World, glad for once to be alone with his thoughts. And he sat for a long time gazing at the view of the Mother of All Worlds that marked the center of this island universe Humanity's tribes had called the Milky Way since time immemorial.

He absentmindedly twisted the light gold chain in one hand and occasionally glanced at the red jewel. He fingered its hard, cold surface and marveled at the way it heated under his finger's pressure. And the longer he held it the more certain he became. A young warrior officer who served as pilot for the ship looked up from his work upon hearing his Elder move; for a timeless moment he locked eyes with Leon before the Elder said to him, "Take us home, pilot." The Elder left the bridge, leaving the young warrior to wonder what could bring such a grave smile to his Elder on such a disturbing day as this. The pilot gave orders. The Repletian ships made a quarter turn in orbit and streaked for their Home Worlds.

CHAPTER 16

Standard Year 2491

She felt the push of her mind threaten to break her. Colors. There were so many colors, she could barely stand; to walk was impossible. The colors held her in their sway. They raced across the landscape to the distant mountains. The grass changed from green to spectral grey to sun red to moon cream. Why couldn't she tear herself away from these colors, even when she knew they would lose her forever? Her hands screamed for comfort, tightening into fists that beat the air and struck her legs. She ignored the pain. There were things she had to remember, memories that teased her mind, driving her to distraction. What was it she had to know? What did her heart ache for? Light and dark, the old woman had said. But *when* and *where?*

How long she stood, she didn't know, but it was enough time to sense a change, to hear sounds from her past. The skies became steel blue. The landscape returned to its dirty gold color. Thunder grew in the distance. At the horizon a great shadow descended, hovered for a moment, and then raced towards her so quickly she flinched. She looked about, but there was nothing she could throw at the alien object.

She watched as the silver shadow landed a hundred yards away. An old word came swimming back to memory; it was the word 'lifter.' A lifter had come for her. She wished it would leave. She felt the thick blood trickle down her legs. She looked down with amazement. Blood. It trailed down her thighs to her bare feet, there to run into the parched soil.

When she looked up, a group of people were walking towards her. As they approached, they formed a semi-circle, as though they thought she would run. What foolishness!

Ten feet away, the leading man stopped. Strange noises came from his mouth. She cocked her head to one side, staring at him. Why didn't he go away and leave her alone?

What more did they want from her?

The man stopped making noises and turned to the uniformed woman on his right. She lifted a small black object that made similar strange sounds before it grew quiet. She moved forward and utterances burst from her mouth, sounds, codes that became increasingly familiar.

"...you Enid Blue Starbreaks? I repeat, is your name Enid Blue Starbreaks?"

Enid (this was her name, she knew it now) chose not to speak. She had no voice with which to speak to these soldiers. And if she could speak, what words would she choose to describe her feelings? Better to be silent.

"Captain, she doesn't seem to understand us."

The man addressed as 'captain' looked at Enid strangely, as if there was something wrong with her. Enid wanted to tell him to get off the planet before it was too late, but something kept her silent.

"Sergeant," the captain spoke again. "Get Ms. Blue Starbreaks something to wear. Christ, does she smell! I'll wager she hasn't taken a bath in years. We need to clean her up. Make the necessary arrangements."

"Aye, sir." The woman gestured for several of her men to take Enid away. Enid felt their danger. She hissed and went into a combat crouch. As the first soldier came near, she spun, her left leg sweep knocking him from his feet. Even as he fell, a surprised look on his face, she leapt up, her fists driving into the second man's stomach. He screamed in pain and the area around Enid became a furious combat zone. Soldiers surrounded her, attempting to pin her to the ground. Several rushes resulted in broken bones and great bruises, not all of them the soldiers'. Several times the soldiers thought they had her. Each time, Enid rose to strike another series of devastating blows. The sergeant watched in amazement as the frail-looking woman before her continued to hold her own against men easily twice her size and weight. She moved with a speed none of the men had seen before. As the seconds wore on, an admiration for her fighting skills changed to fear and hesitation. Enid gave no quarters. Time and again men felt themselves in control of her, sometimes their great arms enveloping her in a bear-like hug, only to find themselves thrown to the ground, the target of punches that broke heavy bones like twigs.

After several minutes, Enid was surrounded by a ring of men who kept their distance. She spun in her place, waiting for the next onslaught. The sudden sharp pain in her neck surprised her; she reached towards the spot and then blackness overcame her, dragging her towards the ground.

The sergeant stood over the still figure as her troops looked down.

"Christ, sergeant, who is she?" a soldier asked. He clutched his side where a rib was broken.

"Classified...Get her to the medical facilities. I want her cleaned up and held until further notice." The sergeant looked at her men with disgust. "And get yourselves patched up while you're there. We're leaving in five minutes, so move your asses."

As her men disappeared into the lifter, the sergeant spoke to her captain.

"Why didn't we kill her and get it over with? There'll be hell to pay when news gets out about our discovery."

The captain asked her to follow him back to the ship. As they walked towards the lifter, he looked down at the ground, bemused. He paused to watch the soldiers take Enid up the ramp into the lifter. He felt the tension drain from his body. The Repletian skirmishes were escalating and the captain wondered for a moment if there would ever be a time when he wasn't so tired, a time when the hostilities between the two human groups would end. Survival was the only thing he could hope for in a war that seemed endless.

He suppressed these thoughts as he had done several times in the past year and returned his attention to his Sergeant: "Sergeant, there may be hell to pay but it won't be us. You know the history..."

"What soldier doesn't? Thirteen years ago, Enid Blue Starbreaks went missing along with the Fourth Fleet. Why wasn't she found here earlier?"

The captain stopped at the threshold to the lifter. He turned from the waiting shadows to look out over the plains.

"Sergeant, once the Fourth Fleet disappeared, we broke some of the Repletian codes. They conducted a full scan of this planet for any survivors. There were no traces of humans. Korel's World was barren of anything but its own life forms."

"Except for one thing."

The captain looked puzzled. "What thing?"

"Well, we have the former admiral of the Fourth Fleet. That's a pretty large miss, if you ask me."

"Yes," the captain sighed. "And then we have Enid Blue Starbreaks. Sometimes I'm glad that I'm only a captain. There's going to be fallout at higher levels when we return her."

"What happens to her?"

The captain thought for a moment and smiled. "They can't afford to kill her, not now. Not when Repletia has gained so much diplomatic and military power. Her death would incense Repletia. I imagine only the admiralty and the Council will know Starbreaks' fate. There won't be a trial. There's no way they could do that and keep her identity secret. Maybe they'll put her in prison and throw away the keys."

"And what do we do? We're privy to that history."

The captain frowned and said, "I don't know. We'd better have a conference with my officers and come up with a plan to cover ourselves. Get busy. We'll meet as soon as we get underway."

Inside the orbiting battle cruiser, the doctor looked through the transparent metal barrier. His eyes scanned the long emaciated body suspended in the tank of saline solution. The woman's head was suspended above the surface. He surveyed the areas where some work on his part was needed. The woman was black from sun exposure. This didn't hide the ribs that projected gauntly from skin that was barely able to hold her frame together. The doctor studied the report. He shook his head in disbelief. He wondered again how the figure that floated in front of him could have fought the way she had against the toughest warriors in the navy. It didn't make sense, but the past few weeks made no sense, from their mad scramble to reach this godforsaken part of the galaxy to the security clamped onto the ship within minutes of the woman being brought on board. Or so it seemed.

"What do you think, doctor?"

"Well, without a scan it's hard to say. But she does need some attention. Was she alone down there?"

The captain looked hard at the doctor before deciding to answer. "She was alone, yes. Now, what do you plan to do?"

"I don't know. Is she important?"

"Very. I want you to do a full analysis on her to verify who she is. We think we know, but I have to be certain. Be thorough."

The doctor hid his annoyance. Even now, the computers were evaluating her DNA tests. Normally, it took seconds to identify people. The doctor glanced at the time on the screen. Five minutes had passed. He had never seen the computer take so long but, even as he watched, the computer reported:

"Analysis complete. Following is a list of necessary repairs to the human."

The doctor read the list and grunted with satisfaction. There was nothing on there he hadn't already guessed.

"Identity has been confirmed."

The doctor waited but the computer was silent.

"Well?"

"Apologies, doctor, but the information is classified."

"Classified? That's nonsense. She's a stray soul from Korel's World."

"Doctor, the information is classified."

The captain interrupted, "Computer, who has access to your findings?"

"Captain, you have clearance to my findings."

"Very well, report your findings."

There was a pause and then the computer spoke. "The female is Repletian. She is fifty years old. She has a fifteen-year-old scar in her left rib cage. She weighs fifty-two point three kilograms. She is severely malnourished. Her name is Enid Blue Starbreaks, former commander of the Fourth Fleet. Her files have been reactivated from the 'deceased' lists."

The doctor whispered, "Enid Blue Starbreaks! Yes, of course. I should have recognized her right away."

The captain, staring at Enid's naked body, turned to the doctor. "I beg your pardon? What did you say?"

"Nothing. It was nothing."

The captain glanced at him, noticing the small beads of sweat forming on the doctor's upper lips, and then spoke to the computer. "Advise the bridge to set a course for the nearest Anphorian Home World. Priority One."

The doctor felt strong fingers grip his shoulders: "Doctor?" The captain's face was inches from his. "Doctor, what you have heard stays with you. Do you understand?"

The doctor nodded. The captain let him go and then walked away. As he disappeared beyond the door the doctor rubbed his shoulders. He took a final look at Enid's floating body. The restraints held her immobile and unconscious while the DNA solution worked on patching her broken bones and skin damage. Given the level of damage inflicted by the fight, and the injuries incurred during her years alone in Korel's World, it would take Enid a full week to be restored to something resembling normal health. He thought of the damage she had done in the past, and whispered, "Fucking Repletian!"

*

"You're certain it's Enid Blue Starbreaks?"

"Aye, sir. The retinal and brain scans verify the DNA analysis. She is older, but it is her."

"I see." Madame President chewed lightly on her lower lips while she thought about the distressing news. What to do? Fuck, just when things between Anphoria and Repletia were stabilizing. Why did it always happen to her? It never happened to her predecessor, no matter that Katina Patriloney's name was feared and hated thirteen years after her death.

"Where is she now?"

"She's in the tank being repaired."

"Did you find the origin of the distress call you received?"

The captain shook his head. "No, like everything connected to that planet, we found nothing to account for the signals. No ship or beacon was in orbit when we got there."

Madame President ended the transmission and sat back to consider her options. She needed to act quickly, but she also had to think. She swiveled in her chair to face the blank wall behind her desk. The weight of the past ten years made her back ache and her hands tremble. She felt something implicitly unfair in the role she had gladly taken back then when the role of president was more of a challenge than a burden. Like her predecessors, she found there was no manual for president, no magic book she could rely on in times of crisis.

Learning to think on her feet wore her down; normally, she was careful and methodical. But the unrelenting advance of the Repletians called for quick decisions. She could turn to only one person for advice, one person she trusted.

"Yes, Madame President?" Former Admiral Lexington's neutral expression was so obviously a mask she laughed. Lexington smiled.

"I see I can't fool you the way I used to do."

Madame President smiled at the memory of her first days as president. The admiral's reputation and stature had intimidated her. In her attempts to assert her own leadership, she fought his reputation by ignoring his advice. The mistakes she made had almost cost her the presidency.

"Do you remember the days when I was a sheep facing a wolf in admiral's clothing? I hated you then."

The admiral gave a slight nod. "Indeed, you were the shy one in those days. I only found out what you were doing behind the scenes at the last moment. I must say I was pleased by your ingenuity, although it almost cost us everything."

"Why didn't you take over when you found out what my plans were? It would have been simpler."

"Madame President, had I chosen the easy way, Anphoria would now be poorer. No, you had to learn the hard way by getting out of problems yourself. The Second Fleet owes its existence to what you did in those three days when Anphoria was at your door howling for your hide."

"Was there no other reason for your hesitation?"

"Well, I may have been an admiral but I couldn't have done what you did in those three days. The academy still studies the methods you used to negotiate the Second Fleet from certain annihilation. I know about military strategy. But in the finer arts of negotiation, I'm like boiling water on ice."

"But I was the one who put the Second Fleet in jeopardy."

"That may be so, but what counted was the result. No school can teach what is unteachable."

"Admiral, I never thought you were one to read the works of Theresa Kuang Hsia."

"No more so than a certain president. In my retirement I have time to read."

"Speaking of which, I have a problem."

Lexington nodded, and a look of pain appeared on his face. He rose from behind his desk and walked to his large window. He stood with his back to Madame President for several moments, his long arms hanging loosely at his sides, contemplative. His voice, when it came, was so low Madame President almost missed what he said.

"What I feared has come about at last. I'm too old to bear this burden."

"You saw this coming?"

"No, not this. What do you know of Enid Blue Starbreaks and me?"

"Only what's on record. Surely there wasn't . . ."

The admiral turned to face her. "No, no. There was nothing like that. She was like a niece to me. I watched her move through the ranks but, when the time came, I didn't know she would suffer terribly for someone else's ambitions. It's not often I'm wrong in my estimation of people. Katina was a horrible exception."

"And now?"

"And now what? Enid is where she is because of me. Anything I did in the past misfired. She's better off without my continued interference, may the Creator have mercy on her."

"Admiral, I don't need this. I need some fucking advice. You're the most qualified..."

The admiral looked directly through the holograph imager at her, his eyes a bright flash of intensity. "I need time to think about this. I'm not one for hasty decisions. In the meantime, I wish you luck."

Before Madame President could protest, his image faded. "Fuck you, Admiral! Fuck you!" She fumed at the holographer and turned away. What to do? She needed to squelch this, or the Anphorian negotiations with Repletia would suffer a severe setback. At the moment, only the captain's ship and the admiral knew. She had to keep it this way for the time being. She needed some rationale for dealing with the former admiral of the Fourth Fleet and she knew what to do.

A quick call confirmed Enid's files were still classified. A few curt commands sorted out Enid's personnel files to make certain discrete entries. Madame President took five minutes to scan the information in Enid's files. She knew that, if her duplicity was eventually discovered, not many people would care. What was important was to complete her negotiations with Repletia. The rest would have to be shelved. She started her holograph screen again, calling up her computer.

"Get me the captain of the *Pleiades* now."

*

The captain left his quarters for the bridge. Once there, he stood on the threshold of the bridge, scanning its occupants. His command crew felt his anger and their talk became muted. Then he strode to his chair, sat down and summoned them.

"What I am going to say is confidential. If our passenger's identity is released to anyone outside of our ship without my clearance, the ship and its crew will be classified as missing in action. Do I make myself clear?" He ignored the intake of breath from his officers.

"Aye, sir!"

"Good. Pilot, set a course for Sandina. Call me when we get there."

Once he had the bridge crew busy at their assigned tasks, the captain walked quickly to the medical unit. As requested, the doctor was waiting for him.

"Well, doctor, we have a problem on our hands and orders to carry out."

"Orders?"

"She's still unconscious. Can we erase her memory?"

"How much time do I have?"

"Twenty hours or less. That's when we reach orbit around Sandina."

The doctor checked his inventories. "We don't have the medications to wipe her memory clean in that amount of time. But we can make sure she loses as much as forty or fifty percent, enough to make most of her recent past a blank. There is a drawback."

"A drawback?"

"Yes. You see, we used chemical memory inhibitors on her when she was a child. The doses we used were effective, but she'll have some natural resistance to chemical inhibitors like TL Phenothiazine."

"Whatever you can do, do it. By the way, doctor, I'm reassigning you."

"I don't understand."

"Based on your involvement with the patient, and your medical experience, you've been reassigned to take command of the medical facilities on Sandina."

The doctor shook his head. "But there's no medical facility on Sandina. Just a god-awful prison."

"Exactly. Upon arrival, you will escort the patient to the prison."

*

As the lifter circled the enormous building, the doctor stared through the window. Sandina, the prison, was a sphere three miles in diameter. The top half of the sphere, that part of it which was above the surface, loomed almost two miles into the dark skies. It contained nearly one hundred levels, almost none of them explored or inhabited. The bottom half of the sphere was hidden beneath the solid granite terrain stretching to the rain-filled horizon.

Sandina was ancient, built by the Nordells. What happened to the Nordells remained a mystery, although people speculated about their abrupt disappearance from Sector Five many years ago. They had left a maze of tunnels boring deeper and further into the planet than anyone had ever explored.

The doctor couldn't see the prison, for it occupied the top half of the bottom of the sphere. Below the prison a series of endless tunnels stretched down and away from the dome. The residents of Sandina called these tunnels the Basement.

The doctor was awed by the immensity of the granite dome. He counted over fifty distinct levels above ground, amounting to over a billion square feet of rooms and corridors. And yet no one lived above ground, for the eternal winds and rains washing over the stone building created a bleak atmosphere. Uneven corridors riddled Sandina's structure, some stretching the entire length of the prison. From the lifter the doctor saw thousands of balconies and windows leading into the dark unexplored parts of the dome.

The lifter shuddered as a gust of wind ripped at the short wings. Rain spattered the windshield. The doctor blinked and shied away. As the wind eddied around and through the dome it sometimes produced high whistling that shrilled against the lifter, and at other times a low moan that bored into the doctor's molars. The doctor saw why humans chose to live beneath and away from this discord of sound. Already he hated this planet, not that he needed any excuses.

The lifter dropped to the ground with a heavy thud, the best the pilot could manage against the strong gusts tearing against the lifter. The soldiers, who had come with the doctor, grabbed the stretcher and bolted into the rain. They made a dash for the nearby open door. The doctor ran with them, and they were soaked in the few seconds it took to get to shelter. Four large prison guards took the stretcher and its patient from the guards, who didn't bother to salute. Instead, they turned and without a word ran back to the lifter, which then streaked upwards out of sight into the black rain clouds. Before the doctor could see the lifter disappear, the door was shut against the weather, leaving a sudden silence that made the doctor uneasy. Again, he wished he had never set eyes on the woman on the stretcher, whose identity he was sworn to keep to himself.

*

Colors. Muted, neutral. A world of slate, charcoal, ochre. A headache hammered at her, made her confused and uncertain. In the cold, her exposed skin broke into goose bumps. An explosion of colors lit her mind and made her grimace with pain. To ease the throbbing, she chased the colors from her mind. An occasional drop of water fell from the ceiling of rough uneven stone onto the floor below. Hollow echoes of feet sounded everywhere. Suddenly a face loomed over her, a face she struggled to recognize.

"Ah, Madame X, you're awake."

She stirred and felt the pain shoot through her legs. The face quickly vanished and then returned as she sat up on the cold metal slab. The doctor hurried back from his workbench. He handed her a steaming cup of brown liquid she didn't recognize. She took a tentative sip, and then a bigger sip, ignoring the pain. As she slowly swallowed the bitter drink, warmth enveloped her. The doctor examined her, using a sound scanner. After a few moments he nodded approvingly and felt for her pulse.

"Where am I?"

"You're on Sandina. It's a prison planet."

Madame X frowned. The doctor smiled at her. She became aware of her nakedness. His eyes scanned her body with evident relish. Her medical records had turned up a surprise, and a pleasant one at that. He had treated Enid as a child, and was now assigned to the *Pleiades*. He looked into her eyes and then gestured; two large men came forward and took hold of each of her arms, lifting her from the table. She almost fell as she again felt the pain in her legs. Her cup dropped to the floor, spilling its contents onto the hard surface, but no one noticed. The doctor looked at the two men.

"She'll be all right. She's a fucking Plete, trash that killed her parents. Take her down to her assigned unit. I'll look in later, once I've talked with the warden."

The doctor watched Enid half-dragged out of the room. Serves her right for sending him to this hellhole. He thought of the times he had held her life in his hands. He should have killed her while he could. Still, perhaps he and the warden could work things out so his stay wasn't wasted. The sight of Enid's long lanky legs brought desire to the doctor's eyes. His posting might work out for the better after all.

*

Much later, after he met with the warden and his family, the doctor said farewell to his escorts and settled into his quarters. The furnishings, while sparse, were better than the doctor could have hoped for. He read an old magazine and then turned on the holograph for news of the night. He was brushing his teeth in the washroom when he heard words that drew him to the living room. An image of the *Pleiades* hovered before him and a low female voice was reading a bulletin.

"...with six thousand crew members missing and unaccounted for. A spokesperson for the admiralty has said that there are no survivors. To repeat, the *Pleiades*, a Class Three vessel, is feared destroyed with all hands on deck. The ship was on a routine mission in Sector Three when it flew into an uncharted meteor field three days out of port. The *Pleiades* was due for reassignment in three months. More news to follow, as it happens."

The doctor felt a chill. He looked nervously about his room. The *Pleiades* had dropped him off hours ago. At full speed it would have taken the Pleiades ten days to reach the borders of Sector Three. Something was going on and it involved the navy. The doctor thought of Enid Blue Starbreaks and knew she was responsible. Highly-placed people were involved. Perhaps he should hold off on his plans for her, at least, until he knew everyone in this prison. With that, the doctor smiled to himself. No need to panic. Everything would work out fine, as they had up to now. Luck was still on his side.

CHAPTER 17

Standard Year 2491

The stone corridor was long and narrow. Low overhead lights cast their dim glow no more than a dozen feet. The rest was veiled in darkness no human eye could penetrate. The occasional drips of water echoed endlessly down the corridors until they faded into silence. Holes riddled the floor, marking where the water had bored into the stone. The rough surface showed its four-thousand-year age. Once these corridors had served as drainage to the great building above, but water table changes over millennia had emptied them.

When Anphorians first found the building, it had been abandoned by its builders. The Anphorians made no attempt to light the innumerable corridors. Only the ones closest to the surface, directly under the black sphere, were lit by human technology. No one knew how far the corridors extended, or whether in fact they ever ended. The original builders had been subterranean creatures who carved channels that made no sense to humans.

For Mole, the Basement was home. Here no one bothered her; no one taunted her or took her food from her. Here she could say anything and nobody ridiculed her. The darkness and the ever-present water kept everyone but the guards from voluntarily entering the maze. And those guards hurried back out after changing the occasional light fixture. So the lights didn't go far and most corridors were dark.

When Mole was first sent here for an off-world crime, the killing of her rich abusive husband, the guards had beaten her. They then dragged her down a long series of steps to the Basement. Two oil drums that stood as high as any person on the planet sat on each side to the Basement's entrance. How long they had been there, Mole never found out, although she marked the spot where the rust had made the pools of water a dirty mud-brown.

The guards hauled Mole along a stone floor to a steel door.

They opened the door and threw her into the corridors beyond. The door was then closed and locked and the lights extinguished, leaving Mole in darkness so complete she thought she had gone blind.

For days and weeks she fought against the darkness, screamed for help, wept until she had no tears. She stumbled about until she found the lights and food. From thereon it was a constant struggle, going from light to light. At each light, once she had eaten the stale food and drank the water, the lights were turned off, leaving her to scramble in search of lights they had turned on in another section of corridors.

She lost track of time. Her knees and hands developed scar tissue from the times she fell, her blood darkening to become one with the mute stone floors. The only fortunate thing about the design of the corridors was they allowed her to walk without having to stoop over. But her walk became a limp as her knees continued to take a beating time and again from her falls.

And then one day out of so many she had lost count, she was weeping for past times when she sensed a change in the texture of the darkness around her. At first, she fearfully looked around.

"Who's there?" she asked, and then screamed. There was no answer but, when she finally stretched out on the cold stone floor to sleep, she felt a sense of warmth and peace flow into her from the stone, almost as though some great animal had lain there. She hadn't known such peace for a long time. As she slipped into a deep and comfortable sleep, she wondered if she were going crazy. Hours later, when she woke up, the gentle darkness retreated, leaving her to the cold, drafty blackness she knew too well.

She shivered and ran after the presence, but it was not there, if it had ever been there. Her feet made a dull echo that fled ahead of her down unseen corridors. And she cursed the darkness and what it contained; it would have been better for her never to know such false hope as she felt now. She tripped and fell, feeling the pain return her sanity to her, if it was sanity she felt. All she could do was to cry, because it crumbled her heart to have the image of her only child becoming a fading memory

Perhaps days passed before she again felt a fleeting presence at the edge of her senses. She was in a sector of the corridors with no light, and it was as if a shadow deeper than the darkness passed before her eyes. There was no sound except her heavy breathing. When she thought to reach out a hand to touch the darkness, it was too late. The blackness hovered before her for a fraction of a second before it receded down the corridors faster than she could follow.

This ephemeral passing hurt Mole, but she kept herself from weeping. Whatever it was, she uncannily found it comforting. The normal darkness was less fearsome, less lonely. Mole smiled into the darkness, not caring if the blackness she had felt would sense her feelings. She knew she was no longer alone in these corridors.

And so it had gone until the guards tired of their games and left a steel door open for her.

Today, Mole had come here to reflect on what she had heard in the commissary. She had snatched her stale bread and old beef jerky quietly, stealing a bit extra to hoard away for her wanderings into the corridors. She preferred this to mingling with the prison population, which was full of cruel people who endlessly teased her. There was one woman in particular who reveled in taunting Mole, even giving her the nickname by which everyone now called her. This woman was large, much larger than Mole, and insisted on demonstrating who was boss.

Two weeks ago a new prisoner had been sent here, a tall thin woman with no past or memories. Evelyn abandoned teasing Mole to assert her authority with the new 'skin.' Madame X, as she was called by the guards, had her eyes to the ground, paid no attention to what was happening around her. She moved with a shuffle and her shoulders slumped, as if she carried the weight of some great internal pain. In the two days she had been here she hadn't said a word to anyone. This fuelled Evelyn's hatred, for the woman was also Repletian.

When her lookouts gave her the okay, Evelyn moved from the wall to block Madame X's path. Madame X looked up, her light blue eyes dull and unresponsive.

"What's the matter, Plete? Ain't we fucking good enough for you? Can't you talk? Or maybe you're too good for the likes of me, eh?"

Madame X lowered her head to stare at the stone floor beneath her. Evelyn, enraged, reached out and slammed a large hand on her slim shoulders, blocking all movement.

"Hey, Plete, I'm talking to you. When I talk, you answer. You ain't going nowhere until you speak."

Madame X remained immobile, and Evelyn gave her a swift shove, launching the smaller woman down to the hard stone. Surprisingly, Madame X rolled to cushion the fall and was on her feet. From ramparts twenty feet above, Mole, who looked down on the scene, saw the bright red streak where Madame X had fallen and skinned her buttocks. Her loose-fitting pants were ripped down the length of one leg. There was blood near the top of the rip and everyone could see the exposed skin even in the low lights. Yet Madame X never uttered a sound, standing as if nothing had happened.

Behind her, Evelyn heard a snicker, but she continued to stare at Madame X. She was about to knock Madame X down again when a lookout gave a shrill whistle, the warning of approaching guards. Evelyn shot Madame X a look full of hate and hissed, "Fucking Plete! I'll show you who's captain here. And you won't forget it."

With that, Evelyn hastened away with her gang. A pair of guards walked past Madame X without a sideways glance at her.

Today Mole had heard Evelyn's gang, who called themselves the Nordells after the species that had carved the sphere from solid rock thousands of years before, planned to trap Madame X in the Basement.

Because guards tended to shy away from the Basement, Evelyn figured she could take her time in beating Madame X into submission.

Mole, who passed unnoticed through most crowds because of her timid manner and quiet movements, had been at the table next to the Nordells during mealtime. While she took no particular liking to Madame X, Mole disliked Evelyn, whose cruelty towards her she would never forget. Yet she could do nothing about Evelyn's plans. No one within the general population bothered the Nordells willingly, although there were rival gangs as strong and as mean, controlling their own sections of the general population. Because Madame X was in the same holding units as the Nordells, she was the Nordells' property.

Madame X sat at another table by herself; she didn't hear Evelyn make her plans, plans based on the fact Madame X was assigned clean-up duties for the areas next to the Basement entrance. It would be easy to force Madame X into a Basement tunnel, but Mole didn't hear which one. So, right after mealtime, while everyone retreated to their various workstations, Mole went to her room to get her gloves. She then scurried to the Basement corridors.

A year ago she had stolen some chalk, and had taken to numbering the corridors she travelled. She became familiar with the network of drainage tunnels under the prison. She ventured into other tunnels, away from the looming presence of the prison above her, but she knew the extent of the corridors would always be beyond her capacity to explore. The corridors not only went out of sight along the surface of the planet, but they extended deep into its womb. They were so deep that once she thought she tasted salt water from a long extinct ocean. It was here where the corridors poured their waters, waters that had been carried into the distant oceans that once covered this barren planet.

Mole discovered a place she knew was safe from anyone's prying eyes. It was a place she guessed was a mile into the tunnels and thirty stories below the prison. It was so remote from the surface there was no chance of discovery here. Nobody dared venture down here of their own volition. The guards thought her crazy; driven to madness due to the initial six months they had kept her isolated in these corridors. Thus, they shrugged off her wanderings as fits of lunacy.

Mole dug into the small mound of articles piled into a dry part of the small circular room that once housed a family of Nordells. She found what she wanted, pulling out a long strip of cloth that was the bottom half of a faded blanket. She had taken the blanket, as she had taken other items,

Clutching the cloth close to her body, Mole climbed through the series of corridors until she sensed she was nearing the entrance to the Basement. There she stopped and listened. At first, all she heard were the fading sounds of her footsteps. She waited patiently, and then heard a faint murmuring. She moved cautiously forward, stopping at each intersection, as she sought the source of the voices. She was heedless of time, for time meant nothing here in the darkness.

Soon the voices became clearer. Screams of anger, the thud of a fist, a body. The light came from a tunnel and Mole panicked. She didn't like fights and knew she was a terrible combatant. But, strangely, the sounds became muted the closer she advanced. Perhaps the fighting was over. But then a scream of pain sent shivers down her spine. It came from whatever was ahead. Frantic, Mole began to quicken her pace, not aware of what she was doing but knowing she had to do something. Without knowing why, she changed her pace and her footsteps raced with a growing and uneven beat. Ahead she heard other voices.

"Listen, what's that?"

"What's what?"

"Something's coming down the tunnels."

"Where?"

"How in fuck should I know? There's supposed to be nothing down here."

"Yeah, well, tell that to whatever's coming this way."

"What do you mean, something?"

"Listen, stupid, we're right at the entrance to this tunnel. Nothing went by us into the tunnels so you tell me what's coming this way."

"Fuck, you're right! I ain't waiting to see what it is. Let's get outta here."

Mole was getting closer to the lighted corridor, and she grunted as loud and as deep as she could, the corridors changing her voice into something inhuman. She was right. She heard the women scream and panic, retreat. Then came the sound of the metal doors slamming shut.

The sight that greeted her as she entered the corridor of light made her stop.

Five women lay scattered, as though by a great wind, over a ten-yard space of stone floor. They lay in dark pools that grew as Mole approached. Puzzled, she stooped next to a body and reached out to touch the liquid. She drew her fingers back and looked at the end of her hand. The liquid was bright red but it thickened in texture and color as she watched. Horrified, Mole wiped her hand on the woven cloth she held in her other hand. She hastily backed away from the body and looked around in fear. The corridor was empty.

Mole huddled against a wall, her eyes large with unspoken thoughts. How long she might have paused on the edge of this hall of death she didn't know, for her senses were drawn to a body that stirred and became still again. Without thinking, Mole scurried to the body and rolled it over to see the face. The ease with which she could do this surprised her, until she saw the exposed ribcage and the thin arms and legs. She knew, without looking at the face covered with blood, this was Madame X. That meant the bodies around her were Evelyn's followers.

Mole cradled Madame X's head in one crooked arm. With the other, she gently wiped at the bloodstained face. After the second swipe Mole paused and almost dropped Madame X's head. A red pool gathered in one eye-socket where eyesight had been robbed. Mole had neither the nerve nor the skills to deal with this injury. There was one thing to do. Mole hauled Madame X's body to the door to the prison basement. She placed her back against that door and pushed it open. Carefully, she dragged the body through the door and then let the body down gently. She straightened to listen, but heard nothing. Evelyn had bolted to higher ground.

Mole looked down at the unconscious body. Whatever else she did, Mole knew Madame X needed quick medical attention. She had to attract the guards without being caught for, while the guards tended to be lax in their treatment of inmates, they also could show a sadistic streak as great as that shown by the inmates. Mole searched the large basement and saw what she needed. Near the top of the flight of stone steps were the two rusty barrels she had first noticed when she was dragged down to the Basement a year ago. One of the barrels now leaned against a wall. The stairs ended forty feet from where Madame X lay, facing away from her, so there was no danger the barrel could hit her.

As luck had it, the barrel was empty. Although it was heavy, Mole found she could move it if she put her back into tilting the barrel from side to side, inching it towards the edge of the first step. Several times she stopped to wipe sweat from her face. Finally the barrel hovered on the edge of the steps. Mole took a final breath and then heaved against the barrel, toppling it over. At first, it rolled down one step at a time but with each bounce it gathered speed. Mole covered her ears as the din thundered through the lower parts of the prison. At the bottom of the stairs the barrel slammed onto the stone floor. One end crumpled under the force, sending the barrel off-kilter to hit the opposite wall, where it smashed apart. In the enclosed space, Mole shook her head as the reverberations of the barrel echoed with the force of a cannon.

As the noise receded, Mole hurried down the steps and raced for the corridors. She jumped over Madame X's still body as she heard the guards running to investigate. Mole scurried into the corridor, leaving the door open for the guards to find the other bodies. Fifty feet down, she snaked through an intersecting passage. She stooped and waited, knowing the guards wouldn't venture this far, not with their hands full of dead and injured inmates. She listened and three minutes later was surprised by the low voices of the guards as they found the bodies. There was fear in their voices, which puzzled Mole.

*

"Whoa, there, Eve. What's the rush?"

Evelyn heard the lead guard and stopped, her followers almost running into her from behind. It was then she noticed the blood dripping from their coats, collars, fingers. She had to come up with something quick or the game was over. She let an edge of panic into her voice, one she didn't have to fake because it was there.

"Oh, am I glad to see you. Something horrible's happened to my girls."

"What are you saying?!"

Evelyn took a deep breath, knowing this would distract the two males and lower their suspicions. "Something devastating, unspeakable just happened. Some of my girls were killed. It was terrible. So terrible. You need to help them."

"Killed? How? How were they killed? Evelyn, you're not making sense."

"They didn't do nothing." We were down looking around, if you know what I mean. They're dead. All dead."

The lead guard looked askance at Evelyn, wondering what she was up to. He was about to say something when he heard a strange sound from the stairs to the Basement. He and the other guard stood motionless as the rattling turned to thunder and then faded. The lead guard turned and signaled. He left Evelyn, who looked frightened. With several other guards, he bolted down the steps.

At the bottom of the long series of stairs, he burst into the Basement. The broken barrel was the first thing he saw, and wondered whatever could have split open such a heavy object. He turned from the stairs and saw the still form of a woman near an open door. Witnessing the blood that covered the floor, he yelled to one of his men, "Get a medic team down here now."

Without turning to see if anyone followed his orders, the lead guard reached the woman's body in a few long quick strides. He felt the rise and fall of her breasts as she struggled to breathe, her breaths coming in hoarse-gargled strains. There was too much blood on her face to identify her, but the lead guard was no longer concerned with her once he saw she was alive. Instead, he peeked into the corridor, followed by a stream of horrified guards who gathered in a ragged line to stare at the carnage in front of them.

*

"Well, Doc, what killed them?'

The doctor looked up from the flat metal table and shrugged. He carefully lowered the knife onto the grey metal beside the body, while he gathered his thoughts. Perhaps it was best to be circumspect.

"It's hard to say. There are indications of great blows to the body, lethal blows to the heart area and to the kidneys. This woman was dead before she hit the floor."

Mykal Leven looked at the doctor. "Could it have been human in origin?"

"I beg your pardon?"

"I asked you if her death could have been caused by another human?"

"Anything's possible. But, why would the blows not be from a human?"

Mykal sighed, "Well, Doc, these women were from Evelyn's gang. It's unlikely Evelyn would kill her own girls."

"What does Evelyn say about this?"

"That's it. Whoever or whatever killed these women has scared the living shit out of Evelyn. She won't talk to anyone about what happened."

The doctor, washing his hands in a large tub, turned the tap off. As he thought over what the warden had just said, he reached for a nearby towel that hung by a hook on the wall. He thought about what he knew about Evelyn.

"Evelyn isn't scared of Satan himself."

"Don't I know that, Doc.? We examined the broken barrel but there were no fingerprints on it. Whatever broke it apart had to be strong. Inhumanly strong."

"What? So you're telling me we have a monster down there?"

Mykal shrugged his shoulders. "Who knows. But I'm placing the Basement off limits until we get to the bottom of this. We can't have a Basement of dead girls."

*

Evelyn repeatedly punched at the darkness. Its smooth featureless texture surrounded her in a blanket that tugged at her soul. She twisted and turned against the darkness, but wherever she turned, there it was, blocking light and sound. She screamed but she couldn't hear herself. She ran until she was out of breath; the darkness continued to cover her, neither impeding her motions nor leaving her alone. Tired, she slumped against the unseen floor and gathered her wits about her. There had to be a way to fight this darkness.

And then a faint sound in the distance beat an unsteady rhythm. At first Evelyn thought it was a trick of her imagination, but the unsteady sounds slowly became louder and louder, closer and closer. A horrid dragging was followed by a boom, as though a huge animal was coming towards her, one of its legs dragging along the surface of the ground. Evelyn heaved herself to a standing position and looked frantically about, but she might as well be blind. The sounds came from all around, echoing in a beat that filled her mind, overcoming her reason. She began screaming and screaming and . . .

"Lords above, Evelyn! Wake up. You're having another nightmare."

Evelyn felt heavy hands on her and tried to shake them off, feeling them turn into talons that dug into her skin. She batted the hands away and then opened her eyes wide with fright, expecting to see the worst. A face loomed over her, a face that looked concerned.

Evelyn grunted, recognizing the familiar face. A dull light came into her room from daylight. Sweat soaked her sheets. She felt groggy, fatigue pulling at her as she struggled to a sitting position. She felt like crying. Life was unfair. She hadn't had a good night's sleep since the night she had ambushed that skinny Plete down in the Basement. Everything had been going fine. The Plete had put up a surprising amount of fight, killing four of Evelyn's best girls, but Evelyn had made her pay for it. She still remembered the thrill of applying pressure to the woman's eyeball as six others held down the woman. The scream of pain (the first sound besides the grunts of the fight), and the sudden give as Evelyn's fingers felt the eyeball cave in to the pressure, came at the same time. Evelyn's hands were covered by the warm liquid that spurted from the Plete's eye. Evelyn lifted her head and was about to give a victory yell when they heard it. A series of slithering sounds beat towards them from the corridors where nothing lived. Fear chilled down Evelyn's spine. For seconds she thought her ears were deceiving her but the echo grew louder.

"What's that?" one of the girls screamed and the next few minutes of terrified running became a blur. Evelyn had almost composed herself by the time she ran into the lead guard; she had her story pat. The five bodies below would need some explaining.

But standing in front of the lead guard, Evelyn was still gathering her wits when the thunderous sounds from the Basement startled her. Her imagination thrilled to what must have come down the corridors, some monster they had stirred in their fight. She was glad when the lead guard broke off his talk with her and left to investigate. She bolted for her room where she huddled in her blankets, feeling exhaustion and fear overcome her. She shivered and tried to sleep, but sleep evaded her. Images, crazy images, swept through her mind. Great drooling beasts with grotesque shapes waited every time she closed her eyes.

Two weeks later the images still haunted her, gradually losing their individuality to become the darkness of the corridors themselves. Cold fear touched her every time she thought of sleep and the waiting darkness, the strange sounds that came with sleep.

She knew she shouldn't feel this way. After all, the fucking Plete had lived. Although on this backward planet, they didn't have the medicine to restore her eye. And it wasn't as if the Plete hadn't had it coming to her, challenging her authority the way she did. She shouldn't feel this way, because she was right in what she had done. She kept telling herself this as one of her girls stood over her, waiting and watching with a look of concern on her face.

CHAPTER 18

Standard Year 2498

In her dreams she felt the tug of hate drive her fingers to pull the trigger. A warm feeling swept over her as she watched the shrouded figure disappear in a haze of red blood. Overhead came the horn blast of triumph. Her arms were raised in victory. Below her, the enormous crowd roared its approval. She turned full circle. Everywhere there were people, filling space to the distant horizon.

The red, bloated sun lowered over the edge of the world. Darkness enveloped, racing towards her at breakneck speed, and into the growing winds she hollered her defiance. Gusts tore at her robes and played havoc with the assembly. People were flung into the skies. Gaps became cancerous black holes that gnawed into the assembly until there was nothing below but the darkness of space. The howling winds became the howl of space, and of something more than space.

The darkness became a great creature hovering on the edge of sight. It hid in dank corridors, waiting while she walked towards it. As others ran screaming down the stone corridors or slumped along its sides, with their mouths frothing, she felt the soothing comfort of its heartbeat. Turning a corner she saw the waters reflect the dark image of someone she knew only too well, and opened her arms to embrace the image as she heard a voice behind her whisper, "No!"

Darkness surrounded her. She knew without opening her eyes it was still night. Outside her open windows the wind rustled through the nearby trees that surrounded her house. The air that swept through her bedroom still held the night's chill. The usual birdcalls were absent, creating a blessed hush in the air. The tiny sound of her manual clock beat its incessant pattern into her mind. She felt her muscles ache from yesterday's exercises. She was old, she thought, but she could hold her own.

Katina moved her right leg and felt the rapturous coolness of the sheets; she then moved to a new spot on the bed, letting its coolness soak through her entire body. She smiled to herself. Perhaps she was slipping. She had forbidden herself such pleasure for most of her life. But then, of course, perhaps she had denied herself for the wrong reasons. There was something to be said for the comforts her wealth and power brought her.

At this thought she opened her eyes to look around. Although it was dark her eyes could make out the dim outline of her room. Overhead, the crystal lights twinkled as a breeze swept through the room. The darkness outside was deep, reminding Katina the usually omnipresent Thiraden moon was in one of its rare oscillations, leaving it below the horizon for three consecutive nights. The light it cast over the waters of this world was one of the wonders within the Anphorian Confederacy. But not tonight. And not for Katina. There was so much work to do.

"How long have you been waiting?" Katina sat up and faced the darkness.

"Deary, it's so hard to move around, so much fuss." The voice from the shadows was deeper than Katina remembered; the figure which stirred was also taller than Katina remembered.

"You seem different."

The other woman laughed. "If it doesn't matter, then my people say that it doesn't matter."

Katina waited, her small figure seated at the edge of the enormous bed.

"It begins in light."

"More riddles? Do you speak of me?"

"Madame President, I speak of what I see in the flames. I'm not here."

"You stand in the dark and speak of fires?"

"As I must. You're a dream to me. So much fuss. So much noise."

"I'm no longer President."

"Titles only. I bring you only this---everything begins in light."

"If you insist on riddles, I have better things to do."

As the shadow faded, its voice filled Katina's mind. "So many things to do. Light."

In a month, the great summit talks between Anphoria and Repletia were due to begin. Hopes were high peace would be established that would serve both groups of humanity well. But Katina thought the new Anphorian Council and President were fools for trusting Repletia to abide by any peace treaty. She would deliver a victory blow for Anphoria that lasted as long as Anphoria existed.

With that, Katina subdued the shadows and scrambled out of bed, denying herself another few minutes of delicious relaxation. So much to do.

In her study, Katina tightened the thin belt around her nightgown. She had the computer switch on a low overhead light. The room was bathed in a soft white glow, enough light to read by, but not enough to disturb anyone else in the house. The computer told her she had five messages. She sipped on a hot cup of tea and made herself comfortable at her desk. A holograph screen came on. As it warmed up, Katina sat back in her chair and closed her eyes to collect herself. Her plans were going smoothly. Over the past several years, once she knew where Anphoria was going, she maneuvered several people into positions of trust within the agencies involved with setting up the Summit. But what she needed now was some distraction, something to take the Council's minds off the Summit.

Katina recalled the Mind Game the Thetans prized so much. Last night she had played the game; at the ninth level she had twice encountered an Elder on the Repletian Council who gave her cause for concern. With the right set of circumstances, Leon Three Starbreaks might yet disrupt her plans. Every other factor was accounted for, but there were people and events among the Repletians over which she had no control. If she were to stop Leon from reaching the Summit in a month, she needed something to distract him. But what?

Katina looked forward to her plan's success. She thought it was unfair to correct the foolish mistakes of those too young to know of the Repletians deceit. Well, no matter. Once she unveiled the deceptions going on behind the scenes, she would be hailed a hero. She thought of an adage, something about the Repletians being nothing but dressed-up animals. For some strange reason, this made her think of her beloved Lawrence of so many years ago. Hadn't he said something like this, or was it something he believed in? Katina wasn't sure, but the memory of him brought a dull pain. She suppressed it and had the holograph replay her messages.

The first two messages were from minor officials who complained of her being behind in her lease payments. Katina, after recognizing the faces of these bureaucrats, shut them off to go on to the next message.

"Madame K," the message began. Her forces knew her by no other name. "This call is secured. A random check of local networks in Sector Two came up with a file that was downloaded three days ago. I await your orders."

Katina, puzzled, downloaded the file from its secured cover and drew a sharp breath as a well-known picture focused on the holograph; she didn't need the information that accompanied it to recognize a face she hadn't believed she would ever see again in this lifetime. And as she studied the picture with hungry eyes a smile came to her face. The data was better than anything she could have hoped for. Yes, she thought, this was the perfect edge she needed to complete her plans for the upcoming Summit. She downloaded the message and contacted her network. She indicated the place where her file had been sent from, a small station at the edge of Sector Two, with the following curt command, 'Delete Source.'

Katina then made a call. She waited until the figure on the other end responded to her signal. "Yes?"

"I have a request."

"Proceed."

"How long before anyone can reach the prison planet Sandina from within Repletian territories?"

"That would be risky. Sandina is in Sector Five, on the other side of Anphoria from the Repletian Home Worlds. They would have to travel with a great deal of security. The added security would slow them down. From the time they received the news, I estimate two or three days to coordinate their route and supplies and another three days to reach Sandina safely."

"And from there to Mickelson's Nebula?"

"Assuming a one day turn around time, another four days."

"So, ten days, then?"

"Yes."

"Good. Here's what I'd like you to do. I'm sending a file to you over secured channels. I want this file broadcast in Repletian space to the attention of one Leon Three Starbreaks, an Elder of the Repletian Council. Make the broadcast untraceable and send it out in twenty days' time."

*

The villa was small, a modest residence compared to the other houses in the neighborhood. It sat on the crest of a large hill. The property was meticulously landscaped with sweeping lawns and bright circular patterns of flowers and bushes. A narrow road cut through this pattern to the foot of the house. An ancient stone wall circled the entire hill. With modern technology such a barrier was more for show than for practicality. No one doubted the faint shimmers of air that clouded the sight of the house were caused by a force field stronger than anything likely to try to force its way onto the grounds. Nor could anyone mistake the small metal objects scattered over the lawn as anything but mechanical recorders equipped with the latest in home guard weaponry.

The villa's decor was glaring. Bright colors swathed the outside walls, pinks and blues forming jagged streaks in imitation of the latest fashions set by the Home World Capital. The surfaces of the walls were simulated wood paneling composed of hardened plastic-metal alloys. The extravagant floodlights lit the villa at night and exposed its owner's wealth. Katina was safe behind the security that protected the house and its contents from the growing number of poor people who filled the city streets.

Over the past two weeks, additional activity went on behind the villa's barriers, but not enough to warrant undue attention. Nearby residents suspected the villa's owner was leaving for some months, not unusual in this neighborhood, where the residents usually owned homes on different Home Worlds.

During this minor flurry of activity, no one saw the woman inside the villa. She was generally perceived as an eccentric widow; rumored to be a wealthy, off-world woman who might have some Repletian blood due to her dark skin and light eyes. Some said that explained her reclusivity; others said she was simply a woman with a tragic past, the victim of some disaster on another world.

But her wealth was not so remarkable as to set her apart from the other affluent citizens who chose to live in the quiet backwaters of a Home World known for its sciences. Others were ostensibly richer and of more influence than the quiet old lady who had stayed by herself for almost a generation now.

The last time Katina had ventured out, she walked the streets of the town with quick certain strides. Several large men with the bearing of fighters surrounded her. They tread lightly and their eyes forever swept the streets and passing people with cold speculation. Three guardian scanners floated above her. Again, this was not unusual. Some townspeople scrutinized her, but most were only marginally curious. The great summit between the Anphorians and Repletians, two weeks away, drew everyone to their holographs, where endless dissections and analyses of the possible outcomes of the summit filled the news.

Katina stopped to drop assorted coins into the hat of one of the beggars who roamed the streets of the town. The beggar thanked her profusely and then scurried away to disappear down an alleyway.

Katina walked into a clothing store. Two guards took up posts ten feet apart on either side of the door while two others followed her in and took up strategic positions from where they could best watch the store and its customers. Katina ignored the curious glances of the few shoppers.

Twice Katina reached out to caress a scarlet robe. A clerk noticed her long slim fingers, aristocratic in their age and untouched by hard work. Her pale arms and hands were a stark contrast to the bright crimson-colored polish that graced each long slender fingernail. Katina took her time, and the clerk knew better than to interrupt her or to offer her services. Such women were resistant to intrusion and seldom returned to stores that suggested anything to them.

At last Katina nodded her head, and one of her guards came forward to take the robe from its hanger. She swept out of the store without so much as a backward glance; a lifter hovered outside the doors and the two door guards helped her climb into it. The door slid shut. Within a few moments, the other two guards, one of them carrying a small box that contained the robe, emerged into daylight and climbed into the lifter.

The sleek ship floated up and then streaked for the outskirts of town, its frame quickly disappearing beyond a hill to the east. No one noticed the beggar the old lady had given money to.

*

As the ship spun through the galaxy, the beggar hurried down the alleyway. He emerged onto a quiet side street and looked around. Seeing no one, he shed his outer clothes and threw them into a garbage disposal. The disposal reduced the clothes to ashes. Satisfied, the man took a breath and pulled back his shoulders, feeling the stress of the last minutes drain from his body. His uniform again felt comfortable. He walked to a parked lifter and climbed in, waiting until its doors were secured. He took the coins the woman had given him, and stared at their dull gold surfaces for a few seconds, admiring their designs. After the scanner assured him no one had followed him, he inserted the largest coin into a slot and watched as a holograph image of Katina focused in front of him. The quiet voice soothed him.

"Commander, I want you to prepare *Threads Way* for star drive. Access codes will follow this message. Stock the ship for a twelve-month trip. I want it ready within twenty hours. Get my people out of their cryogenic chambers. Notify me when you have done everything."

The Commander smiled. He took a final look at the empty street and then gave his lifter its flight coordinates. He watched as the street fell from sight. Within seconds he could see the entire town and then the entire county as his ship streaked for orbit.

*

Near Katina's mansion was a secluded area known only to her, her architect and his constructors, who had built the area to her specifications, and left the planet for other contracts. Katina stood at the edge of the restricted zone. The zone was preprogrammed to provide lethal resistance to any intruder, including Katina. She wore only combat boots, shorts, a sleeveless top, and a weapons utility belt strung around her narrow waist and over her right shoulder. Mobility was her advantage; years of high-level training had pared every spare ounce from her slight body.

Despite her age, Katina looked forward to the rough-and-tumble about to ensue. Her ears caught the tiny whir of the monitors scattered throughout the combat area. Her eyes noted every shadow, every flicker of light or shade. Her steps were quick, carefully planned thirty seconds in advance. Her hands were held close to her belt, one hand always holding a weapon, this time a recoilless handgun made of industrial ceramics and a muzzle velocity more than five thousand yards per second. At that velocity, a grain the size of a rice kernel would punch a hole the size of her head through another person.

Once in the combat zone, Katina did not reemerge for three hours. An observer would have heard the occasional rustle of leaves, the thud of a distant heavy body falling to the ground, the scattered flight of birds from different patches of shrubbery, the heat waves shimmering from puffs of smoke that rose and quickly dissipated in the northeast winds. Nothing else would have led the observer to realize the level of Katina's exercises, nothing to suggest within this small and apparently old woman resided the fiercest warrior Anphoria had ever seen.

*

Three days out from the double star system of Thiraden where she had spent years, the woman who looked forty slipped her small frame through the narrow tube until she reached her destination, the bridge. As she stood up to shake herself loose, Katina felt the star engines rev up. She made straight for her seat, where she activated the holograph screen. The light blinked in receipt of an incoming message. She had the ship record the message while she busied herself setting new coordinates for her small sleek ship. Its size made it faster than any battle cruiser in the galaxy, because the speed of tachyon-driven engines was decided by ships' mass.

She watched the galaxy's center slide into range as her ship rotated on its axis. For a few seconds her mind speculated on that center, wondering if life was possible anywhere near that great blast of radiation. One day she vowed she would find out, but not now. She had too much to do.

Katina thought of the years spent on Thiraden. She had built up contacts over her years as President, many of them unofficial and outlawed by the Anphorian Council. Once free from her role, and at a time when everyone thought her dead, Katina set in motion those people and forces she had spent ten years preparing. Only two people knew of her continued existence. Others had been eliminated quietly and quickly once they were no longer needed.

Thiraden was a stroke of genius on her part. While most people accepted her death, had any doubted her demise, they would not look for her on an Anphorian Home World.

And Katina would have still been in exile there had it not been for the cryptic message she received from a source just days ago. Its implications were staggering, and gave Katina pause for reflection when she first heard of it.

"There can be no doubt as to her identity," she told Sergeant Mathers, who waited on the other end of the holograph transmission. "I want you to watch her for me. And I want her alive."

Now, as she stared out at the place Repletians called the Mother of All Worlds, Katina felt new energy surge through her. She had waited for such an opportunity as Enid Blue Starbreaks offered. Nothing else would do now. "Old friend," she spoke aloud. "Old friend, you and I have so much to finish. So much to tell one another. So much to complete. Where you go, so go I. We're in this together. Nothing in this life will separate us."

Katina thought of her people on the other side of the bridge walls, men and women who would give their lives for her. Thousands of soldiers, hundreds of scientists and technicians. She had gathered and developed this army over the years she had spent in self-imposed isolation, using monies she had stolen from the Anphorian treasury, another of the crimes for which they would kill her, if they knew she was still alive. She would save them despite themselves. Only she knew the threat the Repletians posed.

Satisfied she was on course, Katina swiveled away from the holograph image of the galaxy. Her computer informed her no one had followed them from Thiraden. As far as the Home World was concerned, she was another eccentric widow who travelled from Home World to Home World, in a never-ending search for pleasure. The Anphorian Confederacy was famous for its pleasure worlds, and much of Thiraden was devoted to the more esoteric tastes of Anphoria's wealthiest citizens. Katina had no trouble keeping inconspicuous on such an active planet. Finding her house, a large villa on the outskirts of one of the planet's lesser cities, gave Katina both the privacy she needed and it was in keeping with countless other people who retired to Thiraden. But that was now behind her.

For the next hours Katina sat in her seat and watched the recordings she had made, over the years, of her deeds. Prominent among them was the woman who Katina now travelled to meet. Once Katina had wondered at Enid's abilities; had she been born Anphorian she would have made a first-rate assistant. The curse of her childhood made that impossible to contemplate. Katina watched Enid's final hours, the hours recorded on board *Stars End* and played back throughout the Anphorian Confederacy within days of the Fourth Fleet's disappearance into whatever hellhole the Black Ship had created.

The fact Enid's last moments had shown courage and decisiveness against overwhelming forces boded well for Enid in the long run, once the pain had diminished. Initially, of course, the loss of the Fleet was blamed on Enid, whose ancestry made her an easy target for the Admiralty and the Council.

Katina had the computer play back Enid's last two weeks on board *Stars End.* When the image of Talbot O'Halliran came on, Katina watched his every move, her eyes sparkling with curiosity and interest. She studied the tapes of his encounters with Enid, and listened to words recorded twenty years ago. Katina had the computer do a summary of Talbot's past twenty years to find where he might be now. Katina knew here was someone valuable she could use, once she had more information. Katina found herself staring at a tall athletic lieutenant. His blond hair was cut short in the military tradition; his long lean face was that of a hunter's, the eyes sharp and intelligent, the movements of his body quick and confident. The Navy had done well in shaping this young man, but he was no different from hundreds and thousands of other officers scattered throughout the Navy.

Katina finally turned off the recordings. On her orders the lights dimmed. The red glow from the Centre of the Galaxy filled the bridge with a soft light. It lit Katina's pale face, giving her eyes an eerie wolf-like sharpness.

CHAPTER 19

Standard Year 2491

In the first years of savagery, when the entire prison treated her as the enemy, a Repletian cast to the dregs of Anphorian society, Enid fought hard to survive. But she had no thoughts of seeking haven within protective custody. In the general population she knew her enemies.

Mykal Leven made his position clear at the start of her confinement. A week into her arrival on the planet and a day after the doctor had cleaned her, two guards escorted her to the Warden's office. She didn't know what to expect, except it would be bad. She thought she had prepared for the worst but she was wrong.

The guards led her into a room that looked like a medical treatment center. The guards ordered her to strip. She knew better than to resist. She could have fought them but to what avail? Even if she won where could she go? The prison was a giant castle set within the ruins of a long-departed civilization.

As Madame X she could remember little about the past. It formed a haze through which vague shapes and traces of memory shifted beyond the reach of anything but time. So she stripped and waited.

Mykal Leven came in and she gasped. He was naked and at a nod from him the guards seized her and strapped her into the strange metal table that dominated one corner of the room. They left.

The violation that followed was brutal and short. When he was finished, Mykal looked into her blue-green eyes and smiled.

"You think it's over but it's not. I can and will have you at any time of day or night. You're mine to do with as I see fit. You're only getting what you deserve. Do you understand me, Plete?"

His hissing of the word "Plete" was said with hatred. She gritted her teeth and nodded, trying not to show him how much she hurt inside. Mykal looked into her eyes until she looked away. Satisfied, he climbed off her body and left the room. Madame X winced as the steel door slammed behind him and then she waited for the guards to return.

The chill air was the first thing she felt when she woke up. That, and the ice-cold feeling of the table to which she had been bound for hours. Water made its way through the stone in a never-ending process of erosion, to collect in small pools and rivulets that ran down walls and along floors. The wind that seeped through the stone filled the castle with the strange echoes and murmurs of its wake.

Time became meaningless. When she finally had to relieve herself, she burned with the humiliation of emptying her bowels, the warmth of her waste growing cold with the following minutes. This was the ultimate degradation, the treatment of her body, for others' use. A commodity. She thought she cried then, or perhaps it was only her memories; perhaps she had sworn and raved at the silent walls, hearing her voice thrown back as echoes of her anger and futility.

When the guards finally did return, they showed no emotion as they unscrewed the bolts binding her wrists and ankles. They threw a plastic sheet around her body and then took her into another room, where they tore the sheet from her. They lifted her naked body to bind her hands over her head with a chain connected to a ceiling hook. She twisted in the air as the guards used hoses to wash the smell from her. She screamed as the force of the cold water tore at her skin, spinning her around, drawing blood from her restrained wrists.

Everything became a blur of pain and humiliation, the humiliation worse than anything she thought possible. When it was over, they threw her limp body onto the small cot in her room, Enid shivered for hours. She clutched the blankets for warmth, the mocking voices of the guards filling her with a hate that threatened to take over her soul.

Revenge in all its forms played through her mind---ingenious and terrible ways of disposing of everyone in this prison. Hate for the people who had robbed her of everything precious to her, including her name. Hate for the leering and contemptuous look on the doctor's face, a face that wounded more than it should have, stirring something in her she could not understand. Hate for the Anphorian prisoners who treated her as an outcast they reviled and treated as dirt.

Most of all, the hate ate at her because she remembered nothing. Her sense of emptiness stemmed from the blank wall that faced her whenever she tried to understand what was happening, tried to draw from her past to make sense of the present. As she lay there, for the first time Enid felt the loneliness she knew had been with her all her life.

When the shadow fell over her face, Enid didn't see it at first, so lost was she in her pain. The shadow was still, blocking the light from the single bulb overhead. For minutes it hovered, gradually forcing Enid to become aware of it. A specter hovered near the end of her bed, a pale silent woman whose hair hung in uncombed disarray over a thin narrow face. The great round silent eyes watched Enid's every motion, while loose fingers clutched sporadically at the hem of the tattered knee-length skirt. As Enid stirred, groaning from the pain, the figure almost bolted. Enid became still again, her weight resting on her elbows, watching this figure with a curiosity that grew as she forced her thoughts away from her search for memories.

"M'name is Mole."

Enid kept silent, wondering how this figure had got into her room.

"M'name is Mole."

Enid turned her head and saw the open door, then turned her head back to the specter. Without warning, the woman did a breathtaking series of dips and spins, dancing with complete abandon, before she stopped as quickly as she started. The great round eyes once more stared impassively at Enid.

"M'name is Mole."

"Hello. I don't know what my name is."

Mole giggled, a sharp series of sounds that verged on shrillness. Enid waited, afraid to make any sudden movements. Mole pointed a finger at her and giggled again.

"Your name is X."

"What?"

Mole pointed again. "Your name is X. That's what they call you."

Enid thought about this, and then shook her head. "X. No, that doesn't sound right."

Mole nodded her head vigorously. "Your name is X. Madame X. That's what the guards say. Madame X."

"Madame X."

"Yes, Madame X."

Enid swung her legs from the bed, placing her feet slowly and carefully onto the cold stone floor. She kept her blanket wrapped about her upper body. Mole stepped back, her eyes darting towards the door.

"Mole, how did you get in here? I thought the door was locked?"

Mole ignored the question, her great black eyes staring at Enid. Enid waited, and was about to ask Mole again, when Mole blurted out, "I's saw what they did to you. Saw what they did to you."

Enid thought about this revelation for a few seconds, but no matter how she looked at it, she couldn't remember seeing Mole anywhere before now.

"I don't understand. How did you see me? What did you see?"

"Not nice. No, not nice at all. I's saw what they did to you. To you. Mole cried and cried but wait. Must wait. Guards not see me. People not see me. I's a shadow to every peoples. Every peoples. My friend tells me to wait, so Mole waits. No good if peoples see me. No good for Mole at all."

Enid nodded, going along with Mole. "That's right. Peoples should not see you if you want to be Mole."

Mole made a horrible grimace, baring her teeth, and it took Enid time to realize Mole was smiling.

"Madame X knows. Knows why I can't says anything. I's a shadow and shadow's no good if ever peoples see me. Best not to be seen, like my friend says."

"Your friend? Who's your friend?"

Mole stopped smiling and a look of fright made her eyes rounder, if that were possible. She shook her head. "No," she said in a low whisper, as if afraid of being overheard. "No, Madame X needs not know friend. Needs not know. Friend will come when ready. I brings you some food from kitchen. Madame X needs strong, needs strong for later. Not to give in. No, not to gives in. Mole say bye now. Say bye but I's'll be back. Back later in night."

Enid watched as Mole bent down to retrieve what looked like a small dish holding some small portions of food. Mole placed the dish carefully on the end of the bed, out of Enid's reach. Enid looked at the dish and then to Mole's disappearing figure as she scampered out of the room. The door closed behind Mole, leaving Enid again alone, but this time full of questions.

*

Over the following weeks and years Mole became a constant presence, hovering forever on the edge of Enid's world, ready to dash in to help Enid in any way she could. There were times Mole was absent, when she was drawn inexorably to the tunnels beneath the castle. No one followed her, not after the Nordells' run-in with something that had changed Evelyn to a sullen and remote prisoner who shunned even her followers.

The doctor fuelled the fear. It became known he could not guess what had caused the injuries to the gang members and to Enid, whom everyone knew as Madame X. Lacking the equipment to do more than a cursory examination, all he knew was they had been injured or killed by lethal blows. Evelyn wasn't speaking and although some surviving gang members said Madame X had caused some of the deaths, everyone scoffed.

Mykal Leven sometimes dragged Enid from her room in the middle of the night. His use of her body never went beyond treating her as a receptacle for his lust and hate, from which she learned to detach her mind, soul and feelings. She suspected that, had her injuries down in the corridors not been so disfiguring, he would have made more use of her. As it was, he sometimes had her brought to his office, where she was made to wash down the walls and clean the office while he went about his business. He showed his contempt for her by treating her as if she wasn't there. She hated this, but it was infinitely preferable to those other times when he forced her to watch, chained and secluded, while he raped or punished other inmates, sometimes crippling them, sometimes leaving them shells of their former selves after hours of brutal torture.

Enid lay awake at nights, listening as the darkness enveloped her room. There was never silence, although the halls and other rooms were still. The drip of water into dark pools and the occasional sounds of the wind moving through the halls formed a background to the restless sounds of sleeping inmates who fought their private demons. Guards' footsteps sometimes dully thudded on stone as they paced their endless rounds through the halls. Occasional crude laughter or low conversation filtered through the levels of the prison during the night, different sounds from the day.

Enid became used to the sounds, but she couldn't expunge the sounds of weeping and screaming from those endless hours of watching the Warden have his way with the female inmates. The sight of blood and tears colored her memories and there were times she wished she had died before being sent here. Nothing made sense. She didn't know why she was here except her past damned her and it had so much to do with being Repletian.

Enid thought of the monster that might even now lurk in the dark corridors beneath her, prowling through darkness she could only imagine. When she regained her senses and most of her health following the fighting in the corridors, she found her memories of that fight a blank as deep as her past. She came to believe the rumors circulating about the creature which had attacked Enid and demolished half the Nordells. The stories fit the facts as well as anything else she could imagine.

The most memorable moment of this period was Evelyn's suicide a year after escaping the tunnels.

Standard Year 2492

Sweat. Cold against her skin. Sweat that came from pure fear. She crawled deeper under her single blanket and shivered, not daring to peek out for fear of what she might see. Midnight of another long night. There were stirrings that she didn't recognize, the sound of rustling clothes with their soft swishing. When she had first heard those sounds months ago, she had turned from her cot to stare at the open hallway. No one was in sight and she shrugged, thinking it was an inmate moving about in a nearby cell.

A week later, after lunch, she heard a soft hum in the middle of reading a book in her room, a throbbing vibration that persisted until it broke through her concentration. She placed her book onto the table and got up. The sound came from beyond her doorway. Quickly darting towards it, she found the hallway empty. Confused. she stood still for several seconds. As she turned back into her room an icy draft of air swept over her. She was sure she was being watched. She looked back but the hallway was still empty, the shadows of the afternoon creeping in to darken the natural light of the day.

Evelyn's nerves broke then, the memories of the corridor and the sounds of approach forced a small scream from her as she ran for her cot.

The following weeks and months became an endless series of terrified moments. Sometimes she would be walking by herself when she felt the ice creep along her bare skin, heard the almost inaudible whispers of movement behind her. Evelyn recalled the tales her mother had told her in the middle of the night, tales that thrilled and terrified her. But this was different. For one, she didn't have her mother's warm presence to shield her.

This morning there were no thoughts of leisure reading. The pulsing reverberation pierced through her. And this time she could almost make out what it was. It sounded like voices, like someone calling from a great distance. The memories of her mother's eyes wide with shock as she felt the knife slide into her; the feel of her strength as she grabbed the hand that held the knife; the strange noises that came from her open mouth as her power diminished and slid towards the floor. None of her gang heard anything, although some of them were within a few feet of where she and her mother clutched one another. But now Evelyn knew what her mother had been saying as she slid to the floor. The sounds were the same as the sounds that came from beyond the doorway, the sounds only she could hear, the sounds of something trying to speak her name.

Evelyn screamed but no voice emerged from her lips. And then her eyes widened as darkness, deeper than the darkness of the hallway, crept past the edge of her doorway. Her eyes hurt as she stared into the blackness and she whimpered. Was it her voice she heard as consciousness faded, as a voice pleaded, "Mommy, I didn't mean it! Oh, God, I didn't mean it! I didn't mean it!"

Drawn by the racket, the guards hurried to the room, where the body still swung in long gentle arcs from a rope tied to the single rafter twelve feet above. A small crowd of other prisoners gathered by the doorway but there was nothing anyone could do. The guards spent ten minutes figuring out a way to get high enough to untie the rope from its rafter. Two guards held onto the large body but when the rope slipped free the body fell, its stiff form taking the guards with it. The guards scrambled to their feet and covered the body with the blanket from the cot.

Mykal Leven arrived to take in the scene with a single glance. He ordered the guards to clear the hallway of prisoners. As they followed his orders, Mykal studied the halls. He could see nothing out of the ordinary, although it was a bit dark for this time of day. He blinked and the lights seemed to increase. Mykal didn't like mysteries. He walked into Evelyn's room. A large cot sat in one corner. At the far end, a small night lamp, like the ones most inmates used for reading, illuminated a study table.

A chest of drawers sat perched in another corner of the room. Mykal studied the items scattered carelessly about the top of the drawers. He saw nothing that was remarkable. He stood in the middle of the room, from where he looked up at the distant ceiling. It had to be twelve feet overhead. Mykal turned to a waiting guard.

"Who was the first one here?"

"Me and Edgar were on patrol."

"What did you see?"

The guard shrugged. "Nothing much to say. We heard some sounds like screaming or wailing and we came to look. We found Evelyn hanging there. Wasn't much else we could do but call for help."

Mykal pointed to the rafter. "That's a long way up. Did Evelyn use a chair or ladder to tie the rope to that beam there?"

The guard scratched his head in thought. He looked up and then at the Warden, a look of puzzlement crossing his face.

"Can't rightly say I saw anything like that. No. No, I'm certain there was nothing under Evelyn when we got here."

"Then how in hell did she hang herself?"

The guard backed up a step. "I can't rightly say, sir."

After Mykal dismissed the guards he sat on the edge of the cot and looked vacantly at the opposite wall, his mind racing as he tried to puzzle through Evelyn's 'suicide.' He knew Evelyn. Who could take her without one hell of a fight? There was no evidence of a fight. Further, rigor mortis had already set in. This would have been impossible in such a short time. He was missing something, and he knew it. Somehow it tied in with the incident a year ago down in the Basement corridors. It had to, but he didn't know in what way.

*

The doctor reentered the room. He wore a surgical mask over most of his face and gloves on both hands. He glanced at the still body on the slab of metal. Its head was twisted at an odd angle, leaving no doubt as to the cause of death. Still, the doctor had to complete a cursory autopsy to make Evelyn's cause of death official.

He stripped the blanket from the body and threw the bright sheet onto the floor. Let others clean up after him. Perhaps that bitch Enid Blue Starbreaks, who wasn't much good for anything else since her crippling injuries. He scanned the body for other signs of injury.

The doctor glanced at his watch and marked down the time on his record sheet, another crude necessity on a planet without the most basic quantum processor. He placed the chart onto a nearby table and then leaned over and studied Evelyn's features. Two things struck him at once. The first was the grimace of her final moments of pain. Evelyn's lips were pulled back, baring her teeth. Her bloated tongue protruded from between her teeth. Her eyes were wide with the look of horror, a curious reflex action to the pain, he thought.

The second was the unmistakable smell of rot that almost made the doctor gag. He leaned back, took a deep breath, and grabbed the chart again. Evelyn had died only hours ago, not long enough for the terrible suspicions that cropped up in the doctor's mind. He tried to move an arm but it refused to move, by that confirming the impossibly advanced stage of rigor mortis. The doctor placed his hands around the throat and dug into the flesh, feeling for the broken vertebrae in her neck. Again, he almost screamed as his fingers, despite the slight pressure he used, broke through the skin and sank into a queasy softness. The smell became overwhelming. The doctor released his grip and ran for the basin, where he threw up until he had nothing left to throw up.

By the time Mykal Leven had answered the doctor's urgent call another thirty minutes had passed. Mykal hated the interruption and wondered what caused the panic in the doctor's voice. He signaled for his guards into the autopsy room. As the door slid open an unspeakable odor poured from the room. The doctor raced forward with a set of masks, and led them into the room.

Mykal thought himself a strong man but the black and grey gelatinous mass quivered as he watched, tested him to the limits. The doctor let him look for a few seconds before he grabbed the warden's right arm, exited the room and ripped off their masks.

"What in fuck's name is that?" Mykal asked as soon as his mask was in his hand.

"That is, or was, Evelyn's body."

"But she's been dead for only a few hours. That thing in there looks like it's been dead a month."

The doctor nodded. "You're not far off. I figure three to four weeks of advanced decomposition. Somehow, the process of decay has been accelerated."

"Is that possible?"

The doctor shook his head. "Not even our best labs produce anything like that."

"Are you saying this isn't happening?"

"No. No, what I'm saying is somehow Evelyn's body is decaying at something like one hundred times the normal rate. I'm only guessing at this, but there's nothing else that can explain what's happening to her."

"That's impossible! What in hell is happening to my prison? Fuck."

The doctor just shook his head, his eyes clouded with fear, "I don't know... I really... don't. Know."

CHAPTER 20

Standard Year 2498

Pain filtered through her sleep, bringing with it the unwelcome presence of darkness she abhorred. It was an endless pain. A pain that lay deeper than she wanted to search, yet there it was, an undeniable presence that drew her like a magnet.

She was cold and wet; a cold bone-deep with the chill of stone and nightfall, with the shuffle of her feet and the sight of one eye. Endless patterns of water dripping and wind drafts stirred from the unseen depths. Endless aches brought on by the drag of one foot and the hollow dull pain in her eyeless socket.

Enid thought she had known cruelty in her memories, memories that returned in the lonely cell hours with the slowness of the dripping water. Memories as distant as her past, reaching back through corridors she visited in her dreams, scratching and clawing to evade the open doors of invitation, forced into memories of other rooms, other feelings.

She thought she could handle any feelings after the years alone in these Castle rooms, spurned, hated, vilified by the prison population, following the deaths of so many, in her first years here.

But this fear, anger and isolation was nothing compared to the utter loneliness she felt knowing that she would never again feel the gentle face of the man she had so loved. She knew now what he had felt in a prison of her creation, and now she woke up, in the middle of these dreams of him, with her bed sheets soaked with sweat. There was nothing she could have said to him then, and there was nothing she could ever say to him again. She would have born anything, even this physical nightmare, for a chance to tell him. All of it.

But as silent tears slipped down her raw face, she saw the smiles of two mothers, each now gone forever. The gruff strength of her fathers, each gone forever. Memories of warm familiarity, of clutching a small doll in one hand. The excitement of halls fragrant with newness made her dizzy with happiness.

And with them, the harshness of men taking everything from her. The sight of red and black everywhere in her past. The clear sharp lines of dead trees and windless clouds. The sense of oppressive heat and chilling cold. The need to say and not say what she felt. The vague image of a woman she had never met filled with a hatred that blanketed her world and haunted her with its grief-laden relentless mission.

These memories of her past began on a day when Mole scurried ahead of Enid, her figure flitting in and out of the lights scattered down the length of the corridor. Enid shuffled after her in the best way she could. Her single eye was strained by the constant darkness, but she didn't fall as often as once she had. Her growing knowledge of the Basement kept Mole in sight for most of the time, although Mole sometimes stopped to wait for her to catch up.

Enid found the path difficult, but the quiet and darkness more than made up for the scrambling. She marveled the first few times Mole had brought her to these tunnels. In her cryptic way, Mole over those first few weeks told Enid of the guards' fear and reluctance to patrol the entrances to the tunnels. In part, it was an instinctive fear of the darkness beyond the lights. In part, people had sought refuge in these tunnels never to return. The tunnels were so extensive, Mole had found only a few remains of these first escapees. Their decayed or skeletal remains were always a shock to see.

Finally, Enid's early conflict with Evelyn had created a host of stories about the thing that lived in the tunnels and fed off human flesh. At first, some guards had scoffed at this idea. But when the first body was discovered a month later, its limbs scattered about as though by a great force, even the most skeptical guards began to pay credence to the stories. After hearing the guards' grisly discovery, with her curiosity piqued, Mole took off in search of the body. She told Enid, "Wasn't much more'n a skel'ton. I's figure she died a sittin', leaning 'gainst the wall. Later she fell over and broke up under the wind."

At first Enid had followed Mole with some reluctance, fearing the same things the guards did, for the memories of her first days here were clouded. She thought of Evelyn's fate. No one hid the horror of Evelyn's suicide and the bizarre tales surrounding her death. What if she met whatever had done in Evelyn down here in the tunnels? What happened to Evelyn made Enid, then and now known as Madame X, hated and feared. The warden treated her as his plaything. He relished in her crippling physical injuries and suffering.

But no one dared to confront her. She had the sign of the witch on her, so the remnants of the Nordells insisted. No one disputed them, and no one wanted to incur the curse that had played out on Evelyn. The fact the warden was the only one who dared to mistreat Madame X said a lot for his scorn of their superstitions, for so he considered their beliefs. And although nothing untoward happened to him, there were those who said Evelyn's fate was waiting to catch him up; it was only a matter of time. Mole's voice broke through Enid's reveries.

"This way's. Hurry, we's almost there."

"I'm coming."

Enid looked up to see Mole turn a corner into another corridor. They had been walking for over three hours, and Enid knew she was in strange territory. She was glad for the lights she and Mole had smuggled from the storerooms. Their steady beams prevented them from falling onto the hard surface of the floor beneath Enid's feet. Mole kept her light more as a gesture of goodwill towards Enid. Often, when she was well ahead, Mole turned off her light. Her figure was then visible only when she hurried past an overhead light. Enid wondered how the original Nordells built the system of lights powered by water sources far beneath their feet. A race of tunnel builders should not need such illumination. And certainly it was doubtful they would require light that matched the spectral range of the human eye. Another mystery of this planet.

Enid found herself staring down an unlit corridor. She was about to yell out to Mole, when a pale glow emerged from the right wall of the corridor some three hundred yards from where she stood.

Enid felt the cold bite into her injured left knee joint and knew these were the first signs of an incipient arthritis. Her time down in these cold wet tunnels took their toll on her injuries. A sharp stab of pain throbbed in her absent left eye at this thought. As she moved down the corridor towards the light, Enid decided she would have to tell Mole in the best way she could that it might soon be impossible for her to keep coming down here.

Enid entered a small cave-like room. Mole sat in the middle of the room, a pile of blankets of assorted sizes, shapes and colors surrounded them. Along the walls, canned goods were geometrically stacked; goods clearly gathered over many years. As Enid entered the room, Mole emptied the last of several items from her loose-fitting robes onto a nearby table. She smiled up at Enid.

"I's take some things every times I comes down here."

She cleared a spot against an empty section of the wall for Enid to sit. Enid eased her weight down, careful not to jar her bad leg. Mole's large eyes followed her. When Enid sat with her weight against the wall, Mole grinned widely. Her large uneven teeth made a strange contrast to the darkness that hovered everywhere, despite the small glow cast by the light Mole had hung from a hook in the ceiling above them. Enid felt the pressure of the darkness weigh upon her, but she felt no fear.

Mole twisted the top from a small can of food and passed the can to Enid. She held the side of the can while Mole pressed a heat rod to the bottom of the can, warming it in a matter of seconds. She then gave Enid a spoon and wrenched open a can for herself. After she warmed her own food and began eating, she said between mouthfuls,

"This is Mole's home. No one comes here to bother Mole or makes her cry."

Enid nodded. "Mole's home is nice."

"Thinks so?" Mole grinned her cat grin. "Mole makes the home herself. Takes Mole long time to do."

Enid finished her food faster than she thought possible, feeling the warmth seep back into her body. The ache in her knee subsided. Enid marveled at the sense of peace she felt in the darkness that gradually covered her good eye.

When she awoke, Mole was sleeping beside her, curled against her body. How long Enid had been asleep she didn't know. She raised her head, careful not to wake Mole, and stared down at the small, emaciated woman. Mole's blankets had fallen away in her sleep, revealing the sparse threads that barely held her clothes together. A hole in her robe exposed her pale white skin and the prominence of her rib cage as it rose and fell.

Enid watched Mole for what seemed an eternity. Only when something stirred gently in a corner of the room did she break her gaze. A shadow had shifted among a pile of blankets; perhaps because of the overhead light, although Enid hadn't seen the light swing on its cord.

It took Enid the better part of two minutes to move away from Mole so as not to wake her. Once Enid was clear, Mole stirred in her sleep and rolled over to fill the spot Enid had left. Mole curled into the warmth she felt there and again became still.

Enid dug into the pile of blankets. She felt a small sphere roll into her hands. Surprised, she pulled back, her hands keeping their grip on the object. She raised the ball to eye level and stared into the black sphere. Its blackness was so deep it was the perfect reflection of its surroundings. Its surface felt like glass or metal, but Enid had the odd feeling as she held it that its weight subtly changed. Something about it puzzled her, reminding her of something, but the memory was elusive.

She was struggling with this thought when she felt Mole's right hand on her shoulder. She hadn't heard her wake up, but there she was, looking over her shoulder from behind, staring into the black sphere with an intensity Enid had not seen in her before. The two women held their poses until Mole moved around Enid to take the sphere from Enid's hands. Enid didn't protest.

"Is Mole's. Found it long times ago."

"What is it?"

"Mole's don't know what it is. But it's friend to Mole. Helps her when she needs help."

"That's your friend?" Enid tried not to sound skeptical, but she had to know what the sphere was.

Mole nodded, her teeth bared in a grin. "Is Mole's friend."

"I saw it move just now."

Repeating Enid's earlier gesture, Mole lifted the sphere in both hands until it was at eye level between the two of them. She extended her hands towards Enid, and both women gasped as the sphere floated away from Mole's hands, drifting with the small cool draft of air that sprang from nowhere. Mole was the first to hear the music, and began swaying to it before Enid knew what she was doing. Then Enid, too, heard the low sounds of music. The black sphere began to dissolve in mid-air, and then its shape became amorphous, its darkness increasing until it burned into Enid's single good eye.

Colors. Great swaths of violet to green painted themselves through the room, swooping into her until she felt she could hold no more, and then the faces breathed into her mind, overtaking all conscious thought, The memories hit her so forcefully she fell onto the blankets, holding her head in her hands to contain the pain before it overwhelmed her.

Enid found herself staring into the face of Mole inches away. Another small teardrop fell onto Enid's cheek. Enid smiled as she remembered, remembered everything, and then her body was shaken by the torment and joy of her memories. Mole cradled Enid's head in her lap. She stroked her hair and rocked her head back in forth until her sobs subsided.

"I want to tell you a story," Enid whispered up at the weeping woman above her. "I want to tell you the story of a wonderful man I once knew and loved without knowing it."

Mole listened as Enid spoke of Daegan. Her story was rushed and broken, but Mole sensed the man behind Enid's words. By the time the story ended on the bridge of some magical ship called *Stars End*, Enid had managed to sit up to face Mole, who watched Enid's face come alive with emotion. Gone from Enid's face was the dejection by which Mole had known her for so long, reliving the day she had first cradled Enid in her lap, when Enid's repeated question drew her attention.

"Do you know who I am, Mole?"

"Your name is Madame X, is all."

Enid shook her head. "All my life I've felt I don't know who I am. I don't even know what I want. For the longest time I thought I wanted to be what others wanted me to be, to prove I could be as good as any Anphorian."

"Your name is Madame X, is all your name."

Enid wondered if she should tell Mole what her real name was. But the look of indifference on Mole's face made Enid hesitate; of what use was her name to anyone but herself now? The name would mean nothing to Mole and might pose a danger to Mole. Enid decided to remain silent.

Mole sat on her blankets again, absentmindedly played with one of its edges, not seeing it or anything around her. Still facing her, Enid waited, sensing Mole wanted to say something.

When it came, Mole's voice shook with sadness. "I's once loved a man I's killed. Is why I's here."

"Why did you kill him?"

"He's changed. Once was kind but then he's beat me always. Hurt me bad twice. The last time was the worst. Hits me over the head with an iron. They's say they has to operate to saves me. My head hurt for a long time after that."

Mole leaned towards Enid and parted her own hair, revealing a long hidden scar that ran half the length of her scalp under the hairline.

"That was the last time. Next time he tries it, I stabs him. They's found me sitting there by his body. I feels nothing for the man I's killed, but he's rich so they's put me here, like their laws say they can."

Mole returned to her original position and smiled at Enid. "Sometimes is best not to know all things. You's tell me story of man you love, but you didn't tells him what you felt."

She reached into the blankets folded around her body to pull out the black sphere. It was now inert, merely a dark, dull orb, devoid of its earlier intensity. She tossed it into the pile of blankets Enid had pulled it from earlier. It landed and rolled out of sight into the folds.

"Is time to go back."

CHAPTER 21

Standard Year 2498

Leon stared at the red jewel in his hand. He rotated it so its surface caught the light, sending radiant ripples against the walls. If he stared at it long enough, he saw a dark shadow in the heart of the jewel, a quick fleeting shadow where there had been none before. The shadow reminded him of the woman who had given it to him so many years ago, almost twenty now.

Leon clung to the belief that if Enid was dead, he would know it. This belief had sustained him after the Fourth Fleet's disappearance and the quick rise of Repletia in the following years. That, and Red Dawn's unquestioning love and support.

There had been so much, and so little, to report to the Repletian Council of Elders upon his return. In the Council Chambers, he spoke of everything he knew, and much he guessed at. In the end, the facts gave his words credence. The Fourth Fleet's fate had hurt the Anphorian Confederacy. Repletian warriors who ventured into the border worlds once claimed by Anphoria met with little resistance, and not even the Elders Council could restrain the following rush into the vacuum caused by the demoralized Anphorian retreat.

Fifty border worlds, including Baradine's World, were swept into the Repletian fold before the first wave subsided. Now, twenty years after the so-called Battle at Korel's World, as Repletian forces gathered for another assault on Anphorian space, Anphoria sued for peace, leading to calls for the Summit.

Leon carefully placed the jewel onto the desk beside his writing pad. Golden light poured into the room, casting a dance of luminescence onto his pad. His notes filled half the page. The faint blue ink from the paper's other side traced dim shadows through it, without disfiguring the characters.

"What are you thinking, dear?"

Red Dawn's voice drew him from his reveries. He swiveled in his chair, hearing the creak as his weight shifted around. Red Dawn, a smile on her face, stood in the doorway.

Leon pointed to the red jewel as his wife walked to the desk, where she lifted the jewel from its case. She turned it in her hand.

"She's alive. You know that, don't you?"

Leon nodded: "Yes. Yes, I know that. She needs me, but I don't know how to help her."

Red Dawn moved closer: "When it's time, you'll know in your heart. Everything will happen when it's meant."

Leon laughed. "Careful, dear. You sound an awful lot like Theresa Kuang Hsia."

"I might if I knew her works, which I don't."

"Of course."

Red Dawn cupped the sparkling jewel in the palms of her hands. She held it up to the light and stared for a long time into its depths. Leon watched her, curious to see what she would do or say. After a time Red Dawn lowered the jewel. In that moment, Leon saw the years and the trials, and he stood to hug her. Red Dawn leaned into him, turning her face upwards to look into his eyes.

"I think it's time."

"And what of you? This might take some time."

Red Dawn smiled. "My path is with you. We'll look for her and we'll find her, wherever she might be."

"It'll be long and hard. Perhaps we won't like what we find."

Red Dawn shook her head. "And the price of not looking? She's kin, and she needs her family. Perhaps when we find her, we can perform the Rapac Naming Ceremony."

*

The Senior Elder pushed back the holograph screen and leaned back in her chair. She felt the frustration flow from this seemingly calm man. She couldn't dissuade him but she had to try.

"You're certain, Leon, this is the path you must follow?"

Leon nodded, saying nothing. The Senior Elder studied him for a moment before she indicated the room with a sweep of her right arm.

"And what of this? There's much to do and we cannot afford to lose you. When it comes to dealing with the Anphorians, there's nobody better. You know them; how heavily they depend upon their technology. We need you at the Summit coming up in a month."

"Madame Elder, there's nothing I can do. My heart knows its own path. I cannot choose but to follow. My niece needs me and . . . " Leon hesitated, a frown on his face. ". . . and I need her. She's family, the only blood family I have. I can't leave her, wherever she is."

The Senior Elder gave a curt order. A holograph image of Enid Blue Starbreaks replaced the columns of writing.

"That's it, Leon. You yourself witnessed the suicidal flight of *Stars End*. And it was you who stayed behind to check Korel's World for survivors. Your search came up empty, didn't it?"

"Yes, Madame Elder, it did."

"Then what makes you so certain your niece survived? There's no proof anyone survived."

"I have no proof."

The Senior Elder waited, for she had never seen Leon in such an emotional state. Disconcerting, yet illuminating.

"But I feel in my heart she's alive. She isn't dead."

"All feelings aside, Leon, what can you possibly do? Where in the universe would you even start your search?"

Leon never hesitated. "Korel's World. Korel's World, that's where I'll begin."

"You were there already."

"Madame Elder, you know the history of Korel's World. I have to go there. That's where the trail ended and that's where it begins."

"Why now, Leon? It's been close to twenty years since Korel's World. Why now?"

Leon reached into his tunic and pulled out his gold necklace from around his neck. At the end of the chain hung a brilliant jewel. The Senior Elder stared at the sparkling surface.

"This tells me," Leon said, swinging the necklace in his hand. "Feel it."

The Senior Elder gently touched the jewel. Ice ran down her arm. She quickly pulled her hand back. "What is that?"

"It was given to me by Enid, in our meeting on *Stars End*."

"And why didn't you tell her then who you were? You'd have saved lives."

"It doesn't work that way, Madame Elder. Enid wasn't ready. It would have shamed her before her people, those whom she thought she defended. Moreover, she wasn't ready to believe me, whatever I said."

"And so hundreds of millions died for your reluctance?"

"My conscience is clear. It wasn't me the Fourth Fleet wanted, but the Black Ship. They thought they had the final weapon, a weapon they could use on Repletia. My niece was a pawn in that game. And then there was their President. How the Black Ship knew of her plans to destroy the Repletian Home Worlds, I don't know. But I thank the Spirits of the Universe for knowing, or you and I wouldn't be talking now."

The Senior Elder straightened in her chair. "Perhaps, Leon. Perhaps everything you say is true. Perhaps the Black Ship, in its way, saved us. Perhaps Enid Blue Starbreaks is still alive. Perhaps she's everything you say she is. But if she's alive, where can she be but in Anphorian territory?"

"I have no choice, Madame Elder. Red Dawn and I will take the risks."

"Ah, so Red Dawn is in this with you?" The Senior Elder sighed. "Then there's nothing I can do."

"In this matter, no, there's nothing you can do. I follow the path to the Rapac Ceremonies. For that, Enid Blue Starbreaks is needed."

"Then I have one request to ask of you in the name of the Rapac Ceremonies." The Senior Elder saw Leon tense and she smiled, glad she still had an effect on him.

"What do you want?"

"It's at once simple and difficult. I ask you, Leon Three Starbreaks, on behalf of Enid Blue Starbreaks and Red Dawn, to be careful."

Leon looked surprised, then began to laugh. The Senior Elder extended both palms forward and open to the sky.

"When I give it to you, I give myself. You have my consent. I extend blessings on behalf of all Repletians. I respect your wishes and will keep your trust sacred, no matter the cost."

That night Leon recounted his meeting to Red Dawn. She listened intently, her eyes studying his face as he spoke. When he finished, there was silence. Red Dawn felt the shadows in the room tug at her. Leon felt her withdrawal.

A tunnel extended into the room, a dark tunnel that extended to infinity. As Red Dawn watched him, there was movement, the sound of a small child's weeping. It grew until it filled the bedroom with sorrow. Another silence followed. In the tunnel's distance, something stirred, a blackness deeper than its own dark surroundings. It moved towards Red Dawn. Her eyes hurt, but Red Dawn forced herself to keep watching, fearing more than anything she might lose contact if she let go.

As the shadow approached, the sound of running feet grew louder, a twisted rhythm to their pattern. A clammy feeling crept into the room, the fear of something inhuman that made her tremble. As she was about to cry out, the sounds stopped, fading as bars slammed the corridor shut.

The vision receded. Red Dawn found herself again facing the bedroom wall. Leon waited until she spoke of it, and ended by saying, "This means something. It has to do with our niece."

"The shadows. Your words remind me of the Black Ship."

"And the bars?"

"You mentioned fear and bars and blackness. Maybe there are connections between them."

"There must be. There has to be. But what is it?"

Leon shook his head. "I don't know. I don't know. The small girl crying has me puzzled."

"Think what we know of Enid's childhood. Your brother Samuels and his wife were killed on the Pegasus. Enid must have been five or six at the time. She'd remember."

"Of course! She'd remember. A part of her would always remember."

*

It took a week to get their individual affairs in order and another week to supply the ship and run safety checks on its various systems. Finally, they were ready to leave.

Deep in space, three days out and over two weeks after Leon's meeting with the Senior Elder, their ship again twisted on its axis in preparation for the star drive to kick in. The maneuver took five minutes to complete, spinning it away from the Mother of All Worlds. Red Dawn had never grown used to the view of the galaxy's center. So much energy poured from its heart no human could survive near it, and yet Red Dawn always felt peace flow into her heart whenever she saw the rainbow-hued object.

"Are you ready?"

Red Dawn nodded and settled into her chair, strapping herself in. Standing during a jump was a sport for younger people. She couldn't risk being hurt when Leon needed her. Leon waited until she was safely fastened. Then he pressed the palm of his right hand to the ship console. The imprint of his hand set off a chain of pre-recorded commands, far faster than the mind could follow and then the jump.

Red Dawn felt the sudden drop and twist in her gut, as though she was aboard a lifter in free fall. She had no time to be sick before the ship spun on its axis and settled into the drive.

They had an hour before their ship reached Korel's World. Red Dawn unbuckled her restraints. Leon stared out of the view screen. Blue lines streaked from the center of the screen to its edge, as they chased towards Korel's World on the wave probabilities of their tachyon drive.

"She's out there somewhere, isn't she?"

Leon nodded. "Did you doubt it?"

"No, but then I didn't know until now she's alive, either." Red Dawn looked towards the streaking lights. "So much can go wrong. So many people involved. It scares me."

"I know what you mean. I've tried to forget Korel's World for the last twenty years. It doesn't work. We've explored a tenth of the galaxy and what we've found makes me wonder about our future. There are dead worlds out there that once had races as intelligent as we think we are. And it didn't help them at all."

"Is Korel's World that frightening?"

"Not Korel's World. What happened there happened only to me. But the Black Ship was there. What was it doing there, of all planets? I've replayed a thousand times those last few hours and nothing makes sense. And yet that Ship wasn't evil in any way I could tell."

Red Dawn sat beside her husband. Leon looked at her, his forehead creased with worry. "Don't you see?" he said, "don't you see, I've thought about this in every way I could over the past twenty years.

I can't find it in my heart to think of that ship as evil. But lives are gone. Surely not all of them deserved what happened to them."

Red Dawn felt her husband's excitement. He quickly rushed through his sentences, as though to suspend any interruption.

"I have to believe my niece survived somehow, and if she did, then perhaps the others did. I have to believe in their survival or my niece's life is for nothing."

"But dear, you can't treat human lives like equations. It doesn't work that way. Your niece is alive and we'll find her. And I hope the others are alive. But the only thing we can do is to find her and bring her home."

"That's it. Don't you see? What does home mean to her? The people she served turned on her, and her birth people are nowhere in her life and haven't been since she was a child aboard the Pegasus. Her family must be dead to her."

"Have you wondered why she gave you the red jewel. It's such an unusual gift to give, such a personal gift in such a formal setting. Didn't you say her last words to you were that there were other ways for the two of you?"

"Yes. Yes, she did say that." Leon looked again at the red jewel hanging around his neck and smiled.

They spent the rest of the hour running safety checks. They had to be certain of their ship. Leon said as they dropped from their jump: "Korel's World is the only way to Enid. There isn't any other way."

With that, Korel's World filled the view screen. Red Dawn stared at the green and blue patches moving from right to left across the screen, and remembered Leon's story of his exile on the planet.

"What should we expect to find down there?"

"I don't know," Leon replied. "Probably nothing. Let's see what clues turn up."

Red Dawn unbuckled her safety catches and stood up. The sudden movement made her faint. She grabbed the edge of her chair. Leon rushed over to help her settle back into it. "Be careful, honey. Star jumping is hard on the body."

"I'll be all right. Give me a glass of water and I'll be fine."

Leon went into the small alcove next to their seats. He took a glass from an overhead rack and poured the liquid into the crystal container. He was turning towards Red Dawn when the floor beneath him shook. He tried to grab the counter that separated him from his wife, but failed, and tumbled to the floor. The glass of water shattered, a small piece of glass leaving a bright red streak of blood on Leon's left cheek. Leon felt the warm blood trail down his face. "Damn, what was that?"

Leon pulled himself up to stare through the screen towards a planet turning black with nightfall. After a second he saw the shadow of darkness race across Korel's World faster than the speed of rotation. The darkness deepened until it soaked up light from the galaxy.

"Leon," Red Dawn whispered. "Is this what happened to you when you first came here?"

"No, nothing like this. I've never seen anything like this. It's like watching an eclipse, except we can still see the sun."

"Shouldn't we do something? Anything? Maybe we should get out of here."

"Honey, we came here to find answers. Maybe we're getting one. Let's wait to see what happens next."

They watched Korel's World and both saw the golden star light move from right to left and sweep the darkness away. Red Dawn was the first to notice the difference in the planet below them.

"Where's the land? Dear, there's no land down there."

And then the blue world made sense to Leon. Gone were the mountain ridges and green plateaus. A sheet of water, marked here and there by the odd cloud system, covered the world. No trace of land was visible.

"What does it mean?" Red Dawn asked, her eyes large with fear.

"I don't know."

The couple gazed down at the planet in bewilderment, their faces lit by the pale blue reflection of the world of water. Red Dawn was staring at the eye of a hurricane near the equator when the computer's modulated voice said a ship was nearby.

Ten minutes later a giant shadow covered their ship. *Stars End* hovered over them, dwarfing their three-hundred-foot-long hull. Gaping holes sloped into the flagship's depths. *Stars End* was a bullet sixteen miles long and five miles in diameter.

Probes confirmed the flagship was empty of life, its great engines inactive. A single red lightning stroke, the stroke of the Anphorian Admiralty, ran the length of the ship's outer hull. Leon knew the ship by sight, having watched its fiery path towards Korel's World twenty years ago. The flagship had become lost in the general conflagration that overwhelmed the entire Fourth Fleet.

"I must get into that ship."

Red Dawn shook her head. "It's too dangerous, dear. There's so much we don't know about their ships. And this one's the greatest of them all. It may be full of traps and security measures we know nothing about."

"I have to believe it's here for a reason."

"Yes. But what if it's here to trap or kill you?"

"Look at it." Leon pointed at the scarred hull. "Whatever it was, it's dead now. Broken by the Black Ship, probably beyond repair."

Red Dawn studied Leon's face. She felt the undercurrent of fear.

"I'm going with you. If there's trouble on that ship, I want to be with you."

As their ship approached *Stars End*, a light from inside a gaping hole in the flagship's outer hull glowed. Leon felt the slight jolt as an atmosphere restraining field enveloped their ship. The flagship started its automatic human environment controls, almost a certain sign no one was alive. Leon's ship matched velocity with the rotating outer shell, aligning with one of the bay doors.

Their ship took several minutes to slip into the illuminated bay, where it settled onto an open part of the deck hanger. The wreckage of fighters littered the deck. By this time the flagship had created a breathable atmosphere.

Once their ship settled onto the deck, Leon and Red Dawn ventured onto the cargo bay of deck nine. The floor sloped upwards vertically from the axis of the ship's hull. The rotation created a centrifugal force equivalent to one gee, earth weight. Directly above where they stood, another shell rotated some six hundred feet above their heads. The entire ship was composed of a graduated series of shells within shells, each twenty feet thick, and separated from the other shells by five hundred to a thousand feet. The outer case of each shell was encased in a near-perfect vacuum less than one yard in depth, allowing the shell to spin almost effortlessly. While the shell above their heads was the equivalent of the ceiling for Red Dawn and Leon, the other side of that ceiling would be the floor of an inner shell. Each shell rotated to the equivalent of one gee. Because of this, shells closer to the axis of the ship spun faster.

If the outer double-layered shell was designated as the ninth shell, then every odd-numbered shell was devoted to military, administrative and communication centers. Every even-numbered shell was devoted to habitats, living quarters and recreation areas. The result was over eleven hundred square miles of inhabitable space, over six hundred of it devoted to living space. A million people had lived within the flagship, with half of them marines or soldiers. Despite this knowledge, the rotating shells were so huge a feeling of claustrophobia continually distracted the two Repletians throughout their stay on the flagship.

From where the two humans stood within the walled hanger, they saw a hundred single-person fighters. Some were still hooked to the outer shell, their wings tucked in. Others leaned precariously on broken struts. Finally, others were in smaller pieces, as though a great hand had broken and scattered them around the deck. Not one ship was intact.

In the deck's low lights, Red Dawn shrank from the immensity that greeted her. She clung to Leon as he stared at the wreckage. Though he could see no visible movement, he took no chances and unslung his rifle, a brute rapid-fire weapon that was a direct cousin to the weapon he had taken to Korel's World so long ago. Two hundred yards from them, Leon saw a set of metal doors that stood half open on a set of rails. The hanger entrance, some thirty feet high and forty feet wide, opened into a darkened tunnel. "That's where we're going" he excitedly motioned.

With that, the two made their way towards the door. Their footsteps echoed against the distant walls. The only other sound they heard was their breathing. Leon looked up, watching the door for any signs of movement. The closer they got, the more wary Leon became. When they reached the edge of the five-foot thick door, lights sprang to life on the other side, revealing a seemingly endless tunnel. Leon was about to move forward but Red Dawn held him back.

"Where are you going?" she asked.

"I want to make sure the door is safe. No use both of us getting hurt if that thing slides shut."

Red Dawn laughed nervously. "I've told you before, if we're going to get into trouble, we'll do it together. If this door slides shut with you on the other side, where does that leave me?"

"I see your point. Well, then, shall we do this together?"

Leon placed a foot onto the rails on which the hanger doors

slid. He put his full weight onto the rail, but nothing happened. With that, the two hurried across the doorway and raced down the corridor.

Almost an hour later Leon looked behind him and for the first time noticed the bay door was out of sight. Red Dawn also looked and exclaimed, "This hallway is curved!"

Leon nodded and added, "Not only that, but see how those doors further ahead have their tops missing?"

"So we're also moving up?"

"Exactly. We landed in a bay at this ship's midpoint. Since this ship's sixteen miles long, I'd say we're less than two miles from the bridge."

"But what if we're on the wrong deck? There's a dozen shells that run the length of this ship. Surely they can't all lead to the command center?"

"No, but if any corridors did lead directly to the center, doesn't it make sense it would be those running from the landing bays themselves?"

Red Dawn contemplated this as she looked around. She shivered at the sight of the endless series of doors lining the corridor. "What scares me is there aren't any people. If the Black Ship killed them, where are their bodies?"

"I've been wondering that myself. Maybe we'll find answers when we reach the bridge." Even to himself, Leon sounded skeptical.

They resumed walking, settling into a rhythm that carried them steadily forward, although the pace made Leon's right leg ache from an old injury. He felt relief sweep over him when he saw the corridor end at a door like the one they had crossed over in the cargo bay.

In five minutes the door loomed over them. Leon searched for control panels, but saw none. Red Dawn searched the walls with her hands but she soon returned to Leon's side. "There's nothing that seems to open this door."

"I can't believe we've come all this way to be stopped by something as simple as a door."

"I agree. If there are no panels to run this thing, then it's probably voice-activated."

Leon groaned. "How will we ever find the command words to open it?"

Red Dawn shook her head. "I've been thinking, dear. If this ship was shut down for twenty years, it's unlikely the codes they last used would've remained in the computer's memories."

"That still leaves us back at the beginning. What codes would the computer use as backup?"

Red Dawn smiled. "When I owned that information store, I saw and heard a lot. The Anphorians had backups for everything. Their key codes were simple commands that would place the computers under the command of any survivors."

"All right then, oh, wise one. How many simple codes can you think of?"

"Let's try something only humans would think of in this situation. How about something like 'Home Worlds'?"

"That might work. Let's try it."

Red Dawn stepped back and said in a loud voice, "Home Worlds."

After a few seconds she was about to repeat her words, a reverberant voice filled the hallway.

"You have been identified as human. Please initiate a universal password."

Red Dawn looked to Leon for direction. He shrugged. "It's your choice."

"Computer, the password is 'Enid Blue Starbreaks.'"

Leon laughed and hugged his wife as the computer said, "Your command codes have been installed on all systems. Repairs are being initiated. Flagship command will be transferred to you pending retinal, DNA and name identification. Please identify yourselves. Awaiting further command. Please identify yourselves."

The bridge was smaller than either Red Dawn or Leon had thought possible. A quick survey of the room showed it would comfortably fit ten people. There were six clearly identified work stations, each with its console seat. They formed a half-circle below a raised platform, which supported a swivel chair with the red Admiralty stripe along each of its arm-rests. Leon reached up towards the central chair and gently stroked the soft cloth material. He felt the trace of the person who had sat there during those critical moments twenty years ago.

There was a power there, an energy Leon couldn't explain, but he knew it came from his niece, and so he stared at the command seat. He had been so close to her for that moment in the meeting hall, and here was where she was most at home, if he could call where she lived home. He gingerly eased himself into the contoured chair, which molded around his body.

"How does it feel, dear?"

"Strange. Strange, wonderful and scary. There's a coldness here."

"That would be her military training."

"Yes. Yes, that and more. It's as though something wrapped around her, a darkness from her past. Terrible things happened to her."

Red Dawn sat at a console below Leon. She touched a button. Lights sprang into view, showing a life-size holograph image of herself ten feet in front of the admiral's chair. The image rotated a complete circle and stopped with its face towards them. The ship's computer began its low monologue.

"Your image has been scanned into the command codes of the pilot's chair. How shall I address you?"

Red Dawn realized the computer was waiting for her answer.

"Call me by my name, Red Dawn."

"Done. Do you wish others to have access to your command codes?"

"I wish to have my husband's codes accompany mine."

"Please identify your husband's name."

"He's the one seated on the admiral's chair."

The lights on Leon's seat came to life and he was looking at a holograph image of himself placed besides Red Dawn's still image.

"Please identify yourself for the record."

"My name is Leon Three Starbreaks."

"Do you concur you are co-commander of the flag ship systems?"

"I concur."

"Done. Are there others you wish to have access to all systems?"

Again Red Dawn surprised Leon, who hesitated, only to hear his wife ask, "Do you have records of Enid Blue Starbreaks?"

The holograph images of Red Dawn and Leon faded, to be replaced by a live shot of Enid in her command seat, the one Leon presently occupied. Her dark frame formed a stark contrast to the paler officers who scurried about beneath her as they went about their duties. She was staring directly at the invisible camera hidden in the walls of the bridge. She was oblivious to the camera, having grown used to its presence.

"Is this the person you refer to?"

"Yes, she's the one. Do you have her records on file?" Red Dawn asked.

"Yes."

"She's the only other human who has complete access to ship codes and systems. Please verify this."

"It is recorded, Red Dawn. Ship's controls are now transferred to the bridge and are under your commands. Awaiting further orders."

Leon brought up an image of *Stars End* and studied its

condition. As indicated, the robots aboard the flagship were busy on every deck, placing things back into order and repairing whatever they could.

"Where are the people?" Leon asked the question both he and Red Dawn had wondered since they had boarded the flagship.

"Current status of *Stars End* is as follows. Four thousand two hundred seventy-six Class Five fighter ships are being repaired on decks nine, seven and three. They will be fully operational in five days. Repairs to the outer hull will take three days. There is sufficient food in the storage units to sustain the two humans for their natural lifetimes. Nineteen years, seven months, and fifteen days have elapsed since the flagship's computers went off-line with the disappearance of the ship's complement of humans. The last humans aboard included an estimated ninety thousand civilian support staff, twenty thousand medical staff, and six hundred thirty-five thousand Naval officers and soldiers."

"Scans show the remainder of the Fourth Fleet is not close to Korel's World. All decks are fully functional."

Leon waited for further information, but the images used to update the two humans stopped. Leon turned to his wife, who knew machines better than he ever would. She nodded and took the lead.

"Computer, show us the Admiral's quarters."

A red outline of the bridge rotated ninety degrees. As Leon watched, a green outline formed, shaping a long corridor leading to a set of rooms on the port side of the bridge.

"Do we have access to the Admiral's quarters?"

"Access is available; you may enter at any time."

Once inside Enid's former quarters, Leon stared at the series of pictures strewn in one corner of the large entrance room. The pictures were rendered in pastels or line drawings. Leon knelt to sort through them, studying each set of stark renditions. Trees and dark colors dominated every picture. The pictures were incomplete, although Leon was unsure whether this was intended. Red Dawn, who had toured the other rooms, returned to kneel beside Leon. He passed her the drawings. She saw the scrawled initials, 'e.b.s.' in the lower left corner of the top picture.

"They're hers. I didn't know she could draw."

"Neither did I," Leon said. "She was trying to say something. You can feel it in her pictures."

Red Dawn stared at the scrawled lines and colored textures of each painting. "She's good at this."

Leon looked up from a painting he was studying. "Do you mean these paintings?"

"Yes. Your niece shows originality in these pictures. I'm not sure how she was as an admiral, but she was a good painter. I've never seen anything better."

Leon placed the picture he held onto the small coffee table. "I need to know more about her. Let's find out if the computer has any records on file."

Leon keyed in his commands, and the computer responded in moments. "There are records of everything Starbreaks did until humans disappeared from this ship."

Leon and Red Dawn watched a summary of the Fourth Fleet's mission to Korel's World. The hour-long recording was stunning. Both Repletians watched as Enid went from crisis to crisis, never getting enough time to plan or prepare for the next. The savage personal attack on her in these quarters made Leon stare at the corner of the room where the bed squatted. Unanswered questions remained, and Red Dawn took the initiative. "Are those the last records you have of Enid Blue Starbreaks?"

"There is a nineteen-year gap in my records. Approximately thirty-five minutes before contact with you, my records were activated. Two sets of files were downloaded into the memory banks. One of them originates from a modified signal from Korel's World. It contains a summary of the twelve years Enid Blue Starbreaks spent on Korel's World. The other is a general Repletian broadcast message for Leon Three Starbreaks on coded channels. It contains a brief file on Sandina, a prison planet in the third sector in Anphorian territory.

The two Repletians watched Enid Blue Starbreaks carried on a stretcher. In a world filled with rain, Anphorian guards took Enid through a dark stone door. The sight chilled the two Repletians more than anything they had seen before.

CHAPTER 22

Standard Year 2498

Long afterwards, Enid wondered whether she could have stopped what happened. She spent endless nights mulling over every gesture, word, movement, every clue.

They dragged Enid from the room she called the medical hell. Mykal had been perfunctory in his abuse of her, his mind if not his body seemingly on other matters. He came quickly and left the room without the customary insults. Enid put on her single tattered robe. The guards left her by her open cell door. Not long after, Mole's familiar figure appeared in the doorway. The two walked to the mess hall. Mole was quiet, sensing the hurt, which Enid always suffered after Mykal's abuse of her. They made slow progress through the various groups of prisoners, Mole always looking nervously at everyone they passed.

Enid was silent during their meal, but regained energy as they made their way to the Basement, where the two were permanently assigned for clean-up duty. Not even the guards volunteered to patrol the dark rooms and hallways beneath the prison. For the most part, everyone felt relief someone volunteered for clean-up duties others avoided. Although other inmates suspected the motives of the two women, no one expressed these suspicions, for fear attention would lead to their being assigned to the Basement to replace Mole and Madame X.

Enid kept her identity from everyone but Mole, who listened to Enid's tales of other worlds and other people with a fascination born of ignorance and wonder; ignorance of the names and planets Enid knew and spoke of that showed her familiarity with those things; and wonder at Enid's stories that dealt with matters beyond anything Mole ever hoped to get near.

The two women had made their way so often to the corridors beneath the prison they knew every object, no longer paying much attention to them. Neither saw the cameras that silently swung on pivots following them; recording their every movement and word until they disappeared into the tunnels.

Mykal Leven watched them on his holograph, his face impassive as he heard Mole laugh at something Madame X said before they ducked into the tunnel entrance. After they disappeared, Mykal stared at the empty room for several minutes before he had the computer play back the last few minutes of Madame X and Mole's conversations with one another. The two women were talking of someone named Daegan and just before they left the screen, Madame X spoke of her doubts of ever seeing Daegan again. Mole had turned at the tunnel entrance and laughed, chiding Madame X for giving up before she had even started to search for Daegan.

Mykal turned the holograph off and swore. All this time, the half-blind crippled woman he thought he controlled knew of and did things without his knowledge or consent. No wonder the guards held him in low esteem. Madame X and Mole flaunted their independence despite his deliberate crippling of Madame X in an effort to keep her dependent.

The more Mykal thought about it, the more furious he became. Damn protocol. He couldn't let this continue. He had to do something to reassert his authority. They had to know he saw everything, whether they were guards or inmates. No fucking Plete was going to challenge him without dire consequences.

But Mykal had to be careful. What did he want? Once he knew that, everything else would follow. A goal. Yes, he had to set a goal. And for the next ten minutes, Mykal scribbled rough notes into his diary, finishing the last sentence before cutting work for the day.

In the end, Mykal knew he couldn't physically destroy Madame X more than he had already. He wasn't a fool. He had seen the guards, the use of a Naval ship to bring in the single prisoner. Someone important wanted her to disappear. But they hadn't killed her, which meant sooner or later someone would come to retrieve her. They had also ordered Madame X's memory erased but they'd done a clumsy job.

Perhaps by now, Madame X had recovered enough to remember her previous life as the legendary admiral of the Fourth Fleet. Each time Mykal had her he relished holding such power over her. Mykal's abuse of her was something he enjoyed more than that of the other prisoners, although within the prison population there were women physically far more attractive than the human wreck he had made of Enid.

Mykal rarely thought of Mole, but no one else had bothered much with her, either. However, watching the two women over the past weeks showed Mykal a way to Enid, a way to further damage her. In her weakened state, Mykal wasn't certain how much farther he could push her physically. But he would enjoy the next few hours. The two women would be in their tunnels for five or six hours, he surmised, enough time for him to bring everything to a successful conclusion. The two women were complacent in their isolation, and would emerge from the same tunnel entrance they had disappeared into. Of that, Mykal was certain.

*

Deep within the tunnels, Enid forgot her worries. Mole had misplaced the black sphere several days ago. She finally went into the tunnels the day before, without telling Enid of her plans, there to spend endless hours wandering the dark tunnels. Enid had no choice but to wait. Before Mole reemerged from the tunnels, Enid submitted to the Warden's brutality and contempt one more time.

Mole was radiant when she first saw Enid, but even in her joy she noticed Enid's silent rage. Mole knew Enid needed to get away, and led the acquiescent cripple into the tunnels. Enid began to speak as they neared the tunnel entrance. The dark steps and rooms leading to the corridor entrances looked the same, but Mole felt they were followed. Twice she backtracked to surprise whoever it might be, but always the rooms were empty. The only sounds besides their quiet treads was the endless dripping of water throughout the damp halls.

Enid noticed Mole's caution. After Mole's last cautious loop back to a point they had passed five minutes before, Enid asked her what she was doing.

"Mole feels not safe. Mole feels peoples is watching her."

Enid listened, but heard only the wind softly echo along the twisted corridors.

"I don't hear anything."

Mole cocked her head to one side, closing her eyes in concentration. Enid waited until Mole opened her eyes and grinned at her.

"Madame X's right. Is nothings there. "

"No, don't feel foolish," Enid protested. "It's always better being safe. There's no one following us. But one day there might be."

The two took a final glance the way they had come and then they hurried towards the tunnel entrances. Mole was glad to see her friend smile. After the two hour trip to their safe room in the tunnels she turned and spoke in breathless haste.

"Mole talks with friend. Everything is okay, friend says."

Enid was startled. "What friend? "

"My friend says you's'll be okay. "

"What friend are you talking about?"

"Mole's friend from before. I comes to this room and there's friend. Says you's'll be okay. Peoples come from far away, from places you tell me about."

Enid sat on the familiar blankets and stared at Mole, not understanding what her friend was saying. She tried again.

"Do you mean the friend you met down here is back?"

"Yes. Madame X's right. First friend says Madame X'll be okay."

"But where is your friend now?"

Mole grinned and reached into the blankets beneath her. She pulled out the black sphere Enid had seen for the first time so long ago. She lifted it to eye level and Enid saw the tears streak down Mole's dirty face.

"What's wrong? What did I say?"

Mole wiped her face with her left hand, her right hand holding up the sphere.

"Friend says it must go away."

"Go away? "

"Mole gives friend to Madame X. Friend says it goes with Madame X."

Enid pulled Mole to her, hugging her for warmth and comfort, feeling Mole's bone-thin shoulders shake with silent grief at the loss of a friend. It was Mole who pulled away at last. As she did so, she extended the black sphere to Enid and waited in silence, the black sphere shaking in her unsteady hand. Enid took the black sphere into her own shaking hands. Its weight pushed her hands towards the floor. Mole watched the black sphere descend. She forced herself to look up at Enid, who began to sing a song she could not remember having known before. It was a song from her childhood. Memories came from somewhere deep inside her, tearing away the last curtains of forgetfulness. As she sang, Enid spun the black sphere in her hands and then tucked it out of sight in her long tattered robe.

Mole nodded her approval. "Friend must stay with Madame X."

The two huddled again, and this time they didn't separate until an hour had passed in silent grief. Both felt the passing of something unnameable. Both felt something was happening that was larger than either could know or control.

Their way back towards the surface, towards the Basement,

was made together. The black tunnels reminded Enid of other tunnels. She had travelled such tunnels in her childhood, when she held a small and tattered doll under her arms as she ran within a ship called Pegasus, both of her parents in pursuit.

Enid struggled uphill, her left leg aching at the knee, which had never properly set. The cold hurt, creating a sharp pain that streaked up her leg each time she put weight on it. She hissed with each step, trying not to alarm Mole, but unable to hold the pain in. Sweat ran down her face, clouding what sight she had. The black sphere hidden in her robe gained weight as time passed, until Enid felt like throwing it away. Mole watched her, keeping close to her side.

Once, when Enid stumbled and braced herself against the stone wall Mole hurried to her and reached in to take the sphere. Enid looked up at Mole's cry of pain in time to see Mole's left hand cupping her other hand against her thin chest.

"Mole's hurt. Friends hurts Mole. Only trying to help."

With that desperate cry Mole ran several yards ahead and looked back, the pain and anguish showing on her face. Enid felt Mole's hurt and confusion, but there was nothing she could do about it. The black sphere was beyond her control.

Mole paused, and then came back to help Enid. The two struggled upwards for another hour, until both saw the dim lights that marked the end of the tunnel and the entry into the prison basement. Enid felt the sphere become warm beneath her robe. The warmth gave her added strength to finish the journey upwards, and to sing the song she had sung to Mole when she had first seen the black sphere held in Mole's hands. Mole recognized the song. She beamed with joy. She flitted ahead and then back to Enid in the last yards to the tunnel entrance. Several times she spun; the ragged edges of her skirt and top flaring out, reminding Enid of a bird protecting its young. For some unknown reason Enid began to silently weep. Twenty yards from the entrance, Mole was at Enid's side, taking Enid's weight onto her shoulder for the last time. They were still holding onto one another when they reemerged from the tunnels into lights that flared in front of them, blinding them both.

*

Mykal heard the distant footfalls and singing. He waited with his twenty guards, their weapons drawn. Banks of lights were placed a dozen yards from the tunnel entrance. They were set up to be triggered by any motion near the tunnel entrance. Mykal had the basement lights extinguished. The two women had become so used to the tunnels they seldom needed lights down here.

Earlier, Mykal had trouble trying to get his guards to come down. They spoke of monsters and other nonsense. Mykal called upon his trusted Sergeant Mathers, who rounded up the thugs he depended on the most. Mykal made it clear to them Mole was the target. Mathers grinned at the challenge.

And so they listened now to the approaching footsteps as they had waited for the past two hours. Not even Mathers could intimidate his men into going into the tunnels, which was just as well, Mykal thought, for he had more control in the wider basement spaces.

As the two women came into view, Mykal signalled and the lights sprang on. Both women looked like trapped animals, their eyes blind and staring at the lights. Mathers gave another signal and a guard yelled out to the two women, "Freeze. Don't move or we'll shoot."

Enid gave a cry and moved forward. Mole tried to hold her back but Enid stumbled and fell, feeling the blast of weapons overhead as several weapons opened up, striking Mole as she stooped towards Enid. There was a single agonizing scream of pain and then Enid felt Mole's weight land on her. She fell under the dead weight and her head struck the stone floor. The last thing Enid heard was a voice screaming out, "No!"

Mykal surveyed the scene and grunted with satisfaction. He might not be able to kill Enid, but no one would blame him for capturing two escaped prisoners. That's what the reports would say. Several guards carried Enid's unconscious body from the basement up to higher floors. Others stared at Mole's twisted and charred body, which had been hit by at least eight direct shots.

A guard hurried up to Mykal and saluted. Mykal looked at the guard with some distaste, wondering whether his men cared about personal hygiene. His nose wrinkled at the odours.

"Sir, you have an urgent message waiting for you. There's a ship that's two days out. It's asking for permission to enter orbit over us. Its commander wants to speak to you."

"What's the rush? It's probably a supply ship that's gone off-route."

The guard licked his lips, his eyes darting towards the corner of the room. "No, sir. *Threads Way* looks like a battle ship. And its commander doesn't look friendly."

Mykal cursed. Of all the times to be interrupted by some tinpot captain. He wondered what the urgency could be.

"Help the others to remove that body," he ordered the messenger, pointing to the charred remains of Mole. "I'll be back to figure what to do with Madame X. Meanwhile, guard this place. Make sure no harm comes to her until I decide how to deal with her."

Mykal left the basement chamber. Sergeant Mathers watched the Warden's retreating back and he smiled, licking his lips with pleasure. The next few days promised to be interesting. And he had no doubts about who would win the upcoming battle of wits. Madame K was much too smart for the likes of Mykal Leven.

CHAPTER 23

Standard Year 2498

"Fucking Repletians!"

Mykal Leven turned his bulky frame to confront the group of guards standing next to the row of cells. They stopped talking when they saw his expression.

"Who said that?" Mykal demanded.

The guards remained silent, none of them moving. Mykal glared at them for a minute, but they refused to look at him. Disgusted, Mykal snapped at them, "Listen, you idiots! I don't care what you think of Repletians in your off-hours, but when you're on duty, you leave your feelings behind. Do I make myself clear?"

The guards snapped to attention and yelled with one voice, "Aye, sir!"

"The next time I hear profanity I'll double shift the lot of you. Do I make myself clear?"

"Aye, sir!"

"Then get out of my sight. Back to your duties."

Mykal watched the group of guards split up, each man returning to his post. When the last of them had gone, Mykal continued on his way to his meeting. If he didn't hurry, he'd be late.

He shivered against the drafts as he walked down the long corridor to his office. His hard shoes rang against the stone floor in a quick steady rhythm. His two personal guards kept pace five steps behind him, their shadows flickering against the uneven walls of black stone. Mykal turned a corner and avoided the dark patch where water had gathered in a pool. He hardly noticed this distraction, for his mind was on the person who waited for him on the other side of the door ahead of him.

Mykal had never met the woman, except through the two tapes she had sent him; the first after arrangements were made which set him up for life, and the second twenty years later, when he was asked about a certain prisoner. Each time she hid her identity behind a robe, whose hood hid her face. Mykal knew her voice was altered because of its raspy nature, and he often wondered what she looked like in the flesh. Now, as he neared his office, he wondered if his wish was a wise one after all. Overwhelmed with a sense of foreboding, he forced himself to keep his composure.

A curt gesture from him warned his guards to wait outside the door. He straightened his tunic, pulled back his shoulders, took a deep breath, and exhaled as he told the door to open.

Mykal was surprised to see how small the robed figure was whose back was turned to him. Was his imagination playing tricks on him? At the same time, he was irked because the woman had taken the dominant position in the room, behind his desk. He moved forward as she turned to face him.

"Warden, I'm glad you could find time in your busy schedule to see me."

Mykal shrugged as he tried to see the expressions on her hooded face. "It was the least I could do, after all you've done for me."

The woman grunted. "Just so, warden. I won't tarry. I understand you've had a prisoner in your custody for some time now."

Mykal shivered again, wondering why she stressed her s's. He activated a holograph image and heard a small gasp from the woman as she stared at the image of the woman called Madame X.

"You are certain this is the prisoner you and I talked of ten days ago?"

"Yes, ma'am, she's the one. She was found wandering on a standard survey of Korel's World seven years ago. She's been in our custody ever since. Her memory's gone."

"Yes," the cowled woman said in a slow musing voice. "Yes, I was not told of her until two weeks ago. So much has happened since then."

"In her present condition, what possible use can she be to you? She's a broken shell."

The cowled woman stared at him, her dark eyes gauging his face. "You see only the shell; A shell can be filled with what I need. This time I won't fail."

The woman threw back her hood, startling Mykal. Her face frightened him, for it belied the age in her black eyes: surely only surgery could make her look like she did. Her pupils were narrow wolf-eye slits. Her dark skin was marred by the red gash of her mouth, which was slightly open when she wasn't speaking. Her pale tongue sometimes darted out to lick her upper lips. The red nail polish on her hands was the same shade as her lipstick, if that wasn't the color of her natural skin. Mykal shuddered. The old-young woman smiled.

"The Repletians are of no concern to you, are they, warden?"

Mykal shook his head as she reached out, eerily greeting him with her long narrow nails. All the while her eyes studied him. Mykal would have traded anything not to be in her thrall, but he was years too late.

"Do you wish to see the prisoner?"

The old woman shook her head. " I know everything I need to know. I'll contact you when I've made my decisions."

Mykal blurted out his next words and immediately knew it was a mistake: "You seem familiar to me. Have I ever met you before?"

The old woman stared at him for a long moment and, when she spoke, her voice emphasized every word.

"Warden, your value to me lies in your ignorance. Do I make myself clear?"

Mykal nodded, trying to ignore the single drop of sweat tracing its path down his spine. Despite her fragile appearance, Mykal knew she wielded more power than he could dream of. He apologized. But who did she reminded him of? She stood before him for some seconds after his apology. He knew she saw the flicker of recognition in his eyes.

"Warden, you're dismissed. You can have your office back in two hours. Make sure the woman is not damaged further."

Mykal left his office as quickly as he could.

*

Katina Patriloney watched Mykal beat a hasty retreat. After his departure, she called back the image of the woman. She studied the shattered face with clinical detachment, noting its every feature with a studied familiarity. Although the face was battered almost beyond recognition, there was nothing physical that could not be repaired. But the dull sheen of the eyes exposed a beaten woman. Satisfied, she terminated Enid's image. Only ten days to the Summit remained. By now Leon should have received her message. She had less than a week to arrange matters on Sandina and escape before his arrival. She summoned another coded image. The uniformed man who faced her owed his life to her. Yet, as always, Katina had not asked the naval officer for anything until she needed him, which was now. He bowed to her, disguising his fear behind his military pose. He had waited to be called upon for years. He knew that, once he performed her request, his debts to her would be wiped out. That was the way she worked in her extensive network of operatives.

"Yes, ma'am, how might I help you?"

"We have a problem. The warden recognized me. I trust you know what to do?"

"I'll take care of the matter. Is there anything else?"

"Yes, I want you to replace him with this man." Katina called up the file picture of Talbot O'Halliran. The naval officer stared at the holograph. He studied the serial number and other vital statistics of the young lieutenant. Katina smiled and said, "I believe the ship the lieutenant is on is in Sector Five as we speak. It seems they were rerouted for an emergency call that proved to be a false alarm."

Katina ended the conversation. She sank into the austere brown chair. Its padding was worn and faded, but she scarcely noticed this. She rested her hands on the desk's hard surface and idly looked at the red polish on her fingernails. This was the one habit she had refused to give up after her genetic surgery. The surgery had reduced three inches from her height and darkened her skin. It could cost her her life, for the Covenant of Humanity forbade genetic surgery for military purposes, since the horrors of the Genetic Wars two thousand years ago. She was humored by the fact her skin now so closely resembled those of the people she opposed. Such delicious irony!

In a few moments, Katina dimmed the room lights to sit in the darkness. She called up a holograph image of the woman jailed so many floors beneath. There was not much to see. Katina smiled at the ease with which her plans were falling into place. As she left the office, she wondered about the new warden being sent. She swore this time she would be successful whatever it took.

*

They had cremated Mole's body yesterday. They told Enid, but these days it was hard for her to maintain information. When she could grasp it, the pain was immense. Everyone she had known was taken away from her. Cursed by her ancestry she had been used and spat on, every bone and muscle in her tired body felt the seven years in this prison.

Mole had been the one light, the one friend, who had kept Enid from taking her life.

What kept her going, she didn't know. She didn't eat and sipped only enough water to keep herself barely alive. She waited with a dull expectation for Mykal Leven to mistreat her and gloat over what he had done.

It was not long in coming. They stripped her and dragged her from her cell. She was taken to the medical room, where she was hung by her wrists a foot off the floor. Mykal had come in and over the next ten minutes struck her repeatedly, the final one a blow to the mouth with a steel rod. Enid fainted from the pain. The sharp agony of broken teeth woke her up hours later. She found herself back in her cell, where she hid in her blankets and wept. Sometimes she thought she heard the quick rustle of Mole's tattered robes brushing against the stone floor. But each time, she waited in vain for Mole's bright smiling face to peer around the corner. All she could hear was the steady dripping of the water and the muted conversations of other women in nearby cells. Mole's words flooded her memories, tearing down barriers and building others. What did it matter who she was? She was nothing; she was Madame X, a name as good as any. She was Madame X, known only to herself and to Mole, her dear friend, whose words she clung to with all her being.

And always she kept the black sphere close to her body. It was her connection to Mole, the one thing they had both treasured and shared. The sphere had once filled both of her hands. Now it was smaller, a sphere that could be hidden within her fist.

She stared at the sphere for endless hours, sometimes twirling it in her hand, but mostly just staring at its blackness.

*

Mykal Leven reached Enid's cell. He had spent the better part of two days trying to sort out matters. His family was not of much use, and he ignored his wife's bleating about not letting her help him. Nothing came of his efforts except the realization he was outranked in the old woman's presence. He stared at the woman known as Madame X, who stared down at the stone floor, her one good eye a filmy blue-green, her thin face a mask of fatigue.

"I'm told I should take care of you from now on. Good care of you. I don't know why a fucking Plete is so important, and I don't care. That doesn't mean I can't have you killed in an escape attempt."

The woman never flinched but Mykal hadn't expected her to. He had taken good care of that in the several years she had been in his custody. He had a feeling he was going to lose her in the next few days and thought briefly of making sure no one else could ever make use of her. But the image of the old woman he had spoken to shook him from his state of mind. Mykal was a survivor who knew when he was outmatched. This prisoner's death, he knew, would make him worthless to the old woman. Until then, he would make sure he didn't incur her wrath. But this woman who had so much power over him? Was she the President of Anphoria? But Katina Patriloney died in her aborted attempt to destroy the Home Worlds of Repletia...Perhaps they were related.

"Guards, bring the prisoner with me."

When it came, it came so quickly Mykal never knew it was coming. He was turning towards the door when he felt something cold slide between his ribs. The sharp stabbing pain was quickly replaced by a flood of warmth that covered his hands. He instinctively clutched at his ribs. Then a feeling of cold swept over him. His legs gave way as he lost strength. He felt hands hold him as he fell. He looked up but his vision clouded. Then he felt the darkness, a great blackness, sweep his sight and feelings away.

The men looked at the twitching figure on the floor until its movements stopped. The one holding the dead warden felt for a pulse and shook his head when another guard asked, "Is he still alive?" They turned when they heard a small voice speak.

"Did you kill him? Did you kill him?"

"Fucking Plete! I almost forgot about her. Take her away and get her cleaned up. The new warden is on the way in. He won't like it if he finds out about this mess."

Guards scurried about, several taking the limp form that used to be Mykal Leven to a waiting lifter. They dumped the body in the back and hurried back to find others mopping the floor to wipe away the copious traces of heart's-blood. They grabbed Madame X and led her away to the infirmary, where they stripped her and let the sterilizer clean her. All the while, they tried hard to hide their nervousness, but each of them knew what worried them. Once the new warden saw Madame X, what would he do about the years of brutality they had waged against her?

*

The young Anphorian lieutenant strode down the halls. He felt the chill that pervaded everything, from the dull grey walls to the sparkling white floors of the mess hall. Privately, he wondered again why the navy would dispatch him to take over an ancient and decrepit prison that was about to be torn down.

The more he saw of the prison the less he liked it. What in Creation did they have in mind in sending him here to a backwards part of the Anphorian Confederacy? It couldn't be anything in his recent record of performance. Although only thirty-nine, he had seen a lifetime of battle along the shrinking frontiers of Anphoria. He had hoped to attend the Summit in ten days' time, but that was now out of reach. He had more pressing matters on hand, such as how to assert his control over this prison and its unruly set of guards.

"And so what shall we call you, sir?"

Talbot shrugged. In the five minutes he had spent in the offices of the previous warden, the less he liked the leering attitudes of the guards, barely able to hide their apparent contempt for his youth. Well, Talbot had a way of settling this. The navy had been clear in its orders; establish discipline at any cost as quickly as possible, and await further orders due forty hours after landfall.

"Call me Warden. I trust that's what you called my predecessor?"

"Well, Warden, we don't get many like you on this planet."

"Indeed, so I've gathered. Tell me, who's your best guard?"

"Sir?"

"Your best guard. You know, the one who's called upon the most when trouble needs settling."

"That would be Sergeant Mathers."

"Send for him and get me his file. Dismissed."

"Aye, sir."

As the guards left, they didn't bother to lower their voices. "Poor chap. He's still green. Mathers will make meal tripe of him."

Mathers' files contained no surprises. A brief and inglorious two years of service in the navy. A dishonourable discharge and a beef against the navy ever since. At six feet eleven inches, Mathers was a large man. He was the unofficial leader of the guards. Not even the previous warden had seen fit to challenge him on that. But Talbot couldn't allow two leaders in this prison; he had more to do than to watch his back.

"Sergeant Mathers reporting for duty, sir."

Mathers didn't bother to be polite. He walked into the office, stooping slightly to avoid banging his head on the top of the door frame. Talbot stood up and took his measure of the man. Big, beefy, with arms the size of Talbot's thighs and a belly which had seen a great deal of ale, or what passed for ale on this planet. Talbot noticed the wrinkled uniform, the missing belt, the scuffed shoes, the worn cuffs. His gaze lingered on each part of Mathers' uniform, knowing Mathers would not suffer his open contempt willingly. And he was right.

"Well, warden, have you come to stare at my outfit? Small pleasure it'll give you."

"Indeed, 'small' is the operative word. I haven't seen such slovenly dress since my junior days at the Academy."

Mathers smiled his wicked smile, his two missing upper front teeth making that smile lop-sided. "If you'll give me leave, sir, that couldn't have been long ago, if you get my drift."

Talbot smiled and moved around the desk to within two feet of Mathers, well within range of those massive arms.

"They tell me you're the man who gets things done here. Are they right?"

"If you mean, sir, I get my way, well, then, I guess they're right."

"I've read your military record. Not much there."

"There's enough there to show I know how weak you officers are."

"Indeed. That sounds like a wager to me. Can you back up your talk?"

Mathers smiled and looked at the trim lighter form of the lieutenant. "Against the likes of you, sir, I expect I'd not have much trouble. The last warden knew that, God bless him."

"I suspect the Creator had nothing to do with the makings of the likes of you, Sergeant."

"Maybe not. Would you like to test yourself? It's been some time since I worked up a sweat against an officer. I might like the fun you'd give."

"A challenge. I'd like that. If you win, I'll leave you to your own devices. If I win, you back me up. That's the offer."

"What if I don't like your offer, sir? What's to keep you from breaking your word later?"

"Mathers, I'll be brief. If you don't take up my offer, you'll be off this planet within the next cycle. As for my word, you won't know its worth until you risk it. Do I look like that kind of man?"

Mathers looked the lieutenant over, wondering what the trick was. He couldn't see any and decided to take the new warden up on his offer. He would make the fight quick and merciless. No holds-barred. But no use telling the warden. Let him find out on his own, if he lasted long enough to understand. He nodded in agreement. Talbot saw the cold gleam in Mathers' eyes and knew this man was a bully, but a strong and brutal one. The fight would be as dirty as Mathers could make it. Mathers thought a man like Talbot would fight clean and lose.

"Good. We'll meet in the gymnasium in thirty minutes. Make the arrangements."

Talbot turned his back on Mathers and walked around his desk to seat himself in the warden's chair. He began to write, ignoring Mathers, who stood for some moments, and then hurried out the door. When he had left, Talbot dropped his pen onto the desk. He swivelled around to stare out of his window at the bleak terrain, which lay beyond the prison walls. He wondered again why he had been put in charge of this prison. His career was on the up track. He had performed his duties with flair and efficiency, making him a valued officer the navy would not willingly waste on poor assignments. So what was so important about this planet and this prison? Once he had beaten Mathers, and Talbot had no doubt on this matter, he would spend his time trying to find out. There was something or someone here who meant an awful lot to the navy, or to someone even higher up. Talbot had seen enough of the planet to know it could harbor nothing strategic to the navy, so it had to be a person. Before he left his office he asked the computer to give him an update on prisoners when he returned.

Mathers met him in the gym. Although it wasn't crowded, Talbot recognized several inmate leaders from the profiles he had studied. They were playing basketball when Talbot walked in; they stopped to stand in a ragged semicircle along the edge of the court, watching Mathers shuffle towards Talbot. Some of the prison brigade stood guard along the upper decks. They watched the doings below them, but from their bored looks Talbot knew they expected a beating, a one-sided affair with Mathers keeping his unspoken authority over the guards.

Talbot was no fool. He knew Mathers was a street fighter, someone who used his great size to beat his opponents into submission. Mathers was ten years older than Talbot and, while he was overweight, he was in good condition. If Talbot was to win, he had to win quickly, or not at all.

Mathers stopped ten feet from Talbot and grinned down at the smaller man. Talbot grinned back and waited for Mathers to make the first move. Mathers pointed at Talbot and swung around, addressing the guards in a loud voice: "Take a look at this so-called warden and lieutenant of the navy. He's still green behind the ears."

Talbot was waiting but even so the quickness with which Mathers threw his sucker punch surprised him. He barely evaded it by leaning away from the blow. And then went into action. He fell to the floor and used his momentum, putting his weight into a leg sweep timed to strike Mathers, as Mathers completed his swing. Mathers grunted as he felt his legs swept out from under him. As he fell, Talbot continued rotating on his hands and his other leg swept around in a semi-circle to hit Mathers directly over his kidney area. Talbot felt his foot sink deep into Mathers' side and then Talbot was rolling away as Mathers staggered to his feet, one hand clutching at his side. Talbot, now on his feet, watched as Mathers looked uncertainly about, looking for Talbot even as his vision clouded over. Then the power of the hit sank in and the colour drained from Mathers' face. He opened his mouth wide to scream but the pain overwhelmed him and no sound emerged. He fell over, striking his head hard against the floor, and his body twitched in shock. Two medics came in and hurried to tend to Mathers.

"He"ll need to get to the Tank in a hurry."

Talbot nodded and watched as they strapped Mathers into a stretcher and carried him from the gym. Talbot smiled at the silent guards as he walked out. The guards broke into an uproar as the door slid shut behind him. From now on he knew he would have no trouble with either his guards or with the inmates.

Back in his office, Talbot was scanning the computer files when the Doctor he had met in his first hours on Sandina asked for an audience. Talbot was surprised at how nervous the Doctor looked. Wasn't he the head of the Medical Unit here?

"Sir, I have someone you should see."

"Can it wait, Doctor? I'm reviewing the inmate files."

"That's it, sir. The person I want you to see is an inmate."

"What does he want? I'm busy."

"Sir, it's a 'she.' And I'm sure you'd want to see this one before much longer. She's being transferred off planet and needs your approval."

"Well, then, I guess I'll see her. Bring her in."

"I'll get her, sir."

Talbot turned his holograph off and waited. What could be so important about one female inmate? And then Talbot wondered if she could be the reason for his assignment. He didn't see how it could but then nothing about his transfer to the Warden's position made sense. As he waited, Talbot sipped on a hot cup of Aldean tea.

Just an hour before, he had visited the saline tank that held Mathers; the doctors said the kidney regeneration would take several more hours to mould to the host body. Talbot was reminded again of the primitive conditions he now found himself in. How long would it take to get used to this assignment? And how long would it take to get off this planet for something more meaningful? Talbot was in the middle of these speculations when the doors slid open and the Doctor walked in, followed by an impossibly lean figure whose identity made Talbot almost jump to a standing position.

CHAPTER 24

Standard Year 2498

The flat planet of Diana 5 was known only for ancient Nordell ruins. In five thousand years the entire surface of the planet was riddled with tunnels only the Nordells could safely navigate. Five hundred Standard Years before, the Nordells abandoned the planet, leaving only their buildings and tunnels.

Rains swept over the world in great storms that flooded the lowlands, adding another condition the Nordells prized. Crops were scarce and only a single human group chose to settle on Diana 5. The occasional ore or supply ship orbited the planet, using the planet as a stopping point to more desirable destinations.

It was therefore some surprise to the Thetan Confederate captain, Lisa Lai Jen, when she received a message to make a stop at Diana 5 to pick up a passenger. She double-checked the validity of the message but there was no doubt. The orders came directly from the Thetan Council Chief. The puzzling thing about the message was that the passenger's identity was a secret that would be divulged at a later time, on a need-to-know basis.

After Lisa gave orders for her ship to make the jumps to Diana 5, she sat in her commander's chair and stared at the sheet of paper in her hand. She hated mysteries. She called up the data on Diana 5. The five minute holograph made it harder to understand why anyone important would spend time there. Diana 5's flattened shape was caused by the tug of two distant suns. Rain constantly ravaged its surface, sweeping precious soil into the oceans, killing all but the hardiest plants.

There was a single Thetan township of some fifty people. The township sat on the shores of the largest ocean. Over the town loomed a cliff that ran for fifty miles on either side. Twenty years ago, following the collapse of a part of the cliff only ten miles from the town, the townspeople had spent the better part of a year shoring the cliff above them. Lacking any advanced technology, they built the barrier with their hands.

Almost all the townspeople were loners. They had escaped from Home Worlds in search of a planet that would leave them to their devices and dreams. Some had taken up the ancient practice of growing rice paddies, making use of the abundant rains to grow enough essential crops to keep the township from starving.

Nothing in the holograph tapes showed anyone who might be of the slightest interest to someone like the Thetan Council Chief. But then the most recent tape was five years old. No one on the Home Worlds had seen a need to update Diana 5's files. After all, it was a world that discouraged interest in itself, and was of no great importance to other planets.

In three hours Lisa's ship orbited Diana 5. Lisa secured all stations and made sure the rosters and shift changes were confirmed before she turned over command of the vessel to her second-in-command, with orders to inform the Thetan Council if anything went wrong with Lisa on the planet's surface.

The lifter settled on the eastern edge of the township. Night, such as it was under the baleful orange light of the more distant of the nearby suns, had fallen two hours before. Lisa stepped from the lifter and ten guards quickly followed. She stared at the township. There were three dozen houses built in a single ragged arched line along the shores of the ocean. Several dim lights cast a feeble glow onto the quiet beach. The sound of the waves crashing against the sandy beach was the only thing Lisa heard.

Lisa decided to take no chances. She signalled for her guards to take up combat positions as they moved towards the centre of the arch, where Lisa saw activity taking place. Two guards moved ahead and the rest fell into step beside and behind her, their weapons ready. Lisa was quick to move forward once she selected her destination. The group swept along the beach and then up to the building from which subdued conversation emerged.

Her guards quickly broke into smaller units, two heading for the back of the building while four fanned out to take up stations beyond the lights at the front. Lisa waited until she knew her guards were in position, then directed two to stand by the door. She walked into the building with one guard before her and one behind; the door guards moving aside so as to not block the entrance. At the far end of the large room, opposite to the door she had entered, a counter ran the length of the wall. Behind it, a woman shuttled back and forth, serving several customers who sat on stools. Behind the counter, a square window in the wall showed a kitchen area, from where Lisa heard the clatter of dishes.

Each wall was lined with three booths The booths on her left were empty but the nearest and farthest booths to her right were occupied with patrons eating their food, taking no notice of Lisa's dramatic entry. Lisa had expected anything but indifference. No one looked in her direction. Then finally, the woman behind the counter finished pouring tea into a cup and turned towards her. She made a small bow in Lisa's direction and asked, "What's your pleasure today?"

The people who sat on the stools continued talking. Lisa felt her cheeks grow warm and pulled back her shoulders.

"I'm here to pick up someone."

"That may be, dear. But why do it on an empty stomach? Come on, now, take a load off. Mike's cooking a Special today you'll like."

The woman gestured towards an empty booth to Lisa's left.

"Have a seat and I'll bring you and your people some food. And I won't take no for an answer."

Lisa blinked. "But I'm here to pick someone up."

"Lady, you've said that already. Take a seat. Your friend will be along shortly. She wants you to wait here."

"How do you know who I am?"

"Lady, I may be old but I ain't blind. Nor am I deaf. Your uniform's a dead giveaway. And everyone here heard your lifter. I used to serve in the Confederacy myself. You're a captain, ain't you?"

"I am."

The woman nodded. "Take a seat. Ask your guards out there to come in. No one needs to fear the likes of Theresa Kuang Hsia."

"You know Theresa Kuang Hsia?" Lisa felt faint.

The woman laughed and the others at the counter joined in. Several turned to look Lisa's way for the first time, their eyes scanning her and her guards. Lisa saw curiosity and amusement in their eyes. Before she knew what she was doing, she found herself walking to the middle booth the woman had pointed out to her. Her guards followed. On her orders, the other guards outside came in, taking up the other booths on the opposite side of the room.

The server was over in seconds. She put down the cups of tea she was holding, and then bowed again.

"My name is Margaret Fei Tseng-lu."

Lisa returned the bow and introduced herself and her guards. After the last name, Margaret laughed. "I hope you ain't offended if I don't remember your names. My memory has seen better years."

Lisa warmed immediately to Margaret's easy manners. Margaret looked askance at the other booths and shook her head in mock dismay.

"Such big people. How will I ever manage to feed you? We have such a modest kitchen."

Lisa smiled and shook her head. "My guards don't need food. They ate before we arrived."

Margaret nodded. "Of course. You expected the worst, did you not?"

Lisa was about to deny this but Margaret looked down at the guards' sheathed weapons.

"We didn't know what to expect. We're just here to pick someone up."

Margaret took a deep breath. "Tess has been expecting you. Take good care of her or you'll hear from us." Margaret swept the room with her right arm, surveying the clientele.

"We may not be much, but Tess means a lot to us."

Lisa frowned. "Who's Tess?"

"That's who you're here to pick up. If there's anything you need, yell."

Margaret bowed and left. Lisa took a sip of tea, feeling it fill her with a sense of warmth. She took a second, longer sip, savouring the mild flavor. She had never tasted such tea in her life. As she set the cup down in its saucer, she stared down into it, watching the delicate strands of steam swirl and dissipate into the air several inches over the cup.

"Do you like the tea?"

Lisa jumped at the voice, almost spilling it all over herself. The small slight figure who carried a large knapsack stood before her. Lisa scrambled to her feet as did her guards, who fell in line behind Lisa. In turn, they bowed with the respect they would have shown the Thetan Council Chief himself.

Lisa finished her bow and her right fist moved to her heart.

"I am most honored by your presence, Theresa Kuang Hsia. What is mine is yours."

Lisa was about to unsheathe her weapon to present to Theresa Kuang Hsia, but Theresa shook her head in dismay. "No, no. Don't honor me so. "

Theresa backed away a step and made another bow, deep with the regret she felt at Lisa's greeting. "I don't deserve your feelings. Please, I am only one."

Lisa felt awe sweep through her. And more than awe. She felt the sincerity of Theresa's gesture like a physical blow. She was at a loss as to what to do. For the first time, her sheer size next to Theresa Kuang Hsia's small frame, made her feel horribly awkward. Theresa was motionless, her body holding its position in the middle of a bow of humility. Lisa felt like crying out for forgiveness, which she knew would only worsen the situation. When Margaret emerged from the kitchen, and saw what was happening, she scurried around the counter to Theresa's still form.

"Now what have you done, dearie?" she asked Lisa, not waiting for an answer. She moved Lisa aside and then bowed to Theresa.

"Tess, this woman doesn't know you or your ways. She puts her feet down without looking to see what lies beneath it. But I've served her tea. Your tea."

Theresa straightened from her bow and looked up at Lisa. Her large brown eyes filled half her face, an illusion caused by the impact of what she saw in Lisa. Lisa waited, not knowing what to do or say.

"I ask you again," Theresa said in her low voice. "I ask you again, do you like my tea?"

Lisa nodded vigorously, and felt embarrassed, like a child looking for its mother's approval. But Theresa smiled and reached out her left hand to touch Lisa's right arm.

"I must apologize for my earlier shame. It's been long since I've met others beyond this town."

Lisa took a deep breath and gave a shaky smile. "I understand. I, too, must apologize for my earlier behaviour. I wasn't ready to meet you in this lifetime."

Theresa stepped back and pivoted a complete circle on her left foot. "So, what do you think?"

Lisa was startled by Theresa's move and shook her head. "I don't understand the question?"

Theresa laughed. "Do you think I walk on water?"

Lisa's look of confusion made Theresa laugh even more. "Well, since we've settled that, can I sit with you over tea?"

Theresa didn't wait. She sat in the booth Lisa and her guards had vacated and placed her knapsack down. She gestured for Lisa to join her. Theresa waited until after Margaret had served them tea and the guards took up posts discretely out of hearing range. Her relaxed demeanor put Lisa at ease.

"Tell me, Lisa, what do you know of the Nordells?"

Lisa shook her head. "Nothing. They're some type of alien species, aren't they?"

Theresa reached into her loose-fitting robe and pulled out a small sphere. Its surface was the blackest object Lisa had ever seen, a darkness so deep it became a pure reflection of everything around it. Theresa spun it in one hand. Lisa was staring at the sphere when Theresa threw it into the air towards her. Lisa gasped and reached out without thinking, catching the object before it could shatter on the porcelain floor.

The sphere's warmth surprised Lisa. She lifted it until it was inches from her face. Spinning the object, she noticed two things. First, the object was almost weightless. It felt like a feather, and Lisa had to be careful of her strength, lest the sphere spin from the palm of her hand.

The second fact didn't occur to her until she spun the object several times in her other hand. The object's smooth black texture had the hardness of a diamond. It continued to mirror the room. Lisa found herself wondering where her fingerprints were. The sphere should have become smeared with her hand prints, since she hadn't washed her hands for several hours.

"What is it?" she asked Theresa.

"First, let me tell you something about what I've been doing on this planet. Five years ago I became interested in the Nordells. They were a species of tunnel diggers who disappeared from this part of the galaxy five hundred years ago."

"You mean, left this area of space for good, don't you?"

Theresa smiled. "No, I mean, they disappeared from space. They were set to intrude on human territory and were making final plans when something happened."

"What happened?"

Theresa shrugged, a curious gesture Lisa would not have thought her capable of. Theresa's vast encyclopedic interests and talents were second to none among the ten groups of Humanity.

"There are no records about what happened. One year, the Nordells prepared a simultaneous attack on Humanity and the next year they were gone. Not even a skeleton or picture remained of what they might look like."

"And this black sphere?"

"On each planet where the Nordells were based, I've found at least one of these black spheres. Seven planets, seven spheres. I have them in my knapsack."

"And this one?"

"The same size and weight as the others. I've found each of them in tunnels I've walked through dozens of times. They seem to appear without warning."

"And you've spent five years doing this?" Lisa couldn't keep the dismay from her voice.

"Five years?!"

"Now you know what I mean, perhaps, when I asked you about walking on water. The answer is I cannot be everything I'm made out to be. So I chose not to follow the path others made for me."

"But you have so much to give."

Theresa laughed. She took the sphere from Lisa's hands and dropped the sphere into her knapsack. Although she waited for it, Lisa couldn't hear the sphere hit any other object in the knapsack, not even the spheres Theresa said were in there. Theresa said, "I'm too old to fall for flattery. People won't accept what they aren't ready for."

"They want you anyway. I was sent to get you."

"Oh, yes, I know that. It was I who asked for a ship. And after the Council Chief and I spoke, we agreed speed is essential."

"You spoke with our Chief?"

"Months ago. It was before the Anphorians and Repletians agreed upon trying to settle their differences."

"So you know about the upcoming Summit?"

Theresa finished her tea and stood. Her quick movement caught Lisa off guard, and she felt the incongruity of her talk with Theresa. She knew of important people who never got close enough to the reclusive Thetan to say half the words Lisa had managed to say.

"But I must be intruding upon your time," Lisa apologized.

Theresa began to walk to the door. Margaret yelled after her receding back, "Are you okay, Tess?"

Theresa turned at the door. "I'm all right, Margaret. I'm afraid I'm leaving now."

Lisa hurried after Theresa and she heard Margaret's voice. "Just remember what I told you, captain. She means a lot to us here. Take care of her or you'll answer to us."

Theresa watched the planet become smaller as they quickly rose to Lisa's waiting ship. Her guards stared at Theresa, speaking in low voices, trying not to disturb Theresa's thoughts as she watched Diana 5, perhaps for the last time.

The trip in the lifter was mostly spent in silence, and as it neared its end, Theresa turned her attention from Diana 5 to the approaching ship. Lisa asked her where they were going. Theresa shrugged.

"Our instructions will be given to us once we are on board, and I've confirmed my identity with the Council Chief."

Safely aboard the ship, Lisa unstrapped herself from her safety belt even as they felt the kick of the tachyon drive units. In the five minutes it took them to get to the bridge, the ship dropped from its first jump. Stars spun from streaks of light to single points on the screen.

"No time to say farewell to Diana 5." Theresa's comment was spoken with a tone of regret and sadness, her voice edged with fatigue.

Lisa explained: "We took extra precautions as per our directions from the council chief. No one following us had time to calibrate our jump, so they won't know where we are or where we're going. Not that I know where we're going, either."

*

Lisa was working out in the exercise room when she was interrupted by what seemed to be a pre-recorded holograph message. The Thetan council chief made it clear Lisa's mission was of the highest importance. She was to escort Theresa Kuang Hsia to the Mickelson Nebula, where Theresa would attend the Anphorian-Repletian Summit. Under normal circumstances it was less than two days' travel. But it would take five more days to complete the plans and a further two to put those plans into action. Lisa was therefore to take her time, her only mission to make sure she brought Theresa - the assigned Summit Mediator - to the Summit unharmed.

As the Council Chief's image dissolved, Lisa swore. What was she going to do for seven days? With each day there was an increased risk someone would find the whereabouts of Theresa, and there were enough enemies of the Summit to make this uncomfortable.

Theresa was playing a Thetan mind game involving seven variables at the eighth level when Lisa asked to be let in. Theresa shut down the game as Lisa came into the room. Lisa bowed and Theresa returned the bow.

"I've tried that game. I reached the third level before I thought my head would explode with the variables I had to worry about."

Theresa ordered the holograph turned off. As it followed her bidding, she turned to Lisa.

"That's a high level for a novice. There are lieutenants in our Forces who haven't gone beyond the second level."

"That isn't much consolation. The colonel who beat me gloated for a month after he beat me, I ate sand that day."

"Where is that man now?"

Lisa shrugged. "I don't know. He quit the Forces ten years ago."

"Then his game playing was for nought, wouldn't you say?"

"He sure could play that game."

"What brings you to my quarters, captain?"

"Please, call me Lisa, at least in private."

"All right, Lisa. I'll ask you again, why are you here?"

"We've got a message from the Council. Orders. We're taking you the long way to the Mickelson Nebula off the end of the Sagittarius Arm."

Theresa nodded and turned away to face the screen that gave her a view of the galaxy's outer edges. The ship was between jumps.

"Look out there, Lisa. Out there are over fifty trillion people who have spent over five thousand years spreading out from the original Home World. In that time, we've managed to populate five percent of the galaxy and explore another ten percent. And do you know what scares me? It's the thought those people know my name. They've read my work and I've lived long enough for them to take my writing literally."

Lisa sat on the long narrow couch that moulded to her shape. "Are you saying you were wrong to write those parables?"

"Do you understand metaphor, Lisa?"

"Not extensively. I like reading poetry on occasion."

"Metaphors suggest resemblance. The writing is set around

possibilities I saw in the universe. In those days I thought we were nearing the point where we would find some permanent answers. I blame it on the Formias Rash."

Lisa was startled. "You mean the rash that brings on puberty?"

"Exactly so. It's hard to believe but before the Rash arrived, humans barely lived eighty Standard years."

Lisa shivered. She couldn't help saying, "Yes, but those years were so barbarous."

"And we aren't barbarous? No, the 90 percent of humanity that survives the coming-of-age disease live too long. They live to see the fruits of their labour in their grandchildren and great grandchildren. We weren't meant for this."

"I've read some history books. Nothing but endless wars, poverty and starvation."

"You've read the official versions of those times."

"What other versions are there?"

"Well, for one, there are the original documents themselves. People lucky enough to see their grandchildren wrote of their mortality with more insight and sharpness than we do with our longer lives. I've managed to translate some of those documents. The truth might be shocking to today's Humanity."

Lisa leaned back to stare at the view screen. She would have openly challenged almost anyone in the galaxy for what she'd been told, but Theresa was second to none in her knowledge. Her comments threw Lisa into a quandary. Could she doubt everything she'd been taught at the Academy? Theresa saw her expression.

"Don't get me wrong. There's nothing I can change about our own beliefs. Some of those beliefs were ones I helped build, when I thought I had more answers."

"Why tell me? I'm in no position to do anything even if I wanted to."

Theresa laughed, a sound full of merriment.

"Lisa, if I knew you could do something about the way things are now, I should have to do my best to kill you. No one should have the power to change the beliefs or systems of an entire species. Such power corrupts."

"And yet you're mediating the Summit."

"Yes, but I'm the conduit. My power comes from the fact neither the Anphorians nor the Repletians trust one another. But neither do they fear me. Each will try to use me to get to the other, to win the Summit for their own people."

"But both cannot win."

"Winning is perception. Obvious winners are often history's losers. Time is the only mediator and court of decision. For example, the Repletians are descendants of a number of tribes, the first inhabitants of a place called North America. They were conquered and almost exterminated through a series of barely-hidden genocidal policies. The First Nations of the First Home World continent lost battles but they're still here in their descendants. Time wins."

Lisa left Theresa's quarters. Theresa's words puzzled her, but she had much to do. Her pilot gave her a confused look when Lisa ordered him to plot a seven-day course for Mickelson's Nebula. But he knew better than to question her about the course.

Over the next few days, Theresa craved human company. She explored the ship's wide corridors, delving into every area. She was omnipresent. Her questions were answered by an awed and confused crew, who kept a careful eye out for her safety.

Lisa wondered how Theresa could be so active when she also had to review so much coded information, information flooding daily into her private quarters. Hour-by-hour the situation between the Anphorians and Repletians changed. Tensions grew, but through it all Theresa was oblivious to any pressure. She made contact with one person. No one knew who she talked with but she then emerged from her quarters to prowl the corridors for hours.

Two days out from Mickelson's Nebula, Lisa was resting in her quarters. She found the darkness soothing and relished the warmth of her couch. Covered with her favorite blanket, she watched a holograph rendition of the latest kabuki play. The third act was a stylized rendition of autumn. An actor was about to descend into the restless crowd when the image froze. The computer told Lisa that Theresa stood outside, wanting to see her.

Curious, Lisa suspended the recording and sat up as Theresa entered. The lights brightened to half their full capacity.

Theresa made a shallow bow and hastened to the couch facing Lisa. She made herself comfortable before asking, "What do you know of the military processes of Anphoria and Repletia?"

"Just what I learned in the Academy. I've never had to engage either in combat."

Theresa thought about this for a moment. She wanted to trust Lisa, or anyone, for that matter, who could be a sounding board for her own turmoil. But she had to choose her questions carefully. There were limits to what she could find through the nature of her questions.

"Do you think either side capable of sabotage?"

It was Lisa's turn to pause before answering. Theresa waited, studying this odd product of the Thetan Academy. The warrior class within the Thetan Confederacy was an anomaly, there only to guard Thetan borders from the other human groups who occupied this arm of the galaxy. In her travels Theresa had chances to talk with people like Lisa, but it never failed to fascinate her, to sit like she was doing now, and talk directly to such a person.

"I think both are capable of sabotage."

"So you're saying 'yes' to my question?"

"I guess so."

"Have you thought much about the upcoming Summit?"

"Who hasn't? It's the most important event in human history."

Theresa drew a deep breath before continuing. "I'm afraid you and others exaggerate the Summit's importance."

"Peace between the Anphorians and Repletians certainly are not unimportant."

"If peace was sought, I'd agree with you."

Lisa couldn't hide her confusion. "Are you saying peace isn't what the Summit is about?"

"What I'm saying is the Summit is showcased for something it isn't set up for. My council has informed me someone is out to disrupt the Summit. They don't know who. It could be either side, or both."

"Then your life is in danger!"

Theresa nodded. "But so is the life of everyone there. We have to take extra precaution. Is your crew ready?"

"Say the word and I'll make them ready. They will have to go through me to get to you."

"Yes," Theresa mused. "Yes, they might do that, mightn't they?" She didn't see Lisa's shocked look. There was so much to do in the next two days.

CHAPTER 25

Standard Year 2498

Once she was alone in her set of rooms, Katina smiled. Everything she asked for was here, including the set of cameras the warden had installed to trap Enid and someone called Mole. On her orders, and unnoticed by the warden, Sergeant Mathers had suggested setting up the basement cameras. Mathers had served his purpose and would be removed. Katina couldn't afford slip-ups now.

She had watched the cameras follow Mykal Leven to his death two days ago, a day before the new lieutenant arrived, time enough for Katina to plan her departure with Enid in her custody. Eleven days to the Summit; she would meet with the new warden tomorrow. Timing was tricky, but Katina relished the challenge.

Katina walked out onto the stone balcony to watch the endless rain pour from the black skies. Gusts of wind swept against the stone walls, but the Nordells had been wonderful architects. The balcony ceiling and ramparts folded in front of Katina, sheltering her from the wind and rain. Because of the dome's slope, she couldn't see the ground far below.

Katina let her mind go blank, until she was a part of what she saw. It was her way of relaxing. Earlier in the day, it had taken her an hour to reach the ninth level in that silly mind game the Thetans played, but the challenge was gone. She had dealt with the Leon Three Starbreaks anomaly; every game now ended satisfactorily in the Summit's destruction. She wondered again why people considered it the most challenging game in the galaxy. People were, oh, so much more difficult to manipulate.

To relieve her anxieties, Katina did as her habits dictated. She went into the specially prepared room where she fought a series of lethal challenges in real time. The room was the largest on this floor of the prison, some fifteen thousand square yards, still miniscule compared to the prison's size, but sufficient to hold a few of the more deadly types of machinery Katina demanded for her skills and preferences. The challenges including a knife-wielding automaton, an android weighing two hundred kilograms, and a random selection of industrial laser beams were activated immediately upon the opening of the door, and only deactivated when the door closed a second time. Yesterday, a day following the setup of the room, and despite Katina's personal warnings to the prison staff, a guard had inadvertently wandered into the room in an attempt to locate Katina's personal quarters. Katina had the remains taken by her automatons to the main prison far below, with another warning against the prison staff trying to find her quarters.

The guards had heard of such rooms, always prepared for the elite commanders of Anphoria, who retained their positions based upon their military skills and their combat skills. Anyone wanting promotion had to successfully challenge their commander in hand-to-hand battle. Thus, the senior ranks were among the fittest and most ruthless. But no civilian had ever reached Katina's level of combat training and ability. That she spent an hour or more a day in that room the guards took to calling the Killing Room frightened them more than anything else she did. But, today, after only forty minutes, she emerged from her Killing Room, and stood in the darkness, letting the wind, and the rain spill upon her, soothing her tired muscles.

Occasionally she took a sip of bitter tea from the cup she held in her dark hand, and mused how if not for her size, she could have passed for any Repletian woman. Gone was her preternaturally pale skin. The disguise threw most people off. No one who saw her would think of the grey-haired former President. The skin change, and her black hair, perfectly suited Katina's purposes. Genetic science was her salvation again.

The tea was cold, the way she preferred. As the night deepened around her, Katina sighed and drank the last of the tea. Turning, she paused for a moment to look into her unlit bedroom. She couldn't see where she was going, but she didn't have to. She knew the room's layout to the nearest inch and, without looking, threw the cup over the balcony, not caring where it landed.

Katina's rooms were forty-five floors above the cells on the dome's other side. She enjoyed the hour-long walk to the prison area. No one could find her, unless she told them; there were one hundred levels to the upper half of the building.

Katina had flown her lifter around the building when she first arrived at Sandina. The immense size of the building its brooding rain-streaked bulk fascinated her. She loved its inhuman power. The Nordells had been at home on this barren world. The tunnels beneath the ground were an exact reflection of the half-dome that loomed two miles into Sandina's chilled air. The prison staff and the prisoners preferred the lower floors of the building. The bare rock landscapes that stretched to the horizon intimidated them. They shrank from the mountainous terrain, torrential rains, and deep ravines that covered the planet's surface.

On the second swing around the building, during the initial survey flight, Katina noticed the balconies. They began halfway up the building's visible surface, a half-mile above ground. She studied the building to find the section opposite to the underground prison. She knew better than to choose a place exactly opposite; it would be too easy to find her. So she picked a place three-quarters of the way around the building, three thousand feet above ground. The lifter sent a miniature beacon into the chambers Katina chose. Once afoot, Katina followed the beacon to its source. There her crews had taken five hours to set up everything and leave for the orbiting ship. With the endless storms and distance from the prison, Katina knew no one in the prison had known of her arrival until the time she walked down to the prison, her combat training making the descent relatively easy.

It was late. In bed, Katina read the notes Mykal had sent her before his death. She read through them quickly, noting the information was selective. Missing was the personal intensity, the ongoing hatred of Mykal Leven for Enid Blue Starbreaks, a hatred that would have led to Enid's death if Katina hadn't arrived. Katina marveled people allowed themselves to be ruled by their emotions. She regarded such people with contempt.

A sudden gust of wind, stronger than most, blew into the room, dropping the temperature several degrees. The sturdy balcony doors rattled. Irritated by this distraction, Katina looked up from her reading. The room had become darker. The light from her lamp barely covered the bed and the darkness pushed against the light.

Finally, she pulled back the right corner of her blankets and rose to go to the balcony. A sudden stirring at the corner of her vision startled Katina. She turned towards the motion. Nothing. But it was cold. Katina shivered and ran for the balcony doors, shut them with a triumphant bang, and locked them. In the sudden calm, she heard papers rustle. She turned to see the last notes settle back onto the blankets. Several pieces of paper had drifted to the floor. Katina cursed and ran back to retrieve her scattered notes. It took her almost a minute to gather the notes from the floor, and then she stood over her bed. She stared down at her blankets, puzzled.

They were made up, as though she had not scrambled out of bed to shut the balcony doors. And her notes, they were scattered over the entire width of her bed. Was someone here? Discombobulated, she eased out of the light and stood listening for several seconds. She heard nothing but the muted sounds of the wind and rain outside. Perhaps she'd thrown back the blankets as she got up? There was no other explanation. To be certain, Katina prowled through her rooms, checking every possible hiding place.

She found nothing. Shaken, she climbed under her blankets electing to finish her reading in the morning.

*

Katina watched Talbot O'Halliran's holograph figure. The lieutenant looked troubled as the doctor brought Enid Blue Starbreaks into the room. The doctor moved to one side to allow Enid to collapse into a chair. From there, Katina heard Enid say, "So you's the new warden. What do you wants with me?"

There was a tone of deep bitterness in Enid's voice. Katina wondered if Enid cared for anything in this universe. What would it take to accept such punishment, and not lose everything? There had to be a way.

Talbot dropped his pose to look hard at Enid, until Enid looked up to return his stare. Both of her hands were hidden in the pockets of her torn and unwashed robe. The doctor said nothing. At last Talbot cleared his throat to speak.

"Admiral, don't you recognize me?"

Enid shook her head.

"Admiral, we met almost twenty years ago."

"M'name isn't Admiral. M'name is Madame X."

"Yes, yes. That's what your files say. Don't you remember anything? Anything at all?" Talbot moved away from his desk to get closer to Enid. She smiled and Talbot saw her freshly broken row of upper teeth. "Memory's bad for us. Memory's no good to anyones."

"Who did this to you? Who hit you?"

"When?"

"I mean, who hit you in the mouth?"

Enid grinned. Talbot saw her vacant green-blue eye stare at him. He felt sick, sicker than he had ever felt standing over the remains of a fresh battle.

"They say you's the new warden? What's your pleasure?"

"I wouldn't think of it! I"m not like the last warden."

"Then you's'll not beat me?"

"Doctor, what's wrong with her?"

The doctor moved forward as Enid returned to stare at the floor. She hummed a song that bothered Talbot and the unseen Katina. She wrapped both of her thin arms around herself to rock back and forth in her chair.

"Her only friend was killed in an escape three days ago. Madame X was with her. The warden wasn't pleased. She was punished."

"And this is what they call punishment?" Talbot's face showed his killing fury.

"The warden thought it best to punish Madame X while her escape down below was still fresh in the other prisoners' minds."

"Then why is she like this?"

The doctor shrugged. "I guess her mind snapped with grief. She's been like this since they caught her. Not even the warden's punishment brought her out."

"And then the warden died?"

"And then the warden died," the doctor confirmed. "It's lucky for us you were in the vicinity, ready for reassignment."

"There's something here I don't like. It's almost as though someone's planned this entire series of events."

The doctor was quick to allay Talbot's suspicions. "Who in the galaxy would plan any of this? You've got my report. The warden and his family died of a prolonged contagious disease. We had to isolate and cremate them once they died."

"Yes, I've read your reports."

"Then there's nothing more to say."

"Do you know who Madame X is?"

"No, nor do I care."

"Doesn't it strike you as odd she's the only Repletian prisoner on Sandina?"

"I'm not paid to be curious."

Talbot was puzzled. "Then why did you bring her to me?"

"My superior wanted you to meet Madame X before you met her."

"Who's this superior? I thought I was the new warden."

The doctor chose to ignore Talbot's last question. He pointed towards Enid. "As you can see, Madame X is not well. My superior thinks it best if Madame X is taken from the planet and given the best medical care available."

The doctor's strange insistence on keeping Enid's identity unspoken sounded a bell in Talbot's mind. Had he already betrayed too much in his earlier reference to Madame X as admiral?

"Yes, she's in poor shape. I've looked at your facilities. I must say they're primitive. But why take Madame X off planet? Surely we can call for medical equipment?"

The doctor smirked. "Warden, things aren't always as simple and clean as you'd like them to be. We aren't aboard a Class Two battleship. No one cares about what we do here, so long as we keep quiet about what we do. Most of our prisoners are people the outside worlds would rather forget."

"And this justifies your abuse of prisoners?"

"I follow orders, as you do."

"Well, I'm in charge here. My orders are to keep Madame X here until I can make inquiries."

"That won't be necessary."

The woman's voice startled both men. Talbot turned to the door and saw a small figure standing in the open entrance.

"Who are you?"

"The good doctor here hasn't told you about me?"

"Are you the superior he keeps referring to?"

The woman nodded her head. "I am."

"The doctor says you want to take Madame X off planet for medical treatment."

"That is the general plan."

The woman's soft sibilant voice was low but Talbot had no trouble hearing it. There was an aura of power and authority in the woman's tone of voice.

"Who are you?"

The woman chuckled, a sound marked by the sudden stillness of Enid, who had been rocking in her chair. Enid hid her hands in her pockets.

Talbot had met old people, but the dark brown skin of this woman struck an unnatural glow in the low lights. Anyone looking at her would realize the brown skin was not naturally hers. And yet the woman remained confident behind her obvious genetic alterations. That didn't bother Talbot. After all, older people of wealth underwent genetic changes of various sorts, dependant on their personal inclinations and fears. But this woman's dark skin color made Talbot think of a wolf. The sharp brightness in the woman's black eyes was constant. She looked steadily at Talbot, sizing him up.

"Shall we cut the pretences? My name is Katina Patriloney. I'm sure you've heard of me."

Talbot took a step back, driven by the force of the old woman's voice. She smiled and moved forward.

"Why don't you kill me, lieutenant?"

Talbot heard the contempt in her voice, and something else. He had never met Katina, but her name was known throughout the human race. Katina had died in the firestorm that incinerated her house, leaving Anphoria evenly divided about what she had tried to do against Repletia.

Katina laughed. "You think I'm dead, don't you? Everyone thinks I died of my own doing. Well, in a way, I have died. That suits me fine."

She waited, but Talbot knew she wouldn't have come into this room without protection. She studied his face, before blatantly turning her back on Talbot to face the doctor: "Doctor, unless the young lieutenant disagrees, I have my men waiting outside to escort Enid Blue Starbreaks to my ship. Would you mind taking her?"

The doctor nodded and hurried to Enid, helping her out of her chair and leading her towards the door. He hesitated for a second as Katina said to his back. "Oh, and, doctor, thank you for your discretion over the years."

In those words the doctor knew he wouldn't live out the day. He turned his head to look behind at Katina. She smiled. The same doubts that stopped Talbot stopped the doctor. He looked down and saw Katina's hands were hidden in her long flowing scarlet robes. The door opened before the doctor could decide. Two large men walked in to escort Enid away. She limped between them, her hands still hidden in her robe, her eyes still on the floor. Her breathing was hoarse, as if she had to force herself to breathe.

Two other men stood at the door, leaving the doctor no choice but to leave the room with Enid. Talbot's last glimpse was of the doctor's panic-stricken face.

Katina walked around the desk to sit in the chair owned by the previous warden. Talbot looked around, but saw no signs of a trap. That didn't mean there weren't any.

"I'll ask you again, lieutenant. Why don't you kill me?"

Talbot decided to play along until he knew what she wanted. He said the obvious. "You aren't foolish enough not to have me covered somehow. Not if you are Katina Patriloney."

"Do you doubt who I am?"

Talbot shook his head, staring at the red fingernails on her long slender hands. Her hands were as brown, and as artificial, as her face.

Katina waved towards the seat where Enid had so recently sat.

"Lieutenant, take a seat. We have time."

Talbot felt the faint warmth from the chair's previous occupant as he sat down. "So you're the one who had me assigned here?"

"A good deduction, lieutenant. Yes, I thought it proper you replace the former warden."

"I assume you have something over me, or you wouldn't risk this face-to-face confrontation."

"You learn quickly, lieutenant."

Talbot waited, but Katina was in no hurry to talk.

"Why me? Of what use can I be to your plans?"

"Lieutenant, don't flatter yourself. I have connections. And then, of course, my money buys things sometimes knowledge cannot. I live with that fact. It has proved to be useful."

"You don't have anything on me."

"Is that a question or a statement?"

Talbot gripped the edge of the seat. Katina saw this, and ignored it. "You must have something else because you know I could kill you in less than a second, whether or not you had a weapon."

"Why, lieutenant, I'm surprised at you. I only carry a weapon in self-defense. Here," she gestured at the room, "I do not need any weapons. I'm perfectly safe. I've enjoyed the time I've been here. This planet has so much potential."

"So what is it you have on me. Why don't you just kill me?"

Katina laughed again and leaned forward in her chair, casually placing her hands onto the desk.

"Lieutenant, killing you would be pointless. After I leave, you'll have no means of getting off the planet, or request help from anyone. My men are seeing to that even as we speak. By the time the next scheduled supply ship gets here in two months I'll have had all the time I need."

Talbot felt the slight shudder of the stone floor beneath his feet.

Katina licked her lips, a quick movement that held Talbot's attention. "That would be my men, destroying your lifters. As for my protection, let us say, lieutenant, you have such lovely parents. Just the other day, a friend of mine, who's a close neighbor of your parents, paid them a visit. They had a fine dinner. He wants me to call him to let him know what greetings you want to send. He'll be upset if he doesn't hear from me. And he has such a temper. You know these ex-naval types. So enthused about keeping up the skills they learned in the navy. Poor man feels frustrated since the Repletians took over your Home Planet."

Katina waited, but Talbot was motionless in his chair. He stared at her and she returned his gaze, her black eyes seeming to grow larger the longer he looked. At last he forced himself to turn away. Katina stood up and walked to the door.

"Lieutenant, it was nice meeting you. Look after this prison while you wait for the supply ship. Don't fight it. There's nothing you can do. Oh, and don't worry about the good doctor. I'm leaving a replacement. He's good. We picked him up on our way here. I believe he's Repletian. Don't you love irony? My men have put a twenty-minute time lock on this door. If we were aboveground, you could watch my ship leave. But then, how could the Nordells have had such foresight?"

And, with that, Katina left the room.

CHAPTER 26

Standard Year 2498

Theresa Kuang Hsia watched the stars spin into focus. Lisa busied herself coordinating her deck crew. Theresa watched the larger woman's quick movements, and thought of other times and places.

Mickelson's Nebula bathed Lisa's ship in a red glow. Deep within the nebula, pinpoints of light marked the spots where proto-suns were forged as they accumulated mass. Theresa thought of a womb every time she saw the nebula. Material strung like spider filaments threaded their twisted paths through the nebula.

Lisa finalized her orders. The ship turned and jumped towards the nebula three light years away.

"We should meet the Summit ships in two hours. They're waiting for us."

Theresa bowed, smiling as she completed her motion. "You've done well, Lisa Lai Jen. I'll put in a good word for you and your crew."

Lisa protested. "But I've done nothing but bring you here. My work's done."

"You've done what I asked. Those against me would cripple your ship if they knew its whereabouts."

"Perhaps that's true." Lisa smiled. "But we went through forty separate jumps in the past seven days. No one followed me."

"Of course you're right. Allow an old woman her fears. Emotions keep me going."

"You're barely sixty years older than I."

"Yes, but what years those were!" Theresa laughed. Lisa followed suit, caught up in Theresa's infectious emotions.

The next two hours passed quickly. Theresa returned to her quarters, where she reviewed information sent over secured channels. The Repletians and Anphorians would each have ten ships at the Summit. Each side agreed to limit their ships to Class Four fighters.

The largest ships on either side carried full complements of less than ten thousand.

To help matters, each side also agreed to have the Thetans provide the flagship on which the Summit would take place. The meeting would be broadcast to the ten Groups of Humanity. Nothing like it had occurred for over fifty generations, when the ten Groups had signed the Covenant of Humanity, setting out the terms and conditions by which they would coexist.

As soon as Lisa's small fighter dropped from star drive, the Thetan flagship, the *Samutpada*, greeted Theresa's pending arrival, an arrival eagerly expected by trillions of humans. Theresa read each report sent to her, making notes as she read. On one point she was insistent. While it was customary within the Thetan Confederacy to have the ranking human assume command of any vessel he or she was aboard, Theresa declined. If the worst happened, she wanted the best combat officer in command. She reluctantly agreed to a personal escort and, after quick consultations, she placed Lisa in charge of that escort.

Theresa finished her tasks before shutting down the holograph. She ordered the view screen on and the lights turned off. As the wide port hole's metal screens slid back, the nebula's burgundy red hue flooded her room. Theresa sat back in her chair and slowly sipped her tea. She stared at the furnace of new stars. There was so much matter in the nebula star drives were inoperative. No one went into the cauldron, for the same matter that gave birth to stars were subject to random and massive electromagnetic storms. Attempts at star drive speed within a nebula led to the same spectacular burnouts as ships falling into a planet's atmosphere.

This was the moment of stillness for Theresa. She gathered her thoughts and energy for the tasks that faced her. The next two days leading to the Summit promised to be event-filled days. Any doubts or hesitations Theresa had must be faced now, and not at the Summit, where they would be detected and played upon by both sides. Over the past seven days, she had used her Thetan Mind Game to study the background materials provided her. She thought about the participants, their tendencies and their histories. She analyzed the issues that had dominated both cultures for the past twenty years. And still something nagged at Theresa. There was something missing, something she had overlooked.

What could it be? During endless games at Levels Eight and Nine, she pored over every known fact about the Summit. In every game she lost as events drifted increasingly into disorder, propelled by factors the computer couldn't pinpoint. There were thousands of random elements in the games, but none of them could be faulted for the eventual disruption of the game. Every simulation led to defeat.

Theresa trusted her games, and so she was troubled. She had never lost so consistently. Of the past five games, for example, she had twice reached Level Seven, before the game spiralled into chaos against her best efforts. Each time the Summit ended in conflict. Controlling so many elements led to inevitable headaches. Theresa found her strength draining day-by-day. No matter how much information she fed into the Game, the results were the same. Zero chance of successful negotiations.

Theresa asked for help, and the computer once led her to Leon Three Starbreaks, who controlled events for ten critical minutes on the Seventh Level before he, too, failed. No one else had come close to managing events at this level, and Theresa immediately called up the files on Leon Three Starbreaks.

Leon's history was promising. A young rebel and miner respected by the other miners along the borders, Leon had left his wanderings after an encounter with Korel's World. He became a respected Elder, using his mining experiences to become an archaeologist of the first rank. He had married Red Dawn and the two were happy. Leon had been assigned to negotiate with Enid Blue Starbreaks in an attempt to stave off the Fourth Fleet's feared invasion of Repletian border worlds. Struck by a thought that demanded follow up, Theresa stopped the tapes then. She fed the data into the computer and asked for any known correlations between the former vice-admiral and Leon Three Starbreaks. Theresa knew she was taking a long shot, since she had little information on Leon, and everything on Enid, whose records were part of the military files sent to her.

Five minutes later, Theresa had a partial answer that excited her. The computer informed her there was an eighty five percent probability Leon Three Starbreaks and Enid Blue Starbreaks were direct relatives. Without more information, the computer couldn't be more certain. Theresa sent a scrambled message to the Repletian Senior Elder, requesting an audience with her. While she waited for the reply, Theresa felt her hopes rise. Perhaps there was a way through Leon. Judging by his history, Leon commanded as much respect as did the Senior Elder.

*

"Theresa Kuang Hsia, I am honored."

The Senior Elder sat at a large circular table. Her dark hands were joined, fingers interlocked, on the table. Her blue-grey eyes dominated her face. There was caution and security in them, born of the continual use of power. Theresa had met this look in the past few days, but none matched the Senior Elder's serene look of confidence.

"You do me honor to answer my call." Theresa hoped her voice sounded as confident as the Senior Elder's. She bowed as she said this, a motion the Senior Elder returned with a slight nod of her head.

"Do you seek the advice of a simple Elder?" The Senior Elder's tone of voice was deliberately neutral. She waited for Theresa to make her intentions known.

"Indeed, perhaps you can help me. I need information that may help me at the Summit." Theresa spoke of her need to access Leon's files. She detailed her Game findings over the past week. The Senior Elder listened quietly until Theresa finished.

"This Game you speak of. I have heard of it. I have not heard of any Thetan reaching the Fifth Level. You are what they tell me. But I fail to see how I can be of any use to you."

"Leon Three Starbreaks is a final factor in the Game. I need further information on him. Perhaps he's the clue to help me in my negotiations at the Summit."

Theresa felt the Senior Elder's cold hostility in her next words: "Theresa Kuang Hsia, you are respected throughout the galaxy. Let me tell you my side of this Summit. We don't need this Summit. The Anphorians are losing. The only reason we agreed to the Summit is we want peace, something we can't have while the border disputes continue. And now you tell me you plan to have a game decide the fate of trillions of people. I find this unacceptable. Perhaps you speak in haste. In any event, I hope you consider your position with more dignity and grace than you appear to be doing."

"As for your request for information on Leon Three Starbreaks, let me say Leon's position as Elder entitles him to some privacy. That won't be broken without his personal consent. It's our way. Theresa Kuang Hsia, I wish you good fortunes at the Summit, but I say no more. When I give to you, I give myself."

Before Theresa could respond, the holograph faded, leaving the room bathed in the soft red light that poured in from the nebula.

Lisa was looking through the view screen when Theresa came onto the bridge. Looming in their view was the great flagship, the *Samutpada*. Its form wasn't the sleek bullet-shape that marked the Anphorian flagships. Instead, it was built to house as many labs and housing units as it did military units. The flagship had been recalled from an exploratory trip deep within the Orion arm. Once the Summit was finished, the *Samutpada* would return to its mission.

Three great spheres formed the triangular corners of the *Samutpada*. Each sphere was miles in diameter, connected to each other by an eight-hundred-yard wide set of six-mile-long tubes. One sphere held the military quarters and Command Centre. Another held the labs and research facilities while the third held most of the living quarters for the civilians. Everyone aboard had personal quarters closest to their assigned posts.

The captain of the *Samutpada* gave Lisa and Theresa permission to come aboard. Theresa had no more time for doubt, no chance to resolve the issues raised both by the series of Games she had played.

Lisa and Theresa made their way to the lifter bay. Their departure went without incident. Lisa stared at the immense hull of the *Samutpada* as they made their approach. She had never seen a Thetan flagship up close. The *Samutpada* rotated around its invisible centre of mass. The seven levels within each sphere aligned vertically to the ship's centre of mass. Lisa started to ask Theresa something, but she stopped in mid-sentence when Theresa shook her head.

On board the *Samutpada*, Lisa preceded Theresa off the lifter. She looked around, and saw the military escort standing at attention in a single straight row below her. The landing bay was small by most standards, yet seemed large because theirs was the only lifter present. Except for this line of soldiers, no one was on the deck. Lisa, feeling uneasy, advanced down the small ramp before turning to beckon Theresa. She kept her eyes on the escort, studying every face carefully, committing them to memory, as Theresa came down the ramp. Now was not the time the let down her guard. If rumors were true, someone would try to kill Theresa in the next two days. Lisa vowed they'd have to kill her first.

As Theresa reached Lisa, a man stepped forward from the escort ranks. He marched up to the two women and bowed. As he snapped back to attention, his pale grey eyes stared at Theresa without a flicker of emotion.

"Theresa Kuang Hsia, I welcome you aboard our vessel. My name is Admiral Robert van Troyun."

Theresa didn't bow. Instead, she formally greeted him. She ended her greeting by saying, "I've heard good things about you, Admiral."

"I'm honored by your words, Theresa Kuang Hsia. Let me show you your quarters. We can meet later."

"I'd like nothing better, Admiral. Lead the way."

Van Troyun turned smartly and led the two women from the landing bay. The row of troops fell into step ten feet behind Theresa and Lisa. They walked through empty passages. Lisa wanted to ask the admiral questions, but he kept his stiff military posture for the five minutes it took to reach an innocuous-looking door. He stopped and turned to face Theresa. "Step forward, Theresa Kuang Hsia. The ship's computer will mark your DNA. After this, only you can access your quarters."

Theresa paused. "I'd like Captain Lisa Lai Jen to have the same access to my quarters. I trust there's enough room to have Lai Jen room with me?"

The admiral nodded. "We received your specifications. By your question, you've given the computer permission to allow Captain Lai Jen the same access to your quarters as yourself. I understand," van Troyun looked briefly towards Lisa, "that Captain Lai Jen is your personal body guard for the duration of your stay aboard our ship."

Lisa stared hard at the admiral. Why was he so formal? Aboard his ship he should have dropped his military posturing. Instead, he went to great lengths to hide his emotions, although Lisa knew from her briefings the admiral and Theresa were considered close friends.

"I take my leave. If you need anything, please let me know. While you're on board, you have the full run of the vessel."

Van Troyun left. Lisa waited as Theresa watched the receding group of soldiers disappear beyond a distant door. Only then did Theresa turn to enter her quarters. Lisa was about to ask her a question when Theresa put an index finger to her lips.

They entered their quarters and the double blast doors silently slid shut behind them. The large room lit up under hidden lights. Theresa sat in a single seat chair and gestured for Lisa to sit in a similar chair. She pulled a detector from her large carrying bag and placed it onto the glass table that separated them from each other. The detector's red light stopped blinking and a green light flashed on. Theresa leaned back into her chair.

"That went well, don't you think?"

Lisa felt a thousand questions rise to the surface. "Why didn't the admiral say anything? I thought you two knew one another."

"We do." Theresa smiled at some thought. "Bob handled himself as well as you did."

"I don't understand."

"Since we left your ship, Lisa, we've been under scrutiny."

"Do you mean the admiral was watching us?"

"Not the admiral. Someone else."

Lisa looked around the room with some alarm. "Are we safe here?"

Theresa pointed to the recorder on the glass table. "We're safe while that green light stays on. It's a scrambler."

Lisa looked at the small machine. "But how did the admiral know to keep quiet?"

Theresa smiled. "Don't you remember how Bob greeted us? Pretty formal, wouldn't you say? Even in the military, I would have ordinarily returned his bow. I didn't. You can guess the rest."

Lisa exclaimed, "A signal! You warned the admiral through a signal."

Theresa looked around the central living room. "Lisa, perhaps you should check the rest of our quarters."

Without further bidding, Lisa was up and into the other rooms. Theresa went into the open kitchen area to check the cupboards for their contents. By the time Lisa returned from her security check, Theresa was seated in her chair again. A holograph image of van Troyun hovered above the coffee table. His head turned at the motion on the edge of his screen. "That's Lisa," Theresa advised. "She checked the other rooms."

Theresa glanced at Lisa, who shook her head. "Bob," Theresa continued. "Lisa's found nothing out of the ordinary. Do you think it could've been one of your security guards?"

"I would, except your recorder warned us when you were still aboard your lifter. My crew is busy tracing the origins of the signal, but don't expect them to find anything. We haven't yet, and we've had four other incidents in the last week. It seems our well-kept secret location is probably known to whoever plans to sabotage the Summit."

Theresa said farewell to the admiral and turned off the holograph. Lisa gave her a moment to recollect herself before she spoke.

"There's two sleeping quarters next to each other at the end of the hallway. Each has its own washroom facilities. There's also a separate room they've set up as you requested. It faces away from the centre of this ship. I still don't understand why you chose a set of rooms that faces directly away from the ship's centre."

"I'm playing it safe. If we were on the other side of the ship, anyone could see us."

"Then you fear they'll strike before the Summit begins?"

"Lisa, I've told you already. I'm not certain of anything. Everything I know is limited by my experiences and knowledge, which aren't infinite. Keep a lookout. Of this I know. Whoever it is, they're powerful and they'll strike when least expected, in a moment of their choosing, not ours. We have to believe they've been watching us for years. They know us well."

Lisa grimaced. "The only person I remember from my history who sounded anything like this was that Anphorian President. You know, the woman who killed herself twenty years ago."

"Yes, I'd have to agree with you there. It seems there are others as powerful and determined as she was. I keep thinking of Leon Three Starbreaks, the Repletian Elder. Somehow he fits into this but no one knows where he is. I spoke with the Senior Elder. She's on her way here, but she won't let on where he is, if she knows."

Theresa ordered her chair into a fully reclined position. She looked at Lisa one last time.

"Lisa, whatever happens, the Summit takes precedence. I know how you regard me, but don't let that affect your performance. My life is secondary to the Summit. Remember that, if it comes to making a choice."

Lisa retreated to her room to allow Theresa her rest. Using her holograph, she reviewed details of the Summit , checking the security measures being finalized even now. She didn't remember falling asleep.

"Lisa, it's time."

Lisa heard the voice from a great distance. She had been dreaming of her homeland, which she hadn't thought of for years. Her mother's sad face was replaced by Theresa's anxiety. Lisa struggled to a sitting position. Theresa must have turned the holograph off, for her room was semi-dark.

"How long have I been asleep?" Lisa asked.

"Five hours." Theresa smiled.

"My God, we'll be late!"

"Relax. I've already made other plans. The admiral wants to show us the Summit room. I told him we'd be there in another thirty minutes. Time enough for you to shower and change your outfit if you wish. I'll wait in the living room."

Lisa nodded and headed for the washroom. Something was

important, but she couldn't put her mind on it. Her worries disappeared under the hot streams of water that soaked into her skin and bones. She felt rejuvenated as she dried herself and combed her short hair. She looked into the closet; a row of grey uniforms hung formidably. The uniform she chose fit like a glove.

Lisa walked into the living room. Theresa was watching another holograph. "I'd like to help you, Theresa, but I can't see how," van Troyun was saying.

"I don't know when and where they'll come at me, but if they want to get rid of me, the ideal times are during our rest periods and the Summit."

"I'll assign a squad to your quarters, but they may not stop whoever it is."

"No," Theresa conceded, seeing Lisa in the doorway. "But they'll make the cost of getting to me much harder."

"I see your point. A squad is on its way to you. They'll be there in five minutes."

"Bob, thanks for your help."

Van Troyun smiled broadly. "Anything I can do for you, I'll do. I owe you much more than this."

"I'll see you in twenty minutes." Theresa returned Van Troyun's bow as his image faded from view.

"Do you expect trouble?" Lisa asked as she moved into the room.

Theresa answered Lisa's question with one of her own. "When did you turn off your holograph? I heard it earlier, but it was off when I came into your room."

"I thought you . . ." A chill stop Lisa from finishing her sentence.

"I thought so." Theresa handed Lisa her weapons. "You may need these. Someone has access to our codes."

Lisa was strapping on her weapon belt when a low voice from outside requested permission to enter. Cameras showed a group of five Thetan soldiers led by a short stocky man. It was this man who smiled into the cameras.

"We're here to escort you to the admiral."

Theresa nodded. "Very well. We'll be right out." She turned the holograph off and walked with Lisa towards the exit door. Just before opening it, she whispered to Lisa, "Get ready."

The door slid open as Theresa pushed Lisa to one side and ducked to the other side, barely in time to miss being hit by a bullet that exploded against the opposite wall. Lisa's reflexes kicked in as she cushioned her fall, turning her momentum into a roll that had her on her feet in one fluid motion. Her gun was out and firing into the several men who rushed into the low-lit room. Two went down, but Lisa paid them no attention. She leaped forward into the remaining men as she saw Theresa kick out at the leader, her right leg a blur of motion ending its arced motion deep in the man's guts. The next moments went quickly. There was an eerie silence about the struggle. Each side went at the task of trying to kill the other, no one wasting energy to speak.

Theresa followed her kick with several rapid series punches to the leader's nose and throat. Lisa heard the breaking bones as she fell back into the dark room, away from the falling body of the man she had kicked in the head. A man lunged at Theresa and the two vanished into the darkness before Lisa could shoot him. She looked towards the remaining two men and fell under the punch of one of them. She managed to keep the blow from hitting her on the bridge of her nose by twisting her head at the last moment. Still, the blow landed on her left cheekbone, cracking it and sending a searing wave of pain through her body.

She rolled with the blow, but she lost her balance and fell face first onto the floor. Another blow broke her right leg, the dull snap sounding like thunder to her ears. She grunted from the pain, but she rolled, feeling the assailant's third blow miss her head by bare inches. She was firing up and towards the door as she rolled. A lucky bullet struck her first attacker in his left knee, shattering it. He fell backwards, towards the lit hallway, and the sweeping blow he had started with his left leg caught Lisa in her right arm, the one that held her gun. Her arm was paralyzed and her gun fell to the floor. Lisa found herself staring at the sword the final assailant held with both hands above his head. As it began its lethal arc towards her, she regretted she hadn't helped Theresa survive the fight.

A mist of red blood exploded from the middle of the man's chest. He took flight, his body propelled over Lisa to land several feet beyond her. The sword flew from his hands to bury itself into the opposite wall.

Lights flared up as a group of other soldiers poured into the room. Lisa's last sight, before her pain took over, was of Theresa jumping over the body of her second attacker and running towards her.

CHAPTER 27

Standard Year 2498

Stars End spun into real space on the other side of the giant gas planet. Leon had set the controls for the jump but, during the last minutes before the drop into real space, he took control of the ship. Eleven days had passed since they entered the flagship at Korel's World. Eight of those days passed while the ship's machines worked around the clock to rebuild *Stars End* to Leon's specifications.

Under Leon and Red Dawn's supervision, the automatons removed all but three of the bridge's command chairs, leaving the two humans in control of everything left in the room. Control functions were manual, backed up by automatic controls, instead of the reverse.

On the third day after leaving Korel's World, Leon made his best guess. As the ship dropped out of star drive, he twisted the controls. The nearby planet dwarfed the ship's great structure, and Leon yelled for his wife to hold on. They were closer to the planet than Leon had planned. He turned off the view screen. The green planet spun as Leon's ship steered directly towards its centre. Although Leon knew this was an illusion, his senses told him otherwise.

He stabilized the flagship fifteen thousand miles above the planet's surface. The bright arc of their path dissipated into the vacuum of space. When they swung around the planet to the side facing the sun, their ship no longer left telltale signs of its passage. Leon felt safer as he guided the flagship towards the prison world of Sandina.

Over the past several days, Leon worried he might be too late. He couldn't sleep comfortably. Red Dawn tried to keep him busy organizing their ship to meet their needs in the upcoming days. They left nothing to chance, for while their flagship was now as easy to control as any lifter, it held powers beyond anything they had met before.

Even now, as they made their way to Sandina, Leon and Red Dawn knew only the general outlay and strength of *Stars End.* But they saw why, with such ships, the Anphorians depended so much on technology to operate their ships. Neither sympathized with that dependency, for they thought of it as a weakness, making people the servants of machines rather than the reverse.

Within an hour of their arrival, Sandina spun beneath the immense flagship. Surprise greeted them in the shattered remains of the radio satellite. Chunks of it continued orbiting around the planet.

"Why haven't they come up to fix it?" Red Dawn wondered.

Leon decided to be cautious. Something unexpected had happened here. The coincidence worried him. He had *Stars End* search for electromagnetic signals from the planet's surface. After an hour, they knew something had disrupted the normal lines of communication, which would ordinarily be full with chatter. Their ship searched the planet's surface for signals and found none.

Red Dawn stared at the readouts. "Something's happened to the prison something out of the ordinary."

Leon studied the images of the prison dome. "There's no structural damage to the outside of the prison. But I can't read anything on the other side of those walls. Need better sensors. This ship has sensors deigned for deep space, not planets."

Red Dawn stared at the planet. It looked forbidding from this distance. Great white and black-edged clouds marked the storms that swept over the planet's surface. Red Dawn wondered what type of species could feel comfortable in such a place.

"What do we do now?" she asked.

"We don't have much choice. Our niece is somewhere down there. We have to go down to get her."

"I don't like this. Something destroyed their satellite, and it might still be down there. Maybe it's killed everything."

Leon shook his head. "No. No, I'd know if my niece were dead. I'd feel it. But I feel nothing."

Red Dawn gave in to the inevitable. "The security spheres are ready to send down."

"Well, let's get going. The sooner we start, the faster we'll find her."

Red Dawn gave the command that sent thirty fighter drones streaking for the prison. A lifter containing five hundred security spheres followed in their wake. They headed for the part of the prison which schematics showed was the centre of the human population. Leon and Red Dawn would follow as soon as the spheres secured the prison.

*

Talbot woke up, and felt a moment of dread. An old woman's face still hovered in the darkness, its face a merciless grin of triumph. She held the face of a broken emaciated woman within her long thin fingers. The old woman had said to Talbot, "You can do nothing. She is mine."

Talbot fought to move, but he was held by material that felt like a web. When he moved one part of his body, the web tightened in another part. The more he fought, the tighter the web grew. He screamed for the woman to let her captive go, but the woman chose to ignore him. She turned her back to him, the ultimate form of contempt, and slowly walked away. At the last moment, before Talbot woke up, she turned a final time to stare at him. It was this stare that lingered as Talbot woke up. He shrank from the dark corner of his room. It took him several moments to realize someone was pounding on his door.

He hurried to the washroom, where he wiped the sweat from his face. On his way to the main door, he grabbed his night robe from a chair and put it on, tightening the cloth strap around his waist before opening the door. Cold drafts of air from the hall swept past him, making him shiver.

"Warden, we have trouble."

For an awful moment, as Talbot stared at Sergeant Mathers,

he thought Katina Patriloney had returned. Her face was burnt into his memory, the moment of her departure six days ago something he'd never forget.

"What seems to be the problem?"

"I don't know. One minute we're alone. The next, there's these spheres. They're everywhere. Seven of my men were killed. I was lucky to escape with my life."

More like you were lucky to be able to run away, Talbot thought to himself. If Mathers had overcome his hatred of Talbot enough to come running to him, something serious was happening.

"Wait here. I'll get dressed."

Talbot left the sergeant in the hallway and closed the door. He wouldn't give the Sergeant leeway even in this moment. He quickly dressed and strapped on his weapon belt. On his way out the door, he grabbed a helmet. Sergeant Mathers shivered in the hallway, his eyes still wide with fear.

"Where's the nearest sphere?" Talbot used his voice like a whip to get Mathers' attention.

Mathers didn't respond. Instead, he hurried towards the top half of the prison, where doors opened to the surface world. Talbot followed him, his long strides easily a match for Mathers. Turning a final bend, Mathers stopped and refused to go any further. Talbot didn't wait. He walked to the end of the corridor. A guard stepped away to let Talbot open the door.

A blast of cold wet air blew past Talbot. He struggled to keep the door open. At the same time he saw the small sphere hovering twenty feet from the doorway. Despite the strong gusts of wind that swept around the prison, the sphere bobbed up and down, but remained in its general position.

"You are warned to stay within the walls of this prison. Any human who ventures out will be shot."

Talbot stared at the small sphere. The anger that had mounted over the past week was almost overwhelming. Just as he was about to defy the sphere's orders, a lethal fighter boomed out of the rain and came to an impossibly quick stop over the sphere. Its weapons pointed directly at the door where Talbot stood. Talbot hesitated and, in this hesitation, he heard the fighter's speakers cut through the fury of the storm.

"Please do not leave the premises. By order of *Stars End*, all humans within Sandina Prison are placed in quarantine until the prison has been safely secured. Any interference with the security spheres will be severely dealt with."

Talbot stepped back from the door. As he did so, a long stream of spheres streaked over his head, all but two of them disappearing into the prison corridors. A guard made a move to fire at the passing spheres, but Talbot ordered him to lower his weapon.

"Don't be a fool. We're outnumbered."

"Are you the warden of this prison?"

The sphere that asked this question looked like any of the others. It hovered at eye level ten feet in front of Talbot.

"I'm Warden Thomas O'Halliran. Whoever you are, you are trespassing on Anphorian territory. Identify yourselves."

"The prison has been secured. Stand by for my commander's arrival."

Talbot was about to ask the sphere for more information, but it floated to the ceiling to join the other spheres. A guard came into the room and marched to where Talbot stood. "Sir, the security spheres have taken over the prison. There was no way we could stop them. They've seized our weapons."

"Understood, corporal. Wait here. I'm to expect company from whatever goddamn ship that's sent these spheres and fighters."

Talbot returned to the open doorway and stared into the cloud-cast sky. The rain continued, but in the last five minutes the winds had slowed. Talbot felt the uncertainty in the men behind him; they waited for him to give them orders. He wished he could. But that power had been taken from him with the arrival of the second ship in less than two weeks. Talbot felt the fury of his helplessness. Had Katina decided to clean up after all? Was this her doing? He didn't have long to wait for the answer. Above him the clouds parted to make way for the lifter, its black hull framed by landing lights.

Talbot knew it was Anphorian, but that meant little. Talbot had learned in the past several days some of his people couldn't be trusted. A soldier was about to go out the door but Talbot held him back: "Soldier, we don't know who's in that lifter. But they don't trust us, so keep your guard."

As the lifter came to a landing on the hard bedrock, Talbot knew it wasn't Katina. If it had been, they'd be dead by now. The firepower in the spheres and the drone fighters were many times that of his men. Disarming the prison was clearly more for the safety of the humans in the lifter; they weren't taking chances.

A ramp unfolded onto the slick wet surface of the planet. The door opened and a sphere emerged. From the way rain slanted away from it, the sphere clearly used a force field through which the rain couldn't penetrate. As Talbot stared at the sphere, two people made their slow way into the night air. The man walked with a limp, shocking in this age of medical treatments. The woman who walked by his side was almost as tall. They stopped at the ramp's threshold, staring out in obvious distaste at the inhospitable world. Then they came down the ramp, shielded from the rain by the sphere that hovered five feet over their heads.

Their age showed from the care with which they moved towards Talbot. Both wore the flowing robes of Repletia. Talbot heard the intake of breath from the men behind him. The Anphorian lifter had thrown them off guard. Perhaps they had thought they were about to be rescued. Talbot made a note to himself to be careful in the next few minutes. His men were as skittish as the old couple was confident.

By the time they stopped ten feet in front of Talbot, ten security spheres hovered above them. Even so, the woman stared hard at Talbot and his men, sizing them up. The man was more curious, his grey-green eyes reminding Talbot of nothing so much as the eyes of his former vice-admiral, kidnapped by Katina days ago.

Talbot saluted, and the couple bowed.

"My name is Warden Thomas O'Halliran. I hereby make an official complaint regarding your armed presence on Anphorian Territory."

"So noted, Warden. My name is Leon Three Starbreaks, an Elder of the Council of Repletia. This is my wife, Red Dawn."

The old man's voice was low. Talbot had trouble hearing it over the winds and rains, which continued to sweep the grounds in their relentless bombardment.

Talbot was about to ask more, but the old man made a gesture to show he wanted to discuss this inside. Talbot apologized and stood away from the door to let the two humans enter. His men were lined against the wall, held there by five menacing spheres hovering near the ceiling.

"Are we far from your office, warden?"

Talbot shook his head in the general direction of Red Dawn. "It's not far. Five minutes at most."

"Good. My husband and I would like to talk to you alone, in the privacy of your office. And, as you see, my husband is not in the best of health."

Talbot nodded. He told his guards to await further detail and they escorted the old couple to Talbot's office. Talbot slowed his pace so the older pair of humans could keep up with him. They stared at the granite floors and walls. Once Red Dawn leaned closer to her husband and whispered something that made Leon nod in agreement. Ten security spheres, enough to handle a hundred armed men, hovered above the three humans. Talbot moved carefully, making no moves to trigger the spheres' defense mechanisms. Cold winds swept through the halls, their passage marked by low moaning that occasionally rose to a wail. The winds made the two Repletians nervous.

Talbot took this time to study the two people more closely. Although the wind and the tunnels distracted them, they carried themselves with a confidence borne of years of power. Talbot had seen this walk in others. Red Dawn sometimes let Leon lean on her shoulder to avoid the water that puddled everywhere within Sandina. The woman's red hair contrasted with her dark skin and green eyes. She was tall, but then Repletian women were tall, with noted exceptions like Enid Blue Starbreaks. Her age was indeterminate, but for the fact her walk was slow and deliberate. Her movements were cautious, her eyes sweeping over the soldiers and the looming curved walls of the prison.

Leon, however, was withdrawn. He placed his trust in his wife and followed her lead. Although he limped, he kept up a steady pace. Neither Repletian complained about the cold, the wind drafts, or the many puddles. But their hunched shoulders showed how much they fought against the chill that haunted every corridor.

Talbot arrived at his office door, which opened as he stood aside for the two Repletians. A sphere darted in, its light quickly flashing green revealing it found nothing threatening in the small office. Leon shook his head.

"Warden, please. This is your office. We don't intend to be here long. As I speak, the prison is being searched for a prisoner you've had here for seven years."

Talbot made himself comfortable in his chair and waited as the two Repletians sat on the other side of his large desk. Leon looked expectantly at Talbot: "Do you know who I'm talking about?"

Talbot smiled, sensing their unease. It could only be Enid, but she wasn't here. What would Leon do, once he found out she had been taken six days ago?

"My niece…her name's Enid Blue Starbreaks," Leon said. Talbot gave the barest of nods to show he recognized the name. Leon looked uncomfortable.

"Warden, is she here?"

"Your drones will tell you she isn't. She's been gone for six days."

"Taken? I don't understand. Who would take her?"

"Elder Starbreaks, what do you know of Anphorian history?"

"Quite a lot. I'm a historian of sorts."

"Then the name Katina Patriloney will mean something to you."

Leon nodded. "Indeed. She's been dead for twenty years. Her plan to wipe out our Home Worlds was outrageous."

"That may be so, but she had plenty of support. There are still those who celebrate her memory."

Leon glanced at his wife: "I'd like to sit here and chat all day, but what's your point? What has a dead President got to do with my niece?"

"She's the one who took your niece."

"You're saying someone who's been dead for twenty years has taken my niece?"

As Talbot wondered how to answer, a sphere came into the room to say, "There is no sign of Enid Blue Starbreaks."

Leon looked at Talbot, waiting for an answer. Talbot quickly summarized the last few weeks, starting with his transfer, and ending with the taking of Enid by Katina Patriloney.

"I've heard you for the second time. I still find it difficult to believe a woman who's been dead for so many years can take my niece.

Even pretending Katina's alive, of what possible use could she have for Enid? Where's your proof?"

"I have none," Talbot admitted. "Katina destroyed everything electronic before she left."

Red Dawn spoke next. "So we have to take your word?"

Talbot shook his head. "I don't see you have a choice in the matter. Besides, your own sphere reports her missing. And there's the small matter of our satellite, which you found in pieces over Sandina. I may know the whereabouts of your niece."

"And I assume you want to trade your information for getting off this planet?"

"No trade. I don't work that way. In a way, Enid is why I'm here today, talking with you two."

Leon reached into his long robes to activate a recorder. "You seem to know about our niece and her whereabouts. How did you get your information?"

Talbot tapped his head. "I used logic. Katina once used Enid as a smoke screen to hide her real intentions. The Katina I saw two days ago acted and thought like the Katina of old. And there's only one thing she could be after, using Enid as the bait."

Red Dawn grabbed her husband's right hand in a vice grip. "The Summit! You're talking about the Summit! But the Summit's only three days away!"

Leon stared hard at Talbot. "Could my wife be speaking the truth?"

"Yes, she is. The years have been rough on Enid. She can't put up any fight against the likes of Katina Patriloney."

"What do you want? We have to get to the Summit."

"I want to go with you."

"Why?"

"Well, for one, I'm the only person who recognizes Katina in her genetically altered state. I suspect not many people have lived to say that. I've seen her close up, and I'll know her anywhere."

"You have a point there. But do you have anything on my niece, anything at all? I want to know about her. It's been so many years."

Talbot nodded and reached into the secret compartment of his desk. He took out the recording and handed it to Leon, whose hands shook as he received it.

"I took the liberty of keeping a hard copy of everything over the past weeks. I hope this recording will be of some use to you."

Red Dawn leaned over and put both her hands onto Leon's shaking shoulders. Talbot thought of his parents back on Brian's Planet. He recalled Katina's threats and vowed he'd warn them somehow. He had to warn them. It wouldn't be like Katina to let them live once they were of no use to her. Not for the first time did he wonder how she had manoeuvred the Navy into transferring him here. Talbot closed his eyes, seeing Katina's hooded figure looming behind the broken woman Talbot had idolized all his life.

CHAPTER 28

Standard Year 2498

Katina stared at Theresa Kuang Hsia's holograph image for the last time. She watched the woman in her daily routine, studying every gesture and movement. The way she laughed when she was relaxed, the way she toyed with the strings of her ever-present satchel in her idle moments, or during times of deep concentration, the quick walk that covered distance with a deceptive ease. Katina read every word the woman had spoken in public and a good deal of her words when she was out of the public eye.

With each hour, Katina's contempt for this spiritual leader grew. Expecting a formidable opponent, she met only an old woman who spoke in vague philosophical terms. The woman lacked a hard core, a bedrock of fundamental beliefs to drive her. She was a sentimental human whose words were spoken to a blind and trusting humanity. Katina spun the holograph image and then ended the program. She knew everything she needed to know. People like Theresa Kuang Hsia were laser fodder.

Katina turned to Enid, who sat staring at the floor, mute as she had been for the five days since leaving Sandina. The medics aboard Katina's ship did everything they could to repair the physical damage inflicted upon Enid over the past number of years. But there was nothing they could do to reverse the hell Enid's mind had sustained.

Twenty years ago, Katina had used Enid as part of her plans to destroy the Home Worlds of Repletia. If not for that cursed Black Ship, Katina knew she would have succeeded. Instead, she had spent the last twenty years recovering from that setback. This time Katina wouldn't make the same mistake.

"You'll do well, my dear," Katina spoke absently at the mute woman who called herself Madame X during the bizarre series of events on Sandina. How she'd assumed the alias the good doctor had given her as a ruse seven years ago was part of the previous warden's abuse. In another lifetime, Katina might have grown fond of such a warden, but in this life all Mykal Leven managed to do was to make Enid's usefulness difficult.

Katina left her chair and pulled Enid to her feet. Enid was almost a foot taller than Katina, but it never occurred to her that this woman would try to kill her. And though aware of her renowned fighting skills, Katina was not afraid.

"Follow me," Katina spoke softly. She turned and scrambled through the small tunnel separating the bridge from the rest of *Threads Way*. Enid followed her with ease, her emaciated body slipping through the narrow tunnel as easily as Katina did. They emerged into a large open area lined with padded walls. A group of warriors were in training, whipping their bodies through simulated combat situations. Their synchronized motions were blurs to Katina's eyes; she watched them for several minutes until they came to a natural break in their routine.

"Have you lost it?" Katina asked Enid. Getting no response, and expecting none, Katina moved on, past the training warriors, to a long corridor into which doors opened. As they walked past, Katina paused at each opening, to show Enid the interiors of these rooms. They were large. All filled with people engrossed in their assorted tasks. Some pored over zero point tachyon surveillance devices that mapped the neighbouring parts of the galaxy. Holograph images of the different sections hovered near each station, while men, women and computers studied and plotted various courses through the maze of stars.

Katina led Enid to a large room decorated in the Thetan style. It was an exact replica of the room where the Summit would occur. A great blue carpet stretched from the entrance to the massive centre platform on which conference tables formed a triangle. Ten swivel seats were placed at each table; each equipped with panels built into its right arm. At the apex of the corner furthest from the entrance, a single seat dominated the dais. This would be the Conciliator's chair.

The grey walls were bare except for a series of tapestries hung evenly along the left and right walls. These tapestries depicted various moments of human history, from the fabled first zero point tachyon drive ship to the rendition of the Battle at Korel's World. Each tapestry was edged with the same light blue colour as the Conciliator's Chair.

Katina led the compliant Enid along the carpet and up the five steps of the platform to the table, which parted to allow them into the middle. The tables clicked into place behind them. They were separated from the rest of the room by the heavy wood structures. Katina smiled with pleasure. Everything was perfect.

She gave a command. The room filled with holograph images of uniformed men and women, each dressed to imitate an actual Summit delegate or guest. Three communications spheres, one each from the three main human groups participating in the Summit, came into the room and hovered near the ceiling at the back of the room. Soldiers lined each side of the carpet. On one side stood two hundred Anphorians; on the other side were an equal number of Repletians. Three hundred Thetan soldiers filled the space behind the Conciliator's Chair and the floor immediately in front of the dais, a human shield against any disruption. As was their habit, the Thetan soldiers wore hoods. Ten people dressed as Thetans took their seats at the table directly opposite the Conciliator's Chair. Their backs faced the wall of soldiers lined along the blue carpet. On the right-hand side of the Conciliator's Chair, the Repletian delegates took their seats, while on the left-hand side the Anphorians also took their places. A small woman sat in the Conciliator's Chair, her garb that of the Thetans.

Katina nodded in satisfaction. "There, my dear, is the Summit as it will happen four days from now. Watch and see what I plan to do."

Katina nodded and a play unfolded before Enid's eyes. The participants at the table began talking as though they were in the middle of a meeting that had been going on for some time. None of them noticed the entrance door open, nor did they notice the Repletian woman walk down the carpet. The two lines of soldiers on either side of the aisle were unsure. Soldiers on both sides recognized the tall gaunt figure as it limped towards the dais. Their growing hubbub slowly drew the attention of the delegates at the table. One by one people stopped to stare at the woman. Several delegates rose from their seats to get a better look. As their eyes turned to Enid's simulation, no one saw the Thetan Captain draw his weapon and fire at the Conciliator. The communication spheres fell to the floor as she dropped. The hall broke into a riot. The Thetan captain went down under a hail of fire, but it was too late. Soldiers along the aisle, with no hiding place, went at each other in hand-to-hand combat that engulfed the entire hall.

The lights faded into darkness and then relit to an empty hall. Katina turned to Enid, who had impassively watched the events unfold.

"So what do you think, Admiral?" Katina's voice was low and full of contempt.

"M'name's Madame X," Enid looked down at the floor again.

"Damn you, don't you have anything to say? Nothing about what you are about to do?"

"Madame X's m'name," Enid stubbornly insisted.

Katina glared at her for a few seconds and then smiled, her lips drawing back into a thin line that revealed her feral teeth.

"Never mind. You aren't the real target, anyway. My plans will work out fine."

Katina gestured for Enid to follow her to the bridge. Once there, her computer told her they were an hour from the Summit. She took a final look at Enid. Enid stared at the floor. Katina shrugged. Better this distraction than none. And better that Enid had watched the mock assassination. This knowledge would condition her response at the Summit. Katina hummed to herself for the first time in years. Everything was going according to schedule.

*

The lifter that picked the two humans up barely had room to hold the extra passengers. Katina didn't mind, and she knew neither did Enid. Before she left, she gave specific instructions to the captain of *Threads Way*. Now, dressed like Enid in Thetan garb, Katina wriggled in her seat. She tried to get comfortable with the winding length and tight shoulders of her ceremonial robe. The lifter streaked towards the *Samutpada*, which floated deep within Mickelson's Nebula some thirty light minutes from *Threads Way*. Given the fierce and random electromagnetic storms, the ships within the nebula could keep hull integrity indefinitely, but a frontal faster-than-light assault on them was impossible.

So much security revolved around the Summit there was controlled chaos about the entire event. Slipping the lifter into this beehive of activity was relatively easy, especially since the lifter bore the insignia of the Thetan ships that hovered close to the *Samutpada*. The pilot of the *Samutpada*, nearing the end of his three-hour shift, glanced at the incoming logbook. He saw the lifter was one of the Thetan lifters assigned to patrol the perimeters of the main fleet of ships. He didn't bother glancing at the lifter's pilot, for he saw nothing out of the ordinary.

"So what do we have here?" he asked, more out of routine than from any genuine interest.

"Come on, Li Po. It's Pete. I'm bringing in two more latecomers. Seems like the higher-ups want to add security. Last minute changes, if you know what I mean."

Li Po stared glumly at the two hooded figures who remained as if in deep meditation. He shivered. Their robes marked them as part of the elite fighting force assigned to guard the central dais at the Summit. While Li Po had no records of the request for these late additions to the Summit's security team, neither did he have cause for alarm. He knew these Thetan warriors were said to be matches, one-to-one, with the finest fighters anywhere. They were fearsome, and best not angered unless it was unavoidable.

Li Po fingered the computer screen and nodded. "Come on in, Pete. Dock thirty-five is cleared. See me when you get more time. When this is over, maybe we'll get to swap stories over a drink."

Peter turned as soon as the screen went blank. "We're through," he said to the two women. "I expect a bonus for getting you through this. Especially since I'm also your ticket off the flagship."

Katina nodded, her hood hiding her smile. Pete would never get the chance to "help" them again, let alone collect any bonus. He was part of a trail which was covered up so it would take months, if ever, before anyone could track her movements over the past five years. Access to certain computer banks had proven to be the easiest part of the task of covering her tracks. Next came the elimination of everyone not essential to her current plan. A nuclear device buried deep underneath the prison would destroy Sandina. The young boy-lieutenant and warden, Talbot, was being reduced to elemental atoms along with, Katina hoped, Leon Three Starbreaks, part of a crater three miles wide, marking the detonation of a six hundred megaton device.

Idle regrets, Katina thought. So many promising careers shattered. But she had no choice. History might be kind to her---but that didn't matter. She would break the Summit so completely, peace would no longer be an option. After that, she knew she could depend upon the effects this event would have on the fighting spirits of Anphoria to beat back the Repletians. If Enid could survive what she had, then Anphoria would also emerge victorious from its near defeat. All they needed was that extra push over the edge into true desperation, from which they could tap into the limitless resources of an entire people. And this time no Black Ship would help the undeserving Repletians.

Once docked, Katina led the way through the corridors leading to the personal quarters her contacts had arranged for her. On the way, she stopped in a washroom, where she took off her Thetan robes. She felt more comfortable and cooler, dressed in the loose-fitting simple garbs of a minor Thetan official. She carefully deposited her discarded robe in the incinerator unit and waited until it had reduced her robe to ashes.

In less than five minutes, all anyone saw were two Thetans walking down a corridor, one a minor official and the other a hooded warrior whose limp and slow pace showed he or she had suffered a war injury, not uncommon in these days of border conflicts. Katina felt relief when they arrived at the selected quarters without incident, and apparently without drawing attention to themselves. She needed to rest and finalize her plans in the three days before the Summit began. The holograph light in her quarters blinked, the three messages waiting for her a sign her agents were in place. Katina returned the first caller's message through her coded channel and waited until his face focused through the holograph.

"Captain, I trust everything is on schedule?"

The captain nodded, an expression of hate and fear on his face. "Damn you, yes. Everything is as you requested." He glanced nervously at the figure behind Katina. "Who's that?"

"Relax, captain. She's with me. I have only one more thing to ask of you."

The captain groaned. A bead of sweat trickled along the line of his hair. "I've given you everything you wanted. What more do you want?"

Katina shook her head in mock dismay. "Why, captain! A backbone after all! Your wife is safely in my custody aboard *Threads Way.* You know how I abhor needless violence. All I ask is that you give my ship permission to dock in twenty-one Standard hours. Then I'll deliver your wife to you. That's fair, isn't it?"

"My wife and children. That was the deal!"

"Agreed. Your family will be with you in twelve hours."

"Why should I believe you?"

Katina smiled. "Do you have any choice?" Katina held up a small gold ring with a double inset of diamonds. "Do you recognize your wife's wedding ring?"

"You could have stolen it."

"Yes, I could have, but I didn't." Katina reached into her left pocket and withdrew a small object she held up for him to see. "This is your wife's ring finger. I had to remove the finger to get the ring."

The captain's face whitened and he slumped back in his chair. Katina could hardly hear his next words. "All right. You've got clearance. But they'll be expecting you."

"Yes. I'm sure they are. *Threads Way* has been refitted to look like a food ship. And, despite your flagship's size, food is one of those extras your ship always needs. *Threads Way* has been registered with the Thetan Confederacy as a food ship for fifteen Standard years. Clear her for Dock Thirty-Five."

"But my people! You don't know what you're asking."

"Captain, get me clearance. I don't have time for your compunction."

Katina's next caller was a hooded figure, who sat in the darkness of his quarters. No one else could guess the identity or race of the man, given his voice. Like Katina's, it was randomly scrambled and bounced through fifty different relay stations, in sequences and numbers that changed every several seconds.

"Has the dais been rigged as requested?" Katina fingered the small ring she had shown the captain earlier.

"It has. But the device is small. There's too much security to risk anything larger."

"Will it do the job?"

The hooded figure nodded. "The device will start ten minutes into the Summit proceedings, on my mark. The resulting signals will cover the entire room for forty seconds."

"It'll be tight, but that should give me enough time."

The hooded figure leaned forward, his cowled head growing larger in the holograph. "Madame, I don't care who you are. Be sure you fulfill your end of our agreement and all will go well."

"I'll see you when this is over." In hell, Katina thought. I'll see you in hell.

As the transmission ended, Katina turned to Enid, who had her hands in the pockets of her large robe in a gesture Katina had grown used to.

"Well, Madame X, if that's what you call yourself. I need some sleep. Stay quiet." Katina ordered Enid to lie on one of the two large beds. She then took a set of handcuffs from the table and strapped Enid's left wrist over her head to the wall hook. She tugged at the cuffs and, satisfied it was safe, crawled into the other bed, where she was soon fast asleep.

Enid watched the sleeping woman for some time. She fingered the small sphere she had kept through the changes of clothes over the past few days. The sphere was warm. Enid breathed a soft hum to herself, her calm blue eyes staring at the woman across from her. The computer adjusted the lights until the room sank into darkness from which Enid's hum was too faint to hear, except with the computer's sensory devices. And soon even that faded into silence.

CHAPTER 29

Standard Year 2498

Theresa Kuang Hsia felt the size of the room as she entered. The first thing Theresa noticed were the breathtaking tapestries lining the walls on either side of the aisle. Each tapestry was over a hundred square feet of muted pastel tones. Ten tapestries lined each side of the room. One wall of tapestries showed the ten events considered the most pivotal events in human history, including the discovery of the wheel, the first interstellar flight, the first known fatality of the Formias Rash, and the signing of the Covenant two thousand years ago. The Summit, if successful, would be immortalized with the addition of an eleventh tapestry.

On the opposite wall were the ten most significant human figures in history. Plato was there, as were Confucius and Jesus Christ. Lady Murasaki was there, but not Leo Tolstoy. Isaac Newton was there, but not Albert Einstein. Doctor David S. Formias was there, but not Doctor Louis Pasteur. The tenth, and most controversial, figure along part of the room had been added ten years before. Theresa knew the smooth pale visage of Katina Patriloney as well as she knew her own face. That, and the red nail polish on the long slender fingernails, marked Katina in the final year before her death. The black calm eyes stared down into the room, filling it with the sense of contempt and cynicism that had threatened the safety of the entire human race barely twenty years ago. Katina had come so close Theresa shivered in thinking of it. She knew there were Anphorians who still saw Katina as a heroine who had been foiled in her efforts by the mysterious Black Ship.

The pale blue carpet ran the length of the rectangular room to end at the foot of the dais three hundred feet from the entrance. Theresa's footsteps were muffled by this carpet. Everything in the room was oversized, dwarfing the humans within it. Theresa thought of nothing so much as a cathedral; the atmosphere was the same, as were the hushed tones people naturally chose to use.

In less than five hours, this room would be filled with representatives of three of the ten human groups. Theresa reached the far left side of the dais and walked up the several steps onto the platform. The three large conference tables formed a hollow triangle whose apex was the large central chair furthest from the main entrance. Each table had controls that operated the holographs in the middle of the triangle, as well as giving each table's occupants access to their own databases in other parts of the flagship.

The captain of the *Samutpada* turned upon her approach. His face showed the fatigue of the last several days. Theresa wondered if she looked the same way. She bowed and he returned her bow, although he was slow. Out of respect for her command position, he waited for her to start the conversation.

"Is everything ready?"

"Yes. Your chair is connected to the other chairs; you can cut off any speaker from the controls on the right arm. The left arm controls the computers and holographs. Nothing can be shown or dealt with without going through your chair."

"Excellent. May I try it out?"

"By all means. I've finished coding it to your voice."

Theresa gently placed her large satchel to one side of the swivel chair before she sat down. She overlooked not only the Conference table, but also the entire room. She saw everything from where she sat. The chair moulded to her form. The control panels on the arms of the chair sprang to life, as her DNA and fingerprint identities were confirmed.

"Is there anything else I need to know?"

The captain hesitated for a moment, the stress showing on his face. He shook his head and sighed. "No. No, everything is under your control." He gave her an unfathomable look. "I'm sorry about Captain Lai Jen. She was a good person." The captain's flat neutral tone of voice drew Theresa's attention. She studied his face again but he remained impassive and unreadable.

"She's all right. The medics say she'll recover in two days."

The captain nodded his sympathies, bowed and left, his tall figure striding down the same aisle she had walked.

Theresa watched him go. From the start, the captain had made her uncomfortable . His military reserve was a mask she couldn't penetrate. She had tried to break through that demeanour, his mask, a familiar self-protective defense against past injuries or grievances. Perhaps after the Summit, and before she took a badly-needed rest, she could do something for the captain.

The holograph, in the centre of the hollow triangle formed by the conference tables, sprang to life with the touch of a button. Theresa spent the next hour becoming familiar with each control button. When she felt satisfied she knew what her console could do, she turned the holograph off and stood to leave. A small draft of cold air swept through her short hair. Puzzled, she looked around the room. All the doors were safely locked. A movement drew her eyes to the large tapestry of Katina Patriloney. She felt a chill creep into her spine as the tapestry gently stirred, the portrait of Katina seeming to move, her eyes staring directly at Theresa. Thank the Creator she's dead, Theresa thought as she stooped to pick up her satchel.

Theresa left the Summit room and hurried towards her quarters. Only there did she feel safe from the ever-present danger that loomed larger with each passing hour. The attack a day ago had left her without Lisa Lai Jen, whom she had come to trust and rely on since first meeting her. Something about this worried Theresa, but she couldn't pinpoint the cause.

*

People are so predictable, Katina thought, as she uploaded the last command sequence into the central computer. The holograph lit up to show Theresa Kuang Hsia walking down a hallway towards her quarters. Katina studied the woman for a minute. There was nothing there out of the ordinary. The satchel Theresa had slung over one shoulder weighed her down. Katina smiled. The attack had done its job, knocking her off-centre. The Summit, with its multitudinous tasks, would ensure Theresa wouldn't regain the composure or the distance needed to have any general sense of what was happening to her or to those people around her.

"Captain, I trust all went well?"

The captain nodded, his face worn by what he was doing.

"In a few short hours, you'll be with your wife. All you have to do is go on with your duties."

"You fucking witch! If there's a way, I swear I'll get you for this."

Katina smiled. The long fingers of her splayed left hand reached out towards the holograph. He instinctively pulled back from his screen as her fingers came at him. The red nail polish glittered under the light.

"Captain, threats at this time won't do your wife any favors. Although I must say I enjoy the drama. You've confirmed the reliability of the device?"

"Yes, it's something simple. It's geared to amplify by a factor of ten any electromagnetic energy it detects. That energy is then fed back to the original source, causing an overload. The communication drones and other electric devices in the Summit room will be useless for forty seconds."

"That should give me enough time."

"I ought to shut you down, even if it costs me my wife."

"And your children? Your son and daughter? Your parents? Are you willing to risk your own father and mother? I understand you're close to them, an admirable trait in such a galaxy as we live in. There are long painful lingering ways to die, don't you think?"

The captain groaned and his shoulders slumped in defeat.

"Just go on with your duties. You are no longer a part of this."

Katina switched off the holograph and looked at Enid, who sat to one side of the room, out of range of the holograph cameras. Enid stared at the floor and she hummed the same tune she had been humming since leaving Sandina. Katina stared for a long time at the thin bony figure. The open eye wound and the other facial scars made Enid's visage a grisly one. Katina had once thought of having her medical team aboard *Threads Way* use their DNA and genetic replication methods to restore Enid's health, but she decided against it. Enid in her present state was more effective as a distraction. Even her reticence and her belief she was Madame X worked to Katina's advantage. So long as she didn't seem to know who she was, she was a willing and compliant tool.

"My dear, you'll do fine. There's so much you could have done for me, if there was enough time."

Katina's spoken thoughts were interrupted by her door sensor, warning Katina someone was outside.

"Ah, it's here. Wait here, my dear Starbreaks. I have a present for you."

Katina hurried to the door. A robed figure stood at the entrance. Without a word a small package was handed to Katina. The figure turned and left, seeming to glide, with no visible motion, over the floor. Katina waited until the door slid closed before she turned to face Enid, who showed no signs of interest. She rocked back and forth in her chair and hummed. Katina walked up to Enid and placed a left hand on her rocking head. "Rise, my dear. I have something I want you to wear."

Enid rose without protest and stood with her arms hanging limply at her sides. Katina stepped back. "Take off your clothes, my dear."

Enid undid the rope, which bound her robe to her waist. The robe fell open and Enid shrugged. Katina watched as the light robe slid to the floor, revealing Enid's naked emaciated figure. Starvation was something the doctors couldn't do a thing about. Only time and food could fill in Enid's gaunt body. The leg scar which rendered her a cripple was almost invisible. The doctors had done well and, given more time, they would have eliminated all traces of prison life. But the ghastly eye wound and the scars from the seven years of degradation and abuse on Enid's face were shocking. Enid would create a disturbance, and that's all Katina wanted of her. Time enough to carry out her objective. She hoped Enid remembered the mock assassination that had been staged for her benefit. Katina counted heavily on those memories, although she wasn't foolish enough to rely on Enid's disruptive effects on the Summit.

Katina ripped open the package, revealing a light grey outfit. "Put this on," she ordered. Enid took the tunic, which Katina extended to her. She pulled it over her head and then reached for the grey trousers, and slid into them. Finally, Katina extended a belt that sparkled gold under the room's low lights. Enid tucked the tunic into her pants and then synched the belt around her thin waist.

"Wonderful. Just wonderful. You look like you did twenty years ago. That admiral's uniform suits you perfectly. You'll cause a stir when they see you walk into the Summit. I doubt there'll be anyone who won't know you on sight. Although I must say, your face will cause a shock."

"Sit down. We have four hours before we're scheduled to attend the Summit opening. Here's what I want you to do." Katina spent the next five minutes telling Enid how to behave when she walked into the Summit room. It was impossible to tell if Enid listened to her or would remember what she was told. But Katina trusted her. There was no other way.

*

"Will we get there on time?"

Leon twisted around to face Red Dawn, who stared at him, waiting for an answer. Leon shook his head. "I don't know. The size of this ship slows us down."

Talbot looked up from his screen. "We'll get there at 1200 hours tomorrow. The Summit begins at 0900 hours. Everything depends on when Katina plans to make her move. It will be some time during the first day, because she can't afford progress to happen."

Red Dawn shook her head. "I still don't understand how she's still alive. After all she did twenty years ago, there seemed no way for her to continue."

"She's a strong woman." Talbot looked from Red Dawn to Leon. "I'd like to thank you two again for what you're doing. You didn't have to help me; you could have left me on that planet until the next freighter arrived."

Leon laughed. "For once you're right. I could have left you on Sandina. I wanted to. But my wife said your military training and knowledge would be advantageous, should we need it."

"I thought you'd be afraid of my taking over this ship. It's Anphorian, after all."

"There you're wrong. The shutdown of most of its circuits for twenty years wiped away everything but the most basic capacities. My wife and I have rebuilt much of the programming to respond to us. This ship is for all purposes Repletian."

"I noticed when I tried to operate these controls yesterday."

"A safety precaution. We never expected to share this ship with Anphorian Naval officers. You've been given partial control over some of the ship's higher functions, but ultimate control is still in our hands."

Talbot grinned and ran his hand through his military crewcut. "I'd do the same thing in your position. But I don't have to like it."

"No, you don't have to like it. But it's what we're willing to give you."

"What happens when we get to the Summit?"

"I was part of the planning of the Summit, before I found out my niece was alive and went looking for her. The two sides agreed to keep their delegations to the bare minimum, with no heavy artillery present. They won't have changed in the last month. I'm counting on each side keeping their word. I'm also counting on the fact that, as an Elder, I'm authorized to take part in the Summit. I don't think the Senior Elder has removed my name from her list of delegates."

"You won't have much time to explain yourself. You're in an Anphorian flagship and that's what they'll see."

"I'd love to warn them, but you know I can't. Katina would know of our impending arrival as soon as the others, and she'd also know her plans would be ruined. I need to surprise her or she'll do something more drastic than any of us would like."

"She's planning to destroy the Summit, isn't that bad enough?"

Leon shook his head. "We don't know how she intends to ruin the Summit, or who she's after. But if we let on we're coming, she may decide to take everything down with her."

Talbot felt the knot in his stomach. "What does she want? Why is she trying to do this? It'll hurt her own people as much as it will anyone else."

Red Dawn spoke up. "You never understood her. She's acting not for herself but for what she believes to be right for Anphoria. I don't think she knows the difference between her own motives and those she attributes for the good of your people. In a twisted way, what she's doing might result in what she wants, to make peace between Anphoria and Repletia impossible."

"But she'd have to kill the leaders on both sides."

"Killing people never bothered her before, and I doubt if it will now."

"And your niece is the decoy in this?"

Leon stared at the holograph screen of the stars. "Yes, and my niece is the decoy. Those bastards! How could anyone do what they did to her on Sandina?"

The knot in Talbot's stomach became tighter. "I can't condone what happened to your niece. There's no excuse for it. When this is over, Sandina will be shut down. I'll make sure of that."

Leon looked down from his seat and Talbot bowed his head, trying to hide his misery. The past few days had shaken Talbot's fundamental belief in people's good will. He still hadn't come to terms with what he'd seen on Sandina. He thought such brutality had been a part of Humanity's distant past, but the torture chambers and the crippled victims of the warden and his henchmen had struck something deep inside Talbot he hadn't known was there. And the black anger that came up and ended in his fight with Sergeant Mathers made Talbot sick. He had seen something in himself he hated, and had lost control of, in those few days on Sandina.

Leon saw Talbot's white knuckles and turned to Red Dawn. She moved without a word to Talbot's side. Talbot tried to hold his pain in, but then Enid, the woman he had worshipped as a youth, filled his mind. He recalled his horror at seeing her blindness, the deep scars that criss-crossed her face. But more than anything, more than the physical injuries, he remembered the broken humming, the eternal rocking in her chair of a woman who had once commanded hundreds of millions of people.

Leon watched as Red Dawn led Talbot from the bridge. And for a long time he continued to stare at the closed doors, not seeing them, as his mind wandered far from the great flagship churning its way towards Mickelson's Nebula.

CHAPTER 30

Standard Year 2498

The great doors slid open to the ringing of the bells. The long double-line of Anphorians marched into the room to the watchful eyes of everyone already there. One line consisted of soldiers, the finest within the Anphorian Confederacy. Each resplendent in their crisp uniform. The other line, shoulder to shoulder with the soldiers, consisted of important government and civilian guests, here to bear witness to the historic events, and to give their consent or not to any agreement, on behalf of those they represented. Each civilian wore long red cotton robes devoid of markings. Except for the rhythmic pounding of their feet as the Anphorians marched in stride down the blue-carpeted aisle, there wasn't a sound in the room.

At the head of the procession, the interim President of the Anphorian Council was flanked by the Commander of the Anphorian Armed Forces. She wore her traditional black robes, a long flowing satin cloak that shimmered with each movement she made. She stared straight ahead, her eyes fixed on the figure waiting for her at the end of the aisle.

The admiral wore his formal grey military uniform but, while he kept step with the delegation, his face looked haggard and worn. Once he paused, almost throwing the others behind him into confusion. He quickly recovered, but not before an audible gasp from a guest was heard by the trillions of people who watched this event.

At the end of the aisle, the double-line stopped in unison. The President continued up the steps. She stopped at the top and bowed to the old woman who waited in silence.

"I bring hope, and trust, to work out our differences under your guidance, with the permission of my people, of our Home Worlds and those other worlds within our great Confederacy."

Theresa Kuang Hsia, Philosopher and Conciliator, returned

the President's bow. "Welcome on behalf of humans everywhere. We will work out our differences for the good of all. I greet you and ask you and your delegates to take part in this Summit."

Theresa stepped to one side to let the President and her selected delegates take their places alongside the table. As soon as the last person had lined up to stand beside their chair, the line of Anphorian soldiers saluted and stepped to one side of the carpet, there to stand at attention in silence. The other line of Anphorians stepped through the open gaps of the soldiers to stand in a second line behind them.

Another double-line of people marched into the room. At their head was the Elder's Council, led by the Senior Elder. She was dressed in a long blue satin robe, as radiant as the Anphorian President's. She walked up the steps and bowed to Theresa Kuang Hsia.

"I am here on behalf of the Home Worlds of Repletia. We are here to participate under your esteemed guidance. It is our hope we can come to an honorable resolution of our differences with the Anphorian Confederacy."

"Senior Elder, I welcome you on behalf of humanity. When I give to you, I give myself. On behalf of Humanity, I extend open arms to you and your people."

Theresa moved to one side and the Senior Elder and her Council of Elders moved past her to their selected table. Theresa followed the last of the Elders and made her way to her chair. She turned to the hushed audience.

"My name is Theresa Kuang Hsia. I humbly accept the role of Conciliator of this Summit on behalf of the ten Confederacies of Humanity. Representatives from the other seven Confederacies are behind me. They are here to see and verify the proceedings of this Summit on behalf of their people. I will turn to the Repletian delegation and ask them for formal introductions."

The Senior Elder bowed to the assembly below the dais,

then to the Anphorians facing her and, finally, to Theresa herself. She introduced each delegate at her table. The President of the Anphorian Council followed suit. Theresa waited, her features stiff with the formality the proceedings demanded. After the introductions, which took half-an-hour to complete, Theresa bowed and asked everyone to take their appointed seats. The guards remained standing at ease on either side of the carpeted aisle.

Theresa Kuang Hsia waited until everyone had made themselves comfortable in their chairs. Once she was satisfied she had everyone's attention, Theresa began her rehearsed speech.

"As you know, we have come together to resolve the border disputes between the Anphorian and Repletian Confederacies. Many lives, and much property, have been destroyed on both sides. More will be lost unless we come to a common agreement both sides honor. Does anyone dispute the matters I have stated?"

Theresa waited for the required twenty seconds and then continued: "This Summit needs to have consensus, however long that takes. Are we agreed on this?"

Twenty seconds passed, the silence so intense, everyone could hear the soft whisper of machinery as the three communications spheres at the back of the room recorded this event, relaying what they recorded live to trillions of people scattered throughout the galaxy.

"Silence being consent, let us proceed with initial statements. I yield the floor to the President of the Anphorian Council. Madame President, you may say what you will."

The President rose to her feet and bowed to the Chair before she turned to the spheres and the people below the dais.

"I welcome all who watch this Summit. Know on behalf of the Anphorian Confederacy, we come here as equals. We respect and honor the intents and purposes of the Repletian Confederacy, and hope they in turn respect and honor our intents and purposes."

"The dispute is simple, and the resolution difficult. The times ahead promise to be filled with complex and trying differences between our two great Confederacies, but know here Anphoria will work for solutions fair to all concerned."

"Twenty years ago, we detected what we believed was a new type of military warship within Repletian territory. We had no choice but to assume Repletia was taking their border hostilities with us to a new level of conflict. Our fears were confirmed when we lost two complete fleets with all hands. In our weakened state, we were no match for the well-prepared Repletians, who crossed our borders to rewrite the boundaries agreed to by the ten Groups of Humanity two thousand years ago. Fifty Border Worlds, once called Anphorian, have now fallen under the shadow of Repletia, and for this we ask compensation, justification and rectification. That is our case. I yield the floor to Madame Conciliator."

The President sat down to study the Repletians across from her. She was careful not to show emotions. That would come later.

Theresa turned to the Repletian Council of Elders and yielded the floor to them. The Senior Elder rose to her feet. She was a head taller than the Anphorian President, and much heavier. Her dark brown face complemented her dark blue robe. She, too, turned to face her larger audience. She bowed to the silent assembly below her and then faced the three cameras at the back of the room.

"I extend greetings to Humanity. We come to this Summit prepared to negotiate in good faith, and trust the Anphorian Confederacy sees fit to follow. It is our sincere hope we leave this Summit with peace at hand. Neither side in this dispute will gain everything; both sides must be willing to give to find the centre. So we agree. As testimony to our firm commitment to this process, let me say on behalf of our peoples, I am unilaterally prepared to return to the Anphorian Confederacy five border worlds. When I give to you, I give myself."

The Senior Elder sat down to a storm of voices. Theresa stood up and waited until the voices subsided. When she had everyone's attention, she spoke.

"Madame Senior Elder, I am grateful for your gesture of good faith. Does Madame President wish to say anything in response?"

"I must thank the Senior Elder for being so gracious in returning what was not hers to begin with. We should be so lucky to receive such beneficence."

"Perhaps Madame President would wish for us to withdraw our offer?"

"You fucking witch! You wouldn't dare!"

The Senior Elder rose slowly to stare at her counterpart. "I see Madame President brings her fine gift of oratory. She is right, but for the wrong reasons. I will not withdraw our offer, for that is not our way. However, I must protest, Madame President seems more intent on scoring points than she is in serious negotiating."

Admiral Lexington leaned over to whisper in his President's ear. She nodded and looked to Theresa. "Madame Conciliator, if I am hasty with my emotions, please forgive me. We have suffered long and difficult years, and have lost good people to those who sit across from us."

"I understand. However, I warn you the Conciliator will not tolerate another such outburst. We are here to discuss serious matters, not to win debating contests. That goes for everyone in this room."

"Agreed. May I respond further?"

"Proceed."

"On behalf of Anphoria, I accept Madame Senior Elder's offer."

The Senior Elder, who hadn't sat back down, played a recording of the long borders between Anphoria and Repletia. The areas controlled by Repletia were in blue, while those controlled by Anphoria were in black. Some fifty red dots marked the systems where Repletia had gained control in the past twenty years.

"I ask you to turn your attention to the holograph map before you. This marks the current conditions between our two sides. Twenty years ago, two fleets from Anphoria invaded our territories. They say they were after a ship, which no longer exists. They gave us no fair warning and, as you have all heard from Madame President, they came in the belief the Black Ship was one of ours. I must assume they either intended to destroy that ship or take it into their control. Can you see our situation? If the Black Ship had been one of ours, which it never was, the Anphorians have admitted they were committing an act of war."

"Our forces, scattered throughout our territories, mobilized into loose units numbering from dozens of ships to hundreds. They set out in pursuit of the two fleets. Not finding them, they continued into Anphorian territory."

"But that is not Anphoria's greatest crime. No, we could have handled the two fleets. But their leader," the Senior Elder pointed directly at the President. "Their leader, and her predecessor, deliberately used the Black Ship as an excuse to wipe out our Home Worlds. This goes against the Covenant signed by the Ten Groups of Humanity two thousand years ago. It was a deliberate and unprovoked attempt at genocide."

Theresa held her hand up as the Anphorian President leapt to her feet, and the assembled people below broke into another uproar. It was the President's words more than Theresa's hand that made the crowds grow still. She screamed at the Senior Elder.

"You fucking witch! We had no choice! You could have denied the Black Ship was yours, but instead you mobilized your forces. We had no choice but to think our worst fears were confirmed, that we had found you out, and you were throwing everything you had at us."

"And those star bombs? Were they an illusion?"

"That wasn't us. It never was. Katina Patriloney acted on her own."

"It's said there are Anphorians who wished she had succeeded."

"I can't control everybody. Maybe that's the way you do things in Repletia but that's not us."

"All that aside, Madame Conciliator, we demand simple justice. We are willing to give up twenty-five border systems in return for twenty-five trillion credits, reparation for previous war crimes committed and admitted to by Anphoria."

"Maybe Katina should have blown you up!"

In the quietness of the room the sound of three spheres hitting the floor startled everyone. Theresa, horrified, saw the three communication spheres fall, struck by a force that rendered them inoperative. The delegates at both tables turned towards the spheres, puzzled. In the time it took everyone to turn towards the back of the room, the entrance doors swung open and a tall thin figure hobbled uncertainly into the room. She wore the grey uniform of an Anphorian admiral, but her dark skin betrayed her as Repletian. And as Enid limped towards the dais, people recoiled in horror at the grisly sight she presented, a gaunt skeletal figure with facial scars and an eye wound that made everyone blanch.

Admiral Lexington shouted, "My God, it's Enid Blue Starbreaks!"

"M'name is Madame X. M'name is Madame X."

A single scream forced everyone to turn again to the dais. A robed figure from within the Thetan ranks was wrestled to the floor. At the same moment the entire room noticed the still-twitching figure of the Anphorian President slumped onto the table in front of her.

The pounding of armored feet as a horde of armed men and women ran towards the open door Enid had come through, the sight of another Thetan figure moving swiftly to the Anphorian table, where a hood was thrown back to reveal an old woman who stood and yelled, "Are you with me?" to the ranks of Anphorians, and a small explosive sound coming from beside Theresa's chair, threw the assembly into uncertainty. "Treachery!" sounded from a single voice, then from many, as the room erupted into chaos.

A black sphere struggled to rise from Theresa's satchel, but its colors shifted and its wobbled flight spoke of great effort. Several more rose into the air, but their flights were crooked. One smashed into a tapestry, emitting sparks. A high-pitched scream preceded the death of another sphere. It turned sickly green before imploding, pulling those within ten feet of it into its event horizon.

Katina yelled at the Anphorians at the conference table, "Follow me. My men are here to save you." Another high-pitched scream, and the disappearance of another sphere with an ear-popping implosion, convinced the undecided. As one, they followed Katina as she bolted for the door, where a line of soldiers waited.

*

Theresa knew something was wrong when she saw the first communication sphere bobble. It emitted sparks as it fell with a loud bang, denting the floor. Theresa found her control panels inert. As she rose to call order, she saw Enid Blue Starbreaks' emaciated figure shuffle into the room. Behind Enid, Theresa saw a horde of soldiers running down the large corridor towards the open door. She turned her attention to the conference tables in time to see the arrow thud into the President's heart. The President stared down at the shaft in disbelief. She looked up at Theresa and tried to speak. Instead, blood trickled from her mouth. She fell forward onto the table, driving the arrow through her so the arrowhead emerged from her back.

A hooded figure broke from the Thetan ranks and dashed to the front of the Conference Table, where the hood was thrown back to reveal the dark visage of an old woman, who shouted at the confused Anphorian delegates, "Are you with me?" Theresa was about to try to regain control of the Summit when she heard a small sound at the side of her chair. She looked down to see a small black sphere rise from her satchel. It struggled upwards, rising in spurts. Flashes of energy sparked between its surface and something hidden under Theresa's chair. Theresa stumbled from her chair as the first sphere was quickly followed by the other spheres Theresa always carried in her satchel. Great electric arcs of energy flashed between the chair and the spheres. The harder the spheres struggled, the more energy poured back at them. Their surfaces changed from deep coal-black to a prismatic rainbow of colours.

Cries of "Treachery!" filled the room as pandemonium broke out. Fights erupted among the two groups of people below the dais. The spheres began to disappear with an implosion of energy that sucked in those nearby. Theresa's last clear sight of the room was of seeing Enid Blue Starbreaks grabbed by a group of Repletians. Then Theresa found herself surrounded by Thetan guards, who shielded her with their bodies. She struggled to see what was happening below the dais but the guards refused to let her be exposed to the tumult raging within the assembly. She felt helpless as they carried her to the nearest side exit.

*

The Senior Elder heard the thud of the communication spheres. Puzzled, she looked up, from where she sat writing notes, towards the direction of the sound. The door had opened and an impossible figure, a person from the dead, slowly made her way into the room along the blue aisle. In the hush that followed, the Senior Elder heard a strange hissing sound and another thud, this time from across the platform. She turned to see the Anphorian President try to say something to Theresa.

A Thetan figure was being wrestled to the floor by those near it. But no one was quick enough to stop the Thetan who ran towards the front of the dais. The old woman who emerged from behind the hood looked like a Repletian, but her small frame and black eyes drew the Senior Elder's attention to the last of the tapestries. She saw a dead figure on the wall, impossibly close in appearance to the woman who yelled to the Anphorians, "Are you with me?"

"No! No! This is impossible!" she said to herself. And watched as a black sphere, then another and another, quickly rose from beside Theresa's chair. Something was happening to them, although it was also clear they were weapons in a room that had agreed on leaving weapons outside the room. Large arced flashes of light leapt from the several spheres towards Theresa's chair. A voice yelled "Treachery!" and the entire room broke into hundreds of struggling people.

At this point the Senior Elder remembered Leon Three Starbreaks, and stared down at his niece. Time for action. She bolted from her seat.

"Grab that woman!" she yelled at the top of her voice, at the same time pointing towards Enid. Several Repletians close to Enid heard their Senior Elder's orders and pounced on her, other matters becoming secondary. The Senior Elder turned quickly to assess the situation on the Dais. The old woman who could not be, but had to be, Katina Patriloney, was jumping from the dais. The Anphorian delegates followed her. The Senior Elder heard and saw a third sphere implode.

*

Enid Blue Starbreaks was led to the Summit room by the captain, who waved the guards away from the door. He waited until they had stepped back several paces and to one side of the entrance. He moved in front of Enid to press the coded sequence that opened the doors. They slid open, the captain pointed into the room, and spoke.

"Your mistress calls you. May you both go to hell. I've done my part; now it's your turn. Go in. She's waiting for you." The captain gave Enid a piercing look, his forehead strangely beaded with sweat, before he again pointed into the room. "Please go. I have things I must take care of and I can't help you."

Enid heard the distant sound of voices from within the room, but her eyes were on the captain as he turned and hurried down the corridor. She heard a rumble, a sound of feet running in tandem towards her from where the captain had turned the corner. And then she heard a strange thud, as of some heavy object hitting the floor, within the Summit room. With no choice left to her, Enid took her first few hesitant steps into the room. As she did so, two other thuds sounded and all eyes swung towards her.

She saw the distant figures on the dais and made her slow belabored way towards them. The voices had stopped, but Enid heard the music in her mind grow, extending outwards to fill her vision. Surely the others heard the music, but they gave no signs of hearing. Instead, everything slowed down in her mind. As if in a dream, she saw a hooded figure rise from the people on the dais, rise and point. There was an arrow protruding from a woman up on the dais, a woman dressed in deep black. And the music swelled.

Katina appeared as though by magic, emerging from the people who stood behind the great central chair. Katina moved quickly to the front of the stage, as the figure that had shot the arrow was overwhelmed by those around it. Katina made a sweeping gesture with her arms, pointing simultaneously at the Anphorians on the dais and those on the main floor.

"Are you with me?"

The demand echoed in the shocked room, the pounding of feet were almost at the entrance, and something broke in Enid. Colors swept up from where the great central chair sat, colors and music, which no one else seemed to hear or see. Enid fell under the pounding in her head, her memories striking her with the force of Mole's great staring eyes, the same eyes as those that pierced her soul from the old woman who leaped from the stage.

"Treachery!" rang out, and people around Enid began to fight one another in a babble of voices and bodies that confused her. She tried to stay on her feet as people around her pushed and shoved each other, arms and feet flailing in brutal hand-to-hand combat.

Mole.

Memory.

Music.

David.

Her First Mother.

"No! No! Oh, please, Creator, no! I don't want to remember!"

"Grab that woman!"

And then hands seizing her as she fell her final descent into blackness, even as a sphere near her imploded, taking with it people who disappeared into its event horizon.

*

Stars End flashed into normal space almost on top of the *Samutpada*. And Leon swore as the ship was jolted by missiles aimed at the *Samutpada*.

"What the hell? Red Dawn, what's happening?"

Another jolt almost knocked Leon from his seat. The holograph screen showed the entire area engulfed with fire fights between every ship in the area. The hull of the *Samutpada* was riddled with holes, but its main structures were still operational, as it fired randomly and desperately at everything in its range, which now included *Stars End*.

"I'd hate to see what they call peace!" Talbot yelled from his pilot's seat.

"Shall I launch our fighter drones?"

"Not until we know what the hell is going on. Lieutenant, have we detected where my niece is in this mess?"

Another heavy jolt told Leon their large mass was drawing the attention of the *Samutpada*. "Is she aboard the flagship?"

"No! I've picked her up aboard one of the smaller vessels. She's still alive."

"Which vessel?"

"That one." Talbot pointed to a moving dot in the holograph

screen. There was a heavy concentration of other red dots in the same area, and they coalesced into a more unified whole against the green dots *Stars End* had selected as Anphorian.

"Get me the commander of that ship!"

"Aye, sir."

Talbot sent a general broadcast on Repletian wavelengths. The holograph filled with the vision of the Senior Elder. She appeared calm, although behind her people were running to carry out their duties.

"Elder Three Starbreaks! Greetings. I'm busy at the moment. The Anphorians in their treachery have sent an old flagship against us. Where are you?"

"I have no time to explain. I'm in command of that 'old flagship.' If you want to get out of here in one piece, I can get you aboard our ship. I'm sending the docking coordinates now. Give me your ship codes. Our computer will verify them and allow them into the docking areas. Better hurry. I'm going to star drive in three minutes."

"How delicious! I'll be right there. When we're docked, I'll let you know."

"Get moving!"

The Senior Elder's face was replaced by an overview of Mickelson's Nebula. *Stars End* forged through the nebula as fast as she dared. A string of faster red dots followed her and disappeared from view as ship after ship raced to their selected docking coordinates aboard *Stars End's* nine docking bays. Half the green dots marking Anphorian ships pursued the retreating Repletian forces while the other half continued a suicidal assault on the *Samutpada*. Several Anphorian ships tried to follow the Repletians into *Stars End's* docking bays. But without coded verification, they were destroyed by the flagship's massive pinpoint firepower.

"Can we help the Thetans?" Leon asked. Talbot and Red Dawn both shook their heads. Red Dawn spoke first.

"We've got to get out of here. Katina's planned this well. Somehow she's back in control of the Anphorian forces, which means there may be more Anphorian ships on the way. We've got what we wanted."

Talbot added, "They've got to destroy the *Samutpada*. The people aboard her are the only witnesses other than the two warring human groups who can say what happened. Their word will confirm Katina's role in this. Without them, who'll believe either side? No one, and Katina knows that."

In three minutes the Senior Elder's face reappeared on the holograph screen. "We're in. Let's get out of here, Elder Three Starbreaks."

Stars End boomed out of Mickelson's Nebula with a horde of Anphorian fighters firing uselessly at her thick hull. Leon yelled for everyone to brace themselves, and then he activated the star drive. The Anphorian ships around her acted as increased mass, which slowed the star drive, but not completely. Space time around *Stars End's* hull warped and twisted, pulling apart the smaller ships like taffy.

Red Dawn watched with horror. "If there were only time and another way," she said.

"There isn't," Leon said, and pointed at the holograph. Five great combat vessels were almost on them, vessels green on the screen. In addition, several more great ships were breaking into real space, ships which bore the insignia of the Thetan Home Worlds.

"In no time at all, this'll be a crowded place in the galaxy."

"Leon, dear, Talbot and I can handle things from here. Your niece is down below. She needs you."

Leon couldn't recall the mad scramble to the docking bay. He couldn't remember running up the ramp of the ship, which held the Council of Elders. He never felt the pain shooting through his bad leg from the mad dash along the starship's corridors. All he saw was the still form of his niece floating in the saline tank. Everything up to now had been seen from a distance. But distance no longer proved a barrier. Instead, Leon felt a pain that ripped his world apart as he stared, horrified, at the mutilated thing that was both his blood and the last thing connecting him to his brother and family. He never felt the sharp jab of the needle as it sank into his arm, forcing a blessed darkness as guilt flooded him with its acid poison. Darkness and guilt, poison and pride, the need to ask forgiveness of his niece and his brother for not being there when he was needed. And then he remembered nothing more.

Story concludes in The Black Ship Vol. 2